# CREEPING IN
# REPTILE FLESH

Published by Morrigan Books
Östra Promenaden 43
602 29 Norrköping
Sweden
www.morriganbooks.com

Editor: Kari Wolfe
Editorial Assistance: Amanda Pillar

ISBN: 9789186865184

Cover illustration © Cat Sparks, 2008

First Published by Altair Australia Pty Ltd 2008

Published by Morrigan Books in July 2011

All stories © Robert Hood reprinted with permission of the author

Collection © Robert Hood, 2008, 2011

# CREEPING IN
# REPTILE FLESH

# Available titles from Morrigan Books:

### How To Make Monsters
By Gary McMahon

### Voices
Edited By Mark S. Deniz & Amanda Pillar

### Grants Pass
Edited By Jennifer Brozek & Amanda Pillar

### Dead Souls
Edited By Mark S. Deniz

### The Phantom Queen Awakes
Edited By Mark S. Deniz & Amanda Pillar

### Requiems For The Departed
Edited By Gerard Brennan & Mike Stone

# Coming soon from Morrigan Books:

### The Whisper Jar
By Carole Lanham

### The Ghosts of Unspoken Thoughts
By Karen Newman

MORRIGAN BOOKS

*Ah weak & wide astray! Ah shut in narrow doleful form*
*Creeping in reptile flesh upon the bosom of the ground*
*The Eye of Man a little narrow orb closd up & dark*
*Scarcely beholding the great light conversing with the Void*
*The Ear, a little shell in small volutions shutting out*
*All melodies & comprehending only Discord and Harmony*
*The Tongue a little moisture fills, a little food it cloys*
*A little sound it utters & its cries are faintly heard*

~ William Blake, *Milton*, 1804

# PREFACE

This collection gathers some little-seen stories that thematically resonate — in my mind anyway — with the title novella 'Creeping in Reptile Flesh'. I don't intend to elaborate on those themes here; hopefully, the stories will do that for themselves, though I should warn readers that, with some of the stories, the connections might seem rather obtuse. Moreover, in the titular story in particular, the themes and the story define each other and I don't know that I could adequately articulate all I intended to achieve in it outside the fictional context it creates. Nor should I be able to.

'Creeping in Reptile Flesh' has been a long time in the writing. Its original impetus came from the years I spent as research assistant to a well-known historian, fascinated by the divergent realities I found to exist in the old newspapers I was given to scour. I should point out that the connection between the real-world historian and the one depicted in the story is remote, and neither should be confused with the other in any detail. By the same token, the politicians, political parties and feral creatures depicted in the title story (and in the other stories as well) are fictional creations and not meant to bear any resemblance to persons or creatures living or dead. Even the story 'Casual Visitors', which was inspired by real incidents involving a Sydney-based scifi convention, Harlan Ellison and a flying saucer, is otherwise totally fictitious.

My thanks go to all the editors who felt that the stories re-printed here were worthy of their respective publications in the first place. Thanks, too, to Cat Sparks for her wonderful cover and for her general support throughout the process of bringing the book together.

I would also like to thank Morrigan Books for the opportunity to re-print *Creeping in Reptile Flesh* in this international edition, especially my editor, Kari Wolfe, and Editor-in-Chief Amanda Pillar, who between them tidied the text up considerably. This edition is dedicated to Professor Jim Hagan, with whom I spent many years researching labour history, and many more brewing beer, eating pasta and discussing politics, literature and the State of the Nation. Jim died unexpectedly in November 2009 and I miss him a lot.

Robert Hood
July 2011

Note:
*Creeping in Reptile Flesh was a finalist in both the 2009 Aurealis Awards (for Best Collection) and the 2009 Ditmar Awards (for Best Anthology/Collection). The title story was also a finalist in the Best Novella category of the 2009 Ditmar Awards. The story 'Getting Rid of Mother' was included in the Fifth Annual Volume of Year's Best Australian Science Fiction and Fantasy, edited by Bill Congreve (MirrorDanse Books, 2010).*

# CONTENTS

# CREEPING IN REPTILE FLESH

*"And the feral shall inherit the earth."*
—*"Yipper" Cowling*

The night before they found Alaistair Schow's mutilated body at the shadowy end of a Woolloomooloo *cul de sac*, I dreamt about a naked man wandering alone through an isolated valley. It was a disturbing dream, and though the details faded quickly to a few generalised images, an impression of disruption, of reality in crisis, lingered for a long time afterwards and became part of my memory of the politician's death.

A council worker stumbled upon Schow at about three o'clock in the morning, slumped in a dark pool that was only partially run-off from surrounding buildings; mostly it was blood. I heard about the killing on the radio a few hours later and felt unsettled, although the dream was more insistent and somehow much more disturbing. I found it hard to drag my emotions away from it long enough to feel properly moved. Schow had been a well-liked, if relatively obscure, political identity. Such a death should have been shocking.

Eager to do the right thing by Schow's memory, I forced a dim image of him into my mind: average build; tidy brown hair, neatly trimmed, too much like a toupee to actually be one; tight, cynical eyes; docile manner. His nondescript air was such that I could never figure how he'd managed to work his way as far into the political arena as he had. Influential friends perhaps. But I'd never cared enough to find out.

In the midst of this morbid speculation, George Clarbridge arrived at the door. I thought at first he'd come to berate me about an article I'd contributed to the *Independent Review,* having a go at recent actions by the Government. As it turned out, what he wanted to talk about was twofold: John "Yipper" Cowling, the controversial Independent Member for Arden — and murder.

Up until then, it hadn't occurred to me that the two things might be connected.

## The Commission

My career had been a chequered one, seen as significant by some and inconsequential by others — a judgement largely dependent on which individual agendas I chanced to affect for good or ill over the years. Though technically a journalist, I had been so much more, scavenging below the surface of the political swamp for several decades as an advisor, commentator, spin doctor, de facto conscience — a bottom-feeder, yes, but a bottom-feeder with teeth.

My personal life suffered accordingly. It was my own failing — and the dictates of fate — I had never had a family beyond my biological parents, who died when I was seven, or so I was told, victims of a train derailment, in turn, leading to the political derailment of the then-State Minister for Transport — a nobody I won't even deign to name here. Let myopic academics record his paltry successes and spectacular failures. I have expunged him from my history as all but a personal MacGuffin. Memory of my parents, too, has faded with time. I don't actually recall any special moments spent with them. None at all.

It's all like that, my childhood and adolescence. I don't have any immediate memories of either, only memories based on the memories of others. Even my adopted father's alcoholism is something I have only been told about. I assume the tragedy and pity of it all soured the concept of family for me — or perhaps 'stunted its growth' is a better way of putting it. At any rate, I didn't bond with my foster parents and ran away from home at age twelve. I lived by my wits, alone and homeless, and became the man I am today. Since then, there are women with whom I have assayed a brief liaison — *those* I do remember — but for whatever reason, I have never tolerated their company for long. I cannot relate to them. Isolation is my most natural state. I understand people as political animals; as human beings, however, they remain a mystery.

My relationship with Clarbridge was political; I didn't need to investigate the landscape of *his* soul. His actions were enough.

"So, what are you trying to tell me?" I asked him. His stare seemed particularly intense as he blathered on about the maverick MP. "That Cowling is some sort of subversive?"

"Maybe. Maybe worse than that." He shifted uneasily. "You heard about the murder of Alaistair Schow, I suppose."

"On the radio this morning. I quite liked Schow — though he could be a pain-in-the-arse on committees of review." At which point I remembered the context in which Clarbridge had mentioned this. "You don't think Cowling had something to do with it, do you?"

The directness of the question must have unnerved Clarbridge because he went quite wobbly and shook his hands as though he'd just discovered they were covered in sticky toffee. "Don't know. I really don't. The man's weird. The whole place has been in an uproar since he was elected. Complete uproar. I wouldn't put anything past him. He scares me."

Ridiculous. "For God's sake, George, haven't you been taking your damn meds again? Don't you think that your, shall we say, antipathy to Cowling might have more to do with the fact that his rise has been so meteoric? The man has certainly had impact. Something noticeably lacking in your own career."

Clarbridge huffed contemptuously. "Don't give me that journo bullshit! Cowling's 'Feral' Party hasn't got a hope in hell of challenging us — not at the next election, not ever. I will see to that."

"Not what I've heard."

Clarbridge was a pale, reptilian bloke, with a skull-cap of closely cut, carrot-red hair and a thyroid condition. His normally bulging eyes were bulging quite extravagantly now. "Think what you bloody well want, Leonard. I haven't come to argue about politics."

"What have you come for? Not just to spin some fairy tales, I trust."

He snarled at me, his jowls wobbling unsteadily. "I want your help," he said. "Investigate Cowling for us; find out what he's up to."

"You're asking *me*?"

"You haven't been aligned for some time, Leonard, but this issue is bigger than parties. You were a researcher for Nick Greiner over several years and, before that, Neville Wran. You even wrote independent — and secret — reports for the Carr Government. Don't bother denying it...I've had my eye on you." He shrugged my indignation aside. "You know the ropes. You have contacts. But you also won't be noticed. No one sees you as a threat — they barely even see you at all — even though you're always hanging around the place writing those bloody articles of yours and sticking your oar in where it isn't wanted."

I laughed. "Okay, sure, I could do it, but why should I help you with anything as stupid and as politically sensitive as spying on an MLA?"

Cunning crept over his face as clearly as if there'd been a little window on his forehead flashing a message at me. "You're in debt up to your eyeballs."

"I'm not that desperate."

"Okay, let's do it the hard-arse way." His tone took on the callousness of a gangster from a 40s noir flick. "Certain documents have come into my possession I'm sure you think were destroyed. They provide evidence of the financial status of an insurance company called, amusingly, Thin Ice Limited; these dealings are, shall we say, less than kosher, and suggest a connection with that Daymon bloke. Remember him?"

Daymon's disastrous role in State politics was legendary, if rather elusive when it came down to details.

"I've never had anything to do with the man."

"Not what my sources say. According to the documents, you — and other members of the previous administration — are well-and-truly implicated in some highly dubious dealings. Very sensitive stuff. If you do this job for us, the documents may never come to light."

"You bastard," I said. Clarbridge was rumoured to be in line for the ruling party's top job — ultimately, a sponsored move into the federal arena. It was moments like this that helped me understand why such a promotion might be based on more than longevity.

"You've got that right," he replied.

## Blood and Bones

An idiotic snoop job almost certainly motivated by partisan envy! How did I let myself get dragged into *that* one? What worried me most was the inevitability that, in the end, Clarbridge would want me to do more than find out the Truth about Cowling; he would want information — true or not, serendipitous or planted — that could be used to destroy the man. I wasn't sure the destruction of Cowling was entirely in my interest.

For the time being, there was little I could do to get out of Clarbridge's grip. I'd have to do what I was told. However, there was no way I intended to infiltrate Cowling's inner circle until such a course couldn't be avoided. Instead, I fell back on what I know best —

bottom-feeding.

An initial scouring of the Internet coughed up the usual news stories and political reports, some parliamentary speeches that didn't seem relevant, and assorted unconnected vitriol directed at Cowling by opponents and aggrieved special-interest groups on blogs and Yahoo forums. The only thing that caught my eye was the transcript of a talk Cowling had given at a university graduation ceremony. It was the eccentricity of its central argument that drew my attention rather than any possible light it might shed on my present investigation.

In his somewhat pompous talk, Cowling maintained ferality was a positive evolutionary principle that should be valued, not criticised. Feral animals were the foreign inheritors of environments native species no longer "had the balls" to retain, he said. Change is an irresistible principle, and the complacency of the long-term inhabitant atrophied a species' ability to impose its "conceptual nature" on the world around it. The newcomer, the foreign invader, was driven by transcendent passion — and, as such, was the inevitable winner in any battle for occupancy. "The ontological paradigm the struggle carries with it," as he put it, was more aggressive than that of an occupying species overly comfortable in its stagnating niche. Hence, the inevitable dominance of a feral species. Cowling stopped short of applying this theory to the European invasion of Terra Australis, of course, aware no doubt how such an application would be received in these days of increasingly less than half-hearted reconciliation. But the idea was there in his words as a distinct subtext. Could it be used against him?

I took note of the fact that several times he quoted a book on the subject — *Feral Species of Australia,* by Bindy Daymon, the conservative politician whose career had ended in chaos and infamy a decade or so before and with whom Clarbridge threatened me. I remembered the man clearly, so spectacular had been his rise and fall. But I could not recall ever meeting him. In the end, research into Daymon and lunatic-fringe environmental theories couldn't help me unearth any possible connection existing between Cowling and the recent homicide and so, I gave it up. Instead, I went to the police.

A cop attached to the Major Crimes division, who owed me a favour, supplied all sorts of interesting detail about Schow's death that hadn't made the papers or appeared on the Net. Did I know, for instance, he said, that Schow was torn apart rather than knifed?

"Torn apart?" I queried. "What d'you mean? With bare hands — that sort of thing?"

"Teeth and claws," he replied nonchalantly.

"So, it was an animal?"

His supercilious smirk would have been annoying if indignation had been a viable option for me. "Provided it's an animal with an intricate sense of ritual, sure."

"I wish you'd be less obtuse about this."

Comfortably ensconced in a designer pub within walking distance of Macquarie Street, he took a big gulp of the beer I'd bought him. "Schow's corpse was gutted — using teeth and claws, according to the coroner — in a manner suggesting some sort of ceremony."

"A black mass?"

"Specifically, his entire torso from neck to groin was ripped open, horizontally and vertically, so the skin could be peeled back in four huge flaps. Most of his guts were removed. His heart was taken away and his intestines repositioned in the corpse, carefully but not in their original places. It was as though the killer was reconstructing the victim's insides according to a *pattern*. What happened to the heart we don't know."

"Fucking hell! Any theories?"

"Your guess is as good as ours."

I asked him about forensic analysis of saliva in the wounds.

"Ah, that's unfortunate," he muttered.

"Why?"

"There was a stuff-up. Apparently the test results and the original samples have gone missing. No one's got a clue where they are."

"Sounds fishy to me."

"It would. But you know what bureaucracies are like."

"Can't they get another sample from the corpse? It wouldn't be as fresh, but surely, it would tell you something?"

"Ah, well..." He gestured to a waitress for another beer. "The thing is, the corpse has disappeared, too...believed to have been cremated."

"What? You're kidding?"

He shrugged. "An operational error. An internal investigation has been put in motion."

I had nothing constructive to say on *that* subject, so I asked some further pointless questions that revealed no hint Cowling might be involved, and then gave up on the cops — and the murder. I couldn't even find any evidence of significant political differences between Schow and Cowling; they apparently agreed on most things. It occurred to me Schow might have been the MP Cowling decked on his first day in Parliament — during a minor debate on some issue of electoral re-distribution. In the end, however, I discovered that Schow hadn't even been in the House at the time but was home, sick with the flu.

I skimmed *Hansard* and the newspapers for anything to do with Cowling and his spectacular appearance on the political scene. Apart from the details of his first entry into Parliament, which had been tumultuous but insignificant, there were endless accounts of turbulent doings in the House, altercations with ministers and government lackeys, attention-grabbing statements made to the press, persistent accusations of outrageous or corrupt behaviour, slanging matches...and a steady, inexorable movement toward increased influence within a system normally resistant to allowing independents a real chance of gaining power. One thing I have to admit, though. In the end, reading about Cowling unnerved me so much, I came to think maybe Clarbridge was right. There was nothing definite, just a growing sense of the man's weirdness and a feeling that, beneath his clown-like exterior, he was hiding some dark and dangerous secret.

Ultimately, I knew I had to speak to him, face-to-face. Before then, however, came another dream.

## George Clarbridge Discovers Sin

She sits on the damp grass and gazes up at the mountain.

The woman is perhaps twenty-four, with black hair and a face so gaunt and wistful it seems too fragile to bear his sight.

George Clarbridge kneels, hidden in a dark-green bush a hundred metres away, his hand resting in foliage, steadying him. He's watching the woman, wondering why she's there. A harsh melody carries to him dimly on the breeze, her back curves, her arms twist, her mouth opens widely to emit the moans that form her song. She reaches toward the mountain, but, on the distant slopes, there's no reply, only the sliding shadow of a cloud.

An ache grows along George's spine, fingering at the back of his skull.

Every day for a week, the woman has been there, sometimes sitting, sometimes standing, her intense eyes pleading with the rocky escarpment far above. Her wanting fills George with desire. He doesn't know what she's doing, he doesn't understand her obsession; and hours of watching have brought him no insight. He speculates, sometimes thinks he understands her — but it's a false knowledge, imagination filling a void the woman has created. Ignorance is like an illness and he loathes it, hating himself for refusing to go to the woman and speak to her. He can't. He senses danger and he's not a courageous man.

He continues through the gardens and along the connecting streets toward the City Library, his neck stiff and shoulders aching. Pain is pressing its bony fingers into the soft tissues of his chest.

"Read the *Tribune*," the big man said. "1920 to 1940 or so. Labor grabbed office for the first time in 1910. Grabbed it with both hands, bearing the burden of a platform full to the brim with socialistic promises. It was going to be a new age for the workers, an administration that did not simply patronise them but was made up of men who were of the workers themselves and therefore appreciated the needs of real people. Okay, so we know what happened, there's plenty on that. But I'm concerned to localise our knowledge of Labor's performance during those years. Do you understand what you'll be looking for?"

George Clarbridge nodded. The big man didn't notice. His hands darted restlessly to papers on his desk, eager to continue with what he was doing before George came in. He read one, grunted, tossed the paper aside. The movement turned him back in George's direction and he noticed the waiting assistant again. "Anything that indicates first why people voted for them, and second, what they felt about subsequent events. Understand?"

"Sure," George spoke this time, louder than he should. The big man frowned.

"I'm required to present a seminar paper in June. So busy, busy. Microfilm's in the City Library. I just want the most significant, as you see it, so I don't have to read the lot myself. No time. Any problems?"

"No." George watched him as he slid from his chair. Behind him, through the window, Mount Harma was swathed in mist.

The big man became pensive. "The ALP became a significant force in New South Wales because it organised. It made politics a party game." He chuckled. "Blind man's bluff, maybe." His gesture took him to the door, where he spoke earnestly with his secretary. George shuffled about, shifting his weight from one foot to the other, gazing at the books on the man's shelves. Political histories. Manifestos. Journals of Labour History. Biographies. Election statistics. In the midst of it, he saw an aging *Ellery Queen's Mystery Magazine*. Through the window, a blue slash of sky rose behind the mountain. Light sculpted naked rock above the eucalypt-green forest that carpeted the mountain's slopes.

The big man returned. "You know what you're doing, eh? Bit clearer than mud?"

"Definitely."

"Good. Go to it then. Report to me in a week. Progress, eh? Progress."

George began backing out. The big man disappeared under the desk to rifle through his carry-bag. George took the opportunity to escape. He raised his eyebrows and shrugged when the man's wife, a thin, anaemic-looking person in a flowery house-dress, noticed him. She smiled subversively.

The job — research assistant for Hargrave Colins, a freelance writer of popular histories — was one George got almost by accident because he'd disliked working for the *Southern Times*. The work had been monotonous, not the sort of high profile journalism he'd expected to fall into after finishing his University degree. Petty crime, domestic brawls, sporting results, small-time Council indiscretions and other low-brow, amateur political activities — these were staple fare at the *Times*. The editor was a pompous idiot, not much older than George, who not only considered the *Times* — in reality, an insignificant weekly throw-away — to be some sort of media giant, but his own talents to be the equal of any journalist presently working in Australia. He looked like a beached whale and smelt like a soap factory. He bullied George — that was the thing. George hated it.

One day, Hargrave Colins — a big, meaty bloke with a bull neck and thick wrists — came into the *Times*'s editorial office, where George was sub-editing an advertising feature because the editor himself was too busy eating, and announced that he needed a research assistant, if anyone wanted to give up their current job to take up his offer. "Better conditions," he roared. "And better pay." The editor raged up to him and less-than-politely asked him to get out; but George wrote down the phone number Colins shouted over the editor's head and after work he rang him up.

"I work at the *Southern Times*," George said.

"And now you'd like a real job," Colins suggested.

"I'd like to get out of there. What are you looking for?"

"Researcher. In political history. ALP. I'm writing a book. Interested?"

"I might be. Do you have any connections with the Labor Party?"

"One of Hawkie's nearest and dearest," Colins said jovially. "In his time. Blood-brothers."

"Okay." George laughed. "You're on."

The work was both tedious and compelling. George hadn't imagined old newspapers could be so richly and starkly powerful. While he scanned the headers and closely packed columns for the sort of information Colins was hiring him to find — the speeches of aspiring ALP candidates, the polemics of conservative party spokesmen, accounts of branch meetings, the copious conference reports that appeared each year in the *Worker*, anecdotal tales that gave sudden humanity to abstract political figures — he found his eye wondering to other matters, the wider news that existed beyond the endless accounts of political manoeuvring. Murders, robberies, illicit liaisons, natural disasters, social oddities; he couldn't leave them alone. He'd be reading something about what was happening in Caucus that week and, in a column next to it, he'd come across EARTH TREMOR HITS. COUNTRY RETREAT NO HOLIDAY or GIRLS DESTROYED BY DRUG FIENDS, and he'd just have to delve into it. Sometimes a story would lead him to the next day's issue in pursuit of a continuing narrative. Sometimes it took him on to the day after that. Sometimes the story would continue for weeks, even if sporadically. An endless, real-life melodrama, serialised for his convenience.

One day, his attention was captured by news of a murder. It had taken place in 1924, the body — that of a young girl — discovered in an alley a block from a market arcade in Maroubra. The thirteen-year-old girl, who had been going to the butcher's shop for her grandmother, had been cut open and mutilated — police couldn't even tell if she'd been violated. Something about the story struck him as both fascinating and chilling. It unnerved him that it seemed so familiar, like a memory he'd forgotten. He read more.

The public had been outraged, of course, in those more innocent times, and the outrage fed the story. Clues emerged slowly, though even then there was no certainty they were clues. Men seen in the vicinity. Whispered conversations heard in the local pub. A drop of blood on the footpath a block away. George, fascinated by the tale, followed the story through several weeks of newspapers, until lack of progress caused it to fade, unresolved, from the media. By then, the afternoon had grown grey. George packed up his notes, rewound the microfilm, switched off the reader and left the library. His spirit felt heavy and restive.

She's there again. He hears her singing before he sees her and, against his better judgement, leaves his path and cuts across in the direction of the sound. Evening light is scudding through the trees with him. Thoughts of murder — monstrosities he's been re-constructing in his mind all day — drain from him as he peers through the ring of bushes. There she is! The sun's dying ochre beats against her hair, which is like a shadow that it can't penetrate, so it just slides off. Her large darkened eyes, contrasting with her pale face, gaze pleadingly toward the mountain. Arms outstretched, she cries for some release he cannot, for the moment, grant her. He feels as though he's the one in need of salvation.

Her voice seems to draw him tonight. It always does, whenever he hears it, but this time, it's like an ache in his heart. There's no resistance. He steps out from the bushes.

If she sees him, she makes no acknowledgement. Wind catches the material of her dress and whips it around her legs. Her feet are bare.

He stands, not wanting to interrupt her song, waiting for a break in which he can gain her attention. What will he say? He has no idea and doesn't care — his mind and his heart are full of her, of him being there with her, no longer apart but part of her moment.

Silence. Her dark eyes turn to him.

"I've been listening to your song," he says.

She smiles, slightly embarrassed perhaps, and begins to leave.

"No, wait!" He strides up to her, thoughtlessly grabbing at her bare arm. "Don't go! I didn't want to stop you. The song is beautiful."

She looks at his hand on her arm, then at him. "What do you want?"

"Nothing...um. Nothing. Just..."

"Please let go."

He doesn't have easy control of his muscles anymore. He struggles with his hand to make the fingers release her flesh. It is cold, yet somehow arousing.

"I was intrigued," he says. "Why are you here so often? What's that you're singing?"

Her eyes stare into his. He feels his pulse quicken. He wants to touch her once more, to feel the electricity that shot through his muscles as his fingers made contact with her cold, marble skin. Kiss her perhaps. Feel the smooth invitation of her legs. Soft caress across the curves of her thighs.

"I hold the mountain at bay," she says.

"The mountain?"

"It wants to rise against us. Now's not the time."

Almost against his will, or perhaps to break the hold she has over him, he glances at the mountain. Tufted green slopes, dark shadows that slide on its summit. Wisps of cloud like a cold breath.

She's crazy — that is clear — but, strangely, her madness feeds his desire.

"Rise against us?" he queries.

A soundless rumble shudders through the earth beneath his feet.

When he turns to question her further, she's striding from him across the damp grass. He can sense her panic.

## Fertile Imaginings

I awoke from this dream of Clarbridge on the morning of my appointment with Cowling. Unlike the other dream I'd been having, this one seemed real, like a memory. But why should I remember these particular incidents from Clarbridge's past, even if I'd known them? Clarbridge was not a close friend, perhaps not a friend at all. The only stuff I'd read on him was public knowledge — he'd never told me anything about his pre-political life. I'm sure no one else had.

After a desultory breakfast — Radio National

describing an overnight earth tremor that struck some pissant town out beyond Wagga Wagga — I suddenly realised the peculiarity of it was going to haunt me if I didn't find out whether or not the things I'd dreamt were true. I rang him.

"Bugger it, Leonard," he growled, his voice hissing in my ear as though leaking from the earpiece of the phone. "It's four o'clock in the bloody morning. This better be important. Have you found out something? Can we nail the bastard?"

"Nail the bastard?"

"Cowling, damn it!"

His anxiety levels were still high.

"I wanted to ask you something personal, George. Did you work as a research assistant once, when you were younger?"

"What is this, Leonard? You're supposed to be harassing Cowling, not me."

"Come on! It's a simple question."

I heard him thump something, maybe the wall. "Yes, damn it. So what?"

"Hargrave Colins, right?"

He was silent.

"His Labor Party history. You worked on his goddamn Labor Party history."

"So what if I did? I know it's revisionist junk. If you think you can blackmail me with this—"

"How come you didn't get an acknowledgement?"

"Because Colins is a patriarchal bastard. Look, Leonard, this stuff isn't exactly the secret of the century. The Party machine knows—"

"Don't be so paranoid, George. I'm not looking for

something to attack you with. I had a particularly vivid dream, and it was about that stuff...Colins, the newspaper you worked for...you walked across a park to get to his house. I saw you reading about that murder in Sydney. A little girl."

"My God, Leonard. That's weird. How'd you know about that?"

"I told you. A dream. There was some really strange business with a woman. In the park. She was singing at the mountain. You touched her. Is that true, too?"

"No. No. Of course not. What do you think I am, a pervert?"

I let that pass. "But the other? That was real?"

"It was real. I don't know what you're up to, but if you try anything funny—"

"It was a dream. I swear it."

There was a moment of silence, deep, like a sudden vision of eternal darkness in the middle of a summer day.

"Just get on with the job, Leonard." He hung up.

I smiled at the phone. His agitation exhilarated me, I admit. I didn't know what it meant, or why this knowledge had come to me in a dream, but whatever it was, I would keep it there in a corner of my mind. Everything's useful in the end.

It was too early to bother with the ordinary businesses of life — and I was too restless to settle down to writing the column I contributed to the *Herald*. I brewed some coffee and sat with a cup on my small veranda, staring out across the ocean. The morning was grey and listless. Irregular gusts of wind swept over the water, causing snaking paths of disturbance as though something just under the surface moved indecisively backwards and forwards. I found myself staring at the trails as they flared and faded. Waited for another to occur. Dizziness and a slight nausea shuddered through me.

The air was suddenly cold.

I pulled my eyes away from the ocean and stared into my coffee, as though it might be to blame.

There was a screech of brakes from the coast road that ran between my building and the ocean, followed by the thud of impact. I searched for sign of the accident, but could see nothing.

Wind swept over the escarpment behind me, carrying sea-spray and the grey morning light. Bare rocks along the crown of the cliff-face seemed to flex. The cup fell from my fingers and shattered.

I moaned.

The wind's voice formed words. Words in a language I didn't know. It echoed off the ocean. I turned back to the water and the haze on the horizon was broken by a dark shadow that rolled toward me — a rain shower, I thought. But it was moving against the prevailing wind, so how could it be rain? A meteorological anomaly?

Something was rising. Something unspeakably huge. It appeared from the restless water, runnels like cataracts streaming down its humanoid face and cascading from its shoulders. Its eyes were solid black. Deep and impenetrable. Perhaps the cavernous sockets were empty. If so, its sight came to it independently of physical organs, for it saw me. I could feel its awareness pounding at my skull, aching in my limbs. I couldn't move. The chair under me had become a sucking quagmire. My muscles did not have the strength to break its hold.

From somewhere far away, I could hear a woman's voice, singing.

The giant's attention turned to the escarpment behind me. It opened its mouth and roared a command.

The rocks trembled.

## Blood for the Rocky Ground

When finally he came upon a sign of humanity, it was a real disappointment. The crumbling shed, with its warped boards and broken windows, was more a symbol of passing than of continuity. Yet, there was evidence of present habitation. On a wire, a pair of stained khaki-coloured overalls flapped in the breeze, held in place by broken pegs.

The man glanced around but could see no one. Hunched over, as though hiding in his own shadow, he moved toward the overalls and unpegged them. As he slipped them on, he kept a myopic watch out for their owner.

The air was darkening, a bleak orange-blue that made the spine of mountains defining the valley appear like a sheer wall that hemmed him in. Perhaps the road he'd been following led nowhere. What evidence did he have that this crumbling shed was real? A pair of stained overalls? It could all be a blind, a trick to drain his self-control further, so he might succumb to the despair that lurked within him. That despair wanted out, but the hope he was not alone, that mankind was real...somewhere...offering sanity, kept it in check.

Carefully, he padded up to the shed, and peered through a crack in the wall. Inside, shadows and silence filled the space without giving it form. It was empty. Walls and floor were furnished only with darkness.

He raised his hand. Held it before his face. His fingers spread, taut with anger. His muscles protested as he resisted the impulse to clench his fist and pound it against the wall.

"Damn you!" he growled. Behind him, a rumble of sound echoed through the hills.

"Anyone there?" a voice said. The man's heart leapt.

He tried to determine where the sound had come from; he stumbled, back-to-the-wall, along the line of the shed. Overgrown grass around its base was treacherous with bits of rusted machinery. He stubbed his toe on a sharp edge and swore.

"Who's there?"

Should he say something? Yes, of course, but what? His imagination failed him. He leaned around the corner of the shed. A round, grease-smeared face poked from under the jacked-up rear of a Ford truck.

"Who the hell are you?" it demanded.

What could he say? There was no answer to the question.

A mechanic pushed himself out from beneath the truck. He was wearing filthy overalls and large, shitty boots. He stood, right hand on his hip, left gripping a spanner.

"You fuckin' gonna stand there smirkin' like some bloody goanna?"

The man shook his head. Something rattled in it. "I'm sorry to disturb you," he said. "I was startled. I didn't think there was anyone around."

"Well, I'm around. Damn right I'm around. I'll give you one thing though..." The mechanic leaned intimately — if they'd been closer, he would have been whispering in the man's ear. "Been bloody quiet since that earth tremor this mornin'."

"Earth tremor?"

"You didn't notice?"

"I was...asleep."

The mechanic laughed. "Drunk, ya mean?" This admission of weakness seemed to allay his suspicions. He stuck the spanner in his pocket. "Scared the shit outta me, I'll tell ya. Near pissed me pants. There were fires...right along the horizon. Seemed like it anyways." He pointed back the way the man had come. His hands wiped down his thighs, leaving a greasy smear. "On ya way to town, eh? Hell of a walk. Where you from?"

"Um, up the valley a way. In the hills."

"The Clarbridge place?"

"I'm visiting. Just visiting."

He scratched at his nostril. "The Clarbridge family are the big landowners around here. You must've heard of them." He shrugged. "No? Tell you what, mate...I got a bit of a thirst. You in for a coldie?"

The offer made the man anxious; he felt tension ease up his spine, tugging at his heart. "I've...um, got to be going."

The mechanic came toward him, his lunarscape features stretching into longer valleys. "Bloody hell, have one fa the road. Maybe I'll drive ya to town after." He grasped the man's hand and shook it. "Name's Garry...Gazza." His touch was like an electric shock.

The man stiffened, feeling delicate convulsions in his muscles.

"Okay," he said. "One."

He might've been leaning on an edge that had cut off circulation to his hands. Something was trying to break through their tips.

He followed Gazza inside. Worried his palms against each other. Felt the sweat thicken.

"Get that in ya, mate!" Gazza thrust a chilled VB beer can into his hand. The man gripped it desperately. "Don't cost nothin' to sit." Gazza indicated a wooden chair with a leg partially separated from the joint.

The man felt nausea in his stomach.

He wanted to escape.

But Gazza's rough camaraderie wouldn't let go; the man found himself slumping into the chair, raising and upending the can, feeling the cold liquid spill down his throat. He laughed at something Gazza said about the "bloody weather". While his stomach attempted to deal with the unpleasant acidity of the beer, he watched the dull movement of the mechanic's eyes, the craggy flab around his jowls, grime on his thick neck that failed to hide the flesh beneath it, fullness evident in each and every contour of his body.

"What ya staring at?" Gazza growled. "I got a booger hangin' outta me nose or what?" He stuck his forefinger deep into his nostril.

The man shook his head. Denial. Or loss of control. The mechanic seemed to be swelling with blood, bloating with his own heat. The man's hands ached.

"Funny." Gazza leaned forward, pointing at the man's chest with the finger he'd just extracted from his nose. "You got the same initials as me." *G.B.* was sewn into the denim. "Hey. What the fuck? Those are my bloody King Gees."

Gazza stood. He grabbed at the man, who raised his hand defensively.

"You bloody stealing my stuff?"

Claws raked the mechanic's arm, furrowing channels for the redness that spilled immediately from his punctured skin. He threw himself back, crying out. The man stepped toward him, wanting to reassure.

*Wanting to free his heat.*

Cloth over the mechanic's chest and belly tore apart. "Whatta ya...?" He scrambled backwards, flinging himself out the door. When he thumped down onto the ground, the impact raised spumes of dust. "Fuck off...get the fuck away!"

Far beneath the heat scorching his belly, the man felt cold — an icy breath compounded of fear and something else, something lustful, something that needed the blood pushing on the mechanic's skin. Find it a way out into the world, that's what he had to do. Break through the layers of sediment and filth. Rake in the air. Shout. Feel freedom like an orgasmic shudder.

Gazza screamed as his belly tore open. Blood gushed, splashing onto the ground. The soil took it in as the desert welcomes rain after drought.

The rocks trembled.


**Scars**


Nightmares wracked my sleep.

Their violence was easy to rationalise. The real-world

murder of Alaistair Schow was enough to explain them, I reckoned: shock had hit me at last, the reality that had lain dormant in my heart rising to overwhelm me in the night. I could tell myself that.

But the sea-giant? It had seemed so solid. Not a dream at all. And that couldn't be. There were no giants in the world — and if there were, and one had risen from the sea that morning, why had no one else seen it? Surely, I'd been daydreaming. Weariness — and the strangeness of my dream of Clarbridge — had weakened me, fooled me. I had to push it all aside.

My appointment with Cowling was set for noon. An odd time, that. Politicians were usually involved in business lunches by then. Journalists only got to do lunch if someone wanted a favour. What favour could I possibly do for Cowling?

"Mr Townsend?" A tall, cadaverous woman emerged from the shadows beside the door as I stepped into the parliamentary entrance hall. She scared the shit out of me.

"For God's sake," I growled, retrieving my briefcase. The guard seated a few metres away glanced at us, blinked and returned his attention to the magazine on his lap.

"I do beg your pardon," she said. If she smirked, it was so subtle and ephemeral I could hardly accuse her of doing so, even to myself. "Mr Cowling asked me to intercept you. He has been delayed."

I forced her to look me in the eyes. For a moment she seemed familiar, but the feeling faded quickly. "What's his problem?"

"An electoral matter." She smiled. Her lips were very

pale, as though the blood had drained from them. A silver-grey lipstick perhaps. I noticed that her arms hung at her side the whole time, completely inexpressive. Again she looked uncomfortably familiar.

"And you are?"

"His PA...and researcher." She made an effort of will and her right hand rose. I took it. It was very cold. "Kyla Fauxair."

She was attractive in a distant, chilling way. The ice of her added to the allure. I wondered about her ancestry. She had large dark-blue eyes, immaculately outlined, and skin blanched by a fine, silky powder. Her black hair was pulled back tight, emphasising her sharp facial structure. She might have been a model out of *Elle*.

"Perhaps you can stand in for him until he arrives," I suggested.

She studied me for a moment, as though interpreting my words. "That was his intent, I believe," she said. She took my arm. "But not in here," she added. "This is a deadening place." And swung me toward the door I'd just entered.

We strode along Macquarie Street — or rather she strode and I was dragged in her wake — over the road with barely a glance at the traffic, down King Street and into a marble and metallic cavern called Café Noir. The only black I could see, however, was Ms Fauxair's dress. The café itself flashed primary colours and chrome trim.

"Noir?" I queried.

Kyla touched my chest with a long, manicured finger. Was she trying to tell me something? My heart skipped a beat. What had it meant?

"Irony," she whispered.

A waiter gestured us toward an unoccupied table — the last available, as though it had been saved for us. The place was packed. We ordered coffee — I had mine black; hers was white. I wondered if that, too, was ironic.

"How long have you worked for Cowling?" I asked.

"Long enough for him to have gained my *respect*." The way she said it, the word might have meant something sinister. "He is a remarkable man, Mr Townsend."

"I've heard the stories."

"The truth is much stranger."

I looked into her dark eyes and tried to hold them. "I don't suppose you'll tell me."

She gave her cold smile again. "I suppose not."

We sipped at our coffees in silence. Her gaze never released me, unembarrassed yet undemanding. I couldn't do it. I kept looking away, casually, as though unaware of her attention.

"You are in great danger, Mr Townsend," she said at last.

"From you?"

"I'm not attempting to seduce you — I would not be so obvious." She leaned toward me, gripping my arm. "You are in mortal danger, and you should know it."

"Did Cowling tell you to threaten me? Is this his idea?"

A whisper. "My own, purely my own." She sat back in her chair and, for what seemed the first time, let her attention stray from me. "But he wanted me to." The skin on her neck was smooth, unblemished. I followed it with my eyes to where it disappeared beneath her high-buttoned, black satin blouse. "Do you wish to make love to me, is that what distracts you?"

I was taken aback. Perhaps I blushed — my face was hot. "I don't know what..." I began, but reined in the lie before it went any further. Of course I knew what she meant — and she was right.

"You think I'm beautiful, do you?" she said.

"You are. Like a model. Perfect."

Expressionless, she stared at me. The smile when it came was unsettling. "Nothing is as it seems," she replied. "You imagine my breasts perhaps — their soft, marble perfection, the smooth curves, the crowning nipples like drops of pale blood. You anticipate their exquisite sensuality. But the truth is imperfect."

"Imperfect?"

"This is a world of death and imperfection, Mr Townsend. What place is there in it for perfection?"

This was the strangest seduction I'd ever taken part in. "It's the dream we hold to," I said, reverting to her abstract mode of thought. "We're all scarred, so perhaps we find beauty in the scars."

Her eyes told me nothing. Standing, she looked down at me. "Sit here," she said. "Wait for him." She leaned toward me, her hand cold on my shoulder even through my coat. Her mouth was mere centimetres from my ear. I should have felt her breath, but there was nothing. "My dreams were ended years ago," she whispered. "I hope for nothing. Only Mr Cowling keeps me here. Take care what enemies, and what friends, you make. I must go now."

Then she was striding away. I watched her move to the door of the Café Noir and exit into the street. I didn't follow. The depth of her despair paralysed me.

## The Triumph of Tact

Cowling arrived almost immediately. His long body slammed through the door. Though he managed to avoid colliding with anyone, he gave me an uneasy feeling that disaster could strike at any time.

He looked straight at me and waved. "Townsend," he yelled across the Café. "How are you? Not too civilised, I hope!"

"No, Mr Cowling," I said, smiling in spite of myself. "Not too civilised." It was, I'd been told, his catch-phrase.

"But civilised enough to get on in this bugger of a business, eh?" He towered over me by this time, slamming his big hand on my back. "Call me Yipper," he added. "I prefer to be called Yipper."

"I've always wondered," I said, "is that your real name? I mean, is it the one your parents gave you?"

"Derived from 'Bunyip'," he said. "Traditional thing." He didn't explain further. Instead, he lowered himself into the chair Kyla had been sitting in. "Ah," he exclaimed, "Ms Fauxair has just left."

"She kept your seat warm for you."

"Hardly that." Grinning, he indicated the cup in front of him. "But she ordered me a coffee."

"It's not fresh. I'll get you another."

He fixed me with a stern glance, as though I'd said something wicked. "I like my coffee cold." To prove it, he lifted the cup and, holding my gaze, took a big sip. He grunted. "Still warm. Pity."

"Why don't you order an iced coffee?" I asked.

"It's not the same."

A strange one, that's for sure. He gulped a mouthful of lukewarm coffee and smacked his lips theatrically. "Now, Mr Townsend, what is it you're supposed to be doing? Remind me. A book, is it?"

"On the role of independents in Australia's political history. You, of course, must feature prominently."

He waved his hand, dismissing the notion. "My history has barely begun. I've done nothing but stir up a few of the more complacent of our leaders."

"I think you're underestimating—"

"I never underestimate."

Self-confident enough to deny his own importance, and to sound sincere about it — a dangerous combination. "Be that as it may, I'd like to explore your attitudes a bit, if you'll let me."

He gestured magnanimously.

We talked for some time, about his past — at least as it related to his political career — about his present activities, about his associations. Frankly, I believed very little of it. Sure, it was convincing. Sure, it was internally consistent. But somehow, it wasn't real. It wasn't the substance of it that gave me this feeling, but the tone of it, the ambiance he created for it. It was too pat, too perfectly eccentric and characteristic of him, contrived even in its air of spontaneity. It left me dissatisfied because it meant nothing. It could easily be true, everything he said. Equally, it could be a load of shit. Even if I latched onto some aspect of it, investigated and found out it was a lie, it wouldn't prove anything. I could do the same thing to anyone in the café, and get the same results, and it wouldn't make any of them a murderer. It was all too meaningless. Most of it's gone from my mind now. It was gone five minutes after he said it. Allusions to youthful indiscretion, skilfully elaborated to prove him a man of doubtful, but earned, integrity, or anecdotes about recent larrikinism in the pursuit of ethically dubious ends, just made him interesting and...what? Human, I guess. He made suspect behaviour seem admirable. It never went far enough to provide a basis for suspicion, mingling idealism and frailty in a way that convinced you of his strength — a consummate act because it could so easily be artless.

"You don't know what to make of me, do you?" he suggested after about half an hour of oration.

"You put up a remarkable front," I said.

"Politics is about fronts. So is life."

"But it needn't be anything so superficial, not at all. It might be real."

"We are nothing without our fronts." He laughed. "Nothing but arseholes." He looked into his empty coffee cup, rubbed his finger around the inside and licked off the residue that clung to the tip. "Why don't you ask me something theoretical? A matter of principle."

"Okay. As an independent, how do you see your role in parliament?"

"You mean, do I want to keep the bastards honest?"

"Is that what you're trying to do?"

"It's bullshit. How can politicians be kept honest

when politics is predicated on lies? Using dishonesty to, one hopes, honest ends."

"And not an expression of the will of the people?"

"The People? Merely an abstraction. An abstraction can't have a will. The politician must give form to The People first, as the concept relates to the geographic and sociographic landscape from which he chooses to arise, and, then, to create a will for it."

"So it all comes from the politician. Politics is its own end?"

"Not at all. There is a reality beyond ourselves and it's that which controls us."

"What reality? Truth? Democracy?"

"If I said yes, would you believe me? Of course not. This is an age of cynicism."

"I might believe, but I'd want you to define what you mean by those terms."

"Of course you would, because you're a cynic. Well, I don't mean either Truth or Democracy. I am referring to a spirit vastly more difficult to define and vastly more powerful. And it's not an abstraction."

"I don't understand."

"I don't expect or intend that you should. It's not something we can profitably pursue at this time." He smiled at me in a way that sent chills through me — not because it was sinister, but because it seemed alien, as if he knew I could never understand him. "But I will go back to your original question: I don't want to keep the bastards honest...that's a passive act. I want to bring about change. And I intend to do so."

That sounded more interesting. I caught myself leaning toward him, eagerly. "What change? And how?

Does this relate to your ideas regarding feral invasion?"

He moved away from me in his chair, waving his arms so violently he upset the dried flowers clustered in the centre of the table and sent his empty cup clattering over the floor in the direction of a bemused waiter. "I can't tell you that," he cried, as though I'd threatened him.

The waiter picked up Cowling's cup. "Would you like a refill, sir?"

"What? A refill?" Cowling glared at him.

"Your cup was knocked over." *Was knocked over*. He made it sound as though the act had been committed by some divine providence.

"I don't want any damn coffee!" Cowling growled. The waiter nodded, unfazed, and floated off about his business. "What's he talking about damn refills for?"

I shrugged and he scowled at me. "You were saying?" I gestured for him to continue.

"What?"

"You were about to tell me what sort of changes you wanted to affect."

"I was not. Damned if I'd be railroaded."

"Sorry."

"I can't talk about those matters...yet."

"Too controversial? Too unpopular?"

His big hand reached out and grabbed my wrist. "Politics," he said.

I glanced at his hand and he removed it from my arm. "Politics? I understand that, of course. But if I could follow the progress of your thinking on this matter, watch and record as it transforms or comes into being, I could produce a unique historical document.

Something of great importance. It would significantly enhance your reputation." I made an open gesture — arms wide, fingers spread. "I'll guarantee a personal embargo on anything you tell me now, until such time as you rescind it."

Cowling laughed. "I like you. I really do." Suddenly, the humour dropped away, as abruptly as it had arisen. "If I tell you my plans, I'll be revealing something I haven't told a living soul."

"Just a few dead ones, eh?"

He pushed himself out of his seat, rising like some restless deity. "Not here," he said. "Somewhere private. My electoral office."

"In Mytabin?"

"I have to go back there this evening. Shall we say in two days? Friday."

"But—"

"Can you make it? Yes or no? I'm a busy man, Townsend. I've no time for stuffing about."

"Well, yes," I managed. "I suppose—"

"Good. Noon. Friday." With that, he strode through the café, sidestepping customers with careless aplomb.

I paid the bill.

## Footsteps

I spent the rest of the day in the Parliamentary library, ferreting out everything I could about Cowling. To my surprise (or perhaps not), there was very little. In fact, one would be forgiven for thinking he hadn't existed before he registered as an electoral candidate. Then again, the same could be said for most of the corpses occupying bench space in the House.

At about three, a shock-faced young man in white shirt and tie, blue jeans and Nike cross-trainers handed me a message. "Thanks," I said, and he looked as though I'd spoken in ancient Mesopotamian.

The message read: "Meet me", followed by an address in Maroubra and the name "Kyla".

My naturally suspicious nature urged caution, but the allure of intrigue was stronger. By four, I was driving along a road off Maroubra beach, scanning for numbers. I was expecting an apartment building — one of those art deco places restoration experts like to tart up with pastel paints or a glass-and-metal complex filled with plastic plants — but instead found myself parking down the street from an old-fashioned 1940s brick bungalow. I sat in the car staring at it, unable to imagine Kyla living in a place like that — war-generation quaint, in poor condition, and totally lacking distinction. What connection could she have with it?

Stupid, really, I decided. Why expect a stereotype? Besides, when I thought about it, wouldn't it be appropriately stereotypical for her to have been born in a place like this, part of the fading lower middle-class — until plucked from obscurity by Cowling?

Something banged against the window beside me. I glanced around — there was a small streak on the glass not ten centimetres from my face. Dark red. Perhaps some bird had been eating mulberries. A shadow caught at the corner of my eye, streaking low across the footpath toward Kyla's house. But when I looked in that direction, I couldn't see a thing.

I got out of the car and headed for the front gate. It

was metal and wire, lopsided on one hinge and badly corroded; it creaked when I pushed it, scraping a crevice it had worn in the concrete. If Kyla was watching for me, she gave no sign. I walked along the path and up the stairs.

For a moment, there was no response from knocking. I was about to leave when I heard a faint whisper, as though someone had leaned against the door, singing into the wood. I couldn't make out words, but it was more chant-like than melodic.

"Kyla?" I said, rapping my knuckles on the door. The singing cut off. "Kyla? Is that you?"

There was no discernable response. I pressed my ear hard against the door, hoping to hear breathing or movement. Nothing.

"Kyla? Come on! Open up!" I banged on the wood.

"Leonard?"

The voice came from behind me and startled me so much I scraped my ear on the door and struck the side of my head on the jamb in reaction. Kyla was standing in the path, a look of cold indifference on her face.

"I...um, thought I heard you inside," I said.

"There's no one inside. No one has lived here for many decades." She stepped up to me and waited while I moved away from the door. Then she used a key to unlock it. It swung open; I peered past her into a fussy, darkened hallway, its mustiness disturbed now by daylight and currents of air. "I'm glad you came," Kyla said.

She didn't look glad; if anything, she looked as though my coming was one of the most woeful acts ever perpetrated upon her. Following her through the house — feeling as though the grainy air congealed in her wake by the chill she radiated — I glanced aside at a dark sitting room, its furniture covered in white cloth; on the other side, a closed door; in the hall, a cut-glass cabinet, shrouded in dust and filled with small, twisted ornaments — I couldn't make out what they were. The carpet was old in appearance, but seemed little worn.

"What is this place?" I asked.

Without turning, Kyla answered: "My home."

"But no one's lived here for...well, decades, you said."

Again, she gave no reply, and I followed her to the end of the hallway, which opened into a kitchen area. None of the surfaces gave off a sheen — ancient lino, a Formica table with metal legs and rim, work benches that looked like a continuation of the floor. Dust and mould coated everything.

"My mother and I used to sit in here and talk." Kyla stood near the table. "She'd have cups of tea...I'd drink cordial or milk. She smoked too much, my mother — I remember that clearly."

"Is your mother still alive?" I ventured.

She stared at me, her eyes non-committal. "I don't know," she said.

I didn't pursue it. I sensed a yawning chasm awaited anyone daring enough to venture too deeply into that territory.

Kyla noticed my reticence. Emotion trembled over her face, but was gone before it could work out what it was meant to be. Dragging an old kitchen chair from under the table, she said, "Sit down. Please. You want to know why I asked you here?"

"It crossed my mind." I pulled out another chair and sat leaning on the table. Kyla sat across from me.

"You talked to Mr Cowling, didn't you?"

I nodded.

"And he asked you to visit him in The Scrub?"

"Yes, he did suggest—"

"Will you go?"

I sat back. "Will I go? I guess I will. If I want an interview, I'll have to. Besides..." I shrugged, "...the place intrigues me."

"It shouldn't," she said. "Unless you harbour a desire for self-destruction, unless you want to lose yourself in a sub-imaginative wasteland, steer clear of The Scrub — especially when invited there by Mr Cowling."

I grinned. "Sub-imaginative wasteland? You're being a bit post-modern, aren't you?"

Characteristically, she didn't grin back. "He wants you there. He wants to win you over."

"Me?" Suddenly, I was finding it difficult to maintain my finely balanced sense of the ludicrous. I glanced aside — the walls seemed to be closing in. "What would he want to win me over to?"

"You threaten him. I don't know how. But he's shown me his anger, revealed the deeper recesses of his mind — and you're there, Mr Townsend. You're there in him."

A chill prickled over my skin, even though my rational mind laughed at her B-grade warnings. "I don't understand. What the hell are you talking about?"

"He's not human, Mr Townsend — at least, not human as we...as *you* understand the term."

"Not human?" I stood, causing the chair to

overbalance and crash to the floor. "Look, this is getting too silly. Tell me what you want!"

Her eyes stared up at me, seeing but without passion or recognition. It puzzled me.

"What do you mean he's not human?" I said at last.

"Haven't you felt his power?"

"Sure. He's a powerful man—"

"Not a man." She stood abruptly, grabbing at my arm. Her cold fingers closed on my wrist. "I'm sorry," she said. "I've been with him a long time...a long time. He holds me in a grip tighter than you can imagine."

Were they lovers? "Do you want to leave him?" I ventured.

"There's no answer to that question." She hadn't moved, her hand still attached to me, her eyes and face expressionless. "I can *want* nothing."

"Why are you saying these things then?"

Her hand detached from my arm and fell to her side. It was the only sign of reaction she made. Her passivity — the contrast with her melodramatic words — was beginning to unnerve me.

"Why?" I pressed.

"Because I must. Because Mr Cowling wants it."

"What? But you've been warning me against him."

"As he wishes."

"You said he also wishes me harm. That I will come to harm in The Scrub."

She stared at me without expression.

"It doesn't make sense, Kyla."

Sense? Was I trying to make sense of it? There was a surrealistic logic to the whole thing that fitted well with my dreaming of late — and the senselessness was a basic component. Perhaps it was *me* going crazy after all. I was no longer seeing how my experiences fitted together, nor how the world's elements were interconnected. Nothing could be sensible. Nothing reliable.

"Perhaps I'd better go," I said.

"Come with me!" she replied, holding out her hand — not touching me this time, but waiting for my approach.

"Where?"

"I want to show you something."

I didn't take her offered hand, preferring to remain non-committal. However, I gestured for her to lead on and followed her when she headed out a door on the far wall and down a short corridor. There were inbuilt cupboards on one side, a doorway on the other leading to a bathroom (dank staleness drifted into my nostrils), and at the end, another door. She pushed this one open and went inside.

A bed, single, covered in a mildewed sheet, huddled in one corner. An antique chest-of-drawers, and childish wallpaper stained by paintings no longer there. An old toy box.

"This was my room," Kyla said.

"Really?" What remained of the decor seemed too antiquarian to have been hers. "How long ago?"

"Yesterday. A week ago. Ten years. A century. It doesn't matter. Time has died."

Her words conveyed such sorrow, despite the cold monotone with which they were delivered, that I reached to comfort her. She let my arm encircle her shoulder. "Do you miss those times?"

"I've forgotten them — as life has forgotten me."

"You radiate such pain," I said. "Has your life been hard?"

"Not my life, no."

"I don't understand."

She looked at me. Her eyes were so cold, so empty; they filled me with a grief that was almost fear. "Will you make love to me?" she said. "Here."

I stepped away. "Kyla! I didn't intend to—"

"Seduce me? I would like you to lie with me — it could be important."

She undid the buttons on her blouse and removed it. I couldn't move, paralysed by sexual confusion. Then I saw the scars. One traversed her chest, nipple to nipple, like a sinewy ridge; a second similar scar went in a ragged line from her sternum to her navel.

"How in God's name did that happen?" I stared, against my better judgement — the thing was such a violation. "Surgery?"

"Of a kind."

"I'm sorry," I said.

"It makes me what I am. Such scars repulse you, don't they?"

"No. No."

"I'm not beautiful?"

"You are," I reassured her, sincerely, aware that my heart was racing. In truth, under the scars, her breasts were fine, her skin virginal. "But this is not the place—"

"It is. The perfect place. I lived here. My life was here." She unclipped her belt and slipped out of the sternly cut skirt she wore. In the dim light, filtered through heavily curtained windows, the scars that traversed her torso were easy to ignore, especially as her body was otherwise so perfect.

She came toward me, her hands reaching to unbutton my shirt. I let her undress me. I had no desire to stop her.

When her lips touched me — first my chest, then my belly — their iciness send sparks through my flesh. "You're cold," I said. "Are you sure you want to do this?" She said nothing, merely drawing me toward the bed. The mattress smelt stale and dusty; as I eased myself down beside her, I realised that she exuded no scent at all, neither artificial nor fleshy — either that or the smells of the room overpowered it. But the query was lost when she stroked me, drawing my penis toward her. I ran my hand over her breast (cold, so cold), reached down to stimulate her clitoris; but she brushed my fingers aside and pulled me toward her. I entered her.

The moist warmth I'd anticipated wasn't there. There was no comfort, no human memory. Just bloodless inertia. The chill of lifelessness. My own mortality pounded in my chest, not revealed by a rush of sexual passion, but found in an unexpected wasteland of dead flesh. I pulled away, repulsed.

"What's wrong with you?" I gasped, stumbling to my feet and drawing away from her.

"I told you." She lay staring at the ceiling as she spoke, her body an image of marble perfection — except for the garish scar tissue, which seemed so significant now. "I've been dead for an eternity."

"What in God's name are you talking about? You're sick, surely."

"Dead, Leonard." She rose, her eyes fastening upon me. "This is no metaphor. You felt it. You were in me. Sex is an affirmation of life — but I have no life to affirm. Surely you know that."

"It's impossible." I drew my clothes on, as though being properly covered might shield me from her absurd contention.

"Impossible? There's little that is impossible, and no horror you can imagine that can't be drawn out of an inhuman mind."

"How can you be dead?"

"I *did* live here. Nearly seventy years ago. And I died nearby, slaughtered brutally. I was only a girl. He cut out my heart and ate it. From that time forth, I was his."

"Who? Cowling?"

I never got a direct answer from her. "He forgot me and I was found by another. This one let me grow until I was closer to what he wanted—"

She smiled, perhaps for the first time; then collapsed against the side of the bed, dropping to the floor with a loud thud. "Kyla!" I cried and rushed over to her. Her eyes were still open, though for a moment I couldn't tell if they could see me.

Her lips trembled. "If only...there'd been ...consummation," she whispered. "Your life in me...perhaps I could have..." Her mouth remained open. She wasn't moving. No breath. No pulse. No heartbeat. Whatever she'd been before, she was dead now.

Confused, but unwilling to consider everything she'd said — rather, being more than content to believe that she'd suffered from some bizarre illness — I abandoned her, going outside to ring the police on the mobile phone I'd left in my car. I waited for them outside, because the house seemed to me too sinister a place now — haunted — and I didn't want to go back in, not alone. They came, I explained that I'd received a note to meet an informant there — a woman named Kyla. I showed them the note. Her body's in one of the rooms, I told them.

I half-expected them to find nothing when they went inside. Isn't that what happens in the movies? They would think me crazy, question me with barely suppressed aggression, and send me away afraid of whoever had taken her.

But she was still there, where I'd left her — except the scars across her chest had come unravelled and the flesh was pulled back. There was blood on the floor.

"Been dead for some time," I overheard a white-faced detective say to a fellow officer. "But it's just like that politician, Schow. That makes five."

Five?

## Perpetual Journeys

The road I was following — marked as a major highway on my map — diminished to a dirt track and then a tangle of stunted lantana. I backtracked, certain I must have taken a wrong turn somewhere. It was all very confusing. The GPS system in my car had failed to register Mytabin at all, leaving me to assume it lay in a satellite dead zone. I had resorted to a useless physical directory, its markings failing to correspond with reality at all; at least once I'd passed Gullywater.

An offshoot brought me to a dilapidated gate with a rusted cattle grid. It was a short walk to the farmhouse I spied off to the west. Pounding on the door provoked the frustrated passion of a chained mongrel in the back yard and caused a sad-faced woman blanched by flour to materialise in the shadow of the doorway.

"Help you?" She held up her white hands. "I've been making scones."

"Yes, um...I'm looking for the highway. I seem to have misplaced it."

"Highway? There's a highway back aways — through to Canberra."

"I don't want Canberra," I said. "I'm heading for Mytabin."

She frowned. "Mytabin? That near here? Never heard of it."

"It's in The Scrub. Arden municipality. I'm not sure how close it is. I'd guess a hundred kilometres or so. I thought you might know how I can get back to the Mytabin highway."

She scratched at her forehead, marking it with a streak of white powder. Then she shrugged. "Maybe my husband'd know."

"Can I speak to him?"

She thought for a moment. "Died a year ago," she said at last. Then she added, as though the thought had only just occurred to her. "I miss him."

I ended up driving to Canberra and eventually obtained the information that Mytabin was about 200 kms west, somewhere beyond Narandera, though it could only be approached via a circuitous route that somehow took in Tumbarumba, Culcairn and Urana. It didn't seem to make much sense and was so divergent from directions I'd been given in Sydney I doubted it from the start. Nevertheless, I took a punt and drove around hoping for the way to become clear, though with no result. Once the sun disappeared, I found lodgings outside Wagga Wagga.

Next morning I drove to Narandera and spent the day investigating roads branching off the Sturt Highway. Again, no one seemed able to effectively direct me to Mytabin, though most of those I asked were confident enough in the directions they gave. I got bogged twice and, for an hour or two during the afternoon, was so profoundly lost I began to think I'd have to sleep curled up on the back seat of my car. Then I came upon a bitumen surface and a sign that looked like it had been abused by more than its fair share of trucks, roo-shooters and flung debris gouged out of the crumbling road. The paint was scratched to buggery, though I could make out letters that suggested "MYT" on the left side pointer and was willing to bet what it had once read. A number next to the name may have been intended to offer travellers some slim hope that finding the place was possible after all — though it was indecipherable now. The opposite arrow said, quite clearly, "CANBERRA 84". So close? I muttered complaints to nobody and turned left onto the blacktop.

Night drifted over me through the twisted silhouette of trees along the side of a lazily winding road. It went on and on without hope of a conclusion; kilometre after kilometre as though in an eternal, infuriating loop — road kill and the occasional crow, caught at the edge of my headlight beams, the only sign of inhabitants. My mind went from unspoken rants against Cowling and his infernal electorate to numb despair and a nascent fear. I felt myself slipping, not so much into sleep, I thought, as into a dark fugue state. I reached out to switch on the radio, though with little optimism it would give me anything except static.

"Don't bother," confirmed the man in the passenger seat.

I glanced up. Hovering in the darkness next to me, Schow's pasty face was sculptured out of shadows. "Why not? You got something against country radio."

"Cows and whiney C&W caterwauling. Who gives a shit?"

"I thought maybe I could get some idea where we were."

He laughed. The sound echoed unnaturally around the interior of the car.

"What's so funny?"

"Watch the road, dickhead!"

"What?" Through the night-stained, insect-splattered windscreen, I caught sight of a shape directly in front of me. I rammed on the brakes and swerved, sending the car into a skid. My skull flared with pain as it connected with the side window.

The engine died. Everything went still. I groaned, my bruised skull resting on my hands, still gripping the steering wheel. I wanted to let go, but I couldn't. The muscles had seized. Had I hit someone?

I felt Schow's presence leaning toward me, though I couldn't see him. His lips hovered above my ear. "Be careful," he whispered. The sound of his voice was thin and artificial, as though made of static. I couldn't feel his breath. "You could get hopelessly lost."

I jerked up, making my sight blur and temples throb. "Schow?"

Then, reality struck. How could Schow be in my car? He was dead. Slaughtered. That's why I was going to Mytabin. To investigate the man some wanted to implicate in his death.

"Schow? Are you there?"

The passenger seat was empty. Dazed, I reached over and felt the door. Locked.

Damn. I must've fallen asleep. Lucky I hadn't hit a tree. There were plenty of them. But the car seemed to have stopped in an open area off the road, suggesting, on some level, I'd been conscious enough to recognise a layby and to pull in. I touched the tender spot on my head. No blood. Just a bruise. I'd been lucky.

Outside, the world was still, as breathless as the spectre of Schow that had whispered to me in my semi-conscious state. The area was dark and threatening. Not without some nervousness, I eased open the door and climbed out. The air was so cold it chilled me to the bone without the aid of a breeze, right through my coat. No sounds anywhere. No lights. I could just make out the silhouettes of trees against the sky, but even they were like after-images burned into my retinas from an earlier, brighter time. I shivered and quickly got back in the car.

I had no idea where I was or where to go now. Even the highway had disappeared. I locked the car doors and hunkered down, suddenly gripped by a fear that I was being watched, inhuman eyes lurking unseen among the shadows of ancient forests.

My hands shook badly.

I'd have to wait for morning. Then I'd drive back to Sydney.

Cowling could go to hell — and take Clarbridge and his conspiracies with him.

## The Clarbridge Place

After he'd finished carving up the mechanic, the man stood back and considered his work. The corpse lay prostrate, its chest opened up in four large flaps. Bits of broken rib poked from the flesh and gore. The man raised the mechanic's heart to his mouth, smelling the heady aroma of spilt blood. He bit hard into the warm muscle, chewed and swallowed. Then he tore off another piece and ate it.

When it was gone, a profound lethargy came over him. He yawned, licking the blood from his lips.

The mechanic's house? Would he be safe in there? No. He wouldn't want to be found anywhere near the corpse. Where then? Streaks of night were beginning to leak into the blue sky. He had to find somewhere to hole up.

Yet it had taken him a long time to find this place, this lone evidence of humanity. What hope was there of finding another? He didn't want to hide under a rock or in a hollow tree. He was afraid of the cows, afraid too of other feral animals that might haunt this land. Crows scared him.

Well, he thought, they can feed on what's left of the mechanic.

And as he thought it, he remembered something the

mechanic had said when they'd first talked.

*"Where you from?"*

*"Um, up the valley a way. In the hills."*

*"The Clarbridge place?"*

The Clarbridge place.

That's where he could go. It had to be close by. Up the valley. Not quite back the way he'd come, because he hadn't seen it, but maybe on the western side, in the foothills. He squinted against the setting sun, and as he did so something moved, like a shadow, in the umbra of orange light. Could he make it that far? Half an hour. A hour perhaps.

He'd have to try.

He glanced at the corpse, knowing his act would have consequences. If the flesh and bone remained there, intact, until midnight, it would rise and follow him — he knew that. But if the flesh were too badly eaten — by the crow or by cows — it would never awaken again. Too bad. Frankly, he didn't care. He'd had what he wanted from it and that was enough.

But did he want a corpse trailing after him as he searched for his path? It might be best, at this stage, to limit any servitor functionalities. Besides, the compulsion in him to find human beings or their flotsam was finely balanced against a need to destroy all evidence of the old inhabitants' presence within the valley — he realised, perhaps understood, the tension that confused him, blurred his mind. It was still blurred, his mind and memory, but killing the mechanic and eating his heart had made him feel much better.

Squinting in the failing light, he went to the rear of the truck and examined what was there. Tools, yes, but only car maintenance tools. He strode into the house, searched through it, and, in a room out the back, found what he was looking for.

Using the axe, he chopped up the corpse, so that it could not re-animate and follow him. The dry soil absorbed the blood. As the man severed its last limb, and then cracked apart the body's pelvis, peeling out the backbone and pulling apart the vertebrae, a tremor passed through the bones he held in his hands, the truck parked in his peripheral vision and even, as he discovered when he spun around (sure that he'd sensed movement behind him), the house in which he'd sat and drunk beer with the dead mechanic. Outlines blurred, trembled, began to disperse like desegregating pixels on a computer screen. The man frowned in puzzlement. What was happening?

The bones were gone now, leaving not even a trace of blood. The truck had lost its form and was collapsing into dust. Dust faded into shadow. Shadow was lost in the growing twilight. Now the house went, as though sabotaged by some demolition expert with explosives secreted in the very substance of its walls.

Was the world coming apart?

No, not the world. The man watched until all traces of the mechanic, his truck, and his house were erased from the valley floor. It was an elimination, a cleansing. Apparently humanity no longer belonged here...

Dragging the axe behind him, he headed southward toward the spot on the surrounding hills where he was convinced he'd find the Clarbridge Place. That was where he had to go — it gave him purpose and answered some barely perceived need. His feet ground over the alternately rocky and grassy landscape, eyes peering into the gathering gloom of night. Occasional lightning flashed along the horizon. Two hours went by and, despite his tiredness, he kept on going. Two hours turned to three, flatness turned to slope; the ground became more broken and tormented. Here, the earth's muscles showed as though its skin had been slashed. Its blood was the night. The man mounted a rise as the last light disappeared, still without finding a road. Why wasn't there a road? Surely the Clarbridge Place would have some access leading to it.

The moon rose, but the light it gave to the valley and the hills was sickly and threatening. The man groaned and shivered. He'd lost his optimism now, which had blossomed so powerfully after he fed on the mechanic's heart. He rubbed his lips with the back of his hand and frowned, considering his actions. Was it normal behaviour, eating a person's heart? If so, normal for whom?

He studied his hand in the faded darkness, clenching and unclenching its fingers to the fractured rhythms of his breathing.

## Into the Serpent's Coils

I woke to a face. It was squashed against the glass of the side window, peering in at me. Ugly as sin. With an abruptness that jolted me from my inert wonderment, it grinned, revealing reptilian fangs.

I jerked away, unsure whether I was looking at man or beast. Blinked. Now the thing had gone. A dull green smear on the glass was all that remained as inconclusive evidence of its presence. The stain faded quickly. I checked the locks on the door were still engaged and leaned closer to see where my visitor had gone. Not a sign. Yellow morning light sprayed over the roadside clearing, which was empty except for me and my Statesman. Had the owner of the face slid under the car? Not a nice thought.

I was pondering what to do next, and getting nowhere — thinking only that I was desperate to pee — when a hand slapped against the glass. My heart paused, suddenly unsure whether it should go to the effort of another beat.

"Hey there!"

The face leaning toward me was dark, though not because of Aboriginal ancestry. It was lightless rather than pigmented: an old man's face, weathered and granitite. He looked like he'd been created from the surrounding dirt.

"Whatcha doin' in there?"

The closed window muffled his voice and that fact struck me as rather comforting.

"Got lost last night," I said. "Stopped here."

"Eh?" His left ear turned toward me.

"Got lost!" I shouted.

"Whaaa?"

"Lost!"

He shrugged.

I slid the window open a few centimetres and tried again. "GOT LOST!"

"Yeah?" he said, his dull grey eyes studying me through the gap. "What got lost?"

Sigh. "Mytabin actually."

"Mytabin, eh?" He leaned away and laughed.

I checked around about him for the animalistic phantom I'd seen before this annoyingly human one had turned up.

"Hey," I said. "Is there anything out there? An animal of some kind?"

"No one here but the population of Mytabin," he said, smirking with the self-satisfaction of a good 'joke'.

I looked past him, seeing only bush and dirt and the morning sun.

"What the fuck are you—?"

"I thinks ya found what you was looking for and didn't know it."

"We're in Mytabin?"

"Plumb in the town centre."

A slight wind ruffled through the trees, dragging wisps of morning fog in its wake. There were enough gaps between the trees for me to confirm the only thing beyond the clearing was a scrubby hill. No evidence of a town centre. This old fart was clearly mad. Again, I felt grateful for the door between us.

I looked at him quizzically.

"Look harder," he said.

Against sense, I re-focused beyond him — and sure enough, this time I could see buildings among the trees. In fact, the trees were decidedly sparser than they'd appeared to be. Must have been dawn light creeping through their branches, dispelling shadows. Or had there been more fog than I'd thought? An old 4WD ute rumbled down what was obviously a main street, honking. A woman standing on the front step of a grocery store waved.

"What the hell—?" I muttered. Okay, maybe it was me that was mad. How had I missed all that? Must have been more out of it than I'd thought. I rubbed at my temples.

"It's Mytabin, all right," the man confirmed.

I shoved the door open. The man staggered back, and I scrambled past him out into the street.

If this manifestation was an effect of dawn, it was an effect that had taken way too long to register. Mytabin and its inhabitants had clearly been going about their morning business for some time, by the look of the bustle.

"I need a drink," I muttered.

"Before the Parliamentary bar's even open?"

Startled by the gruff, amused voice emanating from behind me, I staggered around, throwing myself completely off-balance in the process.

"Careful, man." A meaty hand grabbed my upper arm. "Don't want to twist that rubber neck of yours completely out of shape."

"For God's sake, Cowling—"

"Cowling?" He grunted. "Let's have a bit of respect. Call me Yipper."

"And that's more respectful?"

He laughed. The grip on my arm tightened. "Come on."

"Where?"

"I've been waiting. Took you a while to get here. I hope it's not a sign of slackness. I can't abide slackness." He laughed again, releasing his grip, and used the freed hand to slap me on the back. "Anyway, how are you, Townsend?" he exploded. "Not too civilised, I—"

"What the fuck's going on?" I growled, recovering my balance abruptly.

"What do you think's going on? You're here in my electorate. Wanted to know the truth, didn't you? I'm granting you your wish, Townsend."

"That'd be a first."

He laughed — a single hearty yowl.

I followed him out of the rough car park into which I'd apparently guided the car with unconscious attention to protocols, and scampered along in his wake. He strode ahead with vast energetic strides, traversing the main street of Mytabin — which was called Yipper Parade, would you believe? — with determination. The locals were certainly proud of their parliamentary representative; they waved, yelled endearments, stared after him adoringly. A man with a severely withered right arm reached out with his good one to touch Cowling's coat-tails. As his fingers brushed the material, a look of ecstasy flushed over his features. Cowling ignored him. He pushed his way into a well-kept colonial-style two-storey building. I followed. Looking back, I couldn't see the man with the withered arm. There was someone like him at the edge of the adoring crowd, but all this one's limbs were intact.

The inside of the building smelt like vegemite and old apples; it was an open area with vinyl lounge chairs, a wooden counter and a leather-upholstered receptionist. "Good morning, Mr Cowling," the latter said, in a wheezy voice that reminded me of a deflating beach ball.

"Agnetta." Cowling barrelled up to the counter and

leaned over, causing the receptionist to drop back into her chair. "Morning's schedule?"

"Wagtail Primary School, Mr Cowling. Opening the new science block."

"Hmmm." He frowned toward me. "When?"

"Noon. But the mayor was coming around this morning to talk about—"

"Cancel."

"And the school?"

"Leave it in. Science education is vital — have to teach them the facts of life while they're young. Don't you agree, Townsend?"

"Depends which facts you're talking about, Mr Cowling...Yipper."

His grin skewed into a lopsided grimace. "Environmental studies," he barked at me. "The ecology of survival. How to circumvent evolution through a proper knowledge of context."

"Circumvent—?"

"I believe in taking reality by the throat, Townsend — and my kids will learn to do likewise. If the next generation doesn't grow up strong in their own self-confidence, the land will simply consume them. It's a lesson you could do well to learn yourself." He turned away. "Hurry up, man! I haven't got all day."

I tried not to frown outwardly, but inside I was holding back signs of puzzled scepticism. Cowling's rant was sounding like the underpinning of some sort of pseudo-scientific cult. Was I about to have a "Wake in Fright" experience? My attention wandered toward Agnetta, who stared at me dully. Her eyes seemed grey. As she noticed my glance, her lips trembled. I think it was a smile.

"I have one or two things to say to you, Townsend," Cowling declared over his shoulder. "Then Agnetta here will take over."

"Take over?"

"There are things you'll want to see. She knows the ropes. Don't you, Ms Gault?"

I went toward the receptionist, thrusting out my hand. "I appreciate it," I said. Her hand gripped mine. It was cold and dry to the touch.

I let go and pulled away. "Before we do anything else," I said, "I'd like to—"

"Drain the snake?" Cowling yelled boisterously. He directed me toward a washroom. "Ms Gault will get you coffee. How'll you have it? Cold?"

**Truth and Illusion**

What Cowling had to say, he said in his office, energetically and concisely. I sat corpse-stiff, frowning at him as he strode backwards and forwards and roundabout, a bushfly in a bakery, and sipping without enthusiasm at the oily lukewarm coffee his receptionist provided. After a while, Cowling's movement became hypnotic; was it a deliberate technique designed to diffuse memory of his actual words? I felt as though he were brainwashing me using some arcane voice technique.

Afterwards, I couldn't recall anything he said, not exactly — though I thought I had a fair idea of the gist of his rant. It was something to do with the country being at a political crossroads. Hidden enemies and false impressions. Jane Austen even came into it, but I'm buggered if I can remember how. Our enemies are cunning, he said, and often masqueraded as friends.

"Are you talking about terrorists?" I forced an interruption.

He stopped his tarantella long enough to look me in the eye. "Terror hides inside us," he whispered. "It festers in the heartlands — and we take it into ourselves with every heart we consume."

What?

"You must remember, Townsend, we are all terrorists here. Feral beasts in someone else's country. Every race, every species that has existed has been an invader. We struggle for control of what is real and only the winners are considered native to the place they conquer. Once the marsupials were invaders. Once the Aboriginal tribes migrated here over a non-existent land-bridge. Once European colonists came seeking *terra incognita*. There are hundreds of *native* realities, Townsend, no, billions—"

He started up again, moving through a series of intricate verbal manoeuvres, the words I've since forgotten. Though it seemed ordinary enough at the time, now, in retrospect, I recall it as an odd and disorientating experience. But the substance has gone, as evanescent as a town that is not there one minute and then is.

"Townsend!" he barked, snapping his fingers in front of my face. I jerked, physically and mentally, torn from a half-sleep. I stared wide-eyed. His index finger pointed straight at my nose. "You're going to have to make a decision — and soon. Do you want to extricate yourself from the glamour that has ensnared you? Or will you rot away in a barren wasteland of false promises and genetic dead ends?"

I had no idea what he was talking about. It made no sense.

He laughed. "That blank stare of yours speaks volumes. But I remain hopeful."

"Of what?"

"That you'll wake up, my boy." He spun around suddenly, his spider legs controlling his movement perfectly despite the appearance of slapstick clumsiness. His palm crashed against the door. "Ms Gault!" he roared. "Move your lazy arse and take this man where he needs to go! I have work to do."

Then he was close. Facing me. Whispering. I hadn't seen him move.

"You'd do best not to take Clarbridge at face value," he whispered. By rights, his breath should have teased over my face, it was so intimate. But I felt nothing. "Hell's bells, boy, it's best not to take *anyone* at face value, including yourself."

The door opened behind him. Ms Gault's faded enthusiasm poked in through the gap. "You shrieked, Mr Cowling?"

"I did, Agnetta. I did indeed."

He grabbed my arm and thrust me in her direction. "Here, take him to the homestead!"

"Which homestead, your Honour?"

He laughed with extravagant glee. "He'll know. He'll remember."

With that, he rushed away, leaving me bewildered and annoyed. It was getting to be my normal state.

"So..." I said indecisively.

Ms Gault grinned in a manner that suggested such emotional extremes as amusement didn't come naturally to her.

"I was expecting to talk with Mr Cowling," I added. "Not wander the countryside."

"He's a busy man."

"He promised me an interview. That was the point."

She shrugged. One shoulder moved more abruptly than the other, which gave her a puppet-like air. "You'll meet up with him again soon enough. But talk is pointless until you visit the homestead."

"What homestead?"

"Your homestead."

"Mine? I don't come from around here."

Her withered arm patted mine. "Of course you do, sir. Of course you do."

What in God's name was the use in arguing? They were all crazy here. If I wanted to get to the heart of Cowling, I'd have to do what he wanted.

Ms Gault's itinerary was eccentric and pointless. I ended up meeting half the town's populace, whom she introduced with a monotone insincerity that arose from the fact the woman was profoundly monotone by nature. After a while, the sheer volume of introductions caused me to notice an odd consistency: a high proportion of those I met sported the same dull stodginess, a sort of shuffling indifference that was off-putting at best and unnerving at worst. Perhaps it was a small-town thing. I'd never been a great believer in the claim that rural life offers such benefits as a fulfilled life and a meaningful existence.

At one point, I spied a familiar figure through the window of a café. Up until then, I'd considered my earlier conversation with him a delusional product of tiredness.

"Schow?" I said, pushing my way into the ambient smell of coffee, tea and scones.

He looked up. One hairy eyebrow rose above a bulging eye. "Ah," he said. "Ignored my advice, I see."

"Advice?"

"About getting lost. No big deal, Townsend. Everyone ignores me. Everyone gets lost. This is the land of the lost."

"What the hell are you talking about?"

He shrugged and went back to sipping tea.

"What are you doing here, Schow? Everyone thinks you're dead."

His thick lips crinkled upward at one end.

"Cog in the machine, Townsend. Cog in the machine."

I sighed.

"She's after you," he muttered.

"What? Who?"

His eyes looked past me and I turned. Ms Gault loomed in the background, looking impatient in her dull, indifferent way.

"I need to speak to you, Schow..." I said, turning back to him. His seat was empty. I glanced around, but he was nowhere in sight.

"We have limited time," Ms Gault whispered into my

ear. At least, I'd assumed it was Ms Gault. But there was something different about her, voice too low, presence too tall as she leaned toward me, sensed but unseen. I glanced around, already drawing away. Realising who was there, shock propelled me further. My chair slid out from under me and I crashed to the floor.

"Good morning, Mr Townsend."

"Kyla?"

She reached out, tentatively, with an arm that looked like it would shatter if I used it as leverage to pull myself up.

"How can you be here?"

She didn't answer, waiting for me to rise. Eventually I did. Her darkly outlined eyes studied me.

"Have you moved on at all?" she said.

"Moved on?"

"Grown more lucid."

Less lucid and wearier than ever, I slumped into my righted chair. She sat opposite me.

"I don't think so," I managed. "Nothing makes sense."

She smiled weakly. "Then you *have* learned one valuable lesson at least."

I shook my head, feeling a surge of defiance. "No, Kyla. No. That sort of obfuscation is exactly how Cowling operates. It's not enough. Tell me how you're here. You were dead. I saw it."

"I was always dead. I told you that."

"A metaphor..." She showed no sign of confirmation. "Surely?"

"You want me to be here," she said. "Or, at least, you

want me. So, I am here." She stood with the sudden grace of an automaton. "We should go. He will grow impatient."

"Cowling?"

She leaned toward me again. No breath. No scent. "I tried to find an easy way out. But there is none. It can no longer be kept under control."

"What can't?"

She gave a small, tight gesture that may have been intended to indicate the town, the country, the world.

I snarled — it had all gone too far. The dead returning; an elusive town appearing out of nowhere; the possibility I was being led into some kind of trap, a trap lain by a madman disguised as a politician — I didn't believe any of it. But I didn't disbelieve it either. Either way, I'd be a fool to go any further. The unnatural horror would cripple me soon enough if I did.

"I'm leaving," I said. "I don't know who you are or what this is all about, but I'm not playing along anymore."

She reached toward me, offering her hand. Her long fingers seemed to reach into my centre.

I waved her off. "Tell Cowling I'll speak to him in Sydney sometime."

Her hand lowered slowly, as though controlled by a deflating hydraulic lift. A sceptical smile that looked more like she'd succumbed to hopelessness moved on her lips.

And the room became as fog-bound as my brain.

## No Way Out

Tyres slide on loose gravel. He's going too fast. There's panic in the speed, not simple urgency; he corrects the dovetail through chance rather than skill, swiping a roadside post as the tread pleads for a stable surface.

As he tops a crest in the road, the dark silhouettes of trees rush past on either side then fall away suddenly, and he finds himself looking across open, hilly countryside. Night is a vast oil-spill that obliterates both near and distant detail.

Low rumbles vibrate up through the wheels, perceptible despite his Stateman's movement.

"What the hell?" he mutters, feeling the beginnings of a chill he fears will eventually paralyse him completely.

Somewhere ahead lies the main highway — access to Canberra and escape from the insanity of Mytabin. At any rate, he has left the town behind him, and that fact should come as a relief. If he keeps going in the same direction, the whole experience will eventually — hopefully — become an unreal delusion or even a fading dream and he can forget it. Forget Cowling. What was he thinking, giving in to Clarbridge's blackmail? Compared to this mind-fuck nightmare, past indiscretions are meaningless.

The car shudders so violently he can't stop himself from slamming on the brakes. It's just as well; not 50 metres ahead, the road surface bulges and cracks under pressure applied from beneath. Something, something huge, is about to break into the world.

Sitting in his stalled car, he stares through the bug-encrusted windscreen as a giant figure pushes up through the shattered tarmac. Displaced earth nudges his car backwards as a boat is moved by rough seas.

Panic breaks as the giant's shadow collapses over him. The man pushes open the door and rolls out onto the ground, only to feel burning tremors gouge up through his arms and knees, causing his bones to vibrate and crack. Before they shatter completely he scrambles away, gradually finding balance, and runs as fast and as effectively as his legs will allow. Birds and the leaves from broken trees swirl above him in vast sweeping columns, feeding into the darkness of the clouds.

"I'm not the one you want!" he screams.

The giant stamps its clawed foot and the man loses all contact with the ground for a moment. Its loss emasculates him. Tears of blood squeeze from his eyes.

How I got there I don't know, but I returned to consciousness standing on a long-unused, rutted driveway, alone, staring up the final rise at a large country house. In front of me, close, sat a Statesman sedan — dented and dirt-encrusted, its tyres torn and wheel rims sunk into hardened mud. Only one window, the rear-left, remained unbroken. The rest had been blown inward. The roof was crushed on all sides, as though a huge hand had picked it up from above, careless of whatever damage its fingers might cause. I staggered a few steps further and peered into the interior. It was empty.

Part of me immediately accepted this was my car — a fact confirmed by the number plates — though the only possible chain of events that would allow that to be true had to be impossible, surely. I glanced around, jerkily, compulsively. It was late afternoon and a dirty yellow light spilt across overgrown fields, broken fences, starving trees...No one was visible anywhere. In fact, it looked as though no one had been in this place for decades. The half-buried skeleton of a cow was the only evidence that animal life had ever existed here at all.

I looked up...

*...at the house, seeking signs of life in its windows, but its eyes were both blind and impenetrable. A muscle began twitching on his right thigh, so he scratched hard against the course denim of the overalls. They didn't quite fit him and that discomfort seemed symbolic of how poorly this whole world accommodated his presence.*

*His fingernails skidded across a smear of blood...*

I tore myself out of the vision, gasping at this intrusion of my nightmares into the waking world. Took deep breaths. "Calm down, Townsend," I whispered. There had to be an explanation. Whatever it was, it didn't augur well for my sanity.

Cautiously, I looked toward the house. It seemed deserted...no, abandoned. In the dream fragment I'd experienced it had been different: newer, less derelict.

I began to walk toward it. As I did, the scene blurred and another superimposed itself — two visions projected one on top of the other. Focus twitched between the two.

*Trying the doorknob revealed the front door was firmly locked. The man raised the bloody axe he was still carrying and used the blunt side to pound on the polished wood. Its sound reverberated far into an unseen interior.*

*"Is this the Clarbridge place?" he yelled. "I'm looking for the Clarbridge place."*

Again, I forced the imposed vision away. For a moment, the door appeared as it was now — paint worn off by time and wind, cracks where the pressure of heat and cold had stressed the grain beyond its ability to endure, desiccated insect corpses clinging to the bare wood...

*...it opened. Beyond, there were shadows and the dim silhouette of a face.*

*"Who is that? What do you want?" the owner of the face said.*

*"I'm lost. Can you give me directions?"*

*The face scowled suspiciously.*

I rammed my shoulder against the door. The wood was old and rotten and easily crumbled away from the locking mechanism. The stench from inside was of mould and long-decayed flesh. I shoved against the door and tore apart the last splinters holding it to the lock. It crunched open, revealing an entrance vestibule draped with old webs and even older shadows and, at the rear, a large staircase. More numb than brave, I peered into the gloom. Nothing stirred in there except for the faint shifting of dust moved by the air I'd just let in.

"Anyone here?" I yelled, not expecting an answer. The only voice that came back to me was my own, echoing through the emptiness.

*"Who are you? What do you want?"*

*The figure was tall, with reddish hair and large, staring eyes that looked permanently amazed. He appeared to be wearing a dirt-coloured smoking jacket, though as he was peering from around the door most of it wasn't visible.*

*The man in the stolen coveralls rubbed at his temple. "I'm sorry. I've come a long way. Are you Clarbridge?"*

*"Clarbridge? Yes. Who are you?"*

*"I've just arrived here," the man said. "The world is hard to make stable, isn't it? It twists and squirms."*

*"Twists and squirms?" Clarbridge frowned. Then he noticed the axe dragging from the man's left hand and his face blanched. "I think you'd better get off my property."*

*He started to close the door. The man slammed his palm against it, hard. The door crashed inward, pushing Clarbridge halfway across the entrance hall. As he regained his footing, his arrogant nervousness turned to fear. The man strode into the house.*

*"I'll call the police!" Clarbridge warned impotently, backing further away. When he reached the staircase to the upper floor, he took one, two steps up and slumped like an electrocuted fruit bat on the railing. "Please," he whispered, his will dissipating. "I'll help you."*

*The man approached quietly. For a moment, he stood staring at his cowering opponent, vaguely disturbed by his own ability to intimidate.*

*"Does this make you nervous?" he asked, holding up the*

*axe. Clarbridge's eyes widened. The man laughed. "It's irrelevant." He threw it to one side. Its impact reverberated like the death-cry of some cryptozoic freak.*

*"This land is yours?" the man asked.*

*"Land?"*

*"Out there. The hillside and valley."*

*Perhaps Clarbridge saw a glimmer of hope in the simple question. He leaned closer. "Yes, all this. I'm rich. I have influence. There's no money in the house, but I could get it easily. Are you after a job? I need someone to caretake the grounds—"*

*The man gestured impatience. "I don't need money. I need space I can adapt."*

*Clarbridge had withdrawn again, shivering.*

*"Space to usurp the dying soul of humanity," the man added, sneering.*

*"There's lots of space in this country. Why do you want mine?"*

*The man reached a hand toward Clarbridge, muscles tightening, bone pushing outward through retracting flesh. Clarbridge's fear filled him with sudden dark desire. "You can help me," he whispered.*

Images. Memories. Broken and reformed. Why was Clarbridge in this fragment? I had come to believe the man I'd been dreaming about — now affecting me even while awake — was Cowling and, somehow, the dream concerned what he stood for and where he'd come from. But Clarbridge? The dream Clarbridge looked like the Clarbridge I knew, though slightly younger. Yet that didn't make sense. If it was memory and he and Cowling had met like this, it had to have been long ago, long enough for the creature that was Cowling to build a reality around itself, to forge an identity. And why would Clarbridge send me to investigate Cowling if he had, back at the beginning, become one of the politician's puppets?

"See the truth yet, Townsend?" A voice reverberated out of the shadows — a low, inhuman rumble that carried a token humanity I recognised at once.

"Cowling? What the hell do you think you're doing? I came here in good faith and you've been stuffing me around—"

"You came in good faith? I think not. No more than I brought you here in good faith." I could see him now, a thicker darkness coalescing out of the gloom. "What do we have to do with faith, good or otherwise? Either of us."

There was something wrong with his outline. It seemed insubstantial, but inordinately hard-edged. He stepped closer. A shape began to stabilise in the shadows. To one side of him lay the axe the man had carried in my vision, right where he'd thrown it. It was old now, and rusted.

"Maybe not you, Cowling. But I—"

He laughed. "You? You don't even know who you are."

I could see him more clearly by the second. He was monstrous. He looked like a humanoid reptile whose bones had thickened, flesh drying out and tightening around them. His hands were clawed, the skin leathery and nails sharp. Yet, despite his alien appearance, he was recognisably Cowling. There was a spark in his eye, and his lips, though stretched around an extended jawline, were those of the Member for Arden.

"What the hell are you?" I asked, wondering even as I spoke why I was feeling anger rather than fear.

"You and I are cut from the same imported cloth, Townsend," he growled. "Know yourself and you'll know me."

"We're alike? You must be joking! You're closer to the blue-tongue that lives in my backyard."

He laughed, the sound dyspeptic rather than amused. Then he moved, fast and abruptly. I could have dodged away, yet I wasn't afraid of him and remained where I was. His right hand hovered close in front of my face, claws extended. "You were the first, Townsend, but you lost yourself in human blood." I felt his left-hand palm lower onto my scalp. "Surely you remember what happened here..."

*Clarbridge's body gave an involuntary sigh, like a deflating tyre. The man sliced open the flaps he'd mapped out on his victim's bare chest, as blood ran down the torso, forming a pool in its navel indent and spilling onto the floor. Reaching into the rib cavity, the man tore out Clarbridge's heart. He bit into it.*

*As he did, the corpse shifted and the man became aware of movement behind him. He snarled in that direction. But it was only a mirror. For a moment he stared back at his own blood-drenched, animalistic features. His humanity was on the verge of transformation, yet he studied what there was of it with a cold, analytical eye — high forehead, sharp cheekbones, and thin lips.*

*It will have to do, he thought, as he swallowed Clarbridge's heart.*

The vision hit me with migraine violence. Disbelief fought with recognition.

"Ha!" howled Cowling, pulling his hands away. "Now you see it! Now you understand!"

"No!"

"Oh yes, indeed. Clarbridge was yours, Townsend, like many of the others. In the early days, you had a voracious appetite. It's a pity you were so confused."

"It's a lie."

"You know it isn't."

"Why would he send me after you?"

"He's a mere cipher. It was *you* who sent *yourself* after me. Somewhere deep, you knew I was your enemy and you needed to bring that knowledge to the surface."

"And you encouraged it?"

"I need you to re-acquaint yourself with the truth before I consume you, Townsend. Put the potency back into your blood." He grabbed my throat and shoved me against the wall. In the mirror across the passageway — dirty now and streaked with ancient gore — I could see the determined self-awareness that shaped his muscles and bones, contrasted against the ignorance that kept mine weak and ill-conceived. "For a while I thought we might have worked together," he sneered. "Let the native species waste their energy in pointless factional struggles. But, no! Our kind rarely co-exists in peace. There can be only one dominant reality and it shall be mine."

Briefly, I focused past him, drawn by a movement there. Not wanting to alert him, I quickly looked him in the eye again.

"You'd resort to cannibalism?"

"There's a long tradition of it in our species, my lad. Have you become so *civilised* that it disgusts you?"

I struggled against his grip. There was no way I could break it, but if I could just delay him long enough...

"What of Kyla?" I managed.

"Ah, Ms Fauxair! She is a strange one. When you first arrived, when you killed her and ate her heart, she was only a child. The bonding didn't seem to take and so I adopted her, letting her grow into a woman." He sighed theatrically. "She's oddly fey — always obsessing about death — death, heaving oceans and mountains that breathe. A Freudian nutcase, no doubt." He laughed. "Unfortunately I will have to dispose of her. I thought she had become devotedly mine — but her heart was always yours and she rebels."

"A good thing, too," I said.

"Oh? Why's that?"

"Well, it's obvious." I cold-smiled. "Otherwise you would most certainly have killed me." He must have seen the new reality written in my eyes now, because he began to turn.

But it was too late.

The axe in Kyla's hands cut deep into his skull.


**Out of the Sea**

Cowling's heart was hardly haute cuisine, but eating it was a necessary evil. I struggled through with only slight nausea, and that was a reaction to the psychology of the act rather than any genuine physical aversion. Afterwards, I sent Cowling back to his electoral office, the reptile in him forever docile.

Kyla and I returned to Sydney. It was evident; even then, change was creeping through the world in the wake of the Member for Arden's defection from his own party line. I rang Clarbridge and told him Cowling could be rightfully considered innocent of Schow's murder; but he just grunted at me and called me a fool — an attitude I found amusing in light of what I now knew of his hidden incumbencies and subconscious allegiance.

"Murder?" he laughed. "For God's sake, Leonard, have you been pursuing that furphy all this time? It was a mistake. Schow turned up at his office yesterday, alive and only slightly hung over. As for Cowling — he's nothing, a meaningless cipher adopted by crackpots and ratbags too insane to be accepted by the lunatic fringe of either major Party. Find something useful to do with your time."

And that's what I've been doing — something useful with my time. My heritage sings to me from the depths of this flesh I inhabit. I listen to it more often now.

Change is upon us.

Sometimes I stand on my balcony staring out to sea, watching for the giant to rise from deep within that heaving otherworld. They — the old race, the humans — they watch for it, too. But they don't acknowledge why, even to themselves. Absolute truth is not an easy thing to live with.

Much easier when you create it for yourself.

# THE BLACK LAKE'S FATAL FLOOD

If time had been suspended for a moment, he would have seen an almost perfect globe in the air before him; on its surface a diminished version of the world, stretched like a coloured stocking over a bald head. It would have hung there for him to study, but what would he have seen in that diminished world, beyond the surface film, deep in the tiny, watery universe?

Time was not suspended. A drop of water, filtered through the plaster ceiling above him, dripped at his feet with a faint *paf*. Rambler stared at the splatter-pattern it made. "Oh God, Dip!" he groaned. "The roof's leaking." Sheepdip glanced at him from under a droopy eyelid and did nothing. "It's not good enough, mate," Rambler added. "You promised me luxury. Leaky roofs are not luxury."

He'd only been in this hidey-hole a day and already he wanted to be someplace else. That was the story of his life. Rambler by name, rambler by nature. Sometimes, he told people he'd taken up this life of homeless wandering because of his name, but it was a lie. Rambler wasn't his real name; he just liked it. If anyone asked "Who are you, mate?" he could say,

"Rambler by name, rambler by nature." No one ever asked him, of course. In the eyes of normal society, he was useless. He didn't *own* anything, which was Bad, even Irresponsible, and, as a result, he wasn't worth talking to. Rambler didn't care. Who needed superannuation and a credit card anyway? Not him. He didn't need things. He didn't need people. The longest he'd stayed in a place was two months; the only person he'd stayed with longer than a fortnight was Sheepdip. And Sheepdip wasn't a person.

He chucked a cushion at Sheepdip, just because he was thinking of him. The dog growled in a desultory fashion. Rambler got up from the lounge chair and went to the window.

Nice spot though, he thought. If he were going to stay somewhere for longer than it took to munch on a few bread rolls and relieve himself a couple of times, this would be it. He'd stumbled across the small weatherboard house while wandering through bush land in search of one of those marijuana crops he'd heard were scattered along the Illawarra escarpment. The house was isolated, stuck at the butt-end of a long overgrown track, up maybe a hundred metres of cliff and surrounded by bush. Buggered if he knew how they built the thing. A huge tree trunk that must have been a million years old towered above the house. Its roots were so big and knotted, disappearing into and out of the ground; it made him think of a giant squid, rising from the depths to drag the house under the earthy waves.

"Avast!" he shouted. "Get me a harpoon, Captain Nemo!" Sheepdip glanced at him ironically.

The house was on a concrete slab and was furnished, so you'd think someone cared about it. Yet it had the air of a place no one had visited for a decade. There were spider webs everywhere, it was all dusty and untidy and, in the twilight in particular, Rambler thought it seemed rather forlorn.

*Paf.*

He turned at the sound: more water leaking through the roof. There was a tiny puddle in the centre of the room now. Strange, he thought, turning back to the window. It wasn't raining outside, even though the looming proximity of the escarpment was bringing on an early twilight.

In the night, he woke up blind. For a moment, he panicked, fear banishing reason. He strained to see in the darkness — to see anything, even the ghost of a shape. Second after second passed, and there was nothing. Then he heard a movement to his right. He glanced that way as Sheepdip began scratching vigorously. He couldn't see the dog, even though there was light coming through from behind the curtain. Dim light, it was, from a less-than-full moon or something, which allowed him to pick out one corner of the window. "Bloody mutt," he growled. He willed his heart to relax. After a moment, to encourage it as best he could, he reached into his coat beside him on the bed, and extracted the bottle of cheap scotch he'd stashed there. Not much left. He took a measured swig from the bottle and replaced the screw-lid. He'd had that bottle for a fortnight. There was still enough in it to last him two days, if he was careful.

He settled down onto the bed again. He hadn't slept in one for, maybe, six months, and had been anticipating the pleasure of doing so since he'd broken into the place and seen it. That bed was the main reason he stayed, apart from wanting respite from the growing chill of the nights. Unfortunately, the bed wasn't giving him the best night's sleep he'd ever had. He was restless, drifting in and out of slumber like a man kipping on rocks. Maybe beds were a middle-class lie, like everything else.

He slept again, only to be woken some time later by a strange sensation in the back of his skull. It wasn't a headache, though it might have been before it became a vibration in the bone that made his ears hiss.

"That you, 'Dip?" he asked the darkness.

The dog didn't answer. As Sheepdip could hardly have anything to do with a throbbing in the back of his head, Rambler figured he wouldn't bother repeating the question. He got up, steeling himself against dizziness, and went across to the window. Pushing aside the blinds (which were dusty and draped in cobwebs), he could see the huge tree, highlighted and blue-tinged by starlight: a giant crouching next to the house to make a thorough examination of it. Wind was stirring out there. Thicker patches of night shifted as the bush moved.

"I'm hungry," he muttered.

Part of his luck in finding this place was that it was stocked. He'd found food in a cupboard in the kitchen — some of it (like bread and vegetables) so mouldy and rotten it had ceased to smell. But there were cans, too.

He'd read somewhere — or maybe someone had told him, because he couldn't read too well — that cans lasted forever. You could store canned food against a nuclear holocaust.

He stumbled through the darkness now, picking his way past the edges of furniture, tripping over Sheepdip who growled but didn't move, and heading in what he imagined was the direction of the kitchen. It was a bit lighter in that room because there were no blinds, and big open windows looked out over the down-slope of the bush trail leading to the house. He didn't entirely like that; the view made him feel exposed, letting him see too many shapes in the shifting darkness behind the trees. The can opener he'd found was still on the bench. He opened some baked beans by the light of the moon and used a fork to eat them straight out of the tin. There were plates in another cupboard, but he wasn't a civilised man and you had to draw the line somewhere.

*Paf.*

The sound of dripping water from the lounge room nearly made him jump. The noise made the throbbing in his head increase, which was odd because it wasn't that loud. He wandered toward the doorway, peering into the darkness while he ate.

Something moved. He couldn't tell what it was, but a sense of shifting lightness startled him. It took a few seconds before he realised it wasn't in the lounge room: it was behind him. He turned. Through the big kitchen window, Rambler saw the glaring cyclops-eye of a torch, coming up the path. The beam briefly penetrated the glass, though he doubted it would've alerted whoever was holding the torch to his presence. He ducked aside into deeper shadows, out of the direct line of sight.

Must be the owners, he thought. Damn. Why now, when they obviously hadn't visited the place for ages? It was the middle of the night. He wondered if they were dangerous. After all, psychos ruled the world these days. There were psychos on every street and in parliaments around the world. Rambler always kept an eye out for psychos.

Suddenly nervous, he shuffled out of the kitchen. *Paf*, as he passed the drip. It sounded like it had gathered into a large puddle. He skirted the sound so his bare feet wouldn't slosh in the water. He didn't want to leave footprints all over the floor. "Sheepdip," he whispered as he passed the bedroom. In the dark he couldn't find the dog. Probably asleep.

Light swivelled outside the window. He heard voices, though not clearly enough to make out what they were saying. There were two of them, however, and one was a woman. Rambler bumped into something. He stumbled. The noise was so loud he felt sure it would alert his visitors. The handle of the front door creaked.

"Hey, it's unlocked. I thought we'd have to break in."

As the front door opened, Rambler ducked around a doorway that led through to the toilet.

"You hear something, Bill?"

"Just the wind."

Rambler pressed himself against the wall, out of sight but nervous as hell. What if one of them wanted to piss straight away? He heard the front door shut.

"Bloody dark in here."

Light from the torch moved past the doorway. Rambler kept well back, so the beam skimmed by without catching him. He stopped breathing.

"What're we gonna tell Dan if he wakes up and finds us gone?"

"I dunno. Who gives a shit?"

"He's pretty jealous."

"He's a jerk. You can tell him you went out for a leak and got lost. Okay?"

"And you?"

"I'll keep away till mornin'. Tell him I drove into town."

"We were supposed to stay on site till we'd done the whole harvest."

"So, he'll be mad at me. Come on, forget him. That's why we came here, for God's sake."

"Okay, okay. Let's just do it and get back."

Overcome with curiosity, Rambler inched up to the corner and peeked around. They'd put the torch on the back of the lounge, facing away from him, but positioned so the two of them would be partially lit. One was a big bloke, wearing a frayed denim jacket and jeans, with dark hair and cheeks that looked dirty with a day or two's growth. The other was a woman. Her hair was light and there was lots of it. She was wearing jeans and a t-shirt, over which she'd worn a leather coat. The coat was on the back of the lounge now.

"Least it's warmer in here."

"And safer."

"How'd you know about it?"

"Checked it out when we first planted. No one lives in the place. I don't think Greeley has a clue it's here."

"There a bedroom?"

"Sure. Bed's got bugs in it though, and it smells. Forget it. This lounge here'll do."

The woman took off her t-shirt. Rambler gasped as her breasts wobbled in the torchlight: an effect enhanced by the shadows. Luckily neither she nor the bloke heard it over the rustling of their clothes. They were both wriggling out of their jeans. Rambler noticed that the bloke's dick was already erect, like a goddamn battering ram — then the woman was starkers and he wasn't watching the bloke at all. In full daylight, she might have been as pimply and blotchy as the next guy; in this gloom, she looked perfect, like a goddess. Some cellulite around the thighs maybe, but what the hell? Rambler hadn't seen a naked woman for years. It'd been so long since he'd gotten laid, he'd just about lost the incentive. It came back quick enough now, so fierce it felt like pain.

"You're puttin' on weight, baby."

"Am not." She laughed. "That's a great thing to say when you're trying to get into someone's pants."

"Not gonna tell me you need chatting up now, are ya?"

They came together with a wet slap of flesh-on-flesh. Rambler's eyes began moving between the bulge of the woman's breasts pressed against the bloke's chest and the more obscure darknesses where their private bits would be getting together. The damn light wasn't good enough for him to see much, so imagination had to make up some of the difference. They collapsed onto the lounge, but thrashed about so much they soon fell on the floor. That gave them more room to move. The small building was suddenly echoing with grunts and cries of ecstasy (or was it agony?) and the heaving thud of their bodies slapping against each other and the floor. It went on for a hell of a long time — so long Rambler lost interest. Anyway, once they'd hit the floor, they were out of the torch's beam and, in the darkness, became vague shapes not all that exciting to watch. The noises they made were pretty entertaining though. Rambler stopped peering at them and moved fully back around the corner to listen. After a while, he began to consider his own situation. While they were preoccupied with each other's orifices and bulges, he felt he probably should move himself somewhere less potentially conspicuous. Once they were finished, one of them was bound to want to use the bathroom.

Before he'd made up his mind on the best place to move to, however, there was a particularly loud crashing sound, which Rambler recognised as the front door flying open. Without thinking, he glanced around the corner. Someone was striding into the room. He seemed to be trailing darkness like clinging fog.

"What the hell?" a new voice snarled.

Movement on the floor ceased abruptly. The bloke leapt up. Sex had made his legs weak, so he stumbled and tripped, grunting something which Rambler couldn't make out.

"You think I'm a fool?" the newcomer growled.

The woman was still lying on the floor, covered in shadows. Rambler could see her eyes glinting. "Dan?" she said, rather pointlessly — it was obvious even to Rambler this must be Dan.

"Bitch!" Dan said. The word was lost under a roaring

percussion. For an instant, the room sparked light. The woman screamed. Rambler thought he saw her chest tear apart, and then he threw himself back around the corner and retreated as far as he could into the bathroom. A rifle! Dan had a rifle or something, and he'd killed her! Rambler's heart was pounding so hard he thought he'd been hit too, even though the sound of the woman's death scream had filled him so full of fear he knew he couldn't have been hit.

There was a cry, probably Bill's, and the sound of rapid scrambling. "For God's sake, Dan, she was just—" There was another explosion, and the thud of a heavy body striking the floor. This was followed by several more shots. Then the house fell quiet.

Rambler listened, petrified into stillness, blood coursing through his veins like a roaring flood.

"Bitch," the voice muttered.

Scraping noises. Footsteps. More scraping. Something being dragged. *Paf*. Rambler nearly gasped out loud at that, because it sounded distinctly like the leak he'd been listening to earlier. How could he possibly hear a waterdrop from where he was?

"Oh God!" Dan was mumbling to himself, "Oh, God!" What was he doing? "God!" Sound of running feet. The door slammed. Had he gone?

Rambler remained where he was, unmoving, for maybe an hour — it felt like an hour anyway. During that time, even if he'd wanted to move, he wouldn't have been able to, because his legs had been turned to stone. His mouth tasted as though it were full of sand. His temples throbbed.

It was Sheepdip padding up to him and nudging him

on the cheek with his wet nose that made Rambler move. In fact, it startled him so much he yelled like the dickens, leaping a metre into the air. Even before his heart had settled, he realised it was Sheepdip and swore half-heartedly at the dog. He was actually glad to see the stupid mutt; the cold nose brought some reality back into the situation.

"Kept well hidden, eh, did you?" Rambler asked, leaning on the wall while his pulse settled.

The dog huffed.

"Bugger me, Dip. What'd'ya reckon about all that, eh?"

He peered around the corner, just to make sure what he remembered had really happened and wasn't some damn nightmare. Sure enough, there they were: two bodies draped in grey shadow and splattered with darker areas of blood. The fact he could see them so clearly told him morning had arrived. He glanced up through the window; the black of the sky was being replaced by a red-blue haze. He breathed out, as though he'd been holding his breath all this time.

Sheepdip yapped.

Rambler patted the dog's bony head distractedly, and eased himself around the corner. There was no sign of Dan the murderer; just the two corpses, lying in pools of blood, their naked flesh, glowing the way flesh does when early light creeps over it. The bloke didn't have an erection anymore; in fact, there was only a bloody hole where his bits had been shot away. Rambler's stomach heaved. He gulped back the sickness, glancing toward the woman. Her nakedness was no longer erotic, even though most of her body was still intact. One of her breasts had been torn apart by the blast — the left one — but otherwise Dan had let her be. His anger had been directed elsewhere.

*Paf.*

Rambler strained through the darkness to locate the puddle from the leaky roof, then shuffled into the lounge room, keeping to the wall — as far away from the corpses as possible. The torch was lying on the floor, still on. He picked it up and directed its weakening beam toward where he thought the sound had come from.

*Paf.*

Again. His light glinted briefly on a falling drop, and he followed it down to the floor with his eyes. What he saw made him gasp. The water was falling straight into the open mouth of the dead bloke. For a second it looked like the corpse was thirsty, and had placed itself there deliberately. Light caught the ridges inside its mouth and the veneer of mucous on its tongue. Rambler stared at the bizarre sight in the wavering torchbeam for several long moments; there were even bloody marks on the floor, as if the corpse had dragged itself half a metre to the pool.

Or been dragged.

*Paf.*

"Hey!" he yelled. Sheepdip was padding toward the pool of water, tongue hanging out, as though looking for a drink. Rambler screamed at him again, grabbed him by the loose skin on the back of his neck and pulled him away. "Don't drink that, you stupid dog!" Suddenly he just wanted to get out of there, away from the bodies and the water and the atmosphere of growing disquiet that made his knees tremble. Fear swelled in him like a fever. He was heading for the front door, pulling Sheepdip after him, when he heard something move. The sound froze his limbs and yanked his head around so hard he felt the muscles protest. What he saw this time made his bladder give way, and warm urine ran down his leg.

The male corpse was moving. Not fast and only slightly, but, as Rambler stared transfixed, its hands seemed to push at the blood on the floor, clumsily sweeping it across the polished wood. Dark stains mingled with the water in the pool, helping it grow.

What the hell was going on? If the bloke — what was his name? Bill? — if he wasn't really dead, why was he gathering in the blood in this obscene parody of tidiness? Was it some sort of reflex? He certainly looked dead.

Bill made what seemed a huge effort and clamped his stiffened fingers onto the arm of the female corpse. He pulled. The woman moved slightly. He pulled again. Another movement. This went on for some time, with Rambler watching, unable to look away, unable to get his own body to react to the terror flooding through him. Gradually, with unnatural determination, Bill dragged the woman's body to the very edge of the pool, which was now about as big as a medium-size pizza and coloured with a spreading mist of red.

And then, as if it wasn't already bad enough, the scene turned into a nightmare. A ribbon of flesh burst out of the pool of water, making the shallow puddle that was maybe a millimetre deep seem like the surface of a water hole that opened downwards through the floor into a vast subterranean sea. The tentacle was as thick as Rambler's arm and looked as though its skin had been ripped off. It wrapped itself around the head of the woman's corpse then pulled back into the water, taking the corpse with it. No splash. No cries. No fuss. Out, grab, under. At the same time, Bill began to twitch. One arm fell into the water, disappearing beneath the surface — or was it simply *into* the surface?

Years before, Rambler had snuck into a cinema showing a new version of the movie *The Thing*. In that flick, bodies tore open to let loose weird monstrosities of all kinds, and that's what he thought of as Bill's corpse was ripped open from inside, making way for something monstrous. This thing looked like a huge crab, only more flexible, with eyes on stalks and other wriggling fibres sprouting from its back, topped with tiny screaming skulls. Human skulls. Several of them stared at Rambler and snarled and that was too much. Blood drained from his head; the shadows seemed to ignite, were sucked away like pictures on a TV screen when you turn off the set, and Rambler felt himself falling: falling over the edge of something — maybe reality — and suddenly not caring, even if it meant he was going to be pulled into an impossibly deep puddle that was the home of monsters...

There was a gun pointed at his nose. He blinked several times. A snarling face formed in the air behind the gun. Must be a dream, he thought, and I'm still in it.

"Who the hell are you?" said a voice.

The voice was deep and oddly familiar and belonged to the face in front of him.

"How long've you been here?"

Dan, Rambler thought; this must be Dan. He groaned. He wasn't up to this, not on top of his vision of monsters in puddles of water. Dan grabbed him roughly by his coat front, dragging him to his feet. "What've you done with 'em?" he snarled, gesturing over his shoulder with a nod of his head.

He meant the bodies, of course. Rambler glanced past him. There was the pool, still slightly reddened, though more diffusely now. Blood smears on the floor. No bodies.

"I don't know," he croaked.

*Paf.*

He heard water drip in the silence that followed his words.

Dan seemed a bit frustrated. He swore at Rambler, shoved him backwards and aimed the gun at his head again, as though determined to blow the top off it. Rambler was too befuddled to protest. Sheepdip wasn't. Rambler heard his dog's low growl coming from the right. Dan glanced that way, shifting the direction of his aim slightly. "Shut up, dog!" he snarled.

Rambler panicked. He reached toward Dan's arm, though he couldn't quite get a hold on it. "Don't kill my dog!" he pleaded. "He won't hurt you."

Dan looked at Rambler as though he were a squashed turd. "Why would I wanna kill your bloody dog?" he asked. "I got nothin' against your dog. Shit, I don't even wanna kill you."

"Don't you?"

He shrugged. "Might have to, of course. If you don't tell me what happened to the bodies."

Rambler looked at him blearily, trying to come up with something to say that would make sense. But his thoughts turned to nonsense in his mouth.

"'Course, I could *threaten* to kill the dog, seein' how you're so worried about it." Dan pointed the gun at Sheepdip who adopted the stance he always adopted when someone offered to throw a stick for him to chase.

"No!" said Rambler. "No!"

"You gonna tell me."

"I'll tell you what happened," Rambler said. Anticipation and helplessness mingled into despair in his stomach. "You won't believe it."

"Try me."

Rambler did. Sure enough, Dan didn't believe it. Rambler could see the disbelief in his eyes, in his jaw, in the anger starting to wrinkle up his forehead. However, the disbelief didn't erupt into violence. Instead, the killer ran his free hand through his strawy hair and grunted.

"Expect me to believe that, do ya?"

"It's true. Honest. That's what I saw."

"Maybe it is. Maybe it isn't. You an alkie?"

Rambler shrugged. Dan shook his head, seemed to relax slightly, and shoved the gun into the waist of his jeans. "You were here when...when it happened then, eh?" he asked. "Where? Over there?" He gestured at the corner where Rambler had hidden. Rambler nodded.

Dan muttered something. Then, walking over to the bloodstains on the floor, his back to Rambler, he added, "I didn't mean to kill 'em. I was real pissed off, that's all. Crazy mad. I was just gonna scare the shit out of 'em. But when I came through the door and saw 'em there..." He turned, and Rambler thought there was genuine distress in his eyes. "It's like my mind went, you know. It just...went. I started firing...and that was it." He glanced toward the puddle.

"I heard you dragging one of the bodies around," said Rambler, remembering where Bill had been lying, drinking in the water. "Why'd you do it?"

Dan shrugged, with surly annoyance. His anger returned, stronger now. "Shut up, okay. Just shut your mouth!" He looked at the puddle, then at Rambler. "Fuckin' monsters."

*Paf.*

He heard the sound. "Come here!" When Rambler hesitated, he grabbed him and pulled him to the edge of the puddle. "You're tellin' me some bloody great squid came outa here and pulled the bodies in. Bullshit. You can see the floor, for Christ's sake."

Rambler looked and, sure enough, you could see right through the puddle to the boards beneath; the water wasn't even a millimetre deep. Dan squatted next to the water. "There's nothin' there," he said. He reached out with his index finger, intending to poke the puddle. Before it touched the surface, the finger stopped. Dan swallowed and moved away.

"Maybe...maybe I was dreaming," Rambler said.

"Yeah." Dan shoved his chest, making him stumble backwards. "Maybe you're tryin' to make a fool outa me."

"You think I'm crazy. I saw what you did. You're dangerous, mate. What I told you...that's what I thought

I saw. You reckon I wouldn't have made up a better story, if I was meaning to lie?"

Dan scratched at his jaw. "Where's the bodies then? I just wanta burn 'em, so they're hard to identify, ya know? Then bury 'em. So what did ya do with 'em?"

"Nothin', honest."

*Paf.*

Dan glanced toward the sound, watching the ripples on the surface of the puddle where the drop had landed. Then his eyes moved to the ceiling. There was a wet patch the size of a hand. In the middle, another drop gathered weight through seepage, about to break the hold of the surface tension that kept it from falling. The drop was reddish.

Dan looked at Rambler. "In the roof. You put 'em in the roof."

Rambler squinted up at the ceiling. He shrugged. "How would I lug two heavy bodies up there? By myself? You think maybe I'm Arnold Schwarzenegger and not really a sixty year old dero?"

Dan began looking around for a way into the roof and found a trapdoor in the bathroom above the toilet. He stood on the bowl. He glanced at Rambler, who was considering running away while he had the chance. "Try to clear out and I'll catch you easy enough, shitface. Then I'll kill ya. Okay?"

Rambler believed him. He might have made it into the bush, might have found somewhere to hide, but, no doubt, this Dan Greeley knew the area — knew it well — and would track him down as easy as pie. It'd be a big risk. Maybe it was less of a risk than staying here, though, knowing Dan was going to have to kill him anyway because he knew too much.

Suddenly, as though he'd read his thoughts, Dan leapt down, came through and grabbed Rambler by his shirtfront. He dragged him into the bathroom, shoving the gun into his ribs. "Get up there!" he growled.

Entering the manhole was like entering another world. The roof cavity was not as dark as Rambler had expected: sunlight striped the greyness through small gaps and crevices. Dust layered the crossbeams and fibrous boards between them. Scattered patches of blackness added a sense of clutter.

Dan followed him. Together, they crawled further in, looking for the bodies Rambler, at least, knew wouldn't be there. Even trying to determine where the moisture was dripping from proved fruitless. Dan took a rough guess; he flashed the torch around for sign of a leak. Nowhere could they find the dampness the layers of dust should have made blatantly obvious. "It don't make sense," Dan growled. Rambler could only agree.

The dripping continued in the room below. After they'd climbed back down, Dan stood near it, studying the spot in the ceiling and watching as the drip grew to a size where it had to fall. *Paf.* Concentric circles quivered and disappeared on the expanding puddle. "It's like the water starts there, at the ceiling," he said. "Like it's not coming from anywhere."

Rambler didn't comment. After what he'd seen — and he was surer than ever he hadn't been dreaming or imagining things — he hated to think where the water might be coming from, given what it seemed to contain.

"Forget it!" Dan suddenly yelled, as though responding to some thought he'd had. The sound of his voice made Rambler shrink away — it was so full of anger. "I don't know why I've been listening to your bullshit, old man. This..." He took out the gun and waved it toward the puddle. "This is nothing; just fuckin' water. You gonna tell me where the bodies are or am I gonna blow ya brains out?"

From somewhere behind him, Sheepdip growled. Rambler shrank back. "I don't know, honest. I just don't know. If I'm making up the story, where's that drip coming from?"

"A busted pipe...who gives a shit?" He kicked at the puddle. "It's just water. There's nothin' in there that can—"

He never finished the sentence. As his foot hit the puddle, scattering it with a splash, a tentacle emerged from the water and wrapped itself around his leg. His eyes seemed to bulge and the gun went off as his finger tightened automatically. A bullet slammed into the far wall. The gun, released, clattered to the floor. "Shit, no!" he screamed. Already, his leg had been sucked into the water up to the knee. The really odd thing was Rambler thought he could still see the floor on which the puddle was resting; Dan's leg wasn't going through *that*. It just went into the water and disappeared. "Help me!" Dan screamed, fear changing the toughness in his face to a comic grimace.

Rambler couldn't move. As before, terror paralysed him.

"Help! Please."

The terror in Dan's voice was even greater than the emotion churning in his own gut. Dan had been swallowed up to his waist. God knows what was happening to the part of him that wasn't visible. What would it feel like? Rambler took a step toward him. His foot hit something. The gun. He bent and picked it up. Then he took a few more steps, close enough to reach Dan's grasping fingers. Dan grabbed his wrist...and, at once, Rambler felt his centre-of-gravity pulled out of balance. He tried to let go, but wasn't quick enough. Dan was yanked completely into the water. Rambler followed.

For a moment, he was so disoriented he couldn't make out anything. He registered the sudden change in light and shade; the conversion of the stale, old house smell to putrid swamp-stink; the chill that embraced him like a shroud of ice. He didn't even think about where he might be; he just felt a sudden, blinding fear hit him like a club to the gut. Then, in an instant, he saw that he and Dan were hanging suspended above a vast flat expanse: the blackest lake he'd ever seen. It was from that lake that the huge tentacles emerged.

Then, he was falling, no longer suspended. Blackness overwhelmed him as he hit the surface of the lake. His mind rang with growlings and snarlings and bestial exclamations so varied and so multitudinous he couldn't even begin to guess where they might come from. He thrashed about, still gripping the gun, while the water — if it was water — pulled at his clothes and scraped at his skin. What surrounded him felt like water, sure, but it felt like other things, too. Like mud. Like thick porridge. Like poisonous gas. Like some sort of congealed radiation. Like quicksand. Like the rough paws of a million unnameable creatures. He kept his mouth tightly shut, scared to let the stuff into his body. His eyelids were clamped together, too, though, oddly, he could still see the blackness and the murk; and that was the weirdest thing of all. Shapes loomed up at him; distorted monstrosities screamed at him. He pulled the trigger on the gun. Despite the water, the gun fired and the creatures retreated. What were they? Where was this? What had happened to Dan? As the thoughts raced through his mind, Dan's face suddenly appeared a few inches from his own. The eyes were missing and there was no movement to indicate life. Then Rambler saw the rest of Dan's body — a few ragged shreds of bone and gristle — before the whole thing vanished in the murk.

He began beating at the water, vaguely hoping to reach the surface of the lake, though the sort of logic that dictated the 'surface' should lie above him seemed grossly out of place here. His head was throbbing, like it was going to burst. Then he felt his leg gripped, glanced down, and saw that a tentacle like the one that had taken Dan was wrapped around his foot. Panic seized him, making him kick and punch frantically, but there was nothing he could do. The thing was dragging him down, down into the depths of the lake...into whatever maw waited there. He stopped struggling. Maybe it was the extreme nature of the emotions that had overwhelmed him and he was finally exhausted; maybe it was oxygen deprivation; maybe it was some feature of the primordial ooze surrounding him; but, suddenly, Rambler felt calm, relaxed, even *heroic*. He let himself be dragged down while freakish, alien shapes screamed around him, willing him to lose his cool. He scorned them, would have told them to eat his underpants — a fate worse than death even for some disgusting, supernatural freak — except he didn't care to open his mouth to do so. Perhaps they could hear him anyway. Then something gross was in front of him, opening up to consume his body. He shoved the handgun into it and pulled the trigger. Again. And again.

The darkness seemed to explode in flashes of light. Rambler felt himself flung away — whether by the force of the gun's recoil or by the creature's reaction, he couldn't tell. He plunged into thicker mud — the bottom of the black lake? — falling again as it all disappeared and there was daylight and he was looking down at the floor of the small house in the escarpment rainforest. There was the puddle into which he'd been pulled, and the floorboards, and the smears of blood. There was Sheepdip too, next to the pool, just now looking up at him, licking his floppy lips and barking a welcome. Rambler fell, twisting in mid-air so he wouldn't plunge back into the puddle and the black lake that lay beyond it. He struck the floor hard, rolled. There was stillness then, except for the throbbing in his skull. He tried to move, to get further away, but his muscles wouldn't work. Even when he saw huge fleshy tentacles thrashing into the room from the tiny puddle, he still couldn't move. Fear and urgency could only pound at him and make his head throb more.

The dog saved him. Sheepdip sank his teeth into Rambler's arm, pulling him toward the door with quiet urgency. Then pain, and Dip's presence, filled him with energy. He scrambled up and, in a moment, was outside, glancing back at the tentacles that seemed unable to emerge fully into the real world.

Rambler tripped. Something caught up under his feet, clattered, overbalanced him and sent him sprawling on the ground. For a moment, he was dazed, so much so he couldn't get up again. He glanced back. Through the open door of the house, he could see that the drip was no longer a drip, but a continuous flow which came out of the ceiling, splashed onto the floor and turned the puddle into a pool. Its margins began edging toward the doorway.

What would it mean, he wondered, if this water from the black lake got out into the world? He pictured it spilling over the threshold, swirling down the path, trickling over rocks, joining up with creeks, spreading out further and further. Getting into the water supply. Coming out of people's taps. Filling their kettles. Being drunk by them. Splashing into their pools. Lapped up by their pets. Going everywhere.

And each drop an entrance into a world of horrors people couldn't even begin to imagine.

Rambler knew he had to do something. But how did you stop a leak, when the leaking water contained monsters? No plug would hold it because the hole through which it seeped was not a real hole, just some sort of dimensional causeway in the material of the ceiling.

Then he thought: what if there *were* no ceiling?

He glanced around, at his feet, at the cans he'd tripped over. Petrol. Dan had brought it with him to burn the bodies of his victims. *I just want to burn the bodies,* he'd said, *so they'll be hard to identify.*

The tentacles had disappeared, though the stream of water from the ceiling was halfway to the door now. Little time remained to worry about what would and wouldn't work. Rambler forced himself up, ignoring pains and aches. He began splashing petrol around, on the floor, the walls, even into the black lake's water. In the kitchen, he found some old matches; after attempting to light half a dozen of them, one took. Stepping out of the doorway, looking behind him to check Sheepdip wasn't inside, he tossed in the small flame. Petrol burst into sheets of fire.

That was it. Rambler retreated to the edge of the bush and watched the house burn. When the inferno finally collapsed the walls, he felt immense satisfaction. The roof caved in. Soon, there was only a heap of ruins.

He stood on the edge of the smouldering ash-pile and tried to see what had happened to the black lake's flood. Couldn't see a thing. He felt content that he had evaporated the water that had already leaked through, and destroyed the gateway as well.

The world was saved.

But, for how long? If the black lake could break through here, it could break through elsewhere.

Now, whenever people asked him who he was (though hardly anyone ever did), he would say, "Saviour by name, saviour by nature."

They'd smile condescendingly. "What do you save?" they'd say.

"The world," he'd reply. "I save the world."

Though they thought him crazy, they would always ask what he saved the world from, and he would smile knowingly at Sheepdip. "Monsters," he'd pronounce. "I save the world from monsters." They'd laugh, of course, but he didn't care. Being a hero made him feel good, even if Sheepdip was the only person who knew.

And Sheepdip wasn't a person.

# DREAMS OF DEATH

## I

I know what you think, Avarez. A corpse, bullet holes and a matching Smith and Wesson hand-gun are reasonably conclusive as evidence goes; but I tell you it's not murder, despite appearances. For this to be murder, there'd have to be a real body, solid evidence that doesn't disappear with the sun's rising. Blood cloys, wounds don't heal, lips stay cold and tell no tales. Life doesn't go on. That's murder.

Give me a chance and I'll explain.

He was in my outer office when I arrived that morning; the way he looked, he might have slept there. Haunted eyes drifted over me as I shut the door. I thought: This one needs a good feed.

"I want to see Mr Wolfe."

"I'm Mr Wolfe," I said.

"Andy Wolfe? I was told he was a first-rate investigator."

I walked past him, into the inner office, unlocking with practised indifference — briefcase still in hand, no coffee spilt from the Styrofoam cup I'd collected on my way through reception. You can't say I haven't learnt any useful skills since leaving college. I gave the corpse a vampish glance over my shoulder. "Andy Wolfe is a great investigator," I said. "He's also a woman. You want to come in and tell me your problems?"

The foregoing wasn't quite true, of course: I'm exceptional, rather than great. Greatness is a form of immortality that comes through death or fiction — either way, I can't be walking around and still be great. I'd never dealt with any immortal cases, not until that day anyway. And this guy didn't look like the type of client that'd bring me fame. For two years I'd been praying my door would be darkened by someone other than insurance assessors, distraught spouses, worried parents and little old ladies who'd lost their Tiddleses. Two years, and still nothing.

I took off my coat, opened the Venetian blinds and sat behind my desk. He was standing disconsolately on the far side of the door, the bags under his eyes darkening as I watched.

"For God's sake, sit down." I gestured at a padded leather chair. The chair consumed him; it slouched backwards at an angle just severe enough to make clients feel nervous. Gives me a chance to smile reassuringly. Which I did.

"You're a woman," he said.

"So I'm told." It's not a conclusion that's hard to come to, even this close to the Cross. I'm about average height, with short brown hair, large hazel eyes and curves that are unmistakably female, depending on what I wear. On this occasion, I was wearing tight-waisted designer jeans and a blouse with an open neckline. "Does it matter?"

His mouth moved oddly; perhaps it was a smile.

"No, I hadn't expected it, that's all. It's good, a plus, that you're a woman. It'll make things better."

"Oh? How?"

He shook his head and fell quiet, his mind wandering off with the faeries. I cleared my throat and indicated the ball was in his court. Essentially, I like to think my sex is irrelevant in most contexts.

Anxiety passed over his face as he gripped the chair's leather arms tightly. It was an interesting face, if you ignored the despair lying just beneath the surface, ready to turn it to misery at a moment's notice. Lean and hungry, but interesting. Neat black eyebrows, green eyes, receding hairline, and a three-day growth that looked cultivated. I suggested he start with his name.

"My name..." He paused as if it were elusive. Was I about to get a pseudonym? "My name won't mean anything to you."

"I'd rather not call you Thingamy."

The left side of his mouth wrinkled. "Archibald then," he said. "Archie."

"How can I help you, Archie?"

"I might need protection," he muttered. "Could you protect me?"

"I've got a license for this..." I said, rooting around in the top drawer of my desk. The Smith and Wesson was under a pile of bank statements, all un-exciting. I pulled it out and waved it vaguely. I don't like guns; they make me nervous. "Though I'd prefer not to," I added. I put the gun back in the desk drawer. "I don't normally do bodyguard work. Why would you need protection anyway?"

"Promise me — you won't call the police, at least

until you hear me out."

I shrugged. He swallowed again, hesitated, looked at the ceiling, seemed to like what he saw there, and after a moment, reluctantly, dropped his eyes back to me. "I might have killed someone. Perhaps several people."

"What do you mean, 'might'?"

"I have dreams," he said. "Dreams of murder. But I think they're more than dreams. I think they're memories."

## II

Crazy? Of course I thought he was crazy, Avarez, but I listened as he described the dreams. His face seemed to blank out every now and then, as though he were too finely tuned to keep focused for long. It didn't fill me with confidence.

"The main thing about the dreams is that while I'm in them I feel...great joy."

"Joy? What's the cause of the joy? Not the actual killing?"

"Perhaps. I don't know." He looked up nervously. "It's as though I've been...I don't know...set free. Like being released from a cage."

"What are you freed from?"

"I don't know that either."

In his most recent dream, he was standing on a platform at Redfern, waiting to catch a train into the city. As the train pulled in, he pushed a thin man in front of it. He didn't see the man clearly, but he did live out the man's death. He saw, as the victim might have seen it, the bulk of the train and the smeared white dot of the driver's face. The train hit, threw him aside. He saw blood burst across the metal. A few drops reached the ridge of grimy brickwork along the opposite platform edge. He felt his knee break on a sleeper. His head went under a wheel, and, in his final moment of consciousness, he actually heard his skull crack. As the bone shattered, he laughed joyously.

"When I woke from the dream, I was sitting near a fountain, drinking from an old whiskey bottle. I was wearing a filthy cardigan with holes in it. Water was drifting onto me because a strong breeze was blowing."

"Has it occurred to you it might be just what it seems? Vivid, but a dream. Too much booze'll do it every time."

He stood suddenly, proving he was a lot less languid than he looked. His hand slapped onto the desk and withdrew, leaving a thin bundle of fifty dollar bills. "I'm sure it happened, just as I dreamt it. Here's five hundred dollars. Check it out for yourself...and then, find out who the fuck I killed, and who else I might have killed. I want to know why. I'll call back here on Wednesday, if I'm still alive."

"Why would you be dead?"

He breathed deeply, so his throat rumbled. "Maybe these people I'm killing are out to kill me, too," he said.

## III

Part of me wanted to forget the whole thing, Avarez. Give him his money back. Go chase up a lost husband or two. But that part of me hadn't wanted to be an investigator at all. Private dicks are something found in American mystery magazines and Raymond Chandler novels, it said. And women aren't cut out to mimic Humphrey Bogart.

The other part of me sensed more than lunacy in this Archibald character. He didn't seem evil; he seemed like he needed help. Maybe he was right. Maybe someone was trying to kill him and he was retaliating. Maybe an accident had skimmed off his memory. Maybe he hadn't done a thing and was merely the victim of his own imagination. There were a lot of maybes, and I thought, maybe, I'd like to sort out some of them. Archie was kind of cute in a grim, distancing way. And the poor man was desperate and very confused.

I began my investigations with a Redfern station guard — and hit pay-dirt straight off. A bloke had gone under a train on Thursday morning. A real mess. Wrecked the schedules, the guard said. Commuters were bitching for the rest of the day.

"What was this guy like?" I asked.

"Buggered if I know," the SRA man laughed. "Completely mangled." He ground out a cigarette with his boot. I described Archie and asked the guard whether he'd seen him around the station that day. He said, "You must be kidding. What'd ya think I got? Photographic memory or somethin'?"

When I examined the spot where the accident had taken place, I found a stain that looked like blood on the edge of the platform opposite. Archie had known about that spray of blood. Hard to know how if he hadn't been intimately involved.

The body had remained unidentified; nothing on him at all. No one had come forward to claim him though there'd been a bit on it in the papers. I read the article in the State Library. Generalised, nothing helpful. There was a vague picture of police and public milling about some shadowy lumps on the track.

Police records gave the cause of death as *Misadventure*. Witnesses said the guy had seemed to slip. I made a note of their names. If homicide was involved here, as Archibald claimed, one of these bystanders could be the culprit, not Archie. The doctor who'd signed the victim's death certificate told me it was pretty obvious what killed him. No sign of anything else. He smirked. "No bullet holes, if that's what you mean, love."

But, by late Tuesday evening, I still hadn't tracked down the body. Everyone thought someone else had dealt with it. When I pointed out to a rather surly young desk cop that the corpse seemed to have walked away of its own accord, he made a tasteless joke about necrophilia. I said, in some cases, there wasn't much difference between the living and the dead, at least in terms of mental activity.

His immediate superior was just as dismissive. "What's it matter?" the red-faced cop sighed, as though he had better things to think about. Perhaps he did. "We've got the reports. If anyone turns up wanting him, we'll look harder. It was just some derelict who suicided, Miss Wolfe. No one's interested, and there's nothing to find out from the corpse anyway. The head was completely mashed."

After that, I visited one of the witnesses — Mrs Anne Milgate who'd been standing right next to the dead man when he 'slipped' under the train. Being a witness made her indignant. "I'm still having nightmares, dear," she said. "Some of his blood got on my dress."

We had tea in delicate china cups. Mrs Milgate told me how she'd been a metre or so from the man when he went under. "I was looking right at him," she said, biting into a scone. "He just fell forward."

"Was there anyone closer to him?"

"Oh, I think so. It's hard to say."

"Do you think someone might have pushed him?"

She considered the proposition as though I'd asked her whether she'd like another cup of tea. "Murder, you mean?"

"Perhaps just an accident."

"It's possible. I couldn't say."

I described Archie and asked her whether she'd seen anyone fitting his description around about when the accident happened. "Well, dearie," she whispered, nodding her head in a secretive manner. "That sounds rather like the poor man himself, doesn't it?"

Not very helpful, I thought.

## IV

As it turned out, even though I expected he'd regret his decision to bare his soul to me and then go into hiding, Archie was in my outer office when I got there on Wednesday. I told him what I'd found thus far, even the detail of the blood on the platform. "It could have been a guess on your part, of course," I suggested. "It's fairly likely blood would be splashed about in an accident as mutilating as that one."

"But how did I know about the accident at all?"

"The newspaper?"

"I never read newspapers."

"A radio then." I leaned forward, emphasising the point. "Look, the story would have been on the air that morning." I gestured to stop him speaking. "I know you're going to say you didn't hear any news, but, maybe, you just don't remember. A peripheral experience perhaps. Got into your head over a background PA or someone's Walkman. It's, at least, as likely as you killing the guy."

He turned inward, head drooping, green eyes glazing over. The fingers of his left hand began to twitch as though squeezing an invisible rubber ball. "We could prove it by working out your movements," I said. "Mr X died at roughly 9.20 under the train from Sutherland. Where were you then?"

"I don't want you to prove I wasn't there. I killed him. I know it. I just want you to find out why. I want a reason. I want you to prove I'm not just a monster."

"But that's ridiculous. Wouldn't you rather I proved you were somewhere else at the time?"

"No."

"Why not?"

He swallowed, licked his lips. "It's pointless, don't you see? I don't want it to go on forever."

I fell silent, trying to balance out how much trouble he'd prove to be, what his motives were.

"Will you take on the job?" he asked.

"Will you answer my questions honestly?"

He nodded with a foreigner's nervous stiffness.

"Start with your name." I pushed him a pad and a pen. "Your real one. And your address." His tongue crept between his lips, wetting them. That haunted look appeared from its concealment like a mouse sniffing the mingled scent of cheese and cat.

"All right," he said and started to write.

"And I'd like to see some identification." He glanced up, startled. "It's not that I'm suspicious. It's just, well, I don't trust anyone."

"I haven't got any," he muttered. "Not on me and not at home." As he spoke, he was tapping the pen on his palm.

"Driver's license? Credit card? Library card? Frequent Flyers?"

"No." He jabbed with the pen; blood dripped onto the desktop. He didn't seem to notice.

"Well, where do you keep all that money you flash around then?" I said with some exasperation.

"My pocket," he replied, humourlessly.

His name, he claimed, was Archibald Fountain — or, at least, that's what he'd been calling himself for the last week or so, which was as far back as he remembered. The first memory he had of anything except the various deaths he'd dreamed about was of sitting near the fountain in Hyde Park after waking up from his latest dream of murder. Wouldn't you know it? An amnesiac.

"You, my friend, need a doctor, not an investigator," I said when he told me.

"They can't help me. If I find out why I'm killing these people, that'll be the end of it. I know it will." He uttered the words with conviction.

"What about hypnosis?"

"I'll give you two thousand dollars in advance."

"Two thousand...?"

"Please. Aren't you the least bit curious?"

I closed my eyes and sighed. I was curious, no doubt about it, Avarez. In my racket, who wouldn't be?

# V

I began by getting from him a description of all the other dreams he'd had. There were, in all, five dreams of murder: the one at Redfern, another involving a car accident, one featuring poison, one in which he'd held a man against a toilet wall and blown his head off with a sawn-off rifle, and a fall from the top of a multi-storey building. Lots of different deaths. Plenty of telling details to go with each of them.

One problem was, of course, that most of the 'murders' from the other dreams could not be placed as accurately as the train incident. They included no specific place, like Redfern station — which had been identified in his dream by the gardens and a station sign. I assumed the murders, if they were murders, would all have taken place in the Sydney area and checked as well as I could. The car accident was hopeless — there were too many. The poisoning might not have been reported as such; likewise, the fall. The toilet killing was a different story. About three months ago, someone had been killed in a toilet — in fact, one of the toilets in the George Street Hoyts cinema complex. The police report said a patron of the complex (he was there to see *The Evil Dead II*) heard a shot and subsequently discovered the body in an unlocked cubicle. He saw no sign of a murderer. Okay, the fact it corresponded closely to Archie's dream was weird enough, but there were other similarities, too. Firstly, the victim was never identified. Like the bloke who went under the train at Redfern a few months later, he was carrying no means of identification, and no one claimed him. Police assumed the murderer had taken his wallet or he hadn't had one. Secondly, the body told them nothing. It was just a corpse, of average height, slight, perhaps thin in build, dressed in old, unremarkable clothes. The man's head had been blown apart, the corpse examined and buried without ceremony.

As there were no fingerprints on the gun except those of the victim, it looked like suicide anyway.

But, in his dream, Archie, while killing the man, noticed one of the victim's ears was torn off and had landed in the open toilet bowl. You commented on it yourself, Avarez, when I came to talk to you about the death. "You wouldn't guess what I found after we'd shifted the corpse," you said. "The bloke's ear! Lounging like a turd at the bottom of the bowl. Funny in a way, isn't it?"

"Hilarious," I mumbled.

# VI

It's a pity I didn't ask you for the dead bloke's fingerprints, Avarez, because, as it happens, those fingerprints would have broken the case wide open. But I didn't know that at the time and I couldn't imagine exactly what I'd find out from them. Something was nagging at me, but I couldn't think how to resolve the feeling, and so just left it to grow by itself. When you told me your files were unable to put a name to the fingerprints, I simply let it drop.

Meanwhile, I was becoming convinced something weird was happening — and more frustrated; I didn't seem to be able to get anywhere with the case. And my attitude to Archie was changing. At first, I'd thought he was a harmless enough loony; now, the possibility was growing that he might actually be some kind of dangerous ghoul. Coincidences continued to pile up and, like most investigators, I'm naturally suspicious of coincidence. Do you understand what I was thinking, Avarez? Concede he was killing these people — perhaps, if he was, his conscious mind didn't want to know about it, and was making him forget, except deep down in the realm of dreams. If I started to prove it, would I become a target myself? Perhaps that's what he wanted. He made me nervous, remembering his gaunt stare and the twitchy discomfort from which he appeared to suffer.

About then, I decided I'd follow my initial instincts and suss him out. I know what you're thinking: he was my client and investigating him wasn't part of my brief.

But, Avarez, what would you do? Solving the case required me to find out if Archie had actually killed someone — the Hoyts 'suicide' or the Redfern train victim. Or someone else. The corpses told no tales because they weren't available and, when they were, no one asked the right questions. The only thing I knew about them was that nothing was known about them. So, why were these nameless derelicts getting killed? Did Archie have a phobia about derelicts? His intimate knowledge of the deaths must have meant he was the killer; what else could it mean? And who was this Archie anyway, this highly strung amnesiac who had forgotten everything except some gruesome dreams in which he was a killer? Enough is enough. I had to know more about him because there was nowhere else to go.

Archie had given an address in Annandale as the place where he was staying. I went there and found it inhabited by a banshee. The woman who opened the door reminded me of Archie — she looked like she hadn't had any sleep. "Can I help you?" she said. She was holding the banshee, a screaming baby only a few months old.

"Does someone called Archie live here?" I asked.

"Archie? Not unless you mean one of the cockroaches," she laughed lightly, which seemed quite a feat given the circumstances. The baby yelled like an air-raid siren.

"Any men at all? The one I want might have a different name."

"Only my husband Kevin. He didn't get you pregnant, too, did he?"

Now I laughed. "No. I'm an investigator. The guy

I'm looking for's my client. Average height, black hair — what there is of it. Green eyes. He looks sort of weary and unkempt."

"The last bit's Kevin, all right. Not the rest though. Kevin's grossly overweight and has hair like Joanne's." She indicated the baby who stopped crying suddenly and grinned as though she'd just remembered a good joke. Her hair was curly and red.

"Looks like my client made a mistake. I don't suppose you've had anyone staying here?"

She sighed. "Who'd want to? You'd be better off kipping down in the middle of George Street, if you want a good night's sleep." With that, the baby, insulted, began to scream again.

## VII

Archie had lied to me. I wasn't surprised but it did suggest there was more to him than a simple desire to find out why he was killing people in his dreams. I had no idea what 'more' was, but I was determined to find out.

Redfern being the only residential part of the city with which I knew him to be associated, I decided to go there and wander around. There were several doss-houses of one kind or another in the vicinity of the railway station and, given Archie's apparently derelict state, I thought I might learn something in one of them. I was right. The third one disgorged a short, frumpy woman dressed in a floral dress and an old cardigan. She said she was the 'landlady'.

"Yeah, there was this bloke," she said. "Coupla week's ago. Real doped out — they're all like that, mind. Called himself Joe or somethin'."

I watched the lit cigarette she was balancing on her lower lip, fascinated by her remarkable achievement in keeping it there. "Why do you think this person might be the one I'm after? You must get lots of Joes."

"Sure, honey, sure I do. But this one had money. He'd been stayin' 'ere for maybe three weeks, givin' me a hundred bucks for each week's accommodation, like. Then, right at the start of a week he'd already paid for, he went out and was gone for three days straight. I thought he'd just pissed off. But he came back, you see, with blood on 'im, sayin' he couldn't remember a thing."

"That's odd, isn't it? He said he didn't remember a thing, but he found his way back to your...establishment?"

"Yeah. Didn't think of that. Guess that's why you're the detective, eh?"

I shrugged modestly.

"Anyways, he reckoned he was Archie now...and I shouldn't call him Joe. 'Joe's dead,' he said. 'I'm Archie.' Didn't make no difference to me. Archie it was."

"Did he say where he'd been during those missing days?"

"Na. Hardly said bugger-all. Anyways, he'd lost his memory."

"Oh yes. So he had."

She leaned against the doorframe and began scratching away under her right breast. I was standing on the front step where I'd been when my knocking roused her.

"He was a funny bastard," she said. "Got more and more...I dunno...sort of desperate. I thought he was gonna bust a valve or somethin' just before he disappeared that time. That's why I wasn't too surprised, see, when he didn't come back. Sometimes at night, I could hear him screaming in his sleep. Guess he was havin' bad dreams, eh?"

"I guess so," I said.

She couldn't tell me much else. Archie had left her boarding-house about the same time he first came to see me. The landlady reckoned he wasn't long for this world.

"I can tell a sick man when I see one," she mused.

## VIII

Out of some misguided sense of completeness, I'd had prints taken from the arm of the chair Archie sat in last time he'd come to see me. When I got to the office next morning, there was an envelope waiting for me. No real match could be found, it said...sure, it wasn't an official document, Avarez, but I've got friends. One had done a bit of a search and had come up with zilch. He'd written by hand on the report there was a slight correlation with the prints of someone who'd been in prison for stock market fraud about ten years ago — but the crim had hanged himself in prison. Not very useful.

I suppose I was ready to give up when Archie shuffled through the door. He looked all the worse for his two-day's absence — drained, tense and jumpy like a cat that had found itself trapped in the Municipal Dog Pound. He looked at me through his blood-shot eyes, saying nothing.

"Well," I said, "how's it going?"

"You're working for me, remember?" He glanced away to avoid eye contact. "What have you found out?"

I pointed at my log notes, which I'd typed on A4 paper and stored in a folder lying at one side of my desk. The folder was marked 'Archie the Dreamer'. "There's not much there," I said. "You can read it if you like."

He did so, nervously, like a man fascinated by a gruesome pathology report. I'd left out my speculations — they go into my private diary — and the fact I'd been checking out his lodgings and his fingerprints. There wasn't a lot for him to read. His eyes finally left the pages and he glanced around the room as though searching for a place to hide. "Can't you do better than this?" he muttered.

"You haven't given me much to go on. And, as you saw, the bodies of your victims...if you know what I mean...didn't reveal much. They weren't identified and can't be traced now. One of them even seems to be missing."

He looked as though he wanted to tell me something. It's a look I always associate with people who've read to the end of a whodunit and are dying to spill the beans, even though you're only on page fifty-six. "What is it, Archie?" I asked. "Why don't you tell me what you know?"

I think he almost did. His lips trembled, his pupils widened as though he needed expanded vision for the task ahead, his fingers drew patterns in the air. But, as his mouth opened, something grabbed at him from inside his gut, and he drew back again. He shook his head. "I can't remember anything."

I nodded, fancying that, for the first time, I'd seen the schizophrenia hiding out in him.

# IX

When he left a while later, bearing my assurances there were avenues I was yet to explore, I followed him, determined to find out where he went and what he did when he got there. His course was a rambling, purposeless one that took us finally, perhaps inevitably, to Hyde Park. For a long time, he sat on a bench staring at the fountain with its Grecian heroes dripping recycled water. He'd been staring at the bronze statues for a long time, an hour or so, before I noticed he was starting to tremble. The tremors reached a peak and he bent over double, gripping his head between his hands. Then he sat up again, straight and sudden, and screamed. There were words mingled in the scream, though I couldn't hear them clearly. People walking nearby changed their path to avoid him.

He turned.

I was perhaps two hundred metres away, concealed in shrubbery, and, for a moment, I couldn't tell whether or not he'd seen me. My heart sped up as the eeriness of his violent glance twisted in my stomach. Even from that distance, his eyes were spooky.

"You!" he yelled. "Free me, can't you? Free me!"

There was a pause in which our eyes met and held. Then I ducked out of sight, hoping he hadn't been looking at me, hadn't recognised me. I was just someone, a person in the distance. I could deny I'd been following him. I could say I was somewhere else. Surely, he couldn't be sure it was me, not in shadows as I'd been, not half-hidden by trees and the flowering grevilleas. I felt frantic, frantic not to have seen his eyes, not to have heard his words, not to be known to him. I didn't know why. I just wanted to be away from him.

When I looked again, he was gone.

# X

Night fell. I was still in my office, where I'd been since about three. After leaving the Park, I'd gone for a walk on Bondi beach, to be in the sun, to be among people doing nothing but being normal. Water relaxes my mind, which needed relaxing. Archie's eyes scared me and I didn't really know why. The whole case was beginning to scare me. As I saw it, there were several alternatives, one of them being that Archie really was a ghoul, killing people, and suppressing the knowledge, even, perhaps, from himself. After all, here's this guy who's an unknown quantity to everyone. No records available. A stranger to his neighbours. He has money but even he doesn't know where he got it. Perhaps a job he'd forgotten about? He claims to kill people who all appear to have died by accident or by their own hand. Yet he knows all the details of their death, even unpublished details. Weird. Could he be a psychopath?

A hit man? I didn't have a clue, and I didn't like it. It felt dangerous. For a while, I watched the waves foam up the sand, before I got restless and tracked down a phone. My receptionist, Janet, told me there'd been no sign of Archie, not in the building and not in the street outside — not that she'd noticed anyway. So, I returned to the office to try and piece it all together.

Janet left about five-twenty or so, telling me to give myself a break and go home to bed. I only grunted and, two hours later, was still there, reading over my notes and free-associating all sorts of nonsense. Maybe I even drifted off into sleep, because I suddenly sprang awake, startled by a noise that had become indefinable now I was conscious. Darkness had crept into the room, blurring edges and turning the green carpet grey. I shivered, listening intently. Nothing.

Then there was a footfall beyond the closed partition that obscured my waiting room.

"Is there someone there?" I said.

The door opened slowly, but I didn't move. Perhaps I couldn't move. For the first time since I'd opened the agency two years before, I was really scared. Archie had got to me.

When an outline I recognised as his entered through the silently opening door, I switched on the desk lamp. He blinked like a fox caught in a car's headlights.

"Have you found out who I'm killing?" he said.

I slid open the drawer in my desk and froze with my hand resting on the gun there. "Are you sure you want to know?"

"I asked you, didn't I?" Something seemed to have happened to him. He was shaking and breathing irregularly. "You shouldn't follow me. Just tell me if you know who I murdered," he whispered.

"I think you know, Archie. I believe now, for the first time, that you really did kill someone — but I think you already know who and why."

"I don't, for God's sake."

I watched him for a moment, tracing the patterns of tension tightening his body and aching in his face. I could see the age there, decades beyond what I'd thought, fossilised experience beneath the surface of his skin.

"Do you really not know who you are?" I asked.

His breathing was laboured. He looked forlorn.

"Okay, you don't know. Well, I sure as hell don't know either. Here's another question: do you remember hanging around the morgue?"

"Is that what I've been doing?"

"Maybe. In the two real incidents I've been able to trace, one of the actual victims disappeared after the crime, and the other is...well, untraceable." He looked puzzled, painfully so.

"You mean, I stole the bodies?"

"Maybe."

"What am I trying to hide?"

"You tell me."

He made a choking sound deep in his throat as though somewhere in his chest the memories were rising. "I can't," he whispered.

Now I decided to lie. "But you forgot the fingerprints, Archie. They tell us a lot." A gargling moan. I could see it in his eyes; he was starting to remember. I pressed on. "The scientific branch has made a tentative cross-referencing, Archie. What do you think of that?" Archibald twisted, jerking like a marionette. "Who the hell are you, Archie?"

"I can't remember..." he whimpered, crumbling as he spoke. But his eyes gripped mine, filling with remembrance. "You...you can't know what it's like — to dream of death and just feel the dreams pass away with the night. Mostly, I don't remember. I don't want to. Why are you making me remember?"

"You asked me to. Why else would you hire me?"

He choked out the words. I could barely hear them. "Release. To find freedom."

"What do you mean?" I said, seeing the cracks opening him up. My trembling fingers thoughtlessly flipped off the gun's safety catch. "Tell me the truth."

"Nothing's true," he said, his shaking so bad his legs seemed to fold under him. I began to stand, to go to him, but he drew himself up, reforming his body by an effort of will. "You want to know about immortality?" he breathed, like a dying breeze. "Year after year of meaningless living, in a world where there's death you can taste but never gain. For a long time I worked...oh yes, I remember...I've played the stock market ...amassed capital in ways you couldn't imagine. But what does it mean? They all died. My friends, my lovers. I'm more alone than anyone has ever been."

"I don't understand," I said, feeling as though I was suddenly part of a different scenario, one I certainly hadn't written.

"You understand," he groaned. "You just don't want to admit it."

"Tell me then." I stood suddenly. "Cut the crap and

tell me who the hell you're killing!"

He staggered backwards as though my voice had hit him physically. He was shaken by a massive tremor. "Me!" he cried as it faded. "I'm killing me."

Now I was more confused than ever and the confusion manifested as fear, an almost paralysing fear as dark as the night clawing at my windows. "What are you talking about?"

"Suicide. I killed myself." His eyes met mine, and I swear to you, Avarez, after that moment, I know what it's like to stare into hell. Perhaps it was simply madness, but, to me, it felt like damnation.

"That doesn't make sense," I said.

He laughed. "When you're immortal, everything makes sense eventually." He spasmed, then clenched his fists to stop the convulsions. His eyes rose again. "I'm immortal, Miss Wolfe. I can't die — though I want to. It's as simple as that. So, when the pressure builds to a point where I can no longer bear the pain, the isolation...I kill myself, hoping that this time, this time, there'll come an end."

"You're crazy," I muttered what seemed to be obvious truth. Though even as I said it, I remembered the body that had strangely, surprisingly, disappeared.

"Crazy? Yes, I am crazy. And I'm also alive." The emphasis he put on the word turned it to filth.

I decided to try reason. "Surely if your body was destroyed, as the body of the Redfern bloke was, surely you couldn't revive?"

"I can!" he said intensely, straight at me. I retreated, my knuckles whitening around the grip of the Smith and Wesson. "Doesn't work that way. One moment I'm dead...dismembered. Next I'm somewhere else, whole. Just memories of death, none of the reality."

"So what do you want of me?" I said, utterly out of my depth. I'm not a psychologist.

"Release. I came to you because you're immortal, too. You might not know it...but I see it in your eyes."

Denial was useless. "What if I am? How would it help?"

"You've got to kill me!" he growled. "Perhaps if immortal kills immortal, then the curse will end. You're immortal and you're a woman. Women bring us into the world and must be the ones to force us out of it again. So kill me!" He lunged suddenly, his features ancient and mad. I fell backwards, crashing against the chair. My fingers twitched and the gun fired. Several times. A shot tore into his chest, stopping him and pushing him aside. He seemed to recover, leapt at me, roaring. Compulsively, I fired again. The second shot hit his stomach; a third went in his throat. He collapsed with a thud, and lay motionless in a bloody, spreading pool.

I didn't move. I was trembling, shocked by the killing, a killing I hadn't anticipated, in vindication of a belief so ridiculous, no jury would ever convict me of anything except insanity.

But, think about it, Avarez. The lost bodies, the details remembered from his dreams...the pattern that falls so easily into place once you give in to this one possibility. Perhaps it's true. I hope to hell it's true.

His body lay there, doing nothing, but I begged the night that soon it would. Let it shudder, jerk into life, stand to confront me with what I'd done. Then Archie might remember fully, and speak to me again of unending life.

So I wait. You came, Avarez, called here by an interfering neighbour, keen for answers; but, in a while, you'll discover it's been a waste of time. Archie'll get up and there'll be no murder case against me. No corpse. You'll see. In law, death is forever.

Sure, I'm taking risks, gambling with belief. But isn't any risk worth taking in return for the secret of immortality?

# ROTTING EGGPLANT ON THE BOTTOM SHELF OF A FRIDGE

"What's that smell?"

"The only thing I can smell is me."

It was always the same, whenever they returned from being away, never mind for how long. He would regard the house as an alien thing and would be disquieted; for her, the alien thing would be her own body. One would set about searching for the source of his disquiet; the other would head for the bathroom, undress, scour away the residue of distant places.

"Something's gone off. It's coming from the kitchen."

"Check it out yourself. I'm taking a shower."

When Ellen returned, pink and steamy, he was on his hands and knees in front of the open door of the fridge.

"I think I've found it," he said. "Look at this!"

She leaned over him, peering into the fridge's interior. A milk bottle, half full. Various bottles containing sauces and condiments. A half-devoured pile of bones, skin and stuffing they'd bought whole three weeks ago from Red Rooster. Two lamb chops in a bloody plastic bag. Three cans of beer. Some vegetables

— carrots, broccoli, pumpkin. Butter on a dish. A container that held the leftovers of the last meal they'd had at home, three weeks ago. From the outside, it looked like congealed blood. What had it been? Oh yes, chilli con carne.

"What am I looking at?" she asked.

"This!" He flicked his index finger impatiently at something at the bottom, toward the back. She steadied herself, leaning on his shoulders, and squatted down further. There was something purple-black, like a bruise.

"A rotting capsicum," he declared.

She huffed, pushing herself away. "Shows how much cooking you do." She reached in and grabbed the shiny misshapen object. "It's not a capsicum and it's not rotten. It's an eggplant." It felt firm under the pressure of her fingers.

"An eggplant?"

She tossed it at him as she walked away. He felt it and put it back. "I hate eggplant. Why have you got an eggplant in the fridge?"

"I was going to make moussaka."

He made a face. "Well, something smells."

She declared it wasn't her because she'd just had a shower. To prove it, she dropped the towel, so they had to go upstairs and make love — although he insisted on putting clean sheets on the bed first, despite the fact she'd done that the day they left. His fussing nearly quashed her desire, but they got the mood back after a while, made love in an urgent sort of fashion, and he resumed worrying about the smell with a minimum of delay. In the end, she gave in to his worry, as she always did, knowing it was just how he was. No use getting upset about it now. After all, he'd been like that for the twenty-odd years of their marriage.

She said, "Did you check everything in the fridge? What about the meat? Uncooked meat goes off pretty quickly."

He rushed out of the room. While he was gone, she picked up her handbag to get the novel she'd been reading, a detective thing by Patricia Cornwall about a forensic pathologist trying to work out why young couples kept turning up dead. But it wasn't there. Instead her hand emerged holding a copy of Herman Hess's *Steppenwolf*. Damn. Must have swapped them somewhere by mistake. She examined the novel. What was it about? She opened it at random and read. Its sombre mood evoked immediate melancholy in her bones. When her husband came back in, he'd covered himself in a sheet. He had it wrapped around his body like a protective cocoon.

"I checked everything," he said. "None of it's off, not even the chops."

"Not the chops? Are you sure? We've been away three weeks."

"They're okay. So's the milk."

"How can milk not go off?"

"I don't know, do I?"

"The fridge is getting old. I'd be surprised if it worked that well."

"The fridge wasn't running at all."

She frowned at him, wondering if he were having a nervous collapse. She'd heard about people having nervous collapses and, if anyone was going to have a nervous collapse, it would be him.

"Not running?"

"The cord had fallen out. That outlet's been wonky for ages. I keep meaning to fix it."

"Okay, the cord fell out. But you said nothing had gone off."

"That's right."

They discussed how impossible it was for the fridge to have been off but nothing in it to have spoiled, until he started to get angry because the level of her scepticism seemed like a questioning of his ability to tell what was what in the world. She suggested they should forget the whole thing. Who cares anyway? What's it matter? Nothing spoilt, great, and, if they wanted to, they could throw everything out and restock this afternoon because, after all, they were both employed and had plenty of money and they didn't have to be back at work for three days yet. He agreed they should forget it but he wouldn't throw out what was in the fridge because, if it wasn't spoilt, throwing it out would be an unforgivable waste. Okay, she said, and they reminisced about the trip they'd just taken to Gerringong, Mollymook and on down the coast, and forgot the fridge, though he kept sniffing the air and her eyes had taken on a look of cunning.

"I've got to go to the loo," she said at last, but instead, sneaked into the kitchen, where she checked the contents of the fridge. Sure enough, everything was fine. She couldn't smell a thing.

After taking another shower, she decided to go shopping, so she reassured him she wasn't going to throw out and replace what was in the fridge — only the chilli con carne, and, probably, they shouldn't use the milk or the meat, even though they smelt okay, because it had been a long time, whether or not the fridge was working. You could never be too sure. He got a bit tense, but she determined to go anyway, feeling impatient with him.

"By the way," she said, "is this yours?" Holding up the book.

"I read *Steppenwolf* before we got married," he replied, and she couldn't decide whether there was nostalgia in it.

The day was sultry and chilly, both. Behind the nippy autumn wind, there was a sort of putrid heat that might have been generated by the sun, but might, too, have come from the factories breathing out pollutants or the cars with their fevered exhausts. She went along the highway as though headed for Katoomba, disturbed by the anxious bustle of traffic on the old road, but took the PANTHERS turnoff (the sign also read MUSEUM OF FIRE, which she always saw as MUSEUM ON FIRE) and skirted past the club into the centre of Penrith. When she emerged from the supermarket after getting what she wanted, the atmosphere was even more grey and oppressive — worse than she'd ever known it. Maybe there was a storm brewing. That possibility seemed confirmed when she noticed how much wind there was, coming from the east, and how, from the top of a rise, she could see dark shadows in the direction of Sydney. The shadows might have been storm clouds. They swirled and flickered continually, as though lightning was discharging somewhere in the depths of them. If she opened her window, the air seemed to carry noxious smells from far away. High above, there was a hawk, hanging on the wind as though watching her. At one point, she barely missed hitting a dog that rushed out without warning. This near-death experience didn't save it; in the rear-view mirror, she saw it go under the wheels of a gaudily painted panel van that was perhaps fifty metres behind her. The panel van caught up with her, overtook and zoomed away into the distance, doing maybe 180. Words painted on the side read: KERB CRAWLER.

She tried to tell her husband about it when she got home but he was too full of other concerns.

"Come and look at this!" he yelled.

The TV was on. Probably he'd wanted to watch the footie replay, but what he got instead was a special news report. The newsreader was looking uncharacteristically stressed, as though she'd been in a hurry and had tripped over a cameraman on the way to her seat.

"...strange phenomenon which has struck Sydney, as more and more buildings in the CBD succumb to decay. Experts have been unable to explain how diverse buildings, whether old and renovated, middle-aged or no more than a few months old, can all apparently suffer from the same sudden and devastating structural deterioration..."

"It must be an earthquake," she said.

On the screen were pictures of buildings, some of which she recognised — GPO, AMP, Myers in George Street. She watched as they crumbled, sagged, or collapsed inward onto themselves. In the street, people were gaping. Others were running away, screaming, as masonry and showers of dust and dirt turned the air ghostly. The ground did not appear to be quaking.

"So far, over four hundred people have been confirmed dead," the newsreader's voice continued. "Thousands more could be buried under the tonnes of rubble. Robert Calvert reports from the scene..."

Picture of a journalist both shocked and elated.

"I am standing surveying what many describe as the greatest natural disaster ever to strike Australia. Around me, familiar structures, which have stood safely for many generations, are visibly weakening, their foundations crumbling, and the signs of decay growing on their walls even as we watch. Even more bizarrely, new buildings, such as the one behind me — completed only four months ago — are showing the same symptoms..."

"Is this a movie you're watching, Joe?" she asked.

He didn't look around, but she noticed that his hands were trembling.

"It's not possible," he said.

The report continued, possible or not. Shoppers and office workers had been caught in buildings that abruptly collapsed. Others were trampled by panicked crowds. The camera skipped over the body of a man sliced in half by a pane of glass that had fallen from the thirteenth floor of an unnaturally decaying edifice. Vast stretches of George Street and Pitt Street and Elizabeth Street had suddenly been reduced to piles of rubble. The flashing lights of emergency vehicles and police were everywhere. Shocked faces. Bloody faces. Hysterical faces.

But no answers. There were, however, experts who

said "earthquake" or "severe subsidence" or "the effects of some corrosive pollutant". And a psychic named Dave Brock (her husband grunted, as though the name were familiar to him) who claimed the decay was taking place on a spiritual level.

"Is it happening anywhere else, Joe?" When he didn't answer, she grabbed hold of his shoulder and shook him. "Is it happening anywhere else, Joe?"

His face turned to her, lips trembling slightly. "What? Anywhere else? I don't know, do I? How should I know?"

"Have they said?"

"Just in the inner city and King's Cross. That's where the decay's always been."

She rushed to the phone and began to dial frantically.

"What are you doing?"

"Calling our son. My God, Joe, Steven only lives in Petersham. It might be happening there, too."

But the lines were down or clogged or something and she couldn't get through. She wanted to jump in the car and drive to Petersham, right now, but the TV said people from the outer suburbs should not, under any circumstances, approach the city. The highways were already bumper-to-bumper. It was dangerous. Police were arresting looters.

"What if he's been injured, Joe? Or worse."

"He wouldn't have been at home. He works in Canterbury. That's further out."

What about Sharon and the baby? What if she'd gone shopping in the city? Anyway, why had the buildings decided to collapse, right at that point in time? But there were no answers, not even to the smallest and most fundamental questions, let alone the big cosmological ones.

They watched in silence as the reports continued, all the same: decay visibly forming on the façades of buildings, concrete flaking, metal rusting, supports giving way, walls shrivelling like the skins of rotting fruit.

The phone surprised them both when it rang.

"Maybe that's Steven," she said.

She let him take it, but she knew as soon as he spoke that neither Steven nor Sharon was on the other end.

"Simon? No, there's no one called Simon here." He frowned toward her and shrugged. "Simon House? No, no one by that name...Really, you must have the wrong number. Perhaps the lines."

After a moment he hung up. "Wrong number," he said, returning to the TV. "Funny thing is I know the name. Simon House. Keyboard player for Hawkwind."

"What?"

"Hawkwind. A band I used to listen to in the seventies."

If someone could get through with a wrong number, she reckoned, ignoring Joe's revelation, then whatever was wrong with the lines must have been fixed. But when she tried ringing Steven's number again, there was nothing. More buildings collapsed on the TV. The chaos increased. More emergency services vehicles turned up. More police. More reporters.

During an ad, Joe went to the kitchen to get a beer. She heard him open the fridge door, drop something and yell for her. When she went to him and looked in the fridge, her heart nearly stopped.

The white interior was dotted with mould. Items that just a few hours ago she had confirmed to be unspoilt were now useless. The milk in the bottle was thick and yellow. Jars marked THOUSAND ISLAND DRESSING and STIR FRY SAUCE were blackened. The half-eaten chicken was green and maggoty, as were the lamb chops in their bloody plastic bag. Shrivelled carrots, dry, crumbling heads of yellow broccoli, slimy pumpkin. The butter was rancid. The chilli con carne had grown hair.

"My God!" she exclaimed.

"How can it have happened so quickly?" He pushed himself away from the fridge now that his initial surprise was being overcome by the horrible odour. "Were we hallucinating before?"

"Reefer madness," she said.

"What?"

"It's like they used to call it when you smoked too much pot. Reefer madness."

"For God's sake, I haven't touched that stuff for years."

They set about cleaning the fridge, using scrapers to shovel the mould and rancid materials into rubbish bags. The smell was appalling. Everything was off, as it turned out, except the eggplant.

"There's nothing wrong with it." She held it up to his nose, then sniffed it herself.

"Not that we can see or smell. It's probably worm-ridden inside though."

She put it on the bench, not in a rubbish bag. When the fridge had been washed out and disinfected, and the thermostat reset, the eggplant went back in and the new groceries she'd bought followed. He didn't argue. It didn't seem important.

Behind him, through the kitchen door, the TV was shouting news of continuing decay in the inner city. They went in and watched.

"...The strange phenomenon causing buildings to decay and collapse appears to be spreading south and west," claimed a young man in a conservative grey suit and extravagant emerald tie. Underneath him on the screen were the words: ADRIAN SHAW REPORTING.

"Adrian Shaw," her husband said, frowning. "That's odd."

"...Every structure along Broadway from Central to the University has now disappeared into piles of rubble and garbage and as you can see even the Seymour Centre is not immune..." Pan along Military Road to the Seymour Centre, looking as if it were two hundred years old and never in all those two hundred years cleaned or maintained.

"My God," she said, leaping up. "If it *is* heading that way, Steven and Sharon will certainly be in danger. We've got to do something."

"What can we do? The phone's not working. The roads are impassable. Please, Ellen, calm down. The cops are getting people away from the buildings before anything happens."

"What if they don't?"

"It's not as dangerous out of the City. No skyscrapers to fall over on anyone."

"I have to know."

"There are more important questions."

Frustrated by his logic, she tried them on her mobile

and then the home phone again, without success. "I'll start dinner," she said, hoping to keep her mind off things.

Opening the fridge was like an exercise in déjà vu. Mould and decay everywhere. All the new things she'd bought, ruined.

Her husband came and stood in front of the open fridge door, silent, hands hanging by his sides.

"It's not possible," she said. "The eggplant's the only thing that's still okay."

He said nothing, but stared and stared. When she talked directly to him, he snapped out of his trance and headed off through the kitchen door. She asked him where he was going, and he said, "I'll be back in a minute."

He was holding tightly onto a book when he returned, a big book she recognised as one he'd been reading while they were on holidays. It was called *The Strange World*.

"Joe?" she queried nervously.

He didn't look at her. "Listen to this," he said. He flipped through the book, opened it and began reading. "Synchronicity is a different way of viewing coincidence, it says here. Strange stuff happens all the time — like this case I read about once, when three different ships sank in the same place on the same date nearly a hundred years apart, and in each case the sole survivor was a bloke named Hugh Williams. You see? What could cause something like that? Was it the name? The date? The place? The particular conjunction between them? Jung — you know, the shrink — he said synchronicity was 'the simultaneous occurrence of two or more meaningfully but not causally connected events'. In other words, things happen that aren't the result of each other, not in the normal sense, but which, on some other level, are related."

"I don't understand what you're trying to say."

"There's this writer, Charles Fort, who made up a list of really bizarre events and said there was a cosmic joker out there that caused them to happen that way, for no other reason except to create absurd events. There's, like, this passion in the universe for patterns to be set up, bizarre ones. You see what I mean? Microcosm, macrocosm. Little, big."

"Little, big? You think what's happening in our fridge is connected to what's happening in Sydney?"

He flushed red. "I know it sounds ridiculous, but why has everything gone off? Everything except the eggplant?"

"You think the eggplant is doing it?"

"I don't know. Maybe." He flipped through the book some more. "It says here that 'paradigm' is a Greek word meaning *pattern*. An idea or a force, which in magical terms might be expressed in a single object, but, through that object, the paradigm will be able to expand into the larger world. What about that, eh?" He thumbed through the book. "Sympathetic correspondence, that's another one." He found the spot he was after. She thought he looked unhealthily manic; his hands were shaking. "Magic works through the principles of sympathetic correspondence, where doing something to a symbolic object can cause things to happen to something else. Like burning an image of your enemy in order to kill him."

"Why an eggplant?"

He shrugged petulantly. "I'm just saying something weird is going on. Our eggplant might be the cause."

"It's not right. What you're talking about is not the way the world works."

He looked haunted. "Are you sure?"

"Joe, maybe you should lie down for a while," she suggested.

He said nothing, but went into the lounge room and plonked himself in front of the TV, which was showing more scenes of rapid urban decay. He clutched the book to his chest.

"But it's crazy, Joe," she said.

His face, which was pale now and very drawn, turned toward her suddenly. "Every one of the reporters they've had on TV this afternoon has had the name of a member of Hawkwind, that band I told you about. Like the wrong number."

"Hawkwind? What's Hawkwind got to do with it?"

"I don't know," he said.

She was very worried now. As if it wasn't bad enough that terrible, unnatural things were being reported on the TV, and she didn't know whether or not she should be worrying about her son and his family, now her husband was cracking under the strain. It had to be nervous collapse. That was understandable, sure, given what was happening. But why should he think their fridge was responsible?

On the screen was a redheaded woman with big staring eyes and a tailored coat. "This is Simone King reporting for Eye Witness News..."

"*Simon* King," her husband said, without turning,

"...was a drummer in Hawkwind."

She frowned.

The female reporter with a name similar to that of the drummer in a 1970s rock band went on to detail how the 'decay effect' had spread rapidly through the suburbs and was heading for...

"Petersham!" she yelled. "Oh, Joe, look! My God, it's Steven."

Their son, his face dirtied and harassed, was speaking to Simone King on the screen. "It's my wife and kid...they're up there." He was pointing toward the top of a building where tiny figures were milling about without real purpose. "You've got to get them down. Someone's got to do something. If the place collapses..."

*Cracks and visible decay spread around the base of the building. It trembles.*

"We've got to do something," she yelled. "We'll drive there."

Her husband stood. "I've got to destroy the eggplant."

"Eggplant! For God's sake, Joe, our Sharon and Davy are in trouble."

"It's the eggplant," he said.

He pushed past her, ignoring her abuse, and stalked toward the fridge. She followed him.

"Stay back!" he said. "This might be dangerous!"

"An eggplant? How can an eggplant be dangerous? We've touched it more than once and nothing happened."

"We didn't understand it then."

Ring Steven or the police or the hospital or somebody — that was what had to be done. She wanted to reach out to the world and halt the insanity. She wanted to touch her husband's madness, heal his nerves, so that he'd be there for her again — sane, normal.

But she could do nothing.

He opened the fridge.

Swirling darkness picked him up and flung him across the kitchen. His large body crashed into the pantry cupboard, splintering the door and spilling sugar and salt and corn flakes and blood across the linoleum. Stale, rancid smells coalesced into the shape of demons that ripped at the cupboards, scattering plates and cutlery and food in every direction. She felt numb. Her husband lay still amid the storm emanating from the open fridge door.

*"...Rescue workers have not yet arrived and as the stairwells have been destroyed there seems no way for those trapped on the roof to get down..."*

She was kneeling at the edge of a fury of unnatural decay.

*"One man has attempted to climb to safety, but lost his footing and fell to his death. There must be mere seconds left before the entire edifice comes down..."*

She could see the eggplant on the bottom shelf, bigger than it had been and glowing like putrescence.

*"My wife, my child!"* Steven was screaming. *"They'll be killed."*

She reached out and closed her stiff fingers around the handle of a large Staysharp knife. Demon faces leered at her from the stinking maelstrom.

Her husband groaned.

She threw the knife. It spun. Turning and twisting. Slicing the light. A slow-motion ballet. Plunging toward the eggplant.

It struck and embedded itself in the dark-purple skin, driving the object deeper into the fridge. The demonic shapes roared back toward it, dragged as though by a suction tube, but the winds did not abate.

*Cracks widen. Bricks fall away. The building trembles as though with a palsy.*

She clawed over to the fridge, feeling her hair and the skin of her face gripped by the raging wind. Reached in, grabbed the handle of the knife, pulled it toward her — the eggplant impaled on the blade — brought it out onto the kitchen floor, and cut it. Cut it again. Hacked at it. Hacked. Again. Again. Again.

Winds, smell, oppressive presence of decay, they were all suddenly gone. The eggplant was a mushy pile of diced mould and slime on the floor in front of her. It was so quiet now she could hear the throbbing of her own heart.

*"It appears to have stopped! The destruction seems to have stopped! A reprieve for frightened people on the building before us...Reports are coming in now...yes, all across the city the phenomenon has ceased. Of course, we don't know for how long..."*

She wept.

Her husband woke on the couch, where she had dragged him. "Ellen! Ellen!" he moaned, "I've been having a nightmare."

"Yes," she said, "A nightmare."

The stereo was playing one of his old records.

"I know that music," he said. "Hawkwind. *Astounding Sounds, Amazing Music*. Great songs. 'Reefer Madness', 'Steppenwolf', 'Kerb Crawler'...What's that one playing now? I can't remember the name of that one. Something weird."

She was gazing past him, out through the window into a clear, fading twilight.

"'The Aubergine That Ate Rangoon'," she said, tonelessly.

"Oh yeah. Weird title." He paused, as though recalling something. Then he gripped his wife's hand, as though a response to his next question was vital. "Ellen?" he asked, frowning. "What's an aubergine?"

# UNRAVELLING

Simon Nicoya awoke from a dream in which someone had spilled his drink. He remembered yelling and screaming, threatening to smash the fool's nose across the stained surface of the bar. Anger had erupted from him, hot and uncontrollable.

The sheer intensity of his dream lingered in Simon's muscles. He was disturbed by how knotted and strained they felt. Was that normal in the aftermath of a dream? Couldn't be. But, as he readied himself for the hour-long trip to the office, he knew whose fault it was he was such an emotional basket case.

Where was it written he should be the scapegoat for corporate failure? Was it his fault Light-and-Power Enterprises was declining on the stock market? The CEO's unreasonable persecution was so unjust resentment seethed in Simon constantly. Such anger had to come out somehow, and, all things considered, it was probably better it came out while he slept.

The calm never lasted. As usual, pushing through the mindless, aggressive inner-city crowds put Simon in a foul mood, even before he'd reached the building, let alone his office on the 32nd floor. When he got to the lift, the building manager was tacking up a sign that said:

## LIFTS OUT OF ORDER. PLEASE USE EMERGENCY STAIRS. MANAGEMENT REGRETS ANY INCONVENIENCE.

"Morning, Mr Nicoya," the manager said when she noticed Simon. She smiled pleasantly. "Trouble with the electrical system. We'll be re-wiring all day." She shrugged. "Pity you weren't here five minutes earlier. We announced a 9:15 cut-off to give people a chance to get to their offices."

"What announcement?"

"Sent by email yesterday. Didn't you see it?"

Simon's computer had been playing up, restricting access to his mailbox. And no one had told him about the lift deadline. He resisted hitting the manager. Instead, he grinned tightly and muttered, "No worries! These things happen."

He tested the weight of his briefcase in the light of the climb ahead of him. It was inordinately heavy. He sighed. Onward and upward, that was the way to go.

Thirty-one floors later, he was all sweat and aching limbs, his newly pressed suit damp and crumpled. How could he go to the strategy meeting looking like this? He checked his watch, suddenly unnerved. He'd forgotten about the meeting until that momentary thought had flashed across his forebrain. And it was already 9.40, twenty minutes after the conference was scheduled to start.

He forced himself up the final rise of stairs and burst into the company's main suite. Its open plan gave everyone a clear view of his discomfort. Eyes were staring at him from every side.

"You're late for your meeting with the CEO and the gentlemen from NASA, Mr Nicoya," commented the receptionist, handing him a lukewarm cup of coffee she'd prepared some time ago in anticipation of his arrival.

"I'll go straight in," he sighed, taking the cup. "Blue room?"

"Mr Thomas said to tell you not to bother."

"What?"

The woman's gaunt face, plastered with make-up, hid a smug enjoyment. "He was pretty mad. Said he was pulling you off the contract and sticking you on mail sorting. Reckoned the mail boy could do your job better than you. Very unfair, I thought."

Simon's head throbbed, eyes focusing on one demonstratively amused face over to the left behind the copy machine.

"Mr Nicoya, are you all right?" As the receptionist reached toward him to draw his attention, he turned and her arm hit the cup in his hand. He dropped it. Coffee spilled down the leg of his pants and the cup struck the decorative tiles with a sharp, explosive crack.

Simon ground his teeth. *Funny how small things could so easily tip you over the edge*, he thought.

He slammed his briefcase onto the receptionist's desk, scattering papers and stationery across the floor. "Mr Nicoya, this is too much—" the woman began, drawing back, and he snarled at her. The look on his face shut her up.

WHAT CAN YOU BRING TO THE WORKPLACE THIS MORNING? yelled a motivational sign stuck to the wall behind the woman.

Simon sprung the lock catches on his briefcase, took out the loaded Uzi he'd packed into it this morning and began spraying the room with bullets. The receptionist bought it first. As her chest shattered, Simon felt a sense of achievement for the first time in months. He laughed. Then he aimed at the grinning face near the copier. It was no longer grinning, but that didn't matter. Bullets slammed into it and all its expressions became indistinguishable.

When movement caught his eye, he turned, squeezing on the trigger. There would be another flurry of activity then stillness. Simon liked the contrast. He loved the peace that followed in the wake of violence.

At last, drained, he walked carefully over the slimy mess carpeting the floor and headed for the Blue Room, slipping a new cartridge into the Uzi's ammunition chamber as he went. He shot the lock off the door, kicked it open and massacred all the cringing people in the room.

Then he turned the weapon on himself.

Simon Nicoya woke screaming. Sweat covered his face. He swept it from his eyes.

Outside the cabin of his four-wheel drive, lightning cracked through the late afternoon sky. Runnels of water poured across the windscreen in a continuous stream. Damn rainstorm had certainly been fierce! It might have been trying to swamp the domes of his nuclear power plant in a futile attempt to dampen the fires still seething in its reactors.

Simon hadn't meant to fall asleep, and certainly hadn't wanted to subject his already ragged emotions to the violent, excessive dream that had come upon him as he drifted off. But it was something he'd come to expect. Over the past few weeks, his subconscious mind had been throwing up these twisted memories of his past — filled with all the frustrations he'd felt then. He'd never massacred his co-workers, of course, but he remembered the feelings of frustration and anger that had been in him and had never found any sort of expression. His co-workers and bosses had all treated him badly, but he hadn't struck out at them. He'd just worked hard and made connections across the industry, investing wisely and eventually acquiring a majority shareholding. Onward and upward — that was his motto. In the end, he became CEO and that had seemed like a fine revenge.

Yet the frustrations hadn't ended. Instead, they blossomed, personified in a City Council with no foresight and that made courageous decisions with all the backbone of an aging jellyfish. Simon's plans for Nicoya Nuclear Holdings had been grand. What he received from the Council was hindrance and criticism. Even the few Councillors he'd managed to buy hadn't provided him with any loyalty. Public hysteria — cries of nuclear danger and environmental hazard — had quickly turned even the most pliant of them against him. He'd been blocked and betrayed at every point.

In the end, his dreams of a full nuclear network had come to nothing. But that wasn't the worst of it. Spearheaded by extremists within the community, and abetted by his most fervent enemies in the Council, a city-wide movement made its way to the State legislature, urging a complete ban on Nuclear Grid Technologies. After several years of argument, the Federal Court finally ordered his power plant shut down. NGT lawyers explored all legal avenues to appeal, but the company's struggles came to nothing. Sub-atomic flux development was done for and Nicoya Nuclear Holdings faced a hostile stock market over the following weeks. Simon and his company would be ruined.

And it was this damned city's fault.

The rain had eased, so Simon slipped out of his car and headed for the central building. Its forecourt was largely empty at this time of the evening, though he had to find the emotional wherewithal to greet two security guards, a janitor and several scientific personnel as he stalked toward the main offices. No one questioned him, of course. It was his plant, even if it was doomed.

Near the lifts, he forced some coins into the drink machine and it gave him hot chocolate in a cardboard mug. He was chilly and needed warmth. He sipped it as he unlocked the door to his office.

Damp and weary, he slumped into his work chair. Huge bay windows provided a magnificent panorama of the city. Only a few of its row upon row of lights, forming an intricate bauble of energy in the gloom of the twilight, were now powered by NGT. Remaining clients were already arranging for alternative energy sources to feed their hunger. They were hungry still, of course, but not for the energy NGT could supply.

He turned to his desk, reaching to activate his voicemail. Perhaps there'd be good news. His forearm clipped the paper mug he'd placed there and foaming chocolate cascaded over his desktop and onto the phone module. Simon tried to grab the mug and only succeeded in soaking himself.

Fury surged through him. At the same time, frustration crystallised into hard purpose. Cursing, he shook the spilt liquid from his hand and reached into his inner coat pocket. He pulled out his master key and slipped it into a recessed lock on the side of his desk. A panel opened and he entered a code sequence into the pad revealed. Another larger control panel slid from the wall to his right.

Its monitor screen was an intricate pattern of digital information. Following its lead, he spent about an hour entering a sequence of commands few, if any, would have suspected him of knowing. All the while, his cold anger boiled away inside him, encoding itself onto his screen.

In a distant building, an explosion ripped through containment walls and shattered the emergency control system. Alarms began to ring, but it was too late to call for help. Again, Simon glanced out the window, down towards the forecourt, and saw safety and security personnel running about in a panic. His phone rang. He ignored it.

Determinedly, he began work on another sequence of commands, this one designed to cause a nuclear meltdown. The result would be catastrophic — complete destruction of the NGT reactor and a pall of radiation that would saturate most of the city, killing some and maiming many more. There would be explosions, yes. Huge, fiery ones that would rip through the central district and decimate the civic plaza. But Simon's main aim had been the creation of a nuclear poison that would not only annihilate the city but also render it irredeemable for several generations.

Explosions shuddered through the floor.

His work done, Simon returned to the huge windows and calmly watched rising smoke and fire. In his mind's eye, it was as though he could see the waves of radiation slashing outward from this point, destroying everything. He visualised the skin torn from Mayor Bernard's body, flesh and bone melting in the onslaught. He saw the other aldermen, the Town Clerk, the leader of the anti-nuclear community group — all in flames, their genetic structure twisting into hideous 1950s Hollywood parodies of men and women. He saw death. Destruction. The slow painful wastage of atomic poison.

Another explosion rocked the building, very close this time. The paper cup he'd upset earlier rolled off the table and plopped onto the floor.

A wave of destruction shattered the room around him.

President Nicoya awoke with a start, the images vanishing into various corners of the room in an instant. His skin tingled as though nearby fire had tried to burn it. He breathed out. What an extreme, yet oddly appropriate, visualisation of his current frustrations! It felt more like a memory than a dream.

"Mr President, I really must insist that you give me

an answer." The representative from the African States, a short, annoying woman with a voice so deep it made his guts rumble, leaned across the table at him, her eyes intensely dark. Like the rest of the thirty-odd people gathered here in the Security Chamber conference annex, she was always at him, nagging, digging, probing for weaknesses. Simon's shaking hands clenched his chair in frustration, unseen.

He didn't answer her, but, again, glanced up at the huge screen dominating the room. On it, swirling patterns marked the delicate traceries of the World Defence Network. Did they realise he controlled the functioning of that vast web of protection? Had they really considered the implications of continually jabbing at his nerves the way they did?

He was tired of it all. To get where he had, his life had become a continual seesawing between disappointment and determined struggle. Always onward and upward. Sure, he had set out to achieve power, but at what cost to his peace-of-mind? Simon had spent several hours last night talking to Professor Glynnis Jules from New Cambridge, whose work on the Quantum Network was central to its development.

"On a subnuclear level, there is wide-ranging, perhaps infinite connectability between states," she'd said. "That is the system's strength — but also its weakness."

"Weakness?" he'd replied, puzzled.

"Weakness." The Professor pursed her lips. "It's a small thing, but unravel a thread here on Earth and you may unravel another on the far side of the Universe. Theoretically anyway. Perhaps there are a million such threads..."

Scientific bullshit; he had no time for theoretical impediments. Doubt and hesitation were the real enemies. Nicoya flushed Jules' pessimism from his mind.

"Ms G'wanelitan," he said, "you will get an answer when I deem it appropriate to give one." He reached for his cognac and took a sip, letting the action dismiss her whingeing as irrelevant.

"You do not own my people, sir!" she spoke harshly, contemptuously. "We will not be patronised. We can disrupt your plans, and we will, unless you satisfy our concerns."

Others joined in, shrieking, complaining and banging at the gigantic oval conference table.

"You claim levels of safety that are patently deceptive," cried a thin, obnoxious man from the Islamic Sub-continent. "My government feels you must be removed from office."

Everything seemed to stop. Simon glanced at the coloured lines on the screen above, representing the revolutionary but unstable network of protective energy cradling the world in its grip. All he had to do was issue one set of innocuous-sounding orders and he could obliterate not only the Member States but also the entire planet. No one could stop him. Filaments of neo-molecular flux would sweep down through the atmosphere and disentangle the structural stability of entire continents. It would be the end. Apocalypse.

*A small thing really.*

He felt anger boil inside, so deep and so hot he was afraid he wouldn't be able to contain it.

*Not this time, Simon,* he whispered to himself. *Not this time.*

*Yet I must answer their insults,* he thought.

"Are you calling me a liar, Al-Shadan?" he hissed.

The Iraqi ambassador waved a sheaf of papers. "Either that, or a fool. If you doubt our resolve, check the indices for yourself." He threw the bound report across the table. It flapped through the air and slammed down in front of Simon, sliding, knocking over his cognac bubble. The expensive liquid in it splashed over Simon's suit.

For a long, indecisive moment he stared at the fallen glass.

*A small thing,* he thought. *That's all it takes.*

*Onward and upward.*

Somewhere far away, an angry man broke the nose of a drunken fool and the world ended in a flash of shattered glass.

# LO QUE NO ASUSTA

"So how have you been?" I asked, to fill the unpleasant silence.

"Been?" he repeated, staring thoughtfully into an unoccupied corner of the room.

Anthony Relcarne seemed worn out. The charismatic exuberance once so attractive in him lingered as nothing more than an uncertain light that had enlivened his eyes only once over dinner — when I mentioned our days together at university. The rest of the time, he remained dull-eyed and mouthed pleasantries that failed to address the real issue: why I'd received a sudden and unexpected invitation to his home.

"Has something happened?" I asked.

He looked into my eyes. "Something has indeed happened, Alex. Something always happens."

I frowned and he smiled at the silent rebuke. "Yes, I know, I'm being enigmatic." He laughed wistfully. "Twenty-five years, and nothing changes, eh?"

"Tell me what's happened," I insisted.

Instead of answering, he went to the window — the one overlooking the long, patient slope leading to outer Sydney's sprawling suburbs. "Come here!" he ordered in a tone so odd I immediately obeyed.

"What is it?" I squinted past the dim reflection of the

two of us caught in the glass.

"Nothing," he whispered. "Absolutely nothing."

He was right. I couldn't see anything — no trees silhouetted against the night sky, no lights from the thousands of homes and the vast pattern of streets that should have been visible from that window.

"It scares me," he added. "Scares me to the bone."

"It's just a fog."

"Fog?" he scorned. "Everything's disappearing, Alex. I knew it would. That's why I wanted you here at the end."

"What the hell are you talking about?" Impatient, I headed for the front door in order to get a clearer view of the panoramic outlook from his front balcony. But Relcarne moved quickly. His bony fingers grabbed my arm and pulled me back.

"Don't go out there!" he snapped.

I tore from his grip, but didn't continue toward the outside. "What's your problem, Tony?"

Adopting a lighter tone, he suggested we go to his study. "There's some sort of answer there," he said.

"Some sort?"

"But don't expect to feel satisfied by it."

I looked back.

"Don't worry," he assured me. "It's as you say — just fog."

But, as we walked along the hallway, Relcarne slightly ahead of me, I thought I heard him whisper something else — deep-throated, snarling sounds. "What's that?" I asked.

He turned, staring accusingly. "You haven't wondered why I'm here alone." In the dim light, his eye sockets were shadowy, as though the orbs had been removed.

"I wasn't sure—"

"She left," he interrupted. "One day last week, she went away. Sarah was her name."

"I'm sorry."

"No word of explanation...though God knows my constant, pathetic fearfulness would have been enough to drive her from me." He sighed. "She didn't deserve to be tormented. She was never part of it, Alex. Not like you, not like the others."

He wasn't making sense. "What others? Part of what?"

He smiled, not a pleasant smile, no warmth, no welcome — an expression of hopelessness, like everything else about him. "The study," he whispered.

I was worried now. Relcarne seemed barely stable. He'd never been what you would call 'normal', having had an enthusiastic mind that led him into esoteric areas of interest in pursuit of God knows what. As I understood it, the years following graduation had been remarkably successful for him, given his eccentric interests. He'd started some sort of online business, which, while no Microsoft, brought him a comfortable income. There was evidence of that in the house, which was well-situated and comfortably fitted out. But he hadn't been unstable. Not then.

His study was large and full of books. There were two sizeable screens as well, what appeared to be a mainframe computer and some other equipment I couldn't identify. The spaces in-between were crowded with strange abstract sculptures — ancient tribal constructs, suggestive of dark fertility and violence. He gestured for me to sit in a leather armchair and, filled with an irrational expectation, I obeyed.

"What sort of business were you in?" I asked.

"Knowledge storage." He glanced around, the gesture expressive of a distant regret. "And retrieval. All sorts of knowledge. You really have forgotten, haven't you?"

"Forgotten what?"

He strode toward me and slammed a photograph album onto my lap.

"Open it!"

I swallowed my annoyance and did as he asked. Inside were pictures of a group of people — young, with eager, inquiring faces. I was there, too.

"Martina Sanidas," Relcarne said, pointing. "Jonah Frenkel. Koichi Sudiawa. Jill Orwell—"

"I know them. I remember. I may be senile, Relcarne, but a few shreds of memory linger."

I'd run across Jill Orwell perhaps six months before, though I had no intention of telling Relcarne about the meeting. She'd been as frenetic as ever, keen to re-enact some of the sexual adventures we'd had over two decades earlier, during our days as postgraduate students. It was a puzzling but pleasant enough afternoon, though I hadn't heard from her since.

"Do you remember what we did the night we graduated?" Relcarne asked.

"We celebrated. Went to that nightclub — Black Nights or something, it was called. We drank, probably too much—"

He turned away, fetching an old leather-bound book

from his desk. Then, he was back, waving it at me.

"And this? Do you remember this?"

I didn't touch it, reluctant to make contact with the skin-like texture of the cover. But I knew it. "That's the book by...what's his name? The philosopher. Félix Moraleda. He died immediately after writing it."

"Perhaps. Do you remember the title?"

I studied the faded gold lettering. It wasn't readable, even had I been fluent in Spanish.

"*Lo Que No Asusta*," he read. "'That Which Scares Us'."

"Oh, yes. I...I can recall something—"

"Recall something?" He laughed bitterly. "The book contains Moraleda's speculations on the nature of success...his passion to control the essence of fear in the human soul, to harness its strength by seeing it clearly and placing it where we can feed off it rather than letting it feed off us. '*La trampa del miedo*' he called it — the 'fear-trap': a subset of reality, at angles to normal mental processes, where the terrors could be held prisoner. And re-formed into strengths rather than weaknesses."

"Yes, I know. But, so what? What's it to do with me?"

"You were obsessed with the book, Alex." He held it up. "This volume was yours."

"Mine?"

"Yes. You've forgotten, haven't you? I retrieved it from the ruins of Dale Hall. Did you know that the place was gutted a few years back? They've demolished it totally now. No one has been able to explain the cause of the accident."

"I don't understand. Why are you saying this? It's

not even true."

"Of course it's true, and you know it."

"Surely, the book...the obsession...was yours."

His voice was hard. "It was you. I was a mere accessory, before the fact admittedly. And that night, you enticed us back to Dale Hall and the labs. A sort of pact, you said. To see us into the future. To energise us. It was like a lark to us, a joke. But, not to you, I realise now."

I felt too numb to protest. This was both new to me, and ancient knowledge, like faded scribbling on the inside of my mind, slowly revealed as dust settled into its grooves.

Something growled through the air around us, shaking the edges of the room, breathing into its corners. Relcarne glanced up like a startled cat. "God, no!" he said.

"What is it?" I jumped to my feet.

His arms jerked as though his muscles had lost control of the bones they adhered to. The book fell to the floor with a thud. I grabbed him.

"Settle down, for God's sake. You're hysterical."

"It's turning away from me, Alex." His eyes burned with a cold fear.

I held him firmly, to assure him of my support. My old friend was obviously crazy. Yet I felt a compulsion to know everything he had to tell me.

"Finish what you were saying, Tony. I don't understand where you're going with this."

He began to weep. As tears leaked from his eyes, he wrenched himself from me, ashamed. "I'm so scared," he whispered, his back to me.

"Of what?"

"Of the things we put in the fear-trap," he said.

With that, he bent to retrieve the book and lay it gently on the desk.

I got the story from him then — everything that was aching in his mind. He said we'd followed the 'entrapment' procedure as outlined by Félix Moraleda in his book — a procedure the philosopher believed impractical in his own time. Written words were an imperfect medium, he said, too inherently human. To be effective, the endeavour required a mode of recording that would enable words to fully integrate with the subterranean currents of reality...to integrate with them and to reach through them to a new level of interconnection. It needed a new science.

Digital transcription, Relcarne suggested.

We set up a program to send our words into the depths of the cosmos — as primitive as computer science was then. We fed our fears into the paradigm, laughing and giggling darkly — afraid to be serious about them, though they represented the most serious and deeply felt levels of our being. We recorded the things that scared us, recorded them as though engaging in some arcane ritual.

"The medium had still been imperfect then," Relcarne explained. "But it was enough, I believe, to activate a fugue state — some sort of conceptual amnesia — so the knowledge was isolated. Something...I don't know what...knew, that in forgetfulness lay its best chance for survival. It wasn't until I sold my business, and was doing an inventory of old technology, that I found the files containing what we'd written."

"You re-ran the program? Using the new coding and retrieval systems?"

He nodded. "And then it began."

Wind howled outside the room, battering the walls around us. Impossible! The study was in the centre of the house, bound on all sides by more rooms.

Relcarne leaned on his desk for a moment, then reached over to his keyboard and pressed a key. One of the large computer screens came alive. Words formed on it: the names of all of us, all the friends who had graduated together and then engaged in a mock ritual of fear-binding. Jonah Frenkel was first, I was last.

Relcarne looked at me, but I didn't comment.

He moved the cursor to the first name and clicked on it. A new window opened up, containing a dossier on Frenkel: photo, biographical details, stated fears...current history.

Relcarne said, "Back then, Frenkel wrote that his greatest fear was to die in pain. Slowly."

*Pain like hot needles in the flesh, tearing at his bones. Staring down through a dark haze at cracks in the concrete path a metre below, as they filled with his blood. Red tears falling.*

I gasped as the wave of emotion swept over me and then withdrew. What was it? A memory flash? Images from a dream? I glanced at Relcarne, but he hadn't noticed.

"Frenkel was found in a narrow space at the rear of the units where he lived. Police believe he slipped from an upper pathway. He'd been skewered through the gut by a protruding pipe, and hung suspended on it, feeling the unrelenting pressure of gravity on his wound for perhaps two days before he bled to death."

Residue from the images tasted bitter and foul. Relcarne hit the next name.

Jill. I remembered what was to come, sealed within a nightmare. It had lain in my memory, unrecognised, yet when it came, it was almost new.

*She can feel her organs seething with the disease, then dwindling, failing. She has existed, but that is soon to end. Twilight hangs like torn gauze across her windows. A child's voice shrieks.*

"Jill Orwell. What scared her then was AIDS. She was diagnosed as HIV positive a while ago."

I breathed in. "When?"

"Oh, about this time last year."

I shut my eyes for a moment. She'd known. When she came to see me, she'd known!

"Is she —?"

"Dead? Yes. But not of AIDS. She committed suicide about six months ago."

He clicked on another name. I braced myself.

"Mark Scorcini. Mark was a gentle soul. Remember his infuriating diffidence? His greatest fear, he said, was snakes. Clichéd and patently trivial compared to...some." He chuckled.

*Shadows squirm around his feet. He leaps away, crying out for the help he knows isn't there. But the serpents follow, having attached themselves to his arms. No! Please! Get them off!*

"And was he killed by a snake?"

Relcarne shook his head. "A rather large python parked itself out the front of his house one day, no doubt looking for a sunny spot to doze in. He nearly tripped over it. It didn't stay there long, but Mark wouldn't come out. By the time neighbours realised something was up, he was completely mad. He claimed his house was cursed and that his fingers had been changed into snakes. He'd cut them all off and burnt them in the oven."

"You're kidding?"

*Click.* Martina Sanidas. I pressed my hand against the side of my head as though that could ward off the dream-memory I knew would —

*When she glances in the mirror, a stranger stares back at her. She reaches out to touch the glass and feels the cold barrier standing between herself and the monster that has possessed her.*

"Martina was a beautiful woman, wasn't she? A stunner. And utterly vain about it. Her body attracted men like flies to honey, and she revelled in the attention. She worked for it, though — the gym, rigorous diets. Her greatest fear? Not unexpectedly it related to this. She wrote: 'I'm scared my body won't be mine one day. That I'll be trapped in flesh I don't recognise as my own.'"

"And what happened? She got fat?"

"She came down with motor neuron disease. Now she's in a chair permanently. The only muscles she can move at all are on one side of her lip and above the left eyebrow. She dribbles and shits involuntarily. Looking into her eyes is like looking into hell. I know. I went and looked."

I breathed out, having realised that I'd been holding my breath for God knows how long. "I get the picture,

Relcarne, for Christ's sake. They're all the same. But I have to tell you, I've dreamed these things. I already know them."

He nodded, clicking quickly to the file for Koichi Sudiawa.

*Darkness closes around him like intangible hands, strangling, closing him off from the world. The silence of it is unbearable. He thrashes out at the black walls but feels nothing.*

Koichi had said he feared being buried alive. According to Relcarne, he lost all sensory awareness in an industrial accident that destroyed his nerves. Now he lay in a private sanatorium, twitching and raging compulsively; blind, deaf...and utterly alone.

"What about you, Tony?" I asked. "What did you say you feared?"

He lowered his head, pushing at his temples with bony fingers.

"What scared me then?" He laughed bitterly. "The same thing that scares me now." He raised his eyes and I could see how haunted they were. "Sarah and I had a child, did you know that? A beautiful girl. She was ten when she—"

*Tyres screech. Wrenching impact so harsh it seems to shatter reality itself. Her face fills with terror, the pain of sudden awareness. Someone screams.*

"A car crash?" I asked.

He nodded. "My parents were taking her home with them, while Sarah and I...God, I loved them all, Alex — my parents, my child. Coralie hung on for five days, the side of her head shattered. I watched her fade."

"And now Sarah's gone."

He turned away again. "Lost."

"I'm sorry, Tony."

"It was inevitable. None of them belonged to me. I couldn't save them."

I didn't know what to feel. Unreality, like a drug, was dragging me away, keeping me distant. I wanted to say something useful, something to dispel the possibility all this was more than just coincidence and the normal cruelty of the world...

"What do you imagine I can do about this?" I said.

His face was hard as it turned. "You were always strong, Alex. 'Nothing scares me,' you'd say. It was bravado, I guess. Bravado and a sort of theatrical arrogance. I know you well enough to see through the layers of pretence you've built around your precious self-image. It's about control. You wanted to be in control—"

"I control nothing. I'm a freelance journalist. I look on. Stuff happens and I report what I see. I affect nothing."

He grimaced crookedly. "But aren't you scared that one day you might get what you want?"

I might have answered if I could have dredged up some convincing lie, but the possibility passed in an instant. Again the room shook, as though a huge beast had battered in frustration on the external walls. Relcarne's eyes focused behind me and I saw them fill with terror.

I spun around. The walls were dissolving, sucked away into a grey fog.

"Relcarne!" I yelled. "What the hell is this?"

He was cowering against his desk, staring, his hand

pressed back on Moraleda's book. His lips moved, but whatever he was saying was too faint for me to hear. I leaned closer.

"We released something..." Then the words were gone. I blinked, and, in that moment, Relcarne seemed to fall away from me. As I straightened up, I realised he was gone completely, transformed into a dull shadow across the surface of the desk. This wasn't possible. All that nonsense he'd been sprouting was nothing more than the delusion of a sick mind. The ritual we'd performed back then hadn't been mine, I was sure. It had all been his idea. His passion.

Not that it mattered. It was not real.

Yet everything was coming apart.

Someone laughed. It echoed from deep within the fog, low and resonant. The laughter increased my resolve — now, it was up to me. I had to face whatever it was we'd created. I must take control. Whatever was happening, it couldn't be allowed to continue.

I leapt into the drifting dark. Ahead, I could hear something moving, its feet pounding and echoing as though we were in a long hallway. The sound was in retreat. I ran after it, indifferent to the obscurity, careless of the threat. I had to reach the thing we'd spawned...and stop it.

Half-seen movement distracted me. My peripheral vision was alive with it. When I glanced at it directly, it disappeared. When I looked away, it was there again, looming at me, threatening. Yet it swept past into the gloom ahead, dragging me after it.

The distant presence absorbed it all.

"Stop!" I yelled impulsively. "Listen to me, please!"

The retreating footsteps fell silent. I stopped, too. How far away had it been? I took a few tentative steps. Glanced around.

For a moment, nothing happened. For no reason I could articulate, I'd assumed the thing was sentient. Perhaps it was merely reactive...

Then: "What do you want to say to me?" came a voice from somewhere nearby. I couldn't put a name to it, but it was familiar. Another lost memory?

"I want you to stop this."

"What makes you think I can? Is it up to me?"

"It must be. Show yourself."

Fog thickened and swirled, forming indefinite shapes.

"What is happening is simply happening. Fear is not a choice. It is a necessity."

"A necessity?"

Now the fog was dissipating. I squinted ahead, hoping to see the speaker before he thought to move away.

"I can't stop this," he said, "any more than I can stop time. That which scares us drives us on."

I could see him. Stocky. Arrogant. The darkened face became less formless. Still I kept my fear at bay.

"Are you Félix Moraleda?" I asked, desperately. "Is that it? Have we brought you back from the dead?"

He laughed.

My sight had cleared now. I could recognise his features. At last, terror slammed against my heart.

"Was it you all along?" I managed.

I stared at myself across Relcarne's gravel driveway. Beyond lay a glistening suburban lightshow — the city, no longer fog-bound but full of people waiting to be terrorised.

The figure grinned, staring back toward Relcarne's house. Staring at...

*...me*

*I watch. The figure begins to drift apart, like an illusion in fog.*

*"I am that which scares you," I whisper to the empty night.*

# ROTTEN TIMES

## The evening of the third of January

The knife she was using to slice potatoes, slimy with juice, slipped from Louise Delovski's fingers and fell to the bench top. It tumbled, skidded off the edge. The Staysharp blade dug into her kitchen's floor covering, gouging out a divot of red vinyl. The blade hadn't touched her hand. Hadn't even come near it. But, as she stared at the deep cut the knife had made in the floor, Louise felt her palm aching. The fleshy pad at the base of her thumb was lacerated, bleeding a red stream that snaked down her wrist.

Louise was sure the blade hadn't touched her. She blinked, as her vision crumbled. She felt light-headed. Her kitchen appeared to be breaking apart, fracturing into a thousand shattered pieces.

Her heart thumped violently. Heart attack? she wondered in a rising panic. Oh God! I don't want to die. I'm too young. She lowered herself to the floor, rubbing at the cut.

And stopped. Glanced around, fear driving into her gut like ice pellets.

Paint along the side of the bench was cracked and peeling. Scabs of dry-rot flaked off as she watched. That didn't make sense — she'd only painted it, all of it, a little over two months ago. What she was seeing now was the decay of old age.

It was on the floor, too. There, at the edges where she hadn't noticed it before, the vinyl squares were warping, cracking away. Underneath, she could see what looked like the accumulated grease of years of spilled food. Yet, the squares had been laid a week or so after the paint job. Six weeks ago!

She tried to stand, but her legs wouldn't let her. Louise glanced again at her hand — the bleeding one. Her skin was dry and peeling. There was a nasty, weeping growth across her wrist, like a sore that had been festering for days. And her leg, too. No wonder she hadn't been able to stand. She seemed to have hurt her ankle. It looked bruised and swollen, and the foot was at a strange angle, as though its bones had warped.

She began to cry, remembering the old man, the farm, her terror — and any denial she might have made became an empty hope.

**Three Days Before**

"Jerk!"

Eddie Marks grinned as he slammed the side door of his car, providing a dramatic end to the woman's cry. She took refuge behind the protective insulation of the chassis. That was fine with him; she'd made it quite clear what he could do with himself, and *he* certainly wasn't the one who needed a lift back to town.

He turned on the ignition and the engine roared like a frustrated animal. "You getting in?" he yelled, giving her a chance to change her mind. His mother didn't raise her boy to be unforgiving.

"I'll walk!" Venomous. Eddie frowned. He couldn't figure this one out at all. Maybe she was frigid. It wasn't the rejection; it was the extreme reaction to what was, after all, a pretty ordinary request. He'd driven her out here and she'd come willingly enough. He'd parked the car, held her hand, stroked her thigh, felt her pulse starting to race. Then he'd asked if she'd rather go back to his place to do it. She'd said she didn't know that she intended to 'do it' anywhere, not when they'd only just met. He'd said, "Come on, there's no use wasting time, is there? Not getting any younger, you know."

That was when she'd thrown a wobbly, slapped at him, and scrambled out of the car, screaming as though he'd tried to poleaxe her.

Fuck her.

"Walk then!" he snarled, and drove off, deliberately skidding the back wheels and filling the night with dirt. As he went, he glanced into the rear-view mirror. The lonely figure of the woman was disintegrating into darkness and dust.

It wasn't until the rear lights were snuffed out by distance that Louise Delovski suddenly calmed down. She wondered what the hell she'd done.

"Wait on!" she yelled; but she knew he'd never hear her now. He was too far gone. She ground the toe of her right shoe into the dirt.

Around her, the world was dark. There was a sickly moon up there in the sky somewhere, lost in the clouds, but its reflected glow wasn't much help. The air was chilled — weird weather for that time of year, mid-summer, New Year's eve and all that — and it got to her easily; she was wearing a flimsy, shoulder-baring top and a light-weight skirt, that's all. Trance-dance clubs were hot places — they didn't encourage sensible dress. She'd brought a coat, more as an accessory than because she thought she might need it, but had left it in the bastard's car...what was his name? Oh, yes, Eddie.

"Eddie Murphy," he'd said when she asked him at the bar.

"Eddie Murphy is a negro," she'd commented wryly.

"Daylight saving made me fade," he'd replied. Louise had thought the remark funny at the time. Now it seemed juvenile and sinister.

Well, he was a jerk-off, that Eddie, whatever his real name was. What did he have to go and say that for, calling her old? She wasn't that old. It was downright rude, the kind of insensitivity that really pissed her off.

She'd sort of liked him, too. In a desperate sort of way.

Louise began walking along the gravel. On the way there, she'd noticed what looked like a farmhouse, silhouetted on a hilltop off the road. Maybe she could get a lift, or, at least, the farm people might have a phone. Real isolated, it was. Eddie and she hadn't driven that far out of town, but there were hardly any houses. None at all when you came down to it. Just the farmhouse. Where'd that dirt bag been taking her? And how dare he leave her out here, alone. Anything could happen to her out here.

She glanced over her shoulder. Darkness became a

huge, shapeless creature, so she looked straight ahead and walked faster.

She found the turn-off easily enough: dirt furrows, a dried-up wooden gate, rusty wire, an old sign she couldn't read in the dark. There was a chain on the gate with a lock. Both were encrusted with dark flakes of rust. Louise rattled the gate, but it wouldn't give. In the end, she climbed over and began a long, anxious walk up the track toward the distant farmhouse. Everything was overgrown, even the track, which probably would have been lost under the weeds long ago, if the ground hadn't been so compacted and unyielding.

Doesn't look good, she thought. Nothing's been going on here for years.

The 'farmhouse' on the hill turned out to be a derelict shed — that was all. There was machinery in it so old that it had completely fallen to pieces. Looked like a pile of junk. Louise peered in through a rotting hole in the shed door, but it smelt so bad, she didn't attempt to get in. Even the cold would be better than whatever was making that stink.

She turned away, cursing her luck, when she saw what had to be the actual farmhouse, huddled like a stain on the barren pasture land below her. The road she'd followed apparently went over the hill and down again to the farm. Who'd put a farm in a hollow like that? Wind plucked at her skin and she shivered. She didn't care so long as she could get a lift back to town.

Long before she reached the house, she could see it was a wreck, too: old and neglected, blackened by years of fallout from windstorms, boards split with age, windows cracked and broken. Tools and farm implements were scattered here and there. She bent to touch a hoe and it was lumpy with rust. The yard in front was overgrown and pot-holed. Now that she was closer, she could see the carcass of an ancient pickup truck. The tyres were deflated, its chassis worn and pitted, and it looked as though the far-side door hung open on a broken hinge.

Louise climbed the steps leading to a veranda. The boards creaked and gave uneasily. Dirt shifted under her shoes as she went toward the front door. She had to be careful to avoid holes, and her nose picked up the scent of decay and neglect: dampness leaking from gaps in the floor, rot in the boards, dust, the dry tang of age. No way was she going to get a lift here.

Nevertheless, she knocked on the door. A wind was rising and it was bitterly cold; she didn't want to wander in the open all night. If no one was living here, at least the place could provide her with shelter. She knocked harder. The sound reverberated hollowly. No dogs barked, no animals stirred, she heard no indication of living inhabitants at all. Another louder knock and she began calling — but that, too, brought no response. A gust of wind whipped coldness and dirt around her thighs. Okay then — she'd hang out inside the place for the night, safe from the chill. Then, in the morning, she'd walk someplace more civilised and get a ride into town.

She turned the handle and pushed. The hinges squealed. Darkness oozed out around her, thick with staleness. She hesitated, afraid she might catch something because the air tasted so diseased.

Then something moved in the shadows.

Even the fact he couldn't remember her name annoyed him.

Eddie found the parking spot he'd vacated near the club hadn't been taken, and slid his car into the space, angry and tense. So far, the night was a fizzer. *Her* fault, no question. She'd mucked him around and deserved whatever happened to her.

*Louise*, he recalled suddenly.

He'd intended to go back into the dance area and find someone more amenable — after all, this was the fuckin' end of the millennium and he was young and horny. For the moment, he just sat, staring at the street and the neon-smeared night, remembering her name. The whole thing felt wrong. She probably had friends who wanted to know where the hell she was. That was okay, so long as nothing happened to her. But it was quite a way to the spot he'd taken her. What if some sicko pervert came across her walking about in the dark and carved her up? He, Eddie, would be first in line to take the rap, that's what. Last seen with Eddie the Stud, who took her off into the night with his lustful plans neon-flashing all over his face. What a set-up!

There were plenty of weirdos around these days — evidence of the End of the World, Eddie's mum reckoned. "A woman can't stick her head out the door without some loony wantin' to do it to her," she used to say. "There's no order any more. This was prophesied, Eddie." Exaggerated perhaps. At least, he hoped it was — certainly no one in their right mind would want to "do it" to his mum — but the possibility was there.

Anyway, End of the World or not, Eddie didn't want to become the scapegoat for random vendettas launched against Twentieth Century corruption. He glanced at his watch. Just over half an hour and it'd be Twenty-first Century corruption. Even worse.

He cursed, slamming his fist on the dashboard. He was gonna miss all the action, wasn't he? The fireworks. All those women wanting to welcome in the End of the World in proper style. Hand throbbing, Eddie started up his car and backed out of the parking space, watching his headlights flaring on the startled shop window in front of him. There was a screech of brakes. Another car skidded into view in his side mirror. It scraped along his bumper-bar as he jammed a tardy foot on the pedal.

The owner of the other car — a new sports sedan of some kind (not a BMW or something, please!) — was leaping toward him, even before his engine had died.

Louise nearly fell over with shock. She staggered back a few steps to compensate, but found herself unable to run. A man, or parts of a man anyway, appeared in the lighter darkness fractured across the doorway. Louise could see legs and an arm. They looked old and crippled.

"What do you want?" a voice said. During the first instant she heard the words, she was unable to tell whether it was the figure talking or just the sound made by her feet as they scraped on grit.

"I'm, um, lost," she said. "Can I use your phone?"

Wheezing breath, then: "Don't have one."

"I need a lift back to town."

"Truck don't work — like every bloody thing around here."

Louise tried to think. She felt so awkward, standing there on a derelict porch, talking to half a man. She wished she could see his face, but the shadow covering it was too thick. She shivered as wind clawed up her legs and hugged her shoulders.

"You cold?" the voice said.

"Yes."

"Not wearing much, are you?" it said, but in a fatherly manner, without any lascivious overtones — not that Louise could detect anyway. "And you're very young."

Louise smiled. "Am I?"

"Sure. Curse ain't got to you yet."

That puzzled her. She wondered if this old man were perhaps a bit senile. "Curse?"

"You want to come in?" The figure stepped back, disappearing into darkness. "Well, do you?"

"I don't know."

"Too dark for you in here, eh? I like the dark. Stops me from seein' too much. I'll put a light on — have to be an oil lamp. Electricity's out. Wiring's shot." Louise heard him move deeper into the room. "I'd better warn you though, I'm not a pretty sight. Bit of a wreck. Like the bloody house."

Louise felt sad for him. The poor lonely bastard, living here in the dark, unable to look after himself properly, feeling ugly and rejected. Age was a difficult enough thing to have to cope with. "I don't mind.

Really."

"You will, believe me. You will," he said.

Glass and metal clattered together as he fumbled with the oil lamp. He grunted, lit a match. A dim flicker spluttered into life, sending blurred shadows jerking about the room. Louise moved across the threshold, determined to show no revulsion, no matter what he looked like. But she couldn't help it. When he turned to her, she saw how decayed he was and she gasped. The smell only made it worse.

"Told you," he said, grinning over gums with no teeth in a face crumpled like an old newspaper. His skin was thin and desiccated, blotched by stains and cancerous sores. He was so cracked and wrinkled, Louise could hardly make out his features. "It's the Curse." The old man gestured with his only functional hand. His other arm had shrivelled to half its original size and hung limply, as though it had broken down long ago and had never been seen to. Both legs were twisted.

"It's terrible," Louise said. "I'm really sorry. It's not catching, is it?"

He chuckled. The sound was almost jovial — quite incongruous, coming from a source so devastated. "I told you, it's the Curse. Are curses catching?"

"Curse? You mean, like a family curse?"

He laughed. "Yeah. The human family's."

It took Eddie a good half hour to get away from the driver of the sports car — which turned out to be some overly shiny heap of crap. Nevertheless, the bloke was irate and wanted to splatter Eddie's nose right over his face — except, of course, Eddie was bigger than he was. So he satisfied himself with calling Eddie everything under the sun.

"It's a new car!" he yelled. "Now 'cause of some bloody idiot who can't watch where the fuck he's going, the bloody thing's on the scrap heap—"

Eddie barely listened; he was conscious of time running out for Louise. Now he felt sure she was in trouble.

He hitched himself up in a threatening manner. "Look, it's only a scratch for Christ's sake. You're going on like I totalled the thing. Here—" He slapped a piece of lolly paper he'd been scribbling his particulars on into the bloke's hand. "Now get lost before I have a go at mussing up your whingeing face."

The bloke scooted off. His pretentious shit-heap roared down the road.

A moment later, Eddie's car was speeding in the opposite direction.

"Have a guess how old I am?" the man said. He'd collapsed into a wrecked one-seater lounge and was staring intently at Louise.

It was a stupid and embarrassing question. "I wouldn't like to—"

"Sit down." He pointed an arthritic finger at a chair across the room from him. "Keep your distance if you're worried."

Louise felt unable to refuse. Anyway, where could she go?

"You won't insult me," the man went on. "Lost my last shred of dignity ages ago. What's the point of it?"

"I don't—"

"Bet you think I'm seventy or eighty or something, eh?" He looked a hundred and fifty, at least. "Am I right? You plug for eighty? Well, forget it! Thirty-five. How's that grab you?"

Louise grimaced. "It's impossible."

"Thirty-five. Maybe thirty-four. I told you, this ain't old age."

It was obvious he was crazy. Louise knew it then for sure. Senility had withered his brain, trapped his mind in a different time and denied him age as an explanation for his decay. She wouldn't argue with him. She'd just change the subject. "Do you live alone?"

"Who else'd live here? This is me. This is what I am. I hate it, I loathe it. But it's me."

"Couldn't you move?"

"I'm part of it. How can I leave? A month ago, this place was all painted up nice, you believe that? Real nice. The truck worked. The floorboards weren't near so rotten. The paddock out there was greener."

For the first time, Louise glanced around the room. It was shadowy and obscure and would've been that way even if everything were normal — the oil lamp wasn't very effective. But this place wasn't normal. What was probably carpet appeared to be bunched up in the corners, covered in mould. The wooden walls were flaky and dark with rot. Horrible cancerous holes gaped in the floor. What furniture there was seemed on the verge of breaking down into little piles of dust.

"I tried to look after the place," the old man said, following her gaze. "Honest, I did. Tried to keep it whole and clean. Now...well, what's the point? It's got me, no sweat. I'd rather it was over, if I knew what lay at the end of it all. Meantime, I'm trapped."

Louise didn't understand what he was saying. It sounded like ravings, all of it. She'd stopped trying to make sense of it once she realised he was mad. But it made her feel uneasy. Even sick. "Please, is there any way I can get back to town? Any way of contacting...anyone?"

"Only by walking."

Wind howled outside, causing nails to groan in the rotting wood of the house. The man gasped and choked. Pain crushed up his face even more than it normally was. "I hate windy nights," he said. "Too painful. Wind's a destroyer. So's sun. But wind...it can tear you apart."

"Maybe I'd better walk."

"In the mornin', honey. You'll die of exposure, dressed like that. Reckon it might rain."

He was right. Louise could feel the cold on her legs and hugged her arms across her breasts to hold in the heat.

"I'll tell you somethin', if you like," the man said, dropping his head against the back of his seat. Louise thought the mould on it was spreading. She frowned. "I'll tell you about the Curse."

"I don't—"

"Sure you do. It obsesses you, I know. I can tell. You worry a hell of a lot about getting old." He looked at her, his eyes dull and yellow. Louise's heart was pounding. It seemed to shake her whole body, preventing her from replying. "Sure you do. Obsesses you. It's in your eyes, in your words, lying like old makeup in the wrinkles around your mouth. And you're quite right to worry, too. There's decay everywhere. Even as we speak, it's festerin' away in your heart. 'Cause humans are part of the world and the world's rotten."

"Why are you saying this?"

"The devil owns us, and his mark's decay of flesh, decay of spirit."

"It's awful," Louise whispered.

"We've got minds, see? We drag the world around with us, as part of us. So we've got the decay inside. Our minds reach out for somethin', but there's only decay. Maybe that's the Fall, eh? Where our minds took over the place, kicked out the angel of the Lord, started the rot—"

"Stop it!" Louise wanted to run away from this horror. But her legs were frozen with the cold; she couldn't make them obey her, couldn't exert enough will-power to overcome their inertia.

"Stop the decay?" The man laughed and it sounded like wood rotting, stone crumbling. "I can't stop it. I'm its victim — and its servant. Look around. This place is me. As it rots, so do I. Can't you see that?"

She could, but it made no sense. It was a perception that skidded through her mind and failed to find a hold there.

The man became wistful. "Don't know when it began. Decades ago. Yesterday. Time's rotten too. I can feel it. My father brought me here twenty odd years ago — he was a broken man then, marriage, home, career — all destroyed. And he didn't know why. The Curse was on him. I can see its marks in every memory I have. He brought me to this place and he said, 'It's all yours, boy, all of it. Keep it up if you can.' Then he kissed me, passed on what he had—" He laughed hollowly. "Died a month ago — or a century. I tried to maintain the place, to keep *my* place goin'. Painted and mowed and fertilised and greased. Worked my fingers to the bloody bone, knowing how important it was, knowing that unless I did, unless I stopped the rot in the world around me, I was lost. I tried, I tried bloody hard. But I couldn't do it. Machinery breaks down, crops fail, wood becomes brittle in the sun and the wind strips it away. Once the rot sets in, there's nothing you can do about it. These are rotten times."

"But you said a month—" Louise was gripped by his words, despite herself. "You said it was okay then. How can it get like this in a month? This is long-term decay. You're so old—"

He laughed scratchily. "I prayed," he said. "I prayed to God. Stop it, I asked Him, stop this unending decline. I don't want to rot, I said, don't want to rot away. He wouldn't listen. But, the devil now...He's more amenable. Near on a month ago, I found something beneath the foundations of this place, something old and terrible." His legs seemed to crack and strain as he pulled himself up on to his feet.

"What was it?"

"It was under the house. I knew it would be. Knew there had to be some reason why my father hadn't been able to make this place work — why everything just rots away."

"What did you find?"

"I dug in the foundations. Dug with my fingers till they were raw. Dug and dug. And there was this thing—"

"What was it?" Louise repeated, despite the fact her mind was shrinking from what he might say, shrinking from it with terror like a cancer in her chest.

"The Beast," he whispered, turning and indicating something sitting on the mantelpiece over the cold, open fire-place. Louise squinted through flickering shadows.

It looked like a skull, though it was dark and pitted and far too big to be human. Thin humanoid jaw line. Teeth that seemed to grin at her. Large cheekbones. Empty eye-sockets that seemed, nevertheless, to be filled with a malevolence she couldn't see, only feel in the rancid air.

But worse was the pair of chipped, cracking horns that sprouted from its crown.

"Got to be a fake," Louise said weakly.

"Is all this fake?" The man raised his arthritic arm in a bent, awkward gesture. "When I touched that thing, time came unravelled. This is the End of the World. It starts now."

Again, Louise tried to run. She made it to her feet but only managed to stumble perhaps half a metre. Her heart was racing. "Why are you telling me this?" she screamed.

The old man laughed. "It's time," he said. "Must be near midnight, don't you reckon? Midnight of the world."

He came toward her, a scarecrow.

"What are you doing?" she said, afraid.

"Right now," he hissed, wheezing, "you're nowhere down that track. Nowhere. You worry about gettin' old, but you've barely started. I'll teach you about decay — the inexorable work of the Beast."

He was a psycho, no question. Louise struggled to get away, but her will was not enough. As he neared her, she could taste the rottenness in the air, and it paralysed her.

"Decayed in body, decayed in spirit," he said. "I'll be gone soon, this old place can't last much longer. Before I go, I'd like to feel health and wholeness again, even if it's someone else's. Surround myself with sweetness. Your flesh is like an elixir. I'll drink it in, become undecayed for a time. That would be so nice—"

Louise screamed as his withered hand touched her.

She wasn't where he'd left her of course, but Eddie couldn't find Louise along the road either. Where could she have gone? It was possible that someone had picked her up, yeah, possible; but not many people used this road. It was a dead end that finished up at the council dump. No one went there this time of night. It was closed.

Just perverts.

In the distance, beyond the hills, he saw the New Year's fireworks searing the clouds. These were the last moments of the old millennium. Would the new one be different?

He drove slowly back toward town, looking for signs of her passing. Night was a congealing thickness covering the world outside his car like black fog.

The silhouette of a building struck on his awareness too forcefully, given how obscured it was. It was barely visible and his eyes should have skimmed over it. When they didn't, he knew he had to go there. Louise might have seen it, too.

The old gate was padlocked. Eddie got out of his car and checked, shaking the rusty wire in the light-flood of his high-beams. Then he heard a scream. It was distant but shrill, full of terror, and came from beyond the rise like the call of a dying crow.

"Shit!" Eddie whispered and pulled harder on the lock. The scream came again. He twisted viciously and a rusty bar came loose, freeing the gate. Triumphant, he pushed it open, jumped back into his car and accelerated up the track.

The mere touch of the man's rancid skin released Louise from her paralysis. She screamed, giving voice to the fear churning inside her. The man clutched at her more tightly. She kicked out at him, sure she would be too robust for him to withstand, but he was hard and sinewy under her foot and merely stumbled slightly.

"Told you, honey, I'm no geriatric." His breath reeked of mould.

He pressed toward her. Louise pulled herself sideways, trying to escape. "Stay away from me!"

He grabbed at her breast, so that she lost her already tenuous balance, and fell against the chair she'd been sitting on. This time, her weight made it break apart. The legs, rotten and dry, crumbled and collapsed, and Louise dropped awkwardly to the floor amidst the wreckage. She screamed again as he tumbled toward her.

He was harder to deal with than she'd thought. He had a dried-out strength, like compacted earth, despite his obvious fragility. She struck at him with all the force she could muster, her fist connecting with his shoulder. When it crumbled inwards, as though the bones inside the shirt and flaking skin had broken under the blow, determination almost fled from her. Only his stink kept her conscious. His face thrust at her, withered lips pressing to her cheek, finding her mouth as she struggled. Hands like bony pliers squeezed her arms; even his decayed one seemed to find the strength to act against her. She choked, feeling bile rise in her throat, as his spittle mingled with her own.

Eddie's car left the ground as he cleared the top of the rise, and, from that moment, he lost control. The car slewed and bucked as its tyres met the track again. Eddie felt the jarring impact right through to his skull. He fought with the wheel to right the car, but it was a close thing. The heavy vehicle slid at an angle, his mag tyres sending dust up in clouds. Eddie saw the farmhouse — a flickering light was in one window, giving a momentary, vague impression of struggling figures — rushing toward him.

He swore.

The old man clung to her like sticky sap and as difficult to remove. Every time she hit him, or pushed at him, it seemed bits of him shattered — yet he was still there, clinging.

Then he released one arm. She thrashed out, beating at him, pushing, biting. She felt his freed hand groping between her legs. She screamed.

Whether it was her cry, or her knee finding his groin, or something else entirely, she didn't know; but, at that moment, his face twitched with pain and he glanced up. Louise fought harder.

Eddie lost control completely as the house loomed in his headlights. Braking was useless. As he spun the wheel to avoid a piece of rusty machinery, the front tyres hit a pot-hole, tossing the car sideways. Light streamed over the decayed building. Yelling, Eddie rammed his foot hard on the brake pedal. He twisted the steering in an attempt to straighten up. But crumbling earth and his speed defeated him. His car ploughed into the porch of the farmhouse, raising dust and wood splinters. Impact shuddered through his limbs.

"My car!" Eddie groaned.

Chaos settled around him and the whisper of falling dirt took over.

Somewhere tyres crunched dirt, brakes squealed and a deep-throated crash shook the house. Light fractured around the two struggling figures. "My house!" the man shrieked, falling away from Louise at last. She pushed hard, freeing her legs and arms from him, turning to defend herself even as she did. The man retreated from her blind punches.

Desperate, Louise crawled across the dirty, rotting floor, expecting his fingers to tighten around her ankle. But it didn't happen. When she felt safer, she looked back. The old man was banging his head against the floor, whimpering. "What're you doing?" she moaned. He made a gargling noise, a plea. Shaken, Louise moved closer — and felt sickness rise through her chest. The side of his head had caved in; his crumpled face was buckled, cracked, skin ripping, yellow bone crushed inward. Anaemic blood dribbled onto Louise's feet. As she watched, pieces of him broke away as though he were falling apart. For a moment, she saw a hole in the side of his head that seemed to go right through to his brain cavity. Light caught on something greasily wet. Then one of his arms came away.

She screamed as a large piece of powdery plaster crashed to the floor, drawing her attention from the old man. It was then she saw what was happening to the house. Spreading outwards from the area at the front where the porch was — where the impact had come from — the walls and floor were crumbling, falling away, giving up the ghost.

It was all coming down around her.

Immediately, Eddie remembered why he'd been speeding. The girl. She was in the house. Under attack. He fumbled with the car door, forcing himself not to think about the dents and scratches, the gaping wound in his hood caused by the old timber. At least the engine was still running.

Someone came through the front door of the house as he stumbled up what was left of the porch steps. Louise.

"You okay?" he said.

"Get back!" she yelled.

The porch gave under his feet, the wood not just rotten, but visibly rotting. Suddenly a large section of roof heaved inwards.

"Go!" she screamed and shoved at him.

He went. Behind him, as he stumbled down the treacherous steps, the house emitted inhuman groans and grinding noises, a curious and sickening dissonance. Eddie made it to the driver's side of his car and scrambled in.

Louise was slamming the passenger-side door behind her as he turned the key. He'd forgotten in his panic that the engine was still running; the starter motor shrieked.

"Get me away from here!" Louise cried.

He rammed the gears into reverse. As the car skidded slowly backwards, bits of the porch — decaying beams and splinters of wood — scraped along the duco, making it scream. Through the windscreen — which was covered in debris, but remained unbroken — Eddie saw a reddening light escaping from gaps in the walls of the farmhouse.

"It's on fire."

Louise coughed, clearing her throat clumsily. "There was an oil lamp," she said. "It fell over."

Eddie stopped the car about fifty metres along the track. Oddly, he'd expected the house to crumble away entirely or burn to the ground, as they always did in the movies, but the fire seemed to be flickering out and the collapse of the walls and ceiling had reached a sort of equilibrium.

"Was someone in there?" he asked.

Louise stared at the house, eyes wide, chest heaving with emotion. "Yes," she said at last. She was trembling.

"What happened?"

"I was assaulted, that's what." She looked at him. Her features were obscured by shadow. "A man."

"What did you do? Clobber him?"

She gripped his arm, fingers tightening fiercely. "No. But he's dead. Just believe that. He's dead. When you crashed into the house, it killed him. He went mad or something. I don't know."

"I hit him?"

"You hit his house."

Eddie didn't understand that, and he decided he didn't want to. The look on Louise's face, even though it was in shadow, scared him in a way he'd never known.

"Maybe he had a heart attack," he said weakly.

"Yeah. Maybe."

Eddie squinted at her. "What'll we do? We'll have to tell the cops."

"Forget it. They wouldn't understand."

"But—"

"He lived there alone. I don't think anyone even knows he exists. And there's nothing to connect us with the place. He died of old age. So did his house. It fell down."

"Old age?"

"Yeah. That's what anyone who sees him will say. He just rotted away. Come on. Let's go!"

Eddie turned the car and began up the slope in first gear. Behind the roar of his engine, the night was heavy with an oppressive silence. He stopped at the top of the hill and glanced back.

"I don't understand," he said.

Louise said nothing, so he drove on. As they hit the main road, he saw she was rubbing desperately at her mouth, and trying to look at her hands in the darkness.

Very low, she muttered to herself, "Jesus, please. Please, Jesus, no."

**The End**

The world hadn't ended overnight as many had expected it to. The beginning of the new millennium hadn't even been particularly traumatic for anyone other than Eddie.

He opened his eyes, glanced at his car's dashboard clock, and decided he'd stay right where he was for a bit. No use rushing into anything. His head felt very heavy. It was seven o'clock in the morning and he'd fallen asleep in the car after leaving the club the night before. That was odd, because he hadn't drunk as much as usual and had left earlier than he mostly did. Funny. Still, what did it matter? His mum would no doubt be wondering where he'd got to, but she should be used to him by now, and he didn't have anywhere he had to go until that afternoon, when he was supposed to be visiting some relos.

Eddie was thirsty though. Idly, he dropped his hand under the seat, hoping there'd be a can there with a few drops in it. No such luck. His fingers brushed against something soft. He hooked the material and pulled it out — a pair of red knickers. Must've belonged to that Louise. He grinned to himself, remembering. His New Year's night out three days ago had started bad, with Louise being so unresponsive and getting all funny on him, and had got worse with Eddie hitting the Mazda and that. And the business at the farm! Weird. But his luck had got better. Whether it was the shock of killing the old bloke or what, Louise had come over hot and sexy after they got to her place. Eddie was just going to drop her off, but she'd fallen across his shoulder, crying.

"It's the new millennium," he'd said, pointing at the digital clock on his dashboard. She'd just stared numbly at it. So Eddie had slipped off her underwear and they'd played around. Then they'd gone up to her flat, where it was more comfortable. They'd fucked like crazy. Not the best he'd ever had, but it made up for all the other shit they'd gone through. Funny how she'd cried so much though, and wouldn't talk about why. Said it was some crazy idea she'd got off the old man, that's all. Eddie guessed she was badly strung out. He hadn't heard from her since.

He stretched lazily, but the sudden intake of oxygen made his head ache and pain lanced through muscles that obviously hadn't liked sleeping on a car seat. He sat up, thinking he'd drive straight home where he could have a long hot bath, and the first thing he noticed on the way up was all the cracking on the dashboard. It was a nasty jigsaw of splits and tears, like you get when the sun's worked at vinyl over lots of years. Shit, Eddie thought, it was okay yesterday. He cleaned the inside of the car regularly and always used Armorall on the vinyl when he did. What had caused it to get so bad so suddenly?

There were splits on the doors, too — and cracks, actual cracks, in the windscreen. Okay, the car had taken a bit of a battering when it'd run into that old bloke's front porch. But Eddie had had it checked out and the car was booked in at the panel beaters for Friday. Just had to have a few of the side panels and the bonnet fixed up, that's all. The windscreen was unbroken.

It was always the way. You look after a car real well and everything's fine, then something happens and all at once the whole thing starts to go. Shit. It was like some sort of Law.

He twisted the ignition key to start the engine. The car coughed, spluttered, fell silent. He tried again, with the same result.

Now the engine's playing up, Eddie thought, opening the door to go and look under the hood. What next?

The door, its hinges rusted almost to powder, fell away as he pushed, and thudded onto the roadway.

Eddie just stared.

# GROUNDSWELL

"Was that a tree?"

Con Arturo glanced at his partner with a whimsical frown, a look that was more the result of having re-read the Malu file than a response to her question.

"A what?"

Constable Deranne Peret squinted through the side window of their car, pressing against hardened, light-sensitised glass to watch the retreating landscape. From Arturo's point-of-view, the scene was obscured; the road ahead turned upward through stony mountain ridges defined by the car's beams, but, behind them, trailed into unrelieved darkness.

"A tree," Peret repeated. "I thought I saw a gum tree, a big one."

"A gum tree?"

Peret glared over her shoulder, needled by his facetious tone. "Well, it looked like a gum tree. Gnarled thing, a few metres high maybe. That's small, I guess."

Arturo shrugged.

"I read once wild eucalypts could reach seventy, maybe a hundred metres," Peret muttered. Arturo, who was 52, and had seen wild eucalypts in his youth but remained unimpressed by specimens kept alive in Sydney's Botanical Gardens, sighed and tapped at the car's view-field. "We've got a possible murder conspiracy going on here," he said, carefully modulating his voice into sarcasm, "and you're worrying about bloody trees, for God's sake."

"I thought I saw one. I know it's ridiculous, out here, but that's why I mentioned it, Inspector."

Arturo studied her eyes for a long moment, attempting to glean knowledge of her mood from them; he suspected her of game-playing and wanted to know why she might be doing it. Her pupils were an unnatural orange — indicating she'd had cosmetic lens surgery — and quite impenetrable. Arturo hated the fashion. "Maybe it was just a stump — a dead tree," he suggested. "Some've stayed standing. They'll collapse when they're desiccated enough, I guess."

"It had leaves."

"You're imagining things."

The constable nodded thoughtfully. "Maybe." She stared back out the windows. "Might have been a glitch. I read somewhere there's been severe disturbances over the desert air-mass lately. Makes people hallucinate."

"You read too much," Arturo growled.

It's me that's been reading too much, Division Inspector Con Arturo told himself, returning his eyes to the view-field. Page 10 was headed "McGaw"; Arturo scanned the words that followed:

*Patrick Tamrin McGaw, age 63, of Balmain Centre. Shot dead in Rosebank Road, Glebe, on the evening of Thursday, 24 July, at approx. 06.45, by officers of 12 Division investigating report of attempted kidnapping. Deceased carried a Walther Pp6K Special Assault pistol, circa 1998, loaded. Weapon had been fired twice, at arresting police. McGaw's alleged victim, Paul Sandelman, 36, of Epping, was uninjured. Statement taken by Reporting Officer K. Daly at 08.02.*

This was the factual beginning of the Malu file, Arturo supposed, the event that drew him into it.

Its spiritual beginning for Arturo was older, motivated by things he read for the first time when he was about 30. Crime fiction. Mysteries. Books found in a trunk belonging to his father. He'd found them when clearing his father's house for re-sale, had read them — and that was the start. Murder had become, first, his hobby, and, subsequently, his obsession. He'd studied most of the novels of Raymond Chandler and Dashiell Hammett, about fifty anthologies of stories culled from the now-defunct *Ellery Queen's Mystery Magazine* and other journals, books by Agatha Christie, Peter Lovesey, Patricia Highsmith, Robert Bloch, Peter Corris, Fiona Midgeton, Dale C. Thorndyke and a long line of authors who'd kept the tradition alive, even in these days when stories of unnatural death were frowned upon as a source of casual amusement. Arturo's wife, now sadly re-married, had been embarrassed by him and had always interpreted his reading as a side-effect of being a policeman.

"It's sick, Con," she claimed, speaking for a generation. To her, and those she admired, the careless times of uncontrolled mortality had passed; the first quarter of the century had been a period of such extensive violence that many considered mankind had

had a glut of it, that it was wrong to remember the crimes of the past — obscene perhaps.

But, for others, Arturo had said, remembering was a source of comfort. During the Wasting — as events that occurred in the early part of the century were called — death was too close, and its legacies still lingered. But, the guilt had to be borne and it was Arturo's opinion that ignoring it was not healthy — it was, in fact, unproductive and even dangerous.

The ultimate act of murder was committed upon the country itself. Little of Australia's fauna and flora remained. Outside the reserves, the cities and larger towns, the sun was too harsh, the atmosphere too acidic, disease and heat had turned everything, even the mountain rainforests, to desert. Soil leeching on a massive scale, chronic dieback, destruction of the ozone layer, industrial and chemical poisoning, the thinning of forests to such an extent that what survived the woodchippers and the developers had no strength to survive the worsening climate...it all added up, and, in the end, there'd been death and violence and unrelieved crime. Retreat had followed — and a regretful directing of the nation's meagre resources toward salvaging what could be salvaged of the Lucky Country. Governments fell because of an inability to cope with the environmental and legislative problems; it took outside help — interference, some claimed — before white Australian civilisation could feel secure again in the relative comfort it had known since 1788 or so. Pockets of imposed life clinging to a narrow coastline. As for the Aborigines, the koori...some remained in the cities, but the tribes had gone. They proved no more resilient than the rainforests of the north.

"Hasn't there been enough death?" his ex-wife said.

But it hadn't gone away, Arturo claimed. It was all around them.

Luckily, his position in the CID gave Arturo access to files relating to nearly a century of criminal investigation. He'd searched out the most interesting murders and had read up on as many of them as possible. Inspired by what he read — by the sheer recklessness of murder — he'd joined the Homicide Division two years ago. The re-institution of the rule of Law inspired by the Wasting was, if not universally effective, at least, relatively efficient. Law enforcement agencies achieved remarkable success in lowering the crime figures, particularly those relating to murder. The population was smaller, more manageable. Spirits were subdued through years of dying. Methods were more thorough. Sure, there were still a healthy number of domestic homicides, crimes of passion, deaths by manslaughter and the like, but nothing really big. Crime had become as small and unimaginative as the population — as wasted as the land.

Arturo supposed he regretted the lawfulness of his age, and he supposed also that it was wrong to harbour such regret. Yet, murder seemed deeply important, had been a source of legend in earlier times — a symbolic cleansing that allowed for growth. Jack the Ripper, Ned Kelly, Reverend Jones, the Boston Strangler, Charles Manson — they were all profoundly iconoclastic. It fascinated Arturo. Was a richer life made possible by conscious violation of middle-class safety? Was premeditated murder a sort of spiritual fertilisation, a shedding of blood that undermined order and fed the knowledge that life was, after all, both chaotic and precious? For Arturo, the process of detection was a statement of the inexorable rightness of things, a divine patterning — and Arturo, like others before him, wanted to be the high priest of that pattern. To achieve such an end he needed not just murder, but murder that contained within itself some of the ancient power of legend. Something profoundly threatening. Something big. The Malu file seemed to Arturo to fit the bill precisely.

They came upon Anderson's Siding as the sun was rising over the horizon. It was little more than a series of crumbling façades being consumed by the desert, none of the houses lived in for perhaps fifty years. The train track that gave the place its name had itself long ago disintegrated. Arturo noticed the shell of an ancient container carriage behind one building; it no longer looked like something artificial, but had taken on the natural harshness of an outback landscape.

"The sun's coming up," said Peret as she reached out to stop their vehicle. Its computer-systems hummed as they re-adjusted to stillness. The filters and air-coolants registered the imminent heat and pushed levels upward.

"We'll be okay in the car," Arturo commented.

Peret gestured at the control panel. "Look how hot it is out there, Inspector. Can you imagine what it'll be like toward midday?"

Arturo shrugged. "Okay, so the bloody thing'll have to earn its keep. What's the big deal?" Before Peret could speak, he put up his hand. "If it makes you feel any better, we'll hide in one of the buildings, right? Not much, but at least it's shade."

Peret found a high-roofed ground-level building — it'd been some sort of storage depot by the look of it — and Arturo got out of the car to see if he could open the large bay-doors. The atmosphere was hot and oppressive; to breathe it was like inhaling soot — though there wasn't the pervasive petro-chemical smell you always noticed in the cities when you emerged from a purified environment. There was a lock on the door, but it was so rusted it crumbled when he pushed it. Even the wood, which had been thick and hard, gave under his fingers. Dry heat scratched at his face and eyes.

Inside it was cooler, but only just. Tools lined the walls, agricultural implements, all old and rusted, and bags of what once was grain, probably animal fodder, but they were now piles of dusty hessian. The grain probably spoilt and was left to the rodents, back when rodents could still survive out here. There was also evidence of human violence. In the middle of the floor space, there was a skeleton. Arturo took a closer look and found that its skull was smashed at the base. But whatever happened had happened long ago, in the early days of the Wasting, and was outside both his jurisdiction and his interest. Murder committed at that time of universal chaos had no deeper significance for Arturo.

A wave of indirect heat struck him as Peret directed

the car into a concrete loading bay at one side of the building as though she'd dragged hot air in with her. Arturo suddenly felt oppressed and threatened. Stay in your vehicle as much as possible, a Departmental technical officer told them before they left. It cools the air and filters out dangerous radiation. Check levels often. Keep clear of anything you don't understand. Short periods in the open are okay as long as you apply a screening agent to your skin, shade your eyes and drink a lot. But try to avoid direct exposure to the sun. You'll be covered with melanomas before you can blink. And remember, the air's pretty thin on oxygen...

Which perhaps explains why the wood of these buildings doesn't spontaneously ignite under that bloody sun, Arturo thought. It felt like it should.

"Hot?" Peret asked as he climbed back into the car.

"Is the Prime Minister a crook?" he replied.

Time went by slowly. Their instruments registered massive rises in temperature, the very thought of which made Arturo break out in a sweat. They drank water, nibbled at their supplies of Nutri-bars and talked, about themselves — though this was superficial — and about the Malu file. More frequently than he realised, Arturo would say, "When it cools down a bit, we'd better do some exploring," or "I wish to hell we could get on with this." But Peret would reply: "I'd like a cup of tea."

According to antique directories Arturo had found in the Departmental library, Anderson's Siding was the starting point for anyone heading toward the Malu

Valley. Not that anyone had gone to the Malu Valley for a hell of a long time. Malu, which was some Aboriginal dialect word, had been a thickly forested area, but had been logged out of existence before late twentieth-century controversies surrounding Kakadu and Coolangubra had reached a head — and then further ravaged by an international mining concern. Whatever deposits had been in the Malu Valley must have run out quickly because the mine closed after only a few years of operation. Mines still functioned, under incredible difficulties, in other parts of the universal desert, but Malu wasn't one of them.

Because of its history, roads were laid going into the Valley, but they were impassable now — and Arturo's trip would have to be made on foot. It wasn't far, according to the map. Arturo had little inclination to venture any distance from the car, but it was to the Malu Valley that evidence uncovered during the McGaw investigations pointed and to Malu he had to go.

The death of Patrick McGaw was a godsend, Arturo considered. Police looking into the incident became convinced the attempt at alleged kidnapping resulting in his death was not a one-off thing, but part of an ongoing plot. Arturo was brought in on the case when someone discovered that McGaw had driven, at least twice, into the desert with persons now missing. Arturo's own investigations revealed an inordinate number of people had been declared missing over the past year, and that McGaw could just as well have spirited most of them away, too. He was an accounting executive who took frequent, sometimes unplanned, holidays, and travelled often on the roads out of Sydney, pursuing business in Wollongong and Newcastle. His wife said he'd become very odd after one such trip perhaps 18 months previously. He wouldn't talk of what he did except in general, often contradictory, terms, but his car was clocking up mileage, which indicated his claimed destinations were not his real ones. Increasingly, it appeared as though McGaw had been taking people into the desert somewhere and killing them for whatever reason. A reason that, Arturo hoped, would prove to be nicely arbitrary.

A month later, a woman named Trisha Sorrento was arrested and charged with murder; she'd been found with a body in her car. The victim was poisoned. Under interrogation, Sorrento said it was a mistake, an overdosing; she'd only meant to knock the guy out. Why? she was asked. Robbery, she said.

No material proof she'd ever robbed anybody of anything could be found. But she was a licensed prostitute, and several of her known clients had been reported missing. The investigating officer explained that Sorrento had been seen with one of these missing persons in her car, immediately prior to his disappearance.

Any idea where she took him? Arturo asked.

Out of the city, the officer said. North-west. She was often away for days. Exactly like the McGaw case.

Once he was aware some sort of murder ring might be operating, Arturo found more and more evidence — previously undiscovered and in police files — indicating the wave of kidnapping was widespread and was not confined to McGaw and Sorrento. Nobody else was actually identified, but it became clear that others existed. Arturo was determined to find out who they were and what they were doing. He had little to go on — Sorrento died under chemical interrogation before anything was discovered — but Arturo felt if he could find out where they were going everything else would fall into place.

Then, about a week ago, a piece of paper found among McGaw's effects suggested that, at some time, and probably just over a year ago, he had taken a trip "to see Malu".

"Malu? Who's he?" Arturo asked McGaw's wife.

"Not he," the woman said. "It. Patrick was interested in family history — sort of like a hobby. His great-grandfather worked in the Malu Valley during the 1980s, lived in the nearby town — Anderson's Siding, I think Patrick said. Patrick wanted to go there, but I wouldn't let him. I said it was too dangerous. You don't think he went anyway, do you?"

That was exactly what Arturo thought.

"External temperature's dropping," Peret commented.

Arturo had been drifting into sleep when she spoke and her voice made him start. He glanced at the car's clock. "Must be something wrong with the thermometer," he said. "It's only 2.36."

"Ultraviolet levels are falling, too. Maybe it's the clock?"

Arturo checked the view-field's internal timekeeper,

which was on a different circuit. "Says 2.37."

They both studied the external readings. Heat, radiation: falling. Wind velocity, humidity, barometric pressure: on the rise.

"Rainstorm?" Arturo suggested.

"It hasn't rained out here for over a decade, maybe several."

"How do you know?"

Peret squinted at him and frowned. She said nothing.

"Let's back out and have a look," said Arturo.

Peret gave instructions to the computer with a few deft movements of her fingers. The car's engine whined and they moved through the bay doors. At once, they felt wind battering the car. Dust spun about their tyres.

"Looks dry enough," said Arturo. "Fair bit of turbulence though." The sky was clear, more starkly blue than Arturo had expected.

"Doesn't make sense." Peret was sweating. Several drops glistened on her temple. "Temperature's still dropping. It's not exactly cold out there, but it's nearly tolerable. Maybe twenty degrees below what it should be."

Arturo wet his lips. "Let's look around."

The car moved along what had once been the main street of the town, now a shattered row of disappearing shopfronts. "COKE IS IT!" said one sign, in faded, peeling paint. A sudden surge of wind raised the street into the air and both Arturo and Peret cringed as dirt hit the windscreen. The car rocked.

"Getting a bit difficult to see anything," yelled Arturo, though he didn't have to as the car's chassis kept out all external noise.

Then something rose up in front of them, something, impossibly, their scanners hadn't detected from a distance. The car registered the shape almost too late and slammed itself into a sharp turn.

"What was that?" cried Arturo, reaching across to stop the vehicle.

Peret was silent for a moment, squinting out the side window.

"You see it?" Arturo asked.

"I thought...well, a huge kangaroo."

"Kangaroo?" Arturo glanced toward the spot where the shape had appeared and disappeared.

"It looked like one," Peret protested.

"How could it be a bloody kangaroo?"

"I don't know, do I?"

Arturo wondered at that moment, irrelevantly, why Peret had joined Homicide and why she was here with him now. She was a good-looking woman, 26 years old, with friends and lovers and a good future in the developing gene-based forensic sciences. Practical, straightforward. Not an intellectual ratbag like him. As far as he knew, she'd never even heard of Sherlock Holmes. So what was she doing here?

Somewhere deep inside, he knew they were in grave danger. Not from the wind, or the falling temperature, not from Patrick McGaw or someone like him, not from the desert or technical failure; but, from something older, wiser, more elemental than any of these things. He had no reason to think this, could not have rationalised it — he simply understood it to be true, as though a spirit were breathing ancient secrets in his ear.

"Con?" Peret whispered.

"I'm all right." He ordered the car to backtrack slowly; the wind was dropping its load of dust now, the street returning from clouds, and he wanted to find evidence of the "kangaroo" they'd nearly hit. What kind of evidence?

*I don't know*, he muttered.

"You say something, Inspector?"

"No."

It's coming closer, Arturo thought. Whatever it is.

A figure was standing in the middle of the street. Not a kangaroo, but a woman — dark and old, naked under the desert sun. Her hair was black, streaked with white where it mingled in the wind and currents of settling dust. Her limbs were long and knotted, her breasts large and her stomach swollen, as though with pregnancy.

"An Aborigine," Peret said.

Arturo glanced at the temperature gauge. "It's impossible." To him, the miracle was not that this appeared to be a koori woman, but that there was anyone out there at all. No one, white or black, had survived in the outback for more than a few days, let alone lived there, since the Wasting made even the fertile areas barren. It wasn't just the heat, or the lack of food and water, but the unfiltered radiation that burned flesh into cancerous sores.

"Someone must have abandoned her here."

"We'd better help."

Arturo nodded, but neither of them moved. There was something invulnerable about the woman that made it hard for Arturo to see her as a victim. Her weathered skin seemed tough and, at the same time as changeable as the earth's dry surface. She smiled — a calm, knowledgeable smile — and gestured to them.

"I'm not going out there," said Arturo. "Not yet. I don't like it."

"So, don't then."

Silently, the police and the koori woman faced each other for a few minutes — the police within the cocoon of their vehicle, the koori naked under the blazing sun. Arturo wiped sweat from his forehead and scratched at the side of his face — a tic started in the flesh near his left eye. Peret began groaning deep in her throat.

"I wish she'd do something," Arturo whispered, as though afraid to be heard.

The koori woman nodded. She turned, indicating that they should follow, and walked along the main street of the town. Whirlpools of dust trailed her footsteps.

"Do we follow?" said Peret; she sounded afraid of his answer. He nodded.

They stopped the car when the road disappeared under broken rocks and scrap metal, the remnants of a rail track that looked like it had been torn from its bedding, bent grotesquely, and then covered by years of windborne dust. Anderson's Siding was far behind them. The woman continued on, following a narrow path beyond the barrier. Arturo knew they'd have to leave the protection of the car if they were to keep her in sight. She mounted a rise about two hundred metres ahead.

"What are radiation levels like?" Arturo asked.

Peret glanced at the gauges. "Right down. Almost normal."

"Let's go."

He opened his side of the vehicle without waiting for her. She followed more slowly.

"Smell that?" Arturo said. He'd noticed the difference in the air almost at once.

"What is it?"

"Eucalyptus."

Once they reached the rise, they saw the koori woman ahead, standing at the edge of a cliff — but she had become insignificant against a vast, impossible backdrop. In the valley stretching below them was a forest like nothing Arturo had seen before — a rich, windswept sea of green and brown. It spilled along the sides of rugged cliffs, clung to promontories and plateaus many kilometres away, swirled into eddies and corners and swept into the distance. Arturo watched in awe as wind meandered across the reddened tips of trees a hundred metres tall.

"Some of these must be centuries old," he said. "They told us the forests were dead. Lost forever."

"Nothing is lost forever," said the woman, who had approached Arturo while he struggled with fear and disorientation. He looked into her face, and saw that her lips were still. "Hidden — but never lost. The important things return."

"Important things?"

"Life."

"I'm looking for death."

"You've found that, too. They're the same."

In her eyes Arturo saw blood, the blood of...how

many? Perhaps thousands.

"You're the killer? McGaw, Sorrento, others? They were your agents?"

"There's a price to be paid for the forests. In you, in this young woman, there lie the trees, the mosses and ferns, water flowing in creeks that feed rivers and oceans, insects, birds, the animals. Even Malu, the kangaroo. All there, all waiting to be born."

"And you're the midwife?" He stepped closer, drawing his gun. "What have you done with the bodies?"

The woman swept her arm over the Valley.

*His feet slip down a muddy pathway, stumbling on accumulated leaf-litter and over roots, straddling stones covered in moss. Above, the sky is patterned behind clusters of gum leaves and branches like cracks in the blue. Shadow and sun; air heavy with scent.*

*Arturo catches sight of the koori, a darting form interweaving the rich texture of the bush. He fires his Magnum high; the sound smashes the forest and birds flap noisily through the foliage. The huge, knotted antiquity of the gums crowds him, blocking him, holding him back.*

*He fires again, but the woman has gone.*

*Huge rocks, like the shoulders of giants, push up through the forest floor. Their presence unnerves Arturo and he is unable to move across their path; even the trees seem to stand back from them.*

A kangaroo bounds from the bush to one side of the clearing. Arturo's eyes follow the animal as it weaves a course among the boulders.

Forest looms around him, mist trailing through its undisciplined tangle. Ahead the land drops gently, and Arturo can see kilometres of green stretching into a filmy gauze of rain toward the horizon.

"How have you kept this a secret?" he yells.

He stops when memory fails him. Caves open in a tangle of shrub, the darkness leaking from them like the breath of an ancient sleeping creature. Arturo wonders what he is searching for — not this, certainly. He turns aside and runs, chest heaving, across a field of grass and low wattles, his feet crushing its carpet of yellow and ochre gold.

"Peret!' he calls. He cannot remember when he lost her — he can barely recall who she is.

A small creature, furry and squat, watches him from the branch of a tree. A koala. It chews on its meal of leaves, indifferently.

On the edge of the forest, Arturo feels the constrictions caused by thinning air. He leans on the papery bark of a large gum, conscious of it soft against his skin, stares out into land struggling for rebirth, breathes painfully.

"This is the legacy of blood," says the woman from above,

*in the tree.*

When he saw the steel geometry of the Harbour Bridge, Arturo knew they'd made it back alive. Until then, memory had fluctuated between images of desert and dreams of succulent forest, recollections that seemed like death. Neither he nor Peret had spoken much; they'd said nothing of their stay in Anderson's Siding, nothing of what they'd found at Malu. But the need for silence was past.

"We've a lot to do," Peret said.

"We're better situated than the others."

The car slowed as it negotiated the North Sydney overpass. Arturo tapped his forefinger against the view-field screen, drawing Peret's attention. "I've written our report. We found nobody at Anderson's Siding, no clues to the whereabouts of the missing persons. As for the Valley, it was a desert."

"Yes."

Arturo felt the power of Malu in his mind and his body. It was an ache, a potential he couldn't resist.

"There'll be no more mention of the Malu Valley," he said. "And the file will be closed. Random factors introduced. The murder conspiracy theory must appear to be false."

"Yes, Inspector."

"And then..." *And then.*

*And then, he waits in shadows beneath the steel archways of a shopping mall, watching, listening. There are people moving along the footpath, talking of themselves, their aspirations, the successes of the day, hopeful for the future or dismissive of the past. Sydney breathes with sustaining life.*

*Then one man, alone. Malu reaches out, probes the edges of his mind. At last, "That one!"*

*Arturo, his soul dark with murder, emerges from hiding.*

# HEARTLESS

*Walking on a rock platform. Summer. Mid-afternoon. Moments before the dying sun slides behind the escarpment. A gull screeches. Kids in the distance clamber toward a surfing beach on the far side of the point, leaving him isolated. He's glad. He likes being alone with the ocean swell.*

*Someone emerges from the shadow of an overhang. Portly. Rather stiff. A fisherman perhaps. He's carrying a bag.*

*"Superb weather, isn't it?" the stranger says.*

*Dark and crumpled, his suit looks absurdly incongruous framed by sea and sky. His face is bloated, and bears the sort of moustache Clark Gable made fashionable sixty years ago.*

*"Visiting the area?" he questions, sidling up. The hand not holding the bag is pushed into a coat pocket. "With the family?"*

*"Just me."*

*"Oh, good." He's close now. Arm's length away. Intimate. "Maybe you can help me. What's your name?"*

*"Charlie. What's yours?"*

What day was it? What year? Charlie didn't have a clue. Anything was possible. And nothing. As a marker of life passing, time had become irrelevant.

"Morning, Charlie." The psychopath who called

himself a 'radical surgical technologist' appeared in Charlie's field of vision wearing the stupid green (and blood-splattered) gown and equally stupid grin he always wore. He was small but podgy, like a walking mound of fat. Probably stank, too, though it hardly mattered as he'd cut off Charlie's nose days ago — right down to the olfactory nerve buried between the eyes.

"What's on today, Dr Butcher?" Charlie growled nasally.

The technologist, whose name was Wang, didn't look Oriental. When Charlie first heard the name, he'd imagined a Chinese villain from some old-time spy movie. But Wang was born and bred in the hinterlands of the Gold Coast and appeared thoroughly Caucasian. He voted conservative — or, so he said. There was a softness to his face that hid the sadistic cruelty he'd directed toward a succession of victims. Charlie had no idea how many, but the pile of broken bones he'd seen in the cellar wasn't indicative of restraint.

"The traditional centre of being," Wang said. "The arterial mainstay of the body. The pump of life."

Charlie was pleased. This farce had gone on for too long and he was tired. Ripping out his heart would put an end to the slow entropic crawl towards death.

Wang's sausage fingers gripped something shiny and metallic — a thing with sharp edges, corkscrew-like flange and other baroque protuberances that might have made Charlie nervous if he cared.

"Your poetry's as subtle as your surgery, Butch," Charlie commented. For days, his predominant emotion had been weariness; suddenly there was hope, too. Yet he had no intention of sharing that hope with his tormentor. If Wang truly suspected Charlie's delight, he would change his plans.

"My name's Wang," Wang said. "Dr Wang. I am not a butcher."

Charlie raised his eyebrows in mock surprise, as Wang hadn't yet removed them. Wang scowled, but, when Charlie didn't look intimidated, he waddled over to the large chalkboard on the far wall. It was covered in words ending with '—otomy'. Some of them — such as caecotomy, duodenotomy, gastrotomy, and prostatotomy — had neat little ticks next to them. Charlie found it some comfort to know that, given his current occupancy, Wang wouldn't be able to practise 'ovariotomy' or 'hysterectomy' on him.

Wang placed a careful tick next to the word 'cardiotomy'.

He held up the metal gizmo he'd carried into the surgery. "This instrument will revolutionise heart transplants. I made it specially. You'll be famous." He illustrated how the scoop affair carved into the chest, while various do-dads and nobbles on either side separated ribs and flesh and organs, sliced arteries and muscle tissue and channelled blood away, while central pincers gripped the heart for added security during removal. Spring-loaded levers transformed even extreme movements by the operator into delicate manipulations.

"Yeah, very nice," said Charlie. "You're a real artist."

"I am indeed," replied Wang. "I'm so gratified you can appreciate the fact. Surgery should be an art, don't you think? My instruments are more than tools. They are things of beauty. They express and embellish the human spirit." He leaned closer. "Have you noticed," he added conspiratorially, "how the word 'instrument' is used in both surgery and music?"

"You play with yourself so well, too," Charlie pointed out.

Wang smiled happily. For however long Charlie had been there, strapped to Wang's table and subject to his ravings, he'd never been able to penetrate the man's façade. He was immune to sarcasm.

"You know, Charlie," Wang whispered, bending down so that his breath tickled over Charlie's ear like a lover's, "finding you has been of great benefit to me. All my previous patients...had limited usefulness. By the time I'd done a fraction of what I've done to you, they were unresponsive—"

"Dead, you mean?"

Wang nodded. "Yes, dead." He glanced along Charlie's prone body and Charlie raised his head to do likewise. He was (as always) vaguely shocked to see the ravaged landscape of his nether regions. Both legs were gone now, and, instead of a belly, there was a massive, wet cavity that lacked most of the identifiable organs that should have resided there. A few ribs were visible on the left side, sticking out from torn flesh and muscle tissue. "You can talk to me while I perform my...arts. Tell me how it feels. It adds a whole new dimension. And I can go further with you, be more complete in my records, because you don't die."

"Ever wonder how come?" Charlie let his head flop back against the bench. "Aren't you curious? As a scientist?"

"I accept miracles. They add spice." Wang strode

over to a series of large glass containers and began pointing at them. "Your stomach, your liver, your lower intestine, your testicles. I can show them to you, put them in jars, yet you live. What else is this unending life of yours but a miracle?"

"It isn't life, that's for sure," said Charlie. "You can't do this stuff to people unless they're dead. Ever thought of that? You may be learning nothing about the living human body — assuming you have any real interest in such — because I'm dead."

"If you were dead," Wang spoke in a low voice, "your heart wouldn't beat."

Charlie glanced at him cunningly, catching and holding the manic restlessness of the man's eyes. "Ah," he said, "maybe it doesn't."

"I've felt it." Wang reached one gloved hand into the slit he'd made in Charlie's flesh about three days ago. Charlie sensed fingers like heavy congestion in his chest. The movement pained him as pressure bore down on his heart. "It's beating," Wang stated triumphantly. Charlie felt the organ shift.

"Maybe my heart's alive," he said, "but not me."

"Nonsense." Wang grabbed up his instrument and made adjustments.

Charlie watched, smirking. "I've suggested you do a heart removal lots of times. What's made you decide to do it at last?" Wang glanced at him. "You might have cut out my brain. Why not my brain?"

"You're trying to trick me. Without your brain, you'd die. The brain's the key to everything, not the heart. I've seen those movies — you know the ones. With the zombies."

*"Night of the Living Dead? Day of the Dead?* Now you've got it. I'm a zombie. Not living at all."

"Zombies are superstitious fictions. I am a scientist, and you are a scientific marvel." Wang snarled. "The creatures depicted in those populist entertainments are gross and anatomically silly. Mere illusion. But they make a valuable scientific point. Destroy the brain and life ends at last."

"I think you're glorifying it, but never mind. What about my spinal column then? If you could pull it out intact, that'd be a great triumph. It's not much use where it is. No part of my body, no organ, no pound of flesh, is worth a pinch of shit compared to the heart. The heart is everything." Wang frowned, without saying a word, then came toward Charlie with the instrument. That was typical of him. Once he'd made his mind up to do something, no considerations of good sense (or morality either, presumably, though Charlie had never attempted that particular appeal) could deter him. Charlie thought this might be admirable, except that the man's real motivation was simply to inflict cruelties. That's what it was all about. There was no truth in him. He was a simple psychopath, dressed up in scientific jargon — a caricature from 1940s' B-films. "You'll regret it, Wang," Charlie said and meant it. He'd wanted Wang to remove his heart since this nightmare started — since the afternoon Wang attacked him with a loaded syringe and he found himself a captive audience to his own evisceration. Now, perhaps, it would happen and he would be free.

"Surely all those aphorisms about hearts can't be wrong, Wang," he said, perversely enjoying the repartee. With the end in sight, he felt curiously flippant.

"What do you mean?"

"Getting to the heart of the matter. Winning your heart. Heartbroken. Heart and soul. Heartache. Taking it to heart. Love, hate, thought, emotion, life itself — they're all situated in the heart, according to the populist imagery you despise. The heart is the centre of being. *Owner of a lonely heart...*" he sang in his wheezy, oddly disembodied voice, "*Much better than an...owner of a broken heart.*"

Wang snorted. His scorn was palpable. "Yes, yes. Romantic nonsense. Vapid whimsy. With you and your immortality, I'll be able to prove it. I'll take away your heart and you'll still be here. If the heart were the centre of being, you would die for good."

"I told you, I'm already dead. But there may be other consequences. Scientists need to think about possibilities, Wang. Leave nothing to chance."

Wang ignored him. His deco blade sliced carelessly into Charlie's chest, its various appendages separating muscles and ribs. Charlie felt the metal caress him. "Okay, then," he muttered, "don't say I didn't warn you."

"I won't."

"*Take a little piece of my heart now baby,*" Charlie added in a distant sing-song drone.

Wang snorted.

Charlie fell silent as the blade cut arteries, then channelled fatty tissue and the minimal blood into appropriate receptacles. Wang didn't notice Charlie's silence until he stood with the heart cradled before him.

Then he studied his patient's face and bloody chest. "Are you all right?" he asked. Charlie didn't say anything and didn't move. "Uh, oh!" Wang groaned.

He poked the motionless flesh.

Nothing. Charlie was lifeless.

The setback filled Wang with anger. He slashed out with his precision instrument, burying it in Charlie's blank face. The corpse slid up against the ridge around the edge of Wang's operating table in a mock cringe while its heart glopped onto the metal surface, making a dense, wet noise. Over! Over just like *that*.

"Stupid bastard!" Wang yelled. "How dare you die! You gutless, idiotic loser! Together we could have been great. Together we could have turned the medical profession on its head." He brought his face down and held it close to Charlie's, which was as indifferent to him as it was to the blade gouged into its pale flesh. "I had plans, you know. Revolutionary plans! This wasn't about anatomy. No fear! This wasn't just a study of viscera. I was taking you apart, but, afterwards, refined down to your pure living essence, I was going to re-build you. Make you better! Not now! Not now, you fool. It's over. You abandoned me. You ruined everything."

Getting no response from the mutilated corpse — just as he'd provoked no response from endless corpses before this — Wang sighed, the exhalation of breath calming him. The corpse didn't care what he said. It couldn't even hear him. It was dead meat, that's all.

The romantics were right.

The thought filled him with despair. The heart, damn it. Why was the heart where life was centred? Why had reality confirmed the dumb notions of a thousand insipid poets? It should have been the brain. That's what was important. Hearts just pumped blood.

He squinted at the thing on the table. Look at it! Dark and glistening — ugly! And odd. It seemed big and knobbly in a way Wang was sure hearts shouldn't look. Charlie must have been a mutant, a genetic freak. Maybe he'd been one of the living dead after all. Primitive ritual often fixated on hearts as a source of magical power. Perhaps the zombie films were wrong. Not the brain. The heart. Damn! "I should have listened to him," Wang said. There were so many other organs he could have dealt with first, before the heart. So much he could have done. Now he'd have to go back to ordinary people, who died so easily.

Something moved. The heart? Still pumping? Wang leaned closer. The organ smelt nasty — evil somehow. Thinking to cut it open, Wang picked up a scalpel. As he bent over Charlie's heart, squinting myopically to get a better view, one of the thing's severed arteries snagged on his lower lip. The tentacle slid into his mouth.

Wang cried out, shocked by the unexpected attack and appalled by the slimy feel of the tentacle on his lips. His sudden, violent reaction loosened the thing's grip and it fell away from him, scudding across the floor and under a table.

Regaining his composure, Wang bent slightly, hoping to see Charlie's heart lying inert in the corner. He kept his distance, however, and, as a result, could see nothing. He muttered curses under his breath.

Carefully, he pushed at the table, rattling the

instrument array on it like an ill-tuned xylophone. The table moved, revealing about half a metre of grubby floor. No heart though. Must have skidded quite a long way.

"Where'd you get to, you little bastard?" he growled.

Nothing leapt at him and he considered the possibility he'd imagined its movement. He'd knocked the table, making the heart appear to 'move'. Of course, it wasn't alive. How could a heart jump around by itself? All it did was pump blood and, by doing so, kept a body alive, albeit Charlie's miraculously resilient one. *Ker-pump, ker-thump.* A disembodied heart going for his throat? A zombie heart? Ridiculous. Surely that wasn't what doctors meant when they talked about the danger of heart attacks.

"Yoo-hoo! Charlie? Are you there?" He moved the table a bit further. Light from the overhead fluorescent caught on something dark and wet. Wang jerked back, watching it warily.

It didn't move. Only an ordinary heart after all. Dead.

Just the same, there was no way he was going to pick it up. He didn't intend to get that close to the cardial thing.

Watching it all the while, he fetched a broom that was leaning against the wall. The heart didn't move. Gripping the very end of the broom handle, he used the business end to drag the thing into the open where he could see it clearly. As he did, he turned up his lip — it really was an ugly lump of gristle. Gnarled. Bumpy. A sort of greenish red colour.

"You were one weird son-of-a-bitch, Charlie," he

said.

A section of the heart's surface spasmed. Wang took a step back. He adjusted his glasses and tried to focus on it. The larger of two bumps on Charlie's heart was wrinkling up, retracting. What was going on?

Then he saw it! The surface layer pulled back and an eye blinked up at him. The sight was so surreal that for a moment he couldn't register it as an objective experience. It was like holding a Magritte canvas against a photograph of something — he admired its contrivance but knew it was just a whimsy.

The thing on the floor wasn't a painting, or even a disembodied heart, for that matter, but some alien monstrosity with eyes and a thin, featureless mouth that smirked at him and growled. Its inchoate limbs gripped the broom, tearing it from his grip. He was startled. Wanted to run. Didn't have time. The handle jabbed into his solar plexus, winding him, doubling him up. He gasped for breath.

"Bastard!" — a whining hiss.

Then smash! Pain billowed through his head, throwing him sideways. He flailed his arms, hoping to intercept the broom handle. But he missed and it cracked against the side of his skull. Tearing at the air, Wang stumbled over a complex piece of medical equipment — his 'Leg-cutter' — and fell to the floor. His skull bounced against the concrete, causing the room to blur.

"Charlie! Charlie!" he moaned.

Through a haze of confusion, he tried to focus on where he thought the thing was. Colours ran and blended into a bilious grey. He rubbed at his eyes.

Blinked. Movement. A dark blur. Coming closer.

Something grabbed at his lips.

The heart forced open his mouth and, in an instant, while he gagged and spluttered — trying unsuccessfully to pull it from between his lips — propelled itself down his throat. Wang produced a strangled scream, turned red and swallowed compulsively. He felt Charlie's heart slide along his gullet into his chest.

Pain exploded throughout his body. His breast bulged and trembled. He screamed loudly, though as his house was isolated high up a seaside escarpment in the midst of a rainforest, no one was going to hear. He struggled to his feet while a battle still raged inside him. "Stop it!" he yelled, beating at his chest. "Get out of me!"

Tearing agony, like a severe coronary, flung him sideways. He cried out. The pain shifted. Wang felt something moving upward into his throat. Screaming again, he doubled over, desperate to vomit. His body heaved and shuddered. Another compulsive heave and something large and red shot from his mouth, splattering against the wall. Barely conscious now, Wang stared at the organ and realised it wasn't Charlie's heart. It was a heart, sure, but smaller and more ordinary. He collapsed face-down onto the floor.

His last awareness was of a voice, seeming to be inside him, saying: *Don't worry, Doc. I won't stay long. You're not really my type.*

*Walking on the rock platform. Late summer. Mid-afternoon. There's change in the air.*

*Water pounds against the rocks, spouting foam into transient sculptures. A gull screeches. Figures in the distance clamber toward a surfing beach beyond the point.*

*There's someone else here as well. Male. Young, perhaps eighteen. Sitting on a flat rock, just above the heaving waves. Holding a fishing rod. Staring out to sea. Looks healthy. That's what's important. If you're going to be dead, it's best to be healthily dead.*

*Emerging from the shadow of an overhang. Portly. Rather stiff. Intolerably uncomfortable in this flaccid, smelly carcass.*

*Carrying a bag. Other hand in the pocket of the coat. Walking toward the boy. Carefully. Quietly.*

*Shadow falls over him; the youth glances around.*

*Too late.*

*Charlie saying, "Superb weather, isn't it?"*

# SEPARATING LENORE

After its convulsive twitching stopped, Gareth Sutcliffe put his wife's body in four small boxes.

The boxes were wooden and rough, with reinforced joints and a lid that could be nailed down firmly. One of the boxes contained her torso, another her arms, and the third her legs. In the last box, Sutcliffe placed her head, forcing her scarlet hair into the hateful, grinning mouth.

When he'd sealed up the boxes, cleaned his tools and clothes and scrubbed down the bathroom, Sutcliffe buried Lenore in four separate graves at least ten kilometres from each other. This task took all night and well into the next day; it was hard work, especially in his condition. But Sutcliffe knew (because he had looked it up in a book on folklore in the Library) that, in general, demonic creatures only stay in their graves if you decapitate them and bury their heads far from their bodies.

In Lenore's case, he felt it'd be a good idea to take the superstition a bit further, just to be on the safe side.

He'd met Lenore at work, oddly enough. Odd, because she was a demonic creature of some kind, and he worked for the Taxation Department. It had never occurred to him demonic creatures would submit tax returns.

At first, he hadn't known she was weird, of course; that came later when it was too late. At first, she was a sexy redhead who asked if she could have her tax return re-assessed. He'd frowned imperiously and directed her through to his cubicle. On her form S, she was designated a systems analyst; a hefty deduction for computer equipment had been disallowed. Sutcliffe said he'd see what he could do. She left. He passed the deduction, directed appropriate payment to be made, wrote down her address and stuck the file in his out tray. Later, once he was sure she'd received her rebate, he drove to the address on her form. He knocked on the door.

"Hello, Ms Gale," he said, "I was passing and thought I'd drop in to see if you got your money."

"I did." She smiled, her rich lips wet beneath her flicking tongue. "You've been very kind, Mr Sutcliffe. But is there anything *I* can do for *you*?"

There was, of course, and she did it all night and well into the next day.

The relationship that developed was stunning in its sexual intensity. Sutcliffe could hardly believe he'd found such an obliging, stimulating lover. She demanded nothing — and, for several weeks, concentrated on raising him to new heights of libidinous excess. For a while, he fully believed she could reach into his body and inflame his nerves directly; it was only later he realised how true that was.

Often she'd unexpectedly arrive at his desk, just when he'd been thinking about her, take him outside somewhere, and fuck him relentlessly, forcing him to orgasm several times running. He'd return to the office exhausted.

"Go for a bit of a workout, did you?" the section officer would say. "Healthy body, healthy mind, eh?"

On these occasions, Sutcliffe simply nodded.

Certain peculiarities should have warned him. For example, she was considerably shorter than him, but when they fucked against a wall, she'd be just the right height. Odd that, but he was always too preoccupied to question the anomaly. An illusion of passion, he'd say. Her hair seemed to burn more redly in the moment before he came. As a result, any woman with red hair, spied casually on the street, would give him an instant erection. He saw Lenore everywhere. In men's magazines; necks, breasts, navels, thighs and genitalia were all hers, even if the faces weren't. Once he'd surprised her when he walked in on her as she mucked about in the bathroom, doing whatever women do in bathrooms. She'd looked around at him with something approaching hatred — and, in that moment, Sutcliffe thought the figure reflected in the mirror behind her had been someone else's. It was taller, thinner, more gaunt and paler than he liked. And the pubic hair was black, intensely black. He glanced about, expecting to see another woman standing somewhere in the small room. There was no one, of course; suddenly the reflection in the mirror was Lenore's.

She laughed and they fucked on the clothes dryer.

About a week after they met, she moved in with him;

a month after that, they got married. His friends thought it strange he'd given in so readily; he had always been a womaniser and had vowed never to lumber himself with one woman. But he couldn't help it. He suddenly felt he *had* to marry her, before she began looking for someone who would. It had been like a compulsion, a fever that could only be satisfied by cleaving himself to her in this symbolic way. He didn't believe in marriage, had never believed in marriage, but, for a while, its usefulness in keeping her for himself seemed irresistible.

So they were married.

It was an odd ceremony, witchy and esoteric. At the time, she told him it was a form of wedding traditional to her background. Sutcliffe was so besotted with her, so desperate to marry her in any way he could, that he went along with it all. Both wore black; there was a lot of chanting by her relatives, who decorated themselves with very peculiar make-up; Sutcliffe and Lenore submitted their wrists to be nicked so that thick, red blood flowed and the celebrant bound their bleeding wounds together. It was, Lenore said, symbolic. They mumbled odd words after the celebrant, words which sounded normal, conveying ordinary sentiments such as "We will be as one flesh, body for body, blood for blood, soul for soul," but which were said with an intensity that was unnerving. After the wedding, Sutcliffe felt rather like he'd been put through a wringer.

Their wedding night was blistering. Sutcliffe didn't recover for a week, and even then, he was a bit wobbly on his feet if he tried to move too fast.

Then one night, as her hair flamed and he looked into her eyes to see fire burning in them, he asked: "How do you do that?"

"Simple," she said. "I'm not human."

He didn't doubt her words for a second; it was complete truth and he recognised it as such. It let him understand everything...except why she'd made him do it.

"Why me?" he said.

"Because you're a bastard," she replied. "And I like bastards."

A few days after they returned from their honeymoon, Sutcliffe had an affair with the Level 2 receptionist. He chatted her up one lunch-time, rang Lenore to tell her he was working late, took the receptionist out to dinner after work, and screwed her in the back of his car. Next day, he screwed her in the tearoom, and, on Friday, in the supply cupboard, as well as after work in a cheap room down the street. He forced himself on her. It was an act of defiance, a re-assertion of his sense of masculine power. Lenore had tricked him, manipulating him with illusion and magical hocus-pocus. He intended to show her he wouldn't be trifled with.

On Saturday, the receptionist got herself murdered by a psychopath, an unidentified maniac who tore out her heart and nailed it to the wall above the bed where he left her disemboweled corpse.

For the first time, Sutcliffe felt afraid of Lenore.

"Terrible murder last night," she commented over breakfast on Sunday. Her mouth was twisted into a sneering grin — though it may have been the effect of talking with a mouth full of muesli. She chewed, swallowed and read the whole story from the newspaper.

"Did *you* do it?" he asked.

Lenore looked at him — and smiled. "Why on earth would I do that? I didn't even know the poor woman."

Sutcliffe shrugged.

As time passed, he began to get sick a lot. He was vulnerable to every bug that came along, as though his immune system was exhausted, but his doctor told him it was he that was exhausted, not his immune system.

He lost weight. One morning, a month after their wedding, he tried to do up the belt of his pants and found he'd come to the last hole. He made a new one with a skewer.

"There's something wrong with me," he said to Lenore.

"Yes," she said, "You're nearly used up."

"Used up?"

"It's how we survive. We feed off our lovers."

"We?" Sutcliffe was caught between anger and desperation. It choked in his throat. "Like a vampire?" he said at last.

"Pretty close," she replied.

"But there's no teeth marks." He rubbed at his throat.

"We're more subtle than vampires."

"What do you mean?"

"Surely you noticed how strange our wedding was, Gareth, my angel? The ceremony's ancient — old and Satanic, you might say. It joined us into a sort of symbiotic relationship — one body, one flesh. Trouble is, it's all my way. Unfortunate for you, but, as I said, you're a bastard. So who cares?"

He tried to hit her, striking blindly at her stomach. All he felt was a terrible pain in his own gut.

He ran. He left the house carrying his credit cards, ten dollars in coins and the car keys. When a motel sign, blinking randomly in the night, beckoned him to come in out of the darkness, he pulled over and paid for a room.

"How long ya want it for?" the fat proprietor asked.

"God knows," Sutcliffe said.

The man grinned. "Walked out on the missus, eh?"

Sutcliffe gave him a look that would have incinerated thinner hide. "You might say that," he muttered.

Late that night, unable to sleep, he was alerted by a scratching sound. Shadows whispered around him, moving like fog and breathing in his ears. He was getting out of bed when the door, which he'd locked, swung open. A sleek, reddish cat came in and leapt onto the bed. "Hey," Sutcliffe yelled, gesturing at it menacingly. "Get the fuck outa here!"

The cat licked itself once or twice, then said: "Now, now, my angel. Don't be like that! You'll make yourself all uptight and never get to sleep."

Sutcliffe didn't wait to dress. He was in his car and several kilometres away, speeding like a rally driver, before he realised his wallet was in his trousers back at the motel. The highway patrolman who stopped him was most bemused by his lack of identification.

Running away was impossible. Sutcliffe knew that now. He had to find a permanent solution. His strength was failing daily; he estimated he had no more than a month left.

That's when he visited the City Library and read up on magic and its practitioners.

A week or two later, he slipped a poisonous concoction made of various arcane substances into Lenore's evening coffee. She knew he'd got her after the first mouthful.

"Ah, witches' bane," she said, gazing into the brown liquid.

"Yeah." Sutcliffe braced himself for her fury. He hoped she'd drop quickly, before she got a chance to retaliate. He thought a speedy detection of his plot would be the end of him.

But she did not attack. She simply smiled, licked her lips like a gourmet, and said: "Nicely done."

Then the convulsions began.

Once her body was dispersed to its various final resting places, Lenore seemed a lot less potent. Sutcliffe poured a large tequila, neat; he lounged back, staring around the room that was his own again. He felt satisfied.

"Baby," he said, toasting in the general direction of the grave that held her head. "It was fun."

He could say that now; he felt safe. From Lenore —
and everyone else. Few of his friends even knew her;
they considered her an aberration he'd grow out of.
He'd been dropping hints this was happening, so, when
she didn't appear again, he could simply say she'd
skipped out on him. He would be heart-broken, of
course. On the other hand, he'd never even met
Lenore's friends, if she had any. Some were at their
wedding; but apparently, her kind led a solitary life and
none of them had dropped by or shown any knowledge
of where she was when she wasn't at her old place. The
old place was still there; all her papers were registered
under that address. There was no official marriage
license — it hadn't been an official ceremony. So, no
records to cause the State to become suspicious.
Sutcliffe even suspected there would be no official
memorandum of her birth; certainly he'd made sure her
tax file would disappear.

Poor Lenore. For all intents and purposes, she had
never been — and certainly not with him.

"Ciao!" he said, and gulped down the tequila.

For a moment, he was tempted to ring one of the
local agencies and get them to send over a girl or two,
but he knew it would be a mistake. He was weak; it
would take him a while to fully recover, and he didn't
want to pre-empt his enjoyment. Let it come when he
was ready. He had a lifetime to make up for Lenore.

He was asleep almost as soon as his head hit the
pillow, drifting into a pale dawn that was spreading
from the horizon all too soon. Sutcliffe felt something
soft beneath his hand: a breast. His eyes shot open,
straining through the grainy light.

There was no one else in the bed, of course.

"I'm over here," said Lenore.

Somewhere far away he could see her, a shadow, a fragment of breeze drifting in the dim light, a touch of colour in the greyness. She was there, but distant.

"Can't I ever be rid of you?" he growled.

"Soon, angel, very soon."

"What the hell are you doing here? You're dead — dead, carved up, and buried!"

"It's hard to keep a good succubus down."

"You can't come back if you're cut up. The book said so."

"True, as far as it goes. I've come in your dream to ask you to dig me up again. Dig me up and I'll forgive you, I promise."

"Oh no. Forget it! There's no way in the world I'd dig you up again, Lenore. You were a sly, bloody, untrustworthy bitch. Divided up, you can't touch me."

"I wouldn't be too sure."

He could almost see her, grinning at him.

"What do you mean?"

"You never listen to what anybody says, do you? Never think of consequences. You're too wrapped up in yourself, too single-mindedly obsessed with Gareth Sutcliffe."

"Psychoanalysis time, is it?"

"We were married, angel; made one flesh. I told you that before."

"So?"

"So, in killing me, you're simply fulfilling your fondest death-wish, expressing your basic self-loathing."

"What is this crap?"

He could see her now, bending over him, her ivory flesh speckled with gore. Like a patient entering the operating theatre, he couldn't move, but looked on, numbly.

Lenore shrugged. "I've always believed that a lover should put himself in his partner's place, experience the world through someone else's senses."

She reached out, and suddenly, Sutcliffe knew what was happening. He screamed, but the sound turned inward as his mind collapsed.

When he woke it was dark.

His first thought was: *I'm not dead.*

Relief flooded through him in a wave. What a dream! Lenore's presence had been so intense he could still smell her.

He reached out to turn on the bedside lamp and his hand touched raw wood. He tried to sit up but he couldn't; his foot rubbed against a box panel.

He moved his hand to pull away something in his mouth, but again it struck wood. He didn't hear any thud, as though it had happened far away. Then his eyes, adjusted to the dark, focused on a wooden ceiling directly above him, close to his face.

Long black hair spat from his mouth as he screamed. This time, the scream was loud.

But, of course, there was no one around to hear it. Lenore was far away, chatting up one of the women in the Taxation Office.

# GETTING RID OF MOTHER

When the old lady shuffled into their bedroom on Saturday morning, Gary was awake but struggling out from under the debris of a dream. The dream had been full of axes, blood and bits of bodies. He was vaguely aware that the lady was carrying a tray with breakfast on it and this was good because it filled him with contentment rather than fear. He loved it when his mother brought him breakfast in bed. As he moved, he touched Sharon. The touch triggered his memory and the first thing he thought was: *My mother's been dead for five years.*

He sat up. The old lady, dressed in an old-fashioned floral-print dress and black shoes that were very dirty, smiled at him. "Sorry I woke you, Clive dear," she said. "I thought you'd be up already."

Gary and Sharon had moved into the old house in semi-rural Collington only a month before, having bought it from its previous owner on an impulse. Their first months together, living in a small inner-city terrace, were not good. Gary had a delicate constitution and needed someone to watch out for him. Sharon did her best, but she wasn't very good at looking after herself, let alone him, and their life tended to be chaotic. They forgot to pay bills, wouldn't clean up, never managed to undertake even necessary maintenance jobs, frequently ran out of clean laundry, and ate from local takeaways more often than not. Neither felt particularly good about this — it seemed like an admission life was slipping through their fingers. They explained it away easily enough and, as tensions mounted, they blamed their sense of helplessness on city life. "Too much noise, too much confusion. How can anyone expect to cope in this shambles?" they'd said, and moved to the country.

But things hadn't improved. Every morning, Gary dressed for work, noted with a growing unease the derelict condition of the house, remembered the eerie noises under the floor that had kept him awake for hours, stretched and said: "I feel so much better living out here." Sharon would smile and nod wanly.

"I laid out your work clothes, dear, nicely pressed," the old lady was saying. "I hope your new bride won't mind?"

Gary was about to reply that Sharon and he weren't married; but Sharon woke up suddenly, looked at the old lady, shrieked and grabbed hold of Gary. "Who's that?" she yelled.

The old lady grinned indulgently, taking Sharon's slim, white hand in her gnarled fingers. "Did I scare you, love?" She patted Sharon's arm. "It's your mother-in-law. But, of course, you know that, don't you?"

Sharon looked at Gary, bewildered. Gary shrugged.

"Now, the two of you love birds stay in bed for a while...don't worry, you'll get to work on time, Clive. There's no doubt about that."

Gary's eyes darted furtively between Sharon and the old lady. "Um...it's Saturday," he said. "No work today."

The old lady laughed, holding her hand to her mouth. "Saturday? Oh, silly me. Of course, it is. Never mind. All the more reason for you to lie around in bed." She winked. "Newly-weds need plenty of time to get to know each other."

"Newly-weds?" Sharon frowned at Gary. "What's going on?"

"I don't know."

The old lady smiled, and placed the tray across their laps. It contained buttered toast, jam, hot coffee and two bowls of cereal, with freshly-cut fruit and a boiled egg each.

"I simply wanted to get breakfast for my favourite son and my very favourite daughter-in-law," she said, her eyes gleaming contentedly. "So they'll know how much I love them."

The old lady kissed Gary gently on the cheek before he could draw away, and then left the two of them alone, instructing them to relax and enjoy the morning. "I'm going to make a start on this house," she said. "It's an absolute shambles. I don't know, I take a holiday for a few days and, when I come back, nothing's where it should be. Still, not to worry. I know you young people have other things on your minds."

Gary sat unmoving after the door had closed behind the old lady, too stunned to react properly. He'd wanted to question her, but she'd been so earnest, so happy to be there, he couldn't bear to break the illusion. For her to be in the house — Gary and Sharon's house — seemed natural, and he felt anxious about upsetting her.

"Who is she, Gary?" Sharon touched him on the shoulder to focus his attention.

"I don't know, but she seems to feel she belongs here."

"She must be senile or something. This is our house. Why didn't you ask her to explain herself?"

"She thinks I'm her son."

"Gary, she's out there wandering around our house. A stranger. We've got to get rid of her. Go and tell her you're not her son and that she has to leave."

Gary folded his arms defiantly. "Not me. If you want to get rid of her, you do it."

Sharon scrambled out of bed. Her fuzzy black hair sprayed outward, giving her a wild look. "For God's sake!" she said as she grabbed her dressing-gown and swept out after the old lady.

A few minutes later she re-entered the bedroom, looking thoughtful. "Is she gone?" Gary queried.

Sharon collapsed into the bed next to him. "I couldn't do it. She was so concerned about me...Gary, I think maybe this *is* her house."

"What?"

"Remember Mr Sutherland? The man we bought it from? He said the house belonged to his mother, who'd been sent to a nursing home and didn't need it any more. She'd lived here for fifty years or something. His name was Clive and the old lady keeps calling you that."

"Maybe we can find out if Mrs Sutherland's gone missing?" Sharon nodded. Gary fossicked through his sock drawer. "I've got her son's number somewhere."

Just as Gary was about to hang up, convinced there

was no one home, Clive Sutherland answered the phone. He sounded puffed and was surprised when Gary told him who was calling. "Lucky you caught me," he said. "I was just on my way out."

Gary apologised, quickly outlining their problem.

"She's back there?" Clive Sutherland exclaimed, and added: "Stupid old cow!"

"We're not positive it's your mother."

"Who else would it be? She disappeared from the Home last Thursday...they've been looking for her everywhere. Didn't occur to me she'd go back to Collington. I wouldn't have thought she had the presence of mind. God, I hoped I'd seen the last of her."

"Oh...um...She thinks she still owns the house, and that, well...that I'm you."

"Me?"

"Her son. She called me Clive."

There was silence for a long moment, so long Gary began to wonder whether they'd been cut off. "Hello, are you there?"

"What's happening?" asked Sharon, nudging his elbow.

"Look," said Mr Sutherland suddenly, "She's not causing any trouble, is she?"

"No...not at all. As a matter of fact, she...um, made us breakfast in bed, and, at the moment, she's tidying up the house."

"Well, I can't fetch her right now. I've got a brokers' conference in Newcastle today, and an important lunch. I have to leave pronto. I'll get her on Tuesday. Latish."

"Tuesday? That's three days—"

"No problem with that, is there?"

"Um—"

"I mean, if there is, you can ring the cops and they can collect her. In fact, that might be the best idea...I don't like her being back in that bloody house. Might give her ideas."

Gary was horrified. He imagined the sweet little old lady being dragged from what she thought was her home by a couple of gruff policemen. The picture filled him with guilt. The policemen were shoving her into their wagon while she gazed back at Gary helplessly.

"We'll look after her," he said.

"You sure?" Mr Sutherland chuckled. "I should've guessed we'd have this problem eventually. She didn't want to leave the house, you know. Put up a bit of a fuss, but the old dear really couldn't handle it any more. Genevieve and I weren't about to move in to look after her."

"Couldn't you get somebody else?"

"Do you know what a live-in nurse costs these days?"

"She couldn't live with you?"

"I'm a busy man, too busy to have old ladies underfoot." He laughed, as though remembering the happy days of his childhood. "You know, they told me at the Home she'd sit in the lobby all day, dressed and packed up, ready for the bus to take her back to Collington. Kept saying her holiday was over. They'd put her to bed each night, but next day, she'd be in the lobby again. Nothing they said would convince her."

"That's sad."

"You think so? She bullied me for twenty-five years in that house of hers. Now it's her turn. Pity she can't just accept what's what, you know?"

After Sutherland hung up, Gary looked at Sharon helplessly. Once he'd explained what the old lady's son had said, she felt as sorry for her as Gary did.

"Her son must be a great disappointment," she said. "You did the right thing, Gary. She can stay here till Tuesday and *we'll* look after her."

Gary nodded. "It might be fun."

It was, too. Emma was a dear woman whose major concern seemed to be the welfare of her 'son' and 'daughter'. The mess that had filled the house gradually disappeared before Gary and Sharon's eyes, everything moving into recesses and cupboard space they hadn't known existed. During the afternoon, Emma organised Gary to clean the windows and fix up holes here and there in the ageing walls of the house — though, of course, she gave him instructions on how best to go about it. Sharon was directed to manhandle the kitchen into "fit shape for cooking", as the old lady put it.

Later, Sharon and Emma made curtains. "Heavens knows where my old ones got to," Emma said. "They were quite nice and there was no call for anyone to throw them out."

They sat down to a magnificent supper that evening. "One of my specialties," Emma said proudly as the 'newly-weds' tucked into the huge pile of roast lamb and vegetables that covered their plates. They drank wine — "once a week is good for the health," Emma explained — and relaxed to the music of Peter Dawson, the old lady's favourite. Afterwards, Emma reminisced about the happy days when she and Clive's father had been courting — summers of another age that made her happy and even more content.

That night, the noises that had kept Gary and Sharon awake so much began again, a rustling, scratching movement beneath the floorboards and, occasionally, to their horror, inside the roof. Gary felt his despair and helplessness returning, but Emma knew what to do. Gary heard her get up and bash the ceiling and floor with what was probably a broom-handle. "Be quiet!" she ordered. There was increased flurry and soon after that, silence.

"She got rid of them," whispered Sharon, incredulous.

"How does she do it?"

"She knows what's what, I guess."

But there was more to it than that, they knew. There was strength in her that transcended the ageing of her mind and body. Her willpower dominated the house and all its surroundings, both of which knew their place and, generally, kept to it. So long as there was someone there to look after forces from outside the home — bills, Council officers, repairmen — and someone who could do the actual physical things her ageing body forbade her from doing, she was in complete control. Gary and Sharon felt so safe during her visit that they couldn't discuss with each other the possibility of its ending.

She even controlled their neighbour, Mr Blewett.

Blewett was a large, red-faced man with a foul temper and a belief he was always right — the sort of bloke who tossed his junk into their yard and accused them of malicious injury when they attempted to toss it back. Everyone in the street hated him. Gary suspected he often stole their newspaper, and twice, Sharon had seen him sneaking into their overgrown veggie garden in the late evening to pinch cabbages and carrots. His pig-dog would dig up their flower beds, and when they tried to chase the animal away, it'd get nasty and chase *them* into the house. On the day Gary and Sharon unloaded their furniture, Mr Blewett harangued Gary for half an hour about the noise they were making, accusing them of being junkies polluting the neighbourhood with their modern goings-on.

"Flamin' outsiders!" he yelled. "Why don't ya stay in the city where ya belong? We only want decent folk in Green Street."

Twice, he called local police with a story about wild orgies when Gary and Sharon were simply playing music — and not very loudly at that. Luckily, the police knew what a ratbag he was and ignored him. Only last week he had threatened to come over and smash Gary's head in if he didn't "watch his manners". All Gary had done was wave good morning at him as he walked up the driveway.

Early on the Monday Emma was visiting, Mr Blewett began screaming over his fence at them. "Turn off that bloody racket!" he yelled, referring to the radio, which Emma had put on to listen to the breakfast show. "Man can't sleep. If you don't turn it off right now, I'm gonna come over and turn it off meself. With an axe! Ya hear me!" The axe was his favourite threat. Everyone in Green Street had been threatened with that axe.

Gary was getting dressed ready to head off for work — Sharon, worried about leaving Emma alone, called up her office and told them she wouldn't be in. They glanced at each other fearfully when they heard Mr

Blewett's rough voice, but Emma huffed in an exasperated way, mumbled, "Silly man!" and headed for the door.

"Emma!" said Gary, "where are you going?"

"To give that stupid man a piece of my mind." Before he could stop her, she was gone. Gary and Sharon rushed to the kitchen window and watched the fragile old lady approach the big, red-faced man. They were afraid for her. Mr Blewett was obviously surprised to see her; he stopped bellowing straight away and flushed a deeper red. Emma talked at him animatedly for a minute and then retraced her steps. Mr Blewett slunk back inside his house.

Gary and Sharon were amazed. "We won't be hearing from him again," was all that Emma said.

On Monday night, Sharon found Emma sobbing in the spare bedroom. She tip-toed up to her and put her arm around the old lady's shoulder. "What's the matter, Mrs Sutherland?" she asked.

"I'm afraid," Emma said weakly.

"You? Really? What are you afraid of?"

The old lady looked at Sharon with eyes full of tears. "All my things," she said. "They've disappeared. I don't know where they've gone. I'm scared of the people...the ones who took me away last time...I'm frightened they're going to come and take me away again. The bad man will come. The one who hates me. I'll have to go to the dark."

"Dark?"

"Dark and horrible. I hate it. Don't make me go."

"We won't let them take you anywhere," Sharon said without thinking.

"Won't you?"

Sharon swallowed. The old lady smiled encouragingly. "Of course not," Sharon said, feeling trapped.

"Of course not." Emma nodded to herself. "It would be an evil son and daughter who'd send their own mother away, wouldn't it?" Suddenly she gave Sharon a look that had stone in it.

Tuesday morning came like a brooding thunderstorm. Gary and Sharon knew Clive Sutherland would be arriving soon to collect Emma and take her back to the Home, and they couldn't bear to see her betrayed again. The thought of it made them anxious and fidgety. Sharon burst into unexplained tears at the slightest provocation. The old lady caught their mood and was nervous and glum.

"What are we going to do?" Sharon whispered to Gary.

"What can we do? She's not our mother and she has to go back."

Their anxiety was so great, by eleven they felt they couldn't wait there any longer. Both would have liked to go somewhere else — to work or just to the local shops — so they wouldn't have to deal with Clive Sutherland or the tragedy of Emma's departure. But they couldn't abandon her like that — even though abandoning her to Clive was what they must inevitably do.

Emma seemed to pick up on their mood. She came to

them when they least expected it and hugged them.

"It's only Clive," Emma said, suddenly more lucid than she'd been at any time over the past few days. "I'll make sure he doesn't steal anything. You can say goodbye to me now. That way, our stay together won't be sullied by memory of that ghastly man."

"We'll miss you," Sharon commented tearfully.

The old lady smiled. "I've loved living here with you. I love you and Gary...both. You're my children now."

"We'd really..." Gary said spontaneously, overcome, "we'd really like you to stay."

"I know you would, Gary. You are a good man. Knowing that gives me strength."

"Perhaps he'll let you stay."

The old lady's intense blue eyes studied him, wrinkles settling around them like webbing. "He won't. He's an evil, heartless goon. He doesn't love me. He doesn't want me to be happy."

"Surely you could get him to cooperate. He *is* your son."

Her jaw firmed. "No son of mine."

Gary gazed at her for a moment, then looked at Sharon, who shrugged. There was desperation in the shrug. He recognised it. In the few days the old lady had been with them, the atmosphere of their life had changed utterly. Deterioration was replaced by renewal, despair by hope. There was orderliness, not just to the house, but to their lives and thoughts that had never been there before, that, in fact, neither of them had been able to achieve since leaving their respective parental homes. What would happen without the old lady now? The creatures under the floorboards, sensing the departure of the force keeping them at bay, would begin their nightly scratchings; dust would settle, in thicker and thicker drifts; and Mr Blewett and his dog would descend upon them like predators.

"We've got to do something," Sharon said, as though reading his thoughts.

"What can we do?"

"Tell him to go away."

Gary knew, like the old lady, that it wouldn't work. There was something in Clive Sutherland that would insist the old lady should return to the powerless life she'd escaped from. He'd forced that life on her — perhaps because she had always been so powerful here, in her environment, and the child Clive had struggled resentfully against it. Now he sought revenge. Why should he let Gary and Sharon thwart him?

"What can we do?" muttered Gary again.

Suddenly, he felt the old lady's hand, firm now, touch his cheek. He looked at her, fearing what she was about to say. She smiled, her wrinkled, gray lips flushing with blood. "You need not worry," she whispered. "I'll wait upstairs. When he comes, send him to me. I'll deal with him."

"But—"

"No buts." The hardness was there; they couldn't resist her. "Send him to me, then go out."

"Out?"

"Shopping. Have a coffee. Can you do that?" Emma's eyes were like dark coals. "Give me two hours. When you return, it will all be over."

Clive Sutherland turned up later than they'd expected. He was large and sweating, his red face a puffy caricature of the old lady's. He was wearing an ill-fitting beige suit.

"You must be the ones that called me," he said, without proper introduction.

Gary nodded, unable to find words to speak.

"Sorry about this fuss." Sutherland glanced around almost furtively. "Hope you haven't been fretting. I've just come for some...personal items the old...dear left upstairs."

"Personal items?" queried Sharon.

"Yeah. They were left behind when we vacated the house. Hadn't realised before, but, you know, she'd made a note I...uh, they found when they went through her things—"

"Your mother—"

"I know, I know." Sutherland's look of weary sadness was like a bad stage performance. "She was crackers. Sad. Real sad. I'm sorry she bothered you folks. New house and all. Don't need pesky old ladies around, eh?"

"She was no trouble—"

"They found her body over near the highway, you know, a few kilometres from here." He shook his head theatrically. "She was hitch-hiking or something. Hit by a car, they reckon, three days ago or so. They haven't found the driver." He frowned, as though just thinking of something. "Friday night, they said. But you rang me about her on Saturday, so it had to be after you called. Fucking cops!" He narrowed his eyes at Gary. "You should've called me when she pissed off again, you know." Then he laughed. "Never mind though. Better you don't get dragged into the inquest, eh?"

Gary and Sharon looked at each other, disorientation like noxious fumes making them dizzy. What was he talking about?

"But she's not dead," whispered Gary.

"'Fraid so." Sutherland glanced up the stairs. "Didn't you know? Sorry. Point is, I realised we'd left something here...small box...when she moved out. In a sort of alcove behind the inbuilts apparently. Sentimental stuff, you know." He wiped away a perfectly dry tear. "All I got left now."

Gary frowned at him. "I think you're mistaken—"

Sutherland suddenly loomed over him. Gary and Sharon both cringed away. "Tell you what, I'll just go up, grab it and be on my way. No worries."

Before they could say anything, he was off, loping up the stairs two at a time, in complete disregard of his apparent unfitness. He disappeared into the old lady's bedroom with a harsh bang of the door.

Gary and Sharon looked from each other to the upstairs shadows and back again, not knowing what to do.

"Maybe we should call the police," Sharon said at last. "I think he's gone mad."

"No!"

They glanced up at the source of the voice. Emma had appeared at the top of the stairs. Her frail shadow hovered there, gesturing at them. She looked almost translucent in the gloom, like a figure in an old photo.

"Go out!" she said. "Go to the shops. Make sure you are seen."

"But Emma, we can't leave you—"

"Do what I say!" Her voice was irresistible.

They expected the house to be grim and empty when they got back, but, as they pulled into the drive, Emma appeared, wearing an apron and smiling happily.

"Did he change his mind?" Sharon asked, running up and hugging her.

The old lady patted both their cheeks. "I changed it for him." She smiled sweetly. "He's on the back veranda," she said, "waiting for you."

Gary's heart sank. He'd gone away hoping to avoid any further interaction with the horrible Clive Sutherland, only to return to find his worst fears realised. What could he do? What could he say? Maybe the old lady's son would hit him.

"He's mad," Gary said. "He claimed you were dead."

Emma smiled. "He came for his inheritance, that's all. An inheritance he hadn't known was waiting for him."

"I don't understand."

"I left a note for him. It said there was a box full of money in the alcove behind the cupboard."

"But there wasn't, was there?" asked Sharon.

"Oh, yes, dear." She patted Sharon's hair. "The box exists. Enough money to keep us in comfort for a long time to come. But it wasn't his. No. That money is for my dearest children."

"But—"

"We just have to get him out of our lives. Without

him, I can stay here forever."

"And he's on the back veranda?" Gary felt weak with nervous anxiety.

"I've done my bit. Now you must do yours."

"We can't make him do anything."

"I don't think he'll give you any trouble," Emma commented as she led them out.

Gary expected Clive Sutherland to be standing arrogantly against the backdrop of the extensive and overgrown garden, hands on hips, face sneering. But, at first, Gary couldn't even see him. Hope welled up. Maybe he'd left.

"He's lying over there," said Emma, pointing towards the top of the three-tiered stairs that led from the back yard. Sure enough, a big man was stretched out on the wooden planks, on his side, twisted slightly, his back toward them.

"Is he resting?" Sharon whispered as though afraid to wake him. Emma said nothing. Clive Sutherland didn't acknowledge their presence, even when their shoes began clumping across the old boards. He had a towel over his head. Maybe he had a headache.

"Hello, Mr Sutherland." Sharon did not approach him.

"He's dead," Emma said. The young woman looked around, puzzled, saw Emma's hardened face and paled.

"What do you mean?" Gary went towards Clive Sutherland, peering at him as though he were a strange insect. "Are you all right, Mr Sutherland?"

The big, silent man said nothing. He didn't seem to be breathing, but his coat was loose. Gary reached out and touched his hand, which was bent back over him.

As Gary's finger met Sutherland's skin, the young man grimaced and pulled away quickly. Then he noticed a large patch of blood spreading from under the towel out across the old wood. It was dripping through the cracks. "What happened to him?"

Emma pulled away the towel. Gary could see the problem then. Mr Sutherland had an axe buried in the front of his skull. There were little nodules of reddish brain matter gathered around the blade.

Sharon screamed, even though she'd stayed away and couldn't get the full effect of the sight. Gary nearly threw up. He staggered back.

"I thought a little tap on the head might calm him down," said the old lady. "He was getting hysterical."

Sharon, teetering on the edge of a precipice, made a little gasping noise. "Oh, my God," she said.

"It was merciful," Emma continued. "He was far too miserable to live."

Gary and Sharon glanced at each other, aghast and trembling. "Oh, Gary," the young woman whispered, her face white and sickly. "What are we going to do?"

"We'll have to tell the police."

"The police?"

"Yes," said Emma. "You will."

Gary glanced toward her. The old lady had that hard look on her face again — a look that plainly said *It's simple, my boy*. She no longer seemed frail. She'd filled out, wrinkles disappearing like ripples on a pond. "He would've ruined everything. This way, everyone wins. Even his wife will be glad to be rid of him."

"But..." spluttered Gary, sinking into a weather-beaten deckchair. "But...they'll arrest you."

Again, the old lady smiled. Her teeth seemed whiter than they'd been this morning. "Not me. They can't arrest me."

"But you killed him." A sudden thought struck Gary hard. "Or us. They might arrest us."

"They wouldn't arrest you. You two are so sweet...and you were seen this afternoon at the shops at the time he was killed. You *were* at the shops, weren't you?"

They both nodded.

"And you were seen?"

"We talked to Mrs Grahame from the Dentist's."

"There you are then. No, they won't arrest us." She lifted her hand and pointed with one bent, skeletal finger in the direction of their neighbour. "They might arrest Mr Blewett," she said. "He's a loud, violent man. They might arrest him."

Gary felt lightheaded. "But...why would they do that?"

The old lady nodded, wistful acknowledgement of a deeper cunning. "Oh, if they found out that the victim had been killed with Mr Blewett's axe. *And* if they found that he'd earlier gone over to Mr Blewett's house to complain about that annoying dog. Maybe someone heard them arguing."

"Who?" asked Sharon.

"Passers-by. What if passers-by heard them shouting at each other...just before—?" She gestured at the dead body.

"You mean Mr Sutherland and Mr Blewett had an argument?"

"No, dear, but what if it *sounded* as though they did?

It must have been them arguing. After all, you were away. And there was no one else here at the time." She nodded calmly. "Clearly, Mr Blewett followed this gentleman in a temper and used his axe. Only Mr Blewett's fingerprints are on the handle." The lady of the house smiled at them lovingly as the two young people huddled together, their spirits trembling under the gentle timbre of her voice. "Don't you worry about the details, dears. You're my children now, my good children. I won't let anything happen to you. Just do what I say, tell them what I tell you, and there'll be no more trouble. We can stay together forever." She smiled. "You understand?"

Gary and Sharon nodded slowly.

"That's good," she said, and Gary felt like one of the nocturnal creatures Emma could always subdue. He wanted to go and hide in a crevasse.

"After all," the old lady added. "I wouldn't want to think you didn't love me."

The dead man merely looked on.

# THE SLIMELIGHT, AND HOW TO STEP INTO IT

When Harry Freemaker came across a monstrosity in the lane off Queens Park Road, he knew, at last, his luck had changed for the better. He didn't realise his good fortune straight away, of course. At first, he was dead scared, fainting rather theatrically into the refuse from an overturned bin. He'd been picking a tentative course along Raleigh Lane after a night of boozing in the Queen's Bar, his belly and head shifting lazily under the liquid weight of a dozen or so beers. The laneway was dark, but Harry had never been scared of ghosts and murderers, except maybe when he was eight or so, and the shadows behind garbage bins and posts had been bigger than he was. Now, in his prime, there were few murderers who were bigger than Harry's twenty-five stone, and the insubstantiality of ghosts held few terrors for someone as fleshy as Harry.

If thoughts of spectres and killers didn't make him nervous, the idea of amorphous creatures from Outer Space did. Once, when Harry was younger, a school-buddy dropped a container of custard over his head right smack in the middle of the *The Blob* movie. Ever since, Harry had nurtured an aversion for living heaps of slime somewhere in the broom cupboard of his psyche, though he considered there wasn't much need to worry about the problem — amorphous creatures from Outer Space being largely confined to 1950s sci-fi films.

So, when Harry saw movement under the smeared glimmer thrown behind an overturned bin by distant streetlights, and went and looked, the sight of the massive greenish Slimeball froze his heart and made his sinuses pop. Blood rushed in his ears. A single eye, at least as big as Harry's hand, appeared out of the ooze and blinked at him. A mouth dripping with muck opened beneath it, making a few sounds that would have revealed themselves as the initial syllables of ordinary English words if Harry had managed to stay conscious long enough to hear them.

What the creature said was: "But soft! What light through yonder window breaks!" — and it said it with feeling; unfortunately, the creature's only available audience was catatonic before the third syllable was uttered.

When Harry awoke, the nightmare hadn't gone away. Somewhere deep in his delirium, he'd hoped the greenish lump of living slime was an alcoholic will-'o-the-wisp. No such luck. The thing grinned at him as he opened his eyes; when his mouth contorted into a scream, it said; "You're not gonna faint again, are you?" The voice sounded so normal, so familiar, it arrested Harry's terror on the spot and filled him with something resembling indigestion. The Slime-heap's words were formed immaculately, the inhuman lips moving like huge slabs of greasy bacon, but releasing the sound as smoothly as cream from a jug.

Another eye, a smaller one, had decided to join the first through the surrounding tide of ooze, wobbling uncertainly like a piece of fruit in a custard jelly, and though neither looked very stable, both seemed benign enough.

"Who are you?" said Harry, still lying flat on his back.

"I don't have a name." The creature burped and a fetid tang wisped toward Harry's nostrils.

"Where are you from then?"

"Somewhere dark. A place that doesn't have a name."

Harry tried not to notice the dripping and quivering of the creature's jellied flesh — if it *was* flesh. "What do you want?"

The Slime-thing sidled closer, the squirming globules that were its features rising and sinking through the ooze with no apparent rhythm. "I want to be a famous Shakespearean actor," it said. "And I need your help to do it."

Harry was not easily sold on the idea. Sure, it was clear enough the Slimeball wasn't going to make it as an actor on its own — Harry tried to imagine it playing Romeo or Hamlet...or even Richard the First...but his imagination didn't extend that far. Even ignoring this problem, how on earth could Harry help it achieve its ambition? Despite the fact Harry was a member of the South Coora Coora Amateur Dramatic Society, he never got any roles and was never given any responsibilities because he was too fat and ugly and interested in eating — and was a lousy actor to boot. And, if Harry couldn't make it because of his appearance, what chance did the Slime-thing have? Compared to the ugly creature, Harry looked like Robert Redford.

"Besides," explained Harry, sitting with his back wedged against the warehouse wall, "I only joined S.C.C.A.D.S. so I could perve on Wendy Smidmore in the change rooms."

"Oh, no you didn't." The thing extended a tentacle of translucent slime and tapped Harry on the nose. "You can't fool me, you know. You want to be an actor, you want fame, you want fortune. You hate being held in contempt by all the little people that surround you, though, naturally, you've given up admitting it to yourself long ago, because it's easier to give in to appetite and obesity than to struggle for acceptance, knowing it might be turned against you at any time, knowing, perhaps in the long run, the contempt is justified anyway. So, you fulfil your own self-loathing, your self-contempt...you wallow and give yourself sordid excuses for pottering around the edges of a life you'd love to make your own."

Harry nodded. It was true, brilliantly true. He didn't mind admitting the truth when dealing with something that was probably a figment of his imagination anyway. He *did* want to be a famous actor, someone people not only respected, but who entertained them, uplifted them, and changed their lives; someone who gave them meaning by expressing the true nobility of the human soul; someone in immortality's limelight. But why, in the ordinary course of events, would you admit to feelings like those? It was too ridiculous to contemplate. People would laugh.

"So?" he said. "What if I do?"

"So," said the creature, "you help me, and I'll help you. I'm a great actor — the best. A genius to rank with Lawrence Olivier, Ralph Richardson, Richard Burton..."

"You're a bloody slimeball, if you'll pardon me for saying so. How can you play Hamlet?"

"That's exactly the point. I can...with your help."

Harry knocked aside the Slimeball's jellyish tentacle, was repulsed by the slimy feel of it, and drew himself back against the wall. "How the hell can I help? I'm not a theatrical agent."

"You've got a body, and I need one." It globbed into motion, squishing backwards and forwards in front of Harry. "For God's sake, use your imagination, Harry! You've seen all those B-grade monster pictures. What does the invader from Outer Space do? It possesses a human being, of course. What else?"

"You're going to possess me!"

It pushed Harry's chest, forcing him back into a sitting position. "Relax! I can only take over your body if you let me. And you'll still own it anyway. We'll just be sharing it."

"And how does all this help *me*?"

"Ah! Therein lies the rub! Once I'm inside, you'll have my acting ability. I'll make you into a star before the year's out. You'll rocket to the top! Everyone will love you. You'll be adored!"

"Adored?" Harry considered the possibility. He'd never been adored, not that he was aware of anyway. His mother had tolerated him, even hugged him occasionally, but such spontaneous acts of affection had usually come only after the gin bottle was emptied and the soapies were over. She'd never been particularly willing to touch him when he was a kid; then his father had left home to live with a girl he'd met in the laundrette and, for a while, Harry had been a poor substitute. Once Harry developed pimples, she started locking herself in her bedroom with the TV on whenever he came home.

"How do you take me over then?" Harry said.

The Slime-thing smiled — at least, it looked like a smile, a wet, viscous slash in its heaving bulk. "That's the easy part, Harry my dear. You just eat me."

"Eat you?"

"Sure. I taste a bit raspberryish, I'm told."

How he managed the task, Harry couldn't say. Yet, oddly enough, once he got started, it was quite easy. The first few bites were the worst: the exquisite anticipation, revulsion lurking in each swallow, his awareness of the creature's eyes watching him as he lifted the mound of scooped up muck to his mouth, then the texture of slime on his tongue. But, as the living muck squished between his teeth, he discovered the taste was quite pleasant, very pleasant, in fact; and, if he asked the creature to sink its eyes out of sight, he forgot he was eating something sentient, and could pretend he was pigging out on a huge serving of raspberry jelly. Toward the end, he drifted into a Dionysian stupor and must have fallen asleep as the last morsel slid down his gullet. He remembered thinking that the creature was quite uniform in taste and consistency; he found no sign of eyes, nor mouth, nor bones, nor nasty gristly bits. Only jelly. Lots of jelly. That was just as well, he reckoned, because otherwise he might have involuntarily sicked up the masticated creature all over the alleyway.

Harry woke as the light of dawn granulated the air, pushing shadows into dim corners and turning the smog yellow. As his eyes opened, he looked around for evidence of the feast. There was nothing. He felt slightly bloated, that was all — probably the result of too much beer.

"'Struth," he muttered, pushing his bulk into a sitting position, "What a revolting nightmare!" He swayed onto his feet, brushing garbage from his clothes. I must have tripped on this stuff, he thought, tripped and then fallen asleep. What a nightmare!

He considered the adoration the dream-blob had offered him and drew himself up as though to deliver a speech. Instead of dramatic epigrams, a cough hacked from his lungs, setting his belly wobbling. It nearly knocked him down.

"Ridiculous!" he groaned, and heaved himself into motion. When he got to his flat, he went straight to bed; he felt too wretched to eat and the thought of doing anything physical drained the remaining strength from him instantly and completely. His sleep was dreamless.

When next he opened his eyes, he felt a lot better. The extra weight had left his belly, his head was clear, depression withdrawn like a retreating tide, leaving only a few minor stains in the sand to mark its passing. He had a shower, got dressed and decided in favour of breakfast — but there was nothing he wanted to eat in the fridge. The bacon looked disgustingly fatty, the piece of leftover pavlova reminded him of something he'd seen in the rubbish he'd slept on top of yesterday, and the eggs were off. He slammed the fridge door. That was when he caught sight of the notice pinned there by a magnet shaped like a hamburger:

### SOUTH COORA COORA
### AMATEUR DRAMATIC SOCIETY
### AUDITIONS
### MARCH 14 and 15 at 7.30pm

S.C.C.A.D.S. announces auditions for actors and actresses to take part in a production of Shakespeare's *Macbeth* (scheduled for June and July). All parts open. Ring Barbara on 254-6970 for details of audition pieces, or come to the Town Hall Theatre either day and you might end up a star!

### GIVE YOURSELF A GO!

Give yourself a go, Harry thought. Today was March 15. He pondered the coincidence of his having had that particular nightmare last night, and wondered whether it was an omen. Should he try out for this production? It'd be the first time he'd ever auditioned. Naturally, he wouldn't get Macbeth or what's-'is-name, Macbeth's nemesis, but maybe the other one...the one who ends up a ghost. Or, one of the bit parts...something fairly minor. He might have a chance.

*"Go for the lead!"*

Harry looked up, startled. The voice had come from...well, he couldn't tell for sure. The kitchen tidy maybe.

*"It's me, Harry. The Slimeball. I'm inside you."*

Harry looked askance at his stomach. "Oh, no. I'd just convinced myself it was all a nightmare and I wasn't going mad after all."

*"Nevertheless, it's me. And we're going for the lead — Macbeth, the murderer king. It's a great part."*

"I couldn't do it."

*"You won't have to — I'll be doing all the work. There'll be no problem. You know* Macbeth *off backwards."*

"I do not. I've never even read it."

*"You know it backwards! Believe me!"*

"I do not. And I don't intend to audition at all. I wouldn't have a chance. You might — or might not — be inside me, but either way, I'm still fat, awkward Harry, and no one in their right mind's gonna give me a part like that, or any other part either."

*"I make more of a difference than you think, Harry. Try it now. Do the 'Tomorrow and tomorrow and tomorrow' speech."*

"I don't know it."

*"You do."*

"I don't, for God's sake."

*"Try it, Harry. If you can't do it, I'll stop bugging you. If you can do it, you audition. What do you say?"*

Harry, blood boiling at the sheer nerve of this incorporeal voice, nodded, adopted a mock stance and made gulping noises. "See? Nothing!"

*"Just start, Harry. It goes 'Tomorrow and tomorrow and tomorrow creeps...'"*

Harry felt an instantaneous rush of verbiage leap up his throat, propelled from somewhere deep in his gut. "Tomorrow and tomorrow and tomorrow creeps in this petty pace from day to day, to the last syllable of recorded time. And all our yesterdays have lighted fools the way to dusty death." The words flowed easily, not simply remembered, but uttered with passion and despair — Macbeth's despair. "Out, out, brief candle! Life's but a walking shadow, a poor player that struts and frets his hour upon the stage, and then is heard no more. It is a tale told by an idiot, full of sound and fury, signifying nothing." Harry was non-plussed. "I do know it!"

*"You know the whole play,"* said the voice, and chuckled.

Somebody snickered when Harry came up to the table where Barbara Sharkey was taking down the names of those wishing to audition. "You want to audition?" she said. "What for?"

"For a part in *Macbeth*, what else?" replied Harry, glancing nervously around the foyer. Steve Rackmeyer was there, lounging against the tea-serving bar: handsome, slim and cool — a certainty for the lead role if ever there was one. He always got the male lead in

S.C.C.A.D.S. productions. People liked him. Wendy Smidmore was there, too, hovering around Steve. She would be Lady Macbeth no doubt, although Barbara herself would possibly want that role. Barbs was larger than Wendy, who was shapely and youthful; Barbs wasn't a very good actress, but she held the reins of political power within the theatre group, and generally got what she wanted. "They're open auditions, aren't they?" Harry whispered.

"Sure, Harry, sure. What role were you thinking of auditioning for?" Barbara looked at him from under her thick eyebrows, disapprovingly, as though she thought this inclination to challenge his part in the *status quo* quite vandalistic. "One of the soldiers?"

"Um, I was thinking of Macbeth himself."

"Macbeth?"

"I can try for it, can't I?" he said.

She looked at him, as if deciding whether or not he was joking. In fact, everyone within earshot was looking at him. He felt a suffocating urge to run away. *"Stick with it,"* said the Slime-thing's voice. *"Don't be put off by these jerks."*

"Okay, okay!"

"Pardon?" said Barbara.

"What do you want me to do?"

Barbara gestured uncertainly toward a table covered in photocopied extracts. "We're using audition pieces. You can just read them."

"No need for that," he muttered, and stalked through the door into the theatre.

🐾

They sent Harry onto stage third, which was last. Only three people were trying out for Macbeth. Steve Rackmeyer was first; watching him, Harry felt the irresistible futility of his Slime-appointed task. Rackmeyer wasn't brilliant or anything, he wasn't even particularly good, but he had style and grace and a track record that went back through successful productions for several years. Barbara rather fancied him. All during his performance she watched him with a slackness at the edge of her mouth that made her seem to be dribbling.

"He'll get her vote for sure," Harry said — as it turned out, Barbs was going to direct the show, so her vote meant a lot.

*"She's not the only one on the selection panel,"* commented the Slime-voice. *"And besides, she hasn't seen you yet. She might want to get into Rackmeyer's pants, but she'll want you as Macbeth even more."*

Colin Petrie, the local poultry supplier, went next; he was quite good, but reminded everyone of a chook worrying about the sky falling on its head. Suddenly, it was Harry's turn. "You're on, Freemaker," Barbs growled at him, "if you still want to go through with this."

*"Break a leg, Harry!"* said the voice inside him. *"I'll be with you all the way, old man. All the way."*

Harry closed his eyes and stood. He swallowed. Someone snickered, a few people choked back their comments; Harry involuntarily glanced up at Wendy Smidmore on the stage — she was reading in the Lady Macbeth parts — and noticed a look of sheer disgust on her face. He made it up the narrow stairs at the side and gazed down at the dimmed auditorium, trying to give features to the dark blotches that were the selection panel and the other auditionees. The space was vast and fearsome. "What bit do you want?" he managed to say, though his throat was dry and constricted.

"Have you got the audition sheet up there, Harry?"

"No, I won't need it. Just tell me which scene you want."

The whole theatre had gone quiet, waiting for him to entertain them, not in the way he would have liked, but by making a fool out of himself. "Right then. The scene where Macbeth's come from murdering the King. Start from where you speak, Wendy."

"Try not to explode, fatboy," a cry came from the darkened auditorium. "And we'll try not to laugh."

Harry was about to run off-stage when the sound of Wendy's voice saying "I heard the owl scream and the crickets cry. Did not you speak?" grabbed his thoughts in a fist of steel, pushing emotion into his heart, his eyes, his voice. He spun toward Wendy, and suddenly he was a Scottish warrior...

"You were absolutely amazing, Harry. I've never seen you like that before. I forgot who I was while you were speaking, forgot who you were. It was fantastic!"

Wendy Smidmore's enthusiasm stayed with him all week. He hugged it to his heart like a love letter and re-lived it continually. He remembered her face, alight with some emotion he couldn't put a name to...perhaps it was adoration — he wasn't in a position to tell. But the light in her eyes made him hot. For the first time in his life, he felt he could ask her out and not be mocked. He would have done so on the spot, but it was too soon. He needed to get used to the idea first.

He was offered the part of Macbeth, of course; they almost begged him to take it. Everyone was extremely enthusiastic. Even Steve Rackmeyer came up to him afterwards and shook his hand. "Congratulations, Harry," he said. "You're a rotten bastard; if I'd known what sort of a show you were gonna put on, I would've tried harder."

It was the beginning of a new life for Harry. Rehearsals started the next week, and it quickly became apparent Harry needed little direction; in fact, his interpretation of the character moulded the style of the whole production. Eventually, despite her essential arrogance, Barbara Sharkey sought Harry's advice; and Harry gave it freely, even humbly, the Slimeball whispering its instructions in his ear. Every rehearsal night was a gratifying exercise in being adored; the other actors watched him carefully, stunned by his power, even during single line deliveries. When they interacted with him on stage, they showed diffidence and respect. They sought his opinion — and, afterwards, asked him around to their houses, or to the hotel, or to the late night pizza joint, so they could talk to him, get enthusiastic with him, simply be with him. He was invited to S.C.C.A.D.S. parties, to private dinners, and was the centre of the in-crowd. Harry stopped eating and drinking so much (though he didn't lose any weight), went out in the sunlight more often, and was introduced to several prominent politicians.

He was recognised.

The usual rehearsal schedule of three months proved to be far too long. "The Scottish tragedy" was ready to go public in a month; in fact, cast and crew were itching to start. Under strong pressure from everyone, including Barbara Sharkey, the S.C.C.A.D.S. management committee pushed publicity coverage forward and announced a May 1st opening night. The group was restless with suppressed excitement. Dress rehearsals ran smoothly.

At their first public performance, Harry was even better than usual. No one had thought it possible. His thespian skills extracted good performances even from those members of the cast who couldn't perform to save their lives. To Harry, Wendy Smidmore was dazzling, her prettiness and innocence acting in delicious counterpoint to the ruthless pragmatism of her character's ambition. During the murder scene, Harry nearly lost his composure, getting distracted by a smile Wendy threw his way.

*"Cut it out, Harry!"* the jelly-voice shrieked.

Once, Wendy pressed up against him, speaking her lines in a husky whisper. His hand moved down the contours of her body, and, for a moment, she wasn't Lady Macbeth and he wasn't the usurping warrior; an electric current shot across the minimal distance between them.

"After the show, Harry," she hissed in his ear. Then they raged back into their Elizabethan personae.

The large crowd gave Harry a standing ovation. He stood before them, tears in his eyes. "We did it, Slime," he choked, leaving those nearest him to puzzle at his emotion. But the Slime-voice was silent.

At the opening night party, Harry was idolised, his entrance generating spontaneous applause. Everyone wanted to be recognised by him, spoken to, and he spent an hour just re-living the magnificence of his performance. Wendy came in wearing a slinky green dress, off-the-shoulder and open most of the way down her back. Her auburn hair was frizzed out and her eyes caught every spark of light in the room, capturing it and throwing it out again enhanced. Harry really did fall in love with her then. He wanted to go to her, but the crowd held him back.

Barbara Sharkey came up to him and kissed him demonstratively on the cheek. "Congratulations, Harry!" she said. "I've got some good news for you — bad news for us, I think."

"What do you mean?"

"Quentin Phipps was in the audience tonight. Theatre critic for the *Coora Coora Globe*. He loved your performance, Harry, wanted me to tell you that. He had to get back to the office so his review will be in tomorrow's issue. But he knows a lot of prominent people in the theatre world, Harry. Reckons he could get you an interview with one of the professional companies, if that's what you want. How's that grab you? Instant fame, eh?"

The news brought on another round of adulation from the crowd.

Later in the evening, his fans momentarily satisfied and drifting now into a late-night alcoholic stupor, Harry found Wendy sitting alone on a garden chair in the backyard, the breeze shifting her hair like reddish mist around her shoulders. Music pounded dully behind him. He watched her for a while without speaking, entranced by her melancholy and the sensuous curve of her neck; then he moved toward her, reaching out to touch her gently.

"*I'm sick of this, Harry!*" said the Slime suddenly, smashing Harry's silence, though not the girl's. "*Sick of the bloody fawning, the sycophancy, all the boring, contemptible mooning for that bloody tart you insist on indulging in. I wanna go home.*"

"Shut up, will you!" yelled Harry, before he could stop himself. Wendy glanced around, startled.

"Harry!"

Harry flushed. "I didn't mean you, Wendy, honest. It was...someone else." She nodded doubtfully.

"*She's stupid, Harry, and a crummy actress. Forget her. Let's go home!*"

"No!"

"Pardon?" said Wendy, slightly alarmed now.

"Nothing," replied Harry. "Wendy, I wanted to talk to you, to thank you for your efforts. I couldn't have done it without you."

"*What? You must be joking! You could've done it better without her. It's me you should thank!*"

She grinned wistfully. "That's nice, Harry. But it's not true. We're provincial and limited. You made it the great show it was." She reached out and touched him. Even through his sweater sleeve, Harry could feel the flow of excitement rushing from her fingers.

"*Give me a break, Harry! Look at her! She's ugly, she's clumsy. There's not an ounce of fat on her, and what's life without a bit of blubber?*"

"She's wonderful!"

Wendy drew back her hand. "Who is, Harry?"

"You are." Harry had broken into a sweat. A runnel of moisture trickled down the sensitive flesh on his side. His stomach quivered. "I've grown very close to you, Wendy. Very close. I care for you very much."

*"Oh, puke! I can't stand this. What's the matter with you, Harry? I offer you theatrical greatness and you fart around seducing this nobody, this small-town slut!"*

"I warn you!"

"Warn me?"

"Warn you...um...I'm out to get you, Wendy. I love you." The words came quickly, given audacity by Harry's sense that it could all go wrong any minute. The bloody Slime-thing was confusing him.

"Oh, Harry. I thought you'd never notice me." Wendy pressed herself against him; he felt her breasts against his chest, her thighs drawing him in.

*"Now I warn you, Harry,"* the Slime-voice said, cold and menacing. *"I haven't enjoyed any of this. I want to be a great actor, and I thought you could empathise with me enough to overcome the seductions of this backwater sewer-tank. I thought you wanted to be a great actor more than anything else. I thought the desire for it burnt in your soul."*

Harry's mouth trembled over Wendy's; his tongue searched for hers.

*"Bloody S.C.C.A.D.S! What philistines! That production has got to be the greatest travesty I've ever seen. Awful! I hated every minute of it. And you, you're holding me back, Harry! All you want is to fornicate with this thing that couldn't even play Lady Macbeth if her life depended on it! I thought you had vision. Well, I was obviously wrong."*

Harry was lost in the warmth of Wendy's closeness; he barely heard the bleatings of his suddenly-unwilling lodger.

*"Okay, then, that's it, Harry! It'll take me forever to get you out of this place — and there's no fame to be had in bloody South Coora Coora. I'm off!"*

Harry suddenly felt sick. A heaving groan rose from the depths of his stomach, churning his innards like a bad case of colic, muttering in his guts, making his intestines whimper. Pain jerked him away from Wendy.

"What's wrong, Harry?"

He'd gone white as though someone had doused him in baker's dough; his belly bloated like a huge roasting bread loaf. *The Slime-thing,* he thought desperately, *what did it say just then?*

"Sit down, Harry, you look awful. Probably the excitement."

*I'm off! I'm off!* That's what the voice had said. *I'm off!* "Oh, my God!" Harry muttered, feeling sudden panic bloat him further. It wasn't so much the Slimeball's departure that worried him, but how it might do it. Harry had seen *Alien*, had been nauseated along with everyone else as the foetal creature burst from the unfortunate spaceman's abdomen. He recalled the blood, the thrashing about, the agony. "Not that!' he yelled, "Oh, please, not that!"

*"Sorry, Harry,"* the Slime-voice said, *"But when you've gotta go, you've gotta go."*

"I might've known amorphous slime-creatures from Outer Space couldn't be trusted!" Harry shrieked; and threw up all over the back lawn.

Next morning, it was raining. Harry woke hearing the sound of water cascading down his bedroom window; the thud of it made his head ache. All that had happened last night flooded back — Wendy's friendliness, the Slime-creature's sudden temper tantrum, its decision to leave him, the awful heaving sickness in his gut, the first glob of green muck spewing from his mouth. Harry remembered seeing it strike the ground; it quivered as though adjusting to its renewed freedom. He remembered the tiny eye that surfaced from the muck to wink at him. He remembered Wendy screaming something. Then Harry had run. He'd run as more Slime-jelly was ejected from his throat; the miniature creatures had oozed along after him, joining up, getting bigger. He'd finally taken shelter in a reserve that backed onto the house where the S.C.C.A.D.S. celebration party was still in progress. In the distance, Wendy was yelling. Harry, wrenched by involuntary convulsions, sicked up a huge mass of green goo, so much that the twitching seemed to go on forever. The contortions were making his whole body ache.

Then it was over. The Slime-thing, whole again, loomed over the wasted Harry, who was weeping and drawn in upon himself on the ground, like a child who'd been punched repeatedly in the stomach by a school bully.

"Sorry, Harry, but you were a bit of a disappointment to me, you know," the Slime said. Harry just nodded. "Actually the whole business of acting was a bit of a disappointment. I'm beginning to wonder if it's worthwhile. Not much fun being stuck in someone's innards during a long rehearsal period, not to mention the inevitable extended run."

"What'll I do about the remaining performances of *Macbeth*? " Harry gasped out, the difficulties he must now face clarifying out of the misty frenzy of his shock.

"You'll be okay," the Slime said. "Not brilliant, but okay."

With that, it fell silent. Harry had been looking at the ground; when he glanced up, the thing was gone.

"Harry, open the door!"

It was Wendy. Harry forced himself to his feet, feeling as though the weight of the entire house was resting on his shoulders. He had no idea how long he'd been slouched there; the stiffness in his joints suggested it had been quite some time.

"Come on, Harry! Are you all right?"

He slumped against the door, listening to himself breathing in the wood.

"I'm not going to go away, Harry. If you don't answer me, I'll get the landlord to open up. I'm worried about you."

*Worried about you?* Being worried about was another new sensation for Harry. He didn't quite know what to make of it. What he did know was that something disgusting had happened on the night of *Macbeth*'s opening, right in front of Wendy, and, as a result, he no longer had the Slime-thing inside him. He was just

Harry now — fat, ugly Harry.

"Go away, Wendy," he said. "I'm okay. I just want to be left alone."

"Open the door, Harry."

Her voice was so insistent, his desire to see her so intense, he reached out before he could stop himself and released the catch. He stepped back as the door opened. Wendy peered in, frowning slightly.

"Harry?" she said, "What's happened to you?"

For a moment he was afraid to look. Then he glanced down at himself. His belly was smaller.

"I...um...don't know. I seem to have lost weight."

"Yeah. I think you have." She gripped his arm. "Are you really okay? You looked awful when you ran off last night. Positively green."

"I...I...threw up."

"I know. Too much grog, eh? Still, you've had time to get over it. I thought I'd call by to check on you. You want to come with me to the theatre?"

Harry felt his heart thud hollowly, once, and deflate like a leaky balloon. "Theatre?"

"Sure. We've got a performance in an hour. Have you forgotten?"

Ashamed, he turned away, moving for protection toward the kitchen. "I can't, Wendy. I can't get up on that stage again."

"What? Why not, Harry?"

What could he say? The heap of muck that was doing the acting has packed up its genuine talent and gone home? No, she'd think him mad, as well as an idiot. "I'll make a fool of myself. I can't act that well...ever again."

Wendy's hand rested on his shoulder. "I understand,

Harry. But it'll be okay. You'll be terrific. No one expects you to get better each show."

"No, you don't understand." His head slumped. He wanted to explain, but the only words he had were someone else's. "Had I but died an hour before this chance I had liv'd a blessed time: for, from this instant, there's nothing serious in mortality, all is but toys; renown and grace is dead, the wine of life is drawn..." He stopped, realising what he was saying. "Good God," he muttered, "I still know it."

"Of course you do. Did you think getting pissed would blot it all out?"

"No...but I never really knew it."

"Well, it sure sounded like you did to me." She hugged him. "Come on. We'll be late."

Maybe I *can* do it, he thought. He turned to Wendy, smiling wanly. What could happen? At worst, he'd fail. It didn't matter anymore. "OK, I'll give it a go," he said.

From The Coora Coora Globe:

THEATRICAL HIGHLIGHTS
QUENTIN PHIPPS

THE S.C.A.D.D.S. PRODUCTION of *Macbeth*, which is causing a sensation throughout town, has, for this critic at least, improved with every performance. Harry Freemaker's opening night portrayal of the murderer king was certainly a *tour de force*. But it seems to me that, since then, Freemaker has really settled into the role and is now bringing to it a mature and stunning elegance. His second-night Macbeth was not simply a villain caught on the cleft stick of his own ambition, but a man desperately struggling with the spectre of powerlessness. Freemaker's Macbeth has, for this critic, become more human...

# CASUAL VISITORS

I met George in the elevator on my way to the main convention room where special guest Harlan Ellison was giving an address. Ellison writes the sort of left-field sci-fi I enjoy; I was willing to leave Arthur C. Clarke and his school of future realism to the partying accountants and computer programmers clogging the bar. I was looking forward to Ellison's address, though a bit nervous about mingling with the hordes; I even had a copy of *The Fifth Head of Cerberus* for him to sign, if I got a chance to talk to him. I was planning to tell him it was for my son. "My son's name's Clyde," I was going to say, "And he's a big fan of yours,"— and if he asked me mine I was going to tell him it was John.

"Excuse me?" someone said suddenly, squinting around my arm, as though poking his head out from behind a tree. It was a thin, anxious-looking bloke I would have said was pushing fifty. He was grinning. His eyes seemed to take in only my Adam's apple. "It's really nice to meet you."

"Is it?" I said, somewhat bewildered.

"Sure. Is this your first time here?"

"In this lift?"

"In Australia!"

I frowned. "I was born here," I said, and wanted to add, "Not that it's any of your business." But my interrogator looked like he might disappear into his clothes if I did. I felt sorry for him.

"Were you?" he muttered, glancing away toward the buttons on the lift panel. After a moment, he added, "I thought you were American. You wrote all those *Star Trek* episodes."

He believed I was Harlan Ellison, that was obvious. Maybe I looked like Harlan Ellison — I'd never seen a picture of Ellison to know. I was about to laugh and tell him he'd made a mistake when I had a sudden vision of his humiliation — the shrinking, reddening desperation of someone whose self-esteem was so finely balanced that any public mockery would send him over the brink. This man, I thought, rarely goes into public places, and never talks to strangers. If I tell him he's made a fool of himself, he might have a heart attack. I didn't want the lift doors to open on the ground floor to reveal me standing over the body of a dead man.

"Oh," I said, "I am American. I emigrated." I noticed a slight American accent drifting over my words.

"Really?" He shuffled around so that he could face me at a better angle. "I hope you don't think I'm being forward."

"Not at all," I mumbled.

"Didn't you like it in Australia? Why did you leave?"

I shrugged, sifting through my mind for something plausible. "Sure I liked it here. I just had a better offer."

That sounded like business and business was something gentlemen didn't ask each other about. He shut up, though he looked like he wanted me to go on.

"What are you going to talk about for your lecture?" he asked finally.

"Um...oh, you know, this and that."

"Great!" he grinned. "Great! Would you sign my book for me?"

Suddenly there was a copy of *Dangerous Visions* — "You edited it, remember?" — thrust under my nose. I coughed. "I don't know..."

"Please!" he said, his eyes becoming cow-like. "It's for myself, I promise. My son hates science fiction."

I grabbed the book and the pen he'd produced. "My name's George," he said. I smiled and scribbled — in the sort of exuberant handwriting I thought Ellison might use — *To George, all the best with your life, Harlan Elison.*

"Here!" I said as the lift stopped on the ground floor. He wasn't dead; that, at least, was something. "I've got to go."

"Thank you. Thank you so very much."

I smiled in as American a fashion as I could and scurried off. After hiding out around a corner for five minutes or so, I sneaked toward the convention room and, by the time Ellison appeared, I'd forgotten all about George. The American author — dressed in the sort of padded, two-colour baseball jacket you'd expect an American to wear — talked about this and that for two hours: his writing, legal battles, his past, anecdotes about other authors, such as the time Gerry Pournelle burnt his tonsils on the chilli Ellison had been brewing. He had a strong yank accent, was very energetic in his movements, thunderously aggressive like a used-car salesmen, and gave off a powerfully physical air. Seemed like a nice enough bloke, humorous and down-to-earth. He doesn't look much like me though, I thought. Chunkier in build, bigger lips. And, once he referred to the place where he was born — in the States. I remember thinking George must have realised what an ass he'd made of himself by now. Poor guy.

Then this voice said: "Funny bloke, isn't he?" I glanced toward the source of the voice. There was George, staring at Ellison but obviously talking to me. He was gripping the book I'd signed.

He smiled. "I met him in the lift coming down here, you know. We had a bit of a chat."

For a moment, I thought the obvious: he'd seen me, realised his mistake and was letting me know I hadn't got away with anything after all. When I looked at him closely, I realised he meant exactly what he'd said. Sitting next to me was a coincidence. He'd told lots of people he'd talked to Harlan Ellison in the lift. I was just one of many. He looked at me and smiled. I held my breath, expecting him to recognise me.

"He wasn't nearly so funny in the lift," he said. "Must have written this speech especially, eh? I suppose they do that...famous people."

"Suppose so," I replied.

"And you know what?" he continued cheerily.

"What?"

He opened his copy of *Dangerous Visions* to the title page, where I'd signed it. "He misspelt his own name," he chuckled. "Look! He only put one 'l' in Ellison. Just shows you, eh...they're human like the rest of us." He laughed again, without any sign of self-consciousness.

So that's how I met George, through a mingled circumstance of accident and lie. The lie, which he never gave the slightest indication of having seen through, predisposed me to be nice to him when, otherwise, we might have wandered apart again after the crowd in the convention hall dispersed. We went and had a drink together, and that night, because he had come by train, hating every minute of it, I drove him home and went into his house for a cup of coffee. Gail looked like she thought I was a con man. This, of course, wasn't far from the truth. When George went to introduce us, he realised that he'd never asked my name; he flushed.

"John," I said, impulsively, my mind still on Harlan Ellison, "My name's John...John Waits." He called me John from then on; I was too embarrassed to tell him the truth.

I have to admit, I suppose, my relationship to Gail wasn't all that distant. She would often talk to me when George wasn't around. Sometimes she would talk to me when he *was* around, though she spoke as though he wasn't.

"George is just a big baby," she'd say. "I have to do everything for him. It's my opinion — and this is supported by everyone who knows him — it's my opinion he's retarded. Not mentally, you know, but emotionally. I mean, he still reads comics, at his age. Superman! Phaw! And do you think I can get him to show the slightest interest in the kids? No, he'd rather they disappeared down a wormhole or something. It's pathetic. Do you think you can get him to mow the lawn this weekend?"

George would sit to one side, reading, or drawing up plans, or making notes about something going on in his head — but he would never react to these criticisms. When Gail left the room, he'd talk to me though the conversation always fractured off from some apparent *non sequitor*. Something like: "They say people are sometimes drawn back from dying by familiar voices, even when they don't want to come back. What do you think?"

One day, Gail answered the door when I knocked. "George is down the backyard," she said. "Listen, John—"

"Actually, it's Clyde," I told her.

"Really? George has always reckoned it's John. Still, knowing George, there's nothing odd about that. He's had his head up his arse ever since I married him."

"It was just a mistake."

"You're right. Listen, Clyde, I want to ask you something." She took me into the lounge room, sat me down and plonked herself next to me. "Do you think I'm attractive...you know, sexually?"

I didn't know what to say. She suddenly looked like her daughter, who'd sit in the corner and make insinuating noises. "Um..." I said, "Sure."

"So do I. But George doesn't seem to notice me at all, no matter what I do. Has he said anything to you about me?"

"Not really."

"Didn't think so. We fuck all right, now and then, but it's like he's cleaning his teeth or something. Maybe I'm not doing it right. What'd you think?" Her eyes and lips were suddenly very moist; she put her hand on my thigh. "You'd know about women, right? Do you think I'm doing it okay?"

I shrugged. Her hand crept further up my leg. I couldn't help it — my penis stiffened. Gail noticed the bulge and grinned.

"Good," she said. "I want you to test me out."

There was nothing wrong with her technique. But it made me chatty, and I ended up telling her how I'd met George. She laughed when I explained about Harlan Ellison.

"That's great!" she said. "He loves that book. Shows it to everyone."

We chuckled together. I felt very guilty when she finally expelled me through the back door to see George. I wanted to go home, but she said he might find out I'd been there. So George and I discussed aerodynamics or something while sitting in the shed near the back fence, and then I left. I walked down the street to where my car was parked, coat collar turned up against a cold wind, even though it wasn't cold.

Next time I dropped around — a fortnight or so later, and then, only because Gail rang up and said I had to — George dragged me through to the lounge room where he showed me a film he'd recorded the Saturday before. It was *Earth Versus the Flying Saucers* — the old '50s invasion flick, where flying saucers annihilate most of Washington. I'd seen it, of course, but George wanted to watch it with me and enthuse.

"They're perfect!" he cried, bouncing on the lounge as the gleaming ellipsoid shapes rose from behind buildings over the heads of fleeing yanks. That was the beginning of his UFO phase; he read books on the subject, found pictures from sci-fi magazines and stuck them on the wall, and gathered together a collection of films that included *The Day the Earth Stood Still, Close Encounters of a Third Kind* and *War of the Worlds*. He watched them endlessly. It didn't come as a surprise to anyone when he suddenly announced he was going to build a flying saucer.

Of course, he didn't announce it as such; he just started. One Saturday, scaffolding appeared in the backyard — Gail grabbed me as I came in and said, "Find out what the hell he's doing, will you, Clyde?" I asked George, he told me, and I went back in and told Gail.

"For God's sake, why?" she yelled out the kitchen window at George, who was busy fitting all the lengths of piping together. He didn't answer, so she dragged me through to the bedroom and made very intense love to me. "He drives me crazy," she said afterwards. "Do something about it, will you, Clyde?"

What could I do? The whole business fascinated me, and, as the structure grew, taking on a classic disk shape, complete with convex top and bottom and portholes around the rim, I realised this wasn't just some passing fad on George's part, but, in a way none of us could understand, it was an expression of his innermost being. He built that flying saucer with a passion I'd never seen in him before, overcoming obstacles with a sort of zealous determination, showering it with a love he never gave to his family. He drew up plans, complete with mathematically precise structural measurements; he scavenged materials of all kinds and worked to mould them into the form he craved; he fitted them together with precision and an obsessive attention to detail. If something was needed — internal padding, say, or fibreglass for the portholes — he'd find it, no matter what.

"Fibreglass?" I commented one day. "A spacecraft wouldn't have fibreglass portholes. It wouldn't be strong enough."

"It doesn't matter," he said, unfazed. "The molecular reality of the thing is unimportant. It won't fly anyway. So long as it looks right."

He'd even worked out a rationale for the saucer's propulsion system. It was science fiction, of course, packed with the sort of jargonised technicalities that hard-core sci-fi always trundles out to explain the inexplicable, but it sounded right. I was impressed.

"There's a logic to the shape of these saucers that defies reason." He was hammering at the hull just where the curve was most extreme. "They have to be like this, John, even though more reasonable minds have since veered away from the fundamental saucer shape. Like in *Star Wars*."

"Well," I said, "it used to be argued it was an aerodynamically *appropriate* shape, like the '30s rocket — smooth and conical. But aerodynamics is only relevant when there's an atmosphere. In space, any shape's appropriate."

"Physically, sure. But not spiritually."

"Spiritually? What's spiritually got to do with science?"

"Saucers," he said, waggling his finger at me, "...are a spiritual phenomenon. Read Jung. UFOs represent the answer of the collective unconsciousness to our fears about ultimate annihilation. That's why there's so much fuss made over them these days."

"Sounds like bullshit to me."

He gazed at me intently. "Did you know that Bronze

Age Britons used to associate disk-shapes with divine revelation?"

His disk rested on a platform of rusted scaffolding that gave plenty of room to manoeuvre beneath it. By the time he'd completed the main outline of the thing, it was visible over the back fence and quite a distance along the highway. It embarrassed the hell out of everyone. At first they ignored it, suspecting that nothing would come of the idea. I could see them saying to themselves, "George'll tire of it. If I don't mention it, he'll stop." I'm sure they thought he was only doing it to draw attention to himself. But it didn't go away; the superstructure grew and grew, until it obstructed passage through most of the backyard. "I can't get at the fucking clothesline anymore," Gail said to me one day. "Can't you make him stop?"

On particularly hot evenings, George in his singlet tightening bolts, or slapping paint over curving panels, while a Portaflood spun shadows across the yard, his son Greg would stand near the house and yell abuse. I would've felt embarrassed for George, but he didn't even notice — not that he showed anyway.

One day, an officer from the Council turned up and demanded to see the saucer. He insisted it was an extension to the house, like a granny-flat, and said George should have sought Council permission before proceeding.

"It's not a granny-flat, it's a flying saucer," George insisted. "And it's not connected to the house."

The squat Council officer shuffled around the backyard, tapping at the saucer's hull as though he thought there might be a button somewhere that would make it instantly revert to its true shape and purpose.

"It's a granny-flat!" young Greg yelled, leaping out from a bush. "Dad's building it for me. He's gonna keep me locked in it. Tell him to pull it down!"

The officer frowned at Greg. He apparently thought isolating the boy was an action justifiable on compassionate grounds, because he suddenly nodded and said, "Okay, looks alright. There'll be no permission given for electrical connection though."

George looked pleased; everybody else looked dejected.

The beginning-of-the-end was an article that appeared in the local newspaper. The journalist responsible must have heard about the saucer from Council, because he turned up with a photographer a few days after the inspection, wanting an interview with George. Gail apparently told him to piss off, but George ignored her. He showed them around the saucer and talked to them for an hour or so. The article was headed: UFO LANDS IN BACKYARD, and quoted George as saying, "Sometimes I like to imagine I'm just visiting, and was brought here in this saucer. One day it might take me back."

Gail was ropeable. She yelled at me over the phone as though it was my fault, telling me they were getting odd calls from all sorts of loonies — even a couple of pensioners who wanted to book tickets on the saucer when George finally got it off the ground. I told her to calm down; they'd forget about it soon enough.

"God!" she said. "I think George might be right. Maybe he is from outer space — he's off the planet most of the time anyway."

"It'll blow over," I said.

A few days later she packed up and cleared out with the kids.

The first I knew of it was when I went over to see her, worried that I hadn't been very sympathetic. George answered the door, smiled wanly, and nodded for me to come in. "Something wrong?" I asked.

He shrugged. "The saucer's really coming along well."

"Great. Gail okay?"

"I guess so. She left."

I looked at him hard to see if he'd meant what I thought he did. "Left?" I said.

"With the kids. She said she'd had enough. In that note." He pointed offhandedly toward a piece of paper lying on the hall table. "You want to come down and see the saucer? I've just finished the undercarriage."

Before I could answer he was off, striding toward the back door. It slammed behind him. I picked up the note; written in Gail's tight, pedantic script, it read: "See ya, George. You win, after all these years. I just hope the saucer backflips straight up your bum. Don't worry about us — not that you would. We'll find somewhere to bed down. I've been having an affair. Maybe my lover will put me up."

I dropped the note and left, not bothering to say goodbye to George, or to look at his flying saucer. When I got home, Gail and the kids were watching TV in the front room. "How'd you get in?" I said.

Gail leapt up and hugged me. "Greg picked the lock," she said. "I've left George."

"I know. I read your note."

"How's he taking it?"

"Fine. He looked relieved."

She nodded resignedly. I could tell by the distance that appeared in her eyes she'd wanted a different answer; she didn't want to be here with me, she wanted to be with George. But, somehow, it had become impossible. I think we both knew what the truth of it was *she* hadn't left him, *he* had left her.

We argued about whether she should go back — though there was little fire in it. I felt oppressed by a cloud of inevitability, a real pea-soup fog that made me tread carefully because I couldn't see very far ahead. Guilt mingled in it like lumps of suspended coal dust. In the end, she stayed, at least for a while.

A week later, there was a phone call. Gail answered, said nothing, and handed the receiver to me. "It's George," she said.

I took it nervously, covering up the mouthpiece. "Does he know you answered?" I asked Gail. She shrugged.

"Hello?" George's thin voice leaked from the moulded plastic.

"Hi, George," I said. "Sorry to take so long."

"That's okay. I just wanted to tell you, the saucer's finished."

"The saucer?" I felt a surge of anger. "What's with this saucer, anyway? Why aren't you looking for Gail and the kids? They're your loved ones, for God's sake. Aren't you worried?"

"The saucer's the main thing—"

"The saucer's just shit. The bloody thing ruined your life, George."

He laughed. "My life was ruined long ago, Clyde. It's never amounted to much. I've been...very disappointed. With everything."

I said nothing but my sense of what was happening had gone for a tumble. Gail must have told him, I thought. She probably told him about Harlan Ellison, too. Shit. Poor guy.

"I was worried about Gail for a time," he said. "But it's worked out, and she'll be fine. Just fine."

"You can't be sure—"

"I am. Anyway I wanted to say goodbye, that's all. And thanks."

He hung up.

They never did find him, dead or alive. His flying saucer was still sitting in the backyard, all his clothes still in his cupboard — he hadn't even taken a clean pair of underpants. Eventually, Gail learnt he'd had the deeds to the house transferred solely to her name. She dismantled the flying saucer and sold the place. I was against it, and we fought, but she did it anyway. We didn't stay together long.

Naturally, I wonder what happened to George. I guess he went to another city and started a new life for himself under a different name. But, on nights like this, when the sky is clear and cold, I lie staring out my window through the dark lacework of the trees, and I imagine a different scenario:

*There's this spaceship flying along through the stratosphere, scanning the Earth for signs of intelligent life. Suddenly, as the ship passes over the western suburbs of Sydney, one of the crew says, "Hey! Down there! It's one of ours." The alien beings crowd around a porthole and point.*

*Finally one says: "Let's take a closer look!"*
*And George is waiting for them.*

# YOU'RE A SICK MAN, MR ANTWHISTLE

Mr Antwhistle is smiling.

I can see the curve of his lips mingle with shadows given off by the candle in front of him. His thin, white fingers are wrapped around a glass filled with amber liquid — a Scotch and dry probably.

I watch him, my eyes blurring away from the poet standing at the centre of the room's attention.

"Light without a source, the residue of thinking," says the poet, a very serious middle-aged woman with hair adhering to her scalp like soggy strips of newspaper.

Mr Antwhistle plays with the candle on his table. His fingers flutter close to the flame, teasing it then drawing away so the light follows his gesture. The pink of his tongue-tip peeks from between his lips.

The poet finishes; a few people clap. Mr Antwhistle glances up, nodding a brief appreciation. A young woman bearing a guitar replaces the poet. "I wrote this song after I had a vision of a different world, where we love all things," she says, smiling out of the corner of her mouth. "A world of peace." She begins playing the guitar.

Is Mr Antwhistle smiling again? I think so. But his

eyes, what I can see of them, are sad. He mumbles something not meant to be heard then returns to his dalliance with the candle flame.

Mr Antwhistle rarely comes to these weekly readings, maybe six times in the last six months. I'm always surprised when he does. He's short and dapper, and invariably wears a grey suit, though the conservative effect of that is mitigated somewhat by his shoes. Tonight, they are red with a white stripe. He looks like an accountant who feels he must be prepared to balance a ledger at a moment's notice, but who left his calculator at home in the hope no one will ask him to.

The first time he came, everyone drew back spontaneously, reacting to something in his manner — a certain weirdness that wasn't a product of his appearance or his speech. His pudgy face was unsmiling — not unfriendly, but cautious.

"Am I allowed in?" he said to Joan.

"Sure," she replied in her butchest voice. "It'll cost you three bucks if you're employed."

Mr Antwhistle nodded, drawing exactly three dollars from his coat pocket as though he'd had it there, ready. He shuffled through the passageway formed by a table and a row of Joan's gay friends, noticed the bar and went over to it. The two dozen people scattered around the room were silent; hardly anyone was watching him, but I couldn't help feeling those who weren't would have, if they'd understood why the pub had fallen so quiet.

"Scotch and dry please," Mr Antwhistle said to the bartender. His voice was smooth and sweet, with a sharp edge — like a Scotch and dry.

When he'd paid for his drink — the only one he would buy all evening — he went straight to the corner of the room near the front of the performance area. There's a good view of both the readers and the audience from that table; I think that's why he goes there. Every time, he sits in that spot. Once a young woman was occupying the table when Mr Antwhistle arrived. When she noticed Mr Antwhistle, she got up immediately and sat somewhere else. It was a coincidence, I guess, but it was weird anyway.

That was also the night Sandra Gallaway split up with her long-time boyfriend Eddie. It was a very noisy, public affair. Both of them were rather tense when they arrived, and, about halfway through, I noticed Sandra sending mental daggers after him whenever he got up to go to the bar or to talk to someone. Then, toward the end of the third bracket of readings — a tall guy with a myopic squint was intoning a prose piece about steel workers on strike — Eddie suddenly bellowed. "Bloody hell! What was that for?" His voice cut right across the room's attention and impaled the reader. The poor guy gasped, his rhythm lost.

"Don't yell at me, you shit!" That was Sandra. Everyone was watching them by now.

"Look, just shut up, will you! No one wants to hear from you."

"Especially Eddie-bloody-up-himself, eh?"

"I'll pay you back...I said that already. What do you want from me?"

She told him, and I guess it was a lot more interesting than the tall guy's prose piece because he eventually sat down. Joan announced a break though I'm not sure anyone was paying attention to her. Everyone was listening for Sandra. Joan tried to get them to calm down, but it was completely useless. Their voices, irrational with the sort of energy that concentrates in long-term relationships, carried through the renewed chatter of the crowd for at least half an hour. Finally, Sandra threw an ashtray at Eddie, who pushed over the table and might have thumped her in the face except that the bartender came over and suggested they continue the discussion elsewhere.

What interested me about it all was Mr Antwhistle's attention to every detail of the fracas. Once I realised what he was doing, I paid more attention to him than I did to Sandra and Eddie. He'd look up, smile in his odd way, maybe nod. Occasionally, his lips would move, trembling as though words were stealing over them like tiny insects.

Once I thought he said, "That's the sort of fatuous remark we've all come to expect from you." Immediately Eddie shouted, "That's just the sort of bloody fatuous remark I'd expect from you, Sandra dear." The coincidence made me uneasy; that uneasiness has lasted ever since.

On another occasion someone tried to move the piano that sits unused at the back near the toilets. This bloke and a mate got a bit carried away and the piano coasted out of control, gouging a huge hunk of plaster from the wall. The manager of the pub, who'd been morose all night, flew at them like a guard dog given a sudden glimpse of a burglar's exposed rump. He shouted about taking the cost of repairs out of their hide. A scuffle started in which at least a dozen people took part. Most of them were only yelling and screaming, but it caused quite a disturbance nevertheless. Mr Antwhistle was excited. He sat there through the whole thing, watching intently. He had the air of someone taking notes.

That night I spoke to him, making some throw-away remark about the incident. "Quite intriguing," he said. "Some quite unexpected reactions." I asked him his name. "Antwhistle," he replied, nodding gently, "Mr Antwhistle." He smiled, and the intensity in his eyes made me nervous. I moved away on a social pretext.

But, from then on, I watched him carefully. It's always the same: Mr Antwhistle arrives, sits in his corner, waits and watches, some disturbance starts, and, when it does, Mr Antwhistle hangs on every nuance.

Tonight I'm determined to find out something about him — something that can help make sense of the uneasiness he provokes. I want to be near him when whatever's going to happen happens, but, as yet, I haven't worked up the nerve.

Joan comes over and sits next to me, watching me watching Mr Antwhistle. "He's a bloody troublemaker," she says.

I feel uneasiness pounce like a cat onto my lap. "How can you say that?" I look at her eyes, which I'm surprised to find are on Mr Antwhistle. "He never does anything."

"He doesn't have to." She huffs noisily. "His type are always troublemakers."

"His type?"

She's up and away so she won't feel constrained to

answer. She stands out the front and tells everyone the woman singer will play some more of her tunes after a break. I think I hear someone groan.

Mr Antwhistle is sitting back in his chair, gazing around the room. Knots of people untie themselves and drift about, finding new entanglements. There's a group of local drinkers at the bar — unshaven men in greasy jeans, wearing an attitude of determined masculinity. They no doubt think our presence in their pub every Wednesday night is an intrusion. "Pretty exciting stuff, eh?" one says loudly to his mates. "I just love a quiet evenin' of poetry."

Mr Antwhistle sits straighter. That smile appears again, intensifying. I'm suddenly convinced a disturbance is about to begin; the certainty of it is as definite as my awareness of the middy in my hand. I move to Mr Antwhistle's table, sitting opposite him.

"Hi," I say, "Nice to see you again."

"Is it?" he says. His eyes are focussed over my shoulder.

"Sure. You're often here, and that's just great." The emptiness of my remark distracts me; I feel almost panicked. Flickering candle light makes his pupils seem large. "Why do you come here?" I blurt out.

"I like poetry." He shuffles sideways in his chair to see past me. "Do I know you, miss?"

"We met here, that's all."

"Oh."

Behind me, the local boys are getting louder. I glance over my shoulder and see Joan walking toward the bar. She's ignoring the men, keeping her eyes on the bartender and pulling her shoulders back defiantly.

I hear Mr Antwhistle say, "How about a tumble?" Almost immediately, like a fractured echo, one of the men says to Joan, "How about a tumble, honey?"

My heart pounding, I look at Mr Antwhistle though he's ignoring me, gazing toward the bar. His smile is growing and his eyes are almost completely black.

"How about a knuckle sandwich, jerk?" says Joan. The local boys oh and ah. One of them gushes, "Be still my beating heart!"

"You're all a bunch of prickless wonders," Mr Antwhistle whispers.

"Prickless wonders!" Joan's voice echoes from behind me.

The boys' replies are suddenly less jovial. They make coarse jokes about Joan being a dyke. Mr Antwhistle's intensity is now so great I can feel it like a heat. Though frightened of him, I reach out and grab his grey coatsleeve. "What are you doing?" I say.

The contact breaks his concentration. He jerks, a tremor twitching across his face and hands. His eyes latch onto me.

"Leave me alone!" he growls.

"Just stop it!" I shout, though my demand makes no sense to me. Mr Antwhistle frowns. At the bar I hear one of the men say, "Come on, let's get outa here! Might catch somethin'." There are sounds of agreement, and the moment of confrontation dissipates.

Mr Antwhistle is looking disappointed. He glances toward the bar then brings his eyes back to me. The pupils are normal now.

"I beg your pardon," he says. "I thought something was going on." He points over my shoulder. Silence falls between us. I can feel his mind prodding at me like a child exploring a sea-urchin in a rock-pool.

"You're a sick man, Mr Antwhistle," I mutter at last.

He nods thoughtfully.

# BONUS

# NOTE ON SCRUBBED

Sometimes stories grow from earlier stories, not exactly as sequels, but as alternative imaginings of a theme or concept.

'Scrubbed' was written during 2001 for the humorous speculative fiction anthology, *AustrAlien Absurdities*, edited by Chuck McKenzie and Tansy Raynor Roberts and published by Agog! Press. It, in turn, had grown from story fragments and notes I accumulated over many years as a research assistant for Professor Jim Hagan. The story's political satire reflects my reading of reports in 1920s and 1930s newspapers as well as *Hansard* — Australia's official transcription of Parliamentary debates. Some of the ideas expressed in those Parliamentary speeches were so absurd, and suggested a vision of reality that was so surreal, I found it too easy to imagine it all as part of an alien invasion that was another example of the ferality endemic to Australian history.

The title novella of this collection is forged from the same source material. 'Scrubbed' could be seen as some kind of prequel to 'Creeping in Reptile Flesh' in so far as its central character, Bindy Daymon, Member for the imaginary electorate of The Scrub and the author of *Feral Species of Australia*, is referred to in 'Creeping' as part of an earlier period of political chaos. His similarity to the eccentric politician of 'Creeping', Yipper

Cowling, should be obvious. They are clearly of the same species. And of course 'Creeping' offers a more detailed insight into Mytabin and the inhabitants of The Scrub.

I admit that there are differences and inconsistencies in the separate histories of the two stories — differences that make 'Scrubbed' a rather tenuous prequel. The two were not intended to exist together — but I like the fact that they expand on aspects of each other and that the surreal world they both depict can easily be seen as part of the same reality (which is, of course, our own). Apart from anything else, 'Scrubbed' might fill in some interesting gaps in the history of the Antipodean Invasion.

# SCRUBBED

## The Prophet

A single road meanders down from the hills. Patches of withered forest give way to dust and yellowing grass, where the sun sprays heat like malevolence over the ruddy roofs of the settlement there. Mining ceased operation long ago. The families who hang on do so out of habit, working uneconomical farms or living on social security payments that come from towns beyond the horizon.

The houses all look the same: square, peeling and warped, their frontage defined by unmoulded wooden poles, screen-doors and jaundiced curtains. They seem impermanent. Something wants the land they occupy; one day, it will claim it. The people know this without thought, and their listlessness grows in response. They have no purpose, waiting for a solution that never comes.

Pick a house, any house.

In this house, one summer afternoon, a wire door

flung open, violently slammed against the wall. Heat-haze squeezed in, settling indolently onto the lino.

"Keep that bloody kid quiet. I'm tryin' to sleep." The voice that came from the adjoining room was old and spiky with intolerance. Granddad hadn't worked since the mines closed down ten years before; he'd forgotten the energies of youth. There was, to him, something sinister in the boy, something that sent him fearfully into a doze or suspiciously into the folds of the out-dated weekly newspaper that reached them. His voice died off in mumbles.

The subject of his displeasure remained quietly in the centre of the kitchen for a moment, frowning. A woman who stood by the stove, stirring the greenish contents of a battered pot, looked at the boy, but said nothing.

Sending up a wave of dust, an old Bedford rattled by on the road outside, and the mangy dog down the street barked indignantly, its slumber disturbed.

The boy's face stretched as he walked toward his mother. "Hey, mum," he grinned, holding up a small flat object — very dirty and very dented — as an offering. "See what I found."

"Nice," said the woman, turning back to her pot. The township sprawled thinly across the valley in all directions, and, at the moment, she wished her small son anywhere, except here. She was too tired, it was too hot and he was too young.

"You didn't look, mum." The boy shuffled his feet.

"Yes, I did, dear."

"No, you didn't, mum."

"Oh, for...all right!" She turned around, looking without seeing. "Yes dear, very nice." She went back to her cooking.

"What is it, mum?"

"I don't know, dear."

"It belongs to a man I met out the back of Bradys'."

"I hope you didn't pinch it."

"Found it in the grass. Finders keepers, I reckon."

"Who was it? Jim Brady — drunk, I suppose."

"It weren't nobody. A stranger. But he don't want it — he's dead."

"He's what?"

"Dead, mum. He was only little and thin, with real long arms and legs, and he was sorta green. Sorta like a lizard. A space lizard, I reckon."

"Oh, I see."

"Bit burnt though."

"Who was?"

"The lizard man." The boy paused, then added with conviction: "He stank funny."

"I'm sure he did."

The boy wrinkled up his lips. "There was a dead chook near him too, and one of the lizard man's eyes was pecked out—"

"Not while I'm cooking, dear!"

"You don't think he was murdered, do ya, mum?"

"Go and play somewhere else, dear."

"Where do you reckon he might've come from?"

"I don't know, dear. Mars?"

The boy squealed in delight and zoomed around the room with his arms outspread, roaring like a jet. He smashed into the floor at his mother's feet. "I reckon that fallin' star the other night was his spaceship."

"It was a meteor, dear."

"Maybe he just got out of the spaceship before it exploded and he was comin' to look for help — maybe he wanted to eat a chook 'cause he was hungry. You don't think he eats boys, do ya?"

"Oh for Pete's sake...there's no such thing as green lizard men from outer space."

"What would you know? I saw it on telly once."

"Don't you use that tone with me, young man, or you'll get your bum kicked!"

Silence scored through their talk, underlain by the gurgle of the soup, the swish of the woman's spoon as she stirred, and the distant drone of the cicadas. After a while, the boy said: "What do you reckon this thing is?"

"Go outside and play with your green lizard man friend or something! I'm busy!"

("Where's my bloody soup?" from the outer room.)

"But he's dead."

"Yes dear."

"He is."

("Everything's goin' to the bloody dogs. I want my soup!")

"I said okay."

"I reckon it's some sorta weapon — a zap gun like in the comics."

"It didn't do him much good against the chook then, did it?" The boy was silent. *One point to me,* the woman thought.

"Maybe he liked chooks. Maybe it only zaps things he doesn't like."

"Just go outside, dear. I'm really not interested in your lizard man. Mummy doesn't want to play."

"Maybe I'll press one of these buttons and find out

what it does."

"Fine." She stirred the soup tensely and watched a fly battering itself to death on the window.

The kettle began shrieking. The sound was strident and made her teeth ache. She felt as though all the tension in her was being drawn out and sprayed across the walls.

"Mummy! I've pressed it now."

"Good!" she screamed.

A road tip-toes down the hills surrounding the valley scrubland. Bush gives way to rich soil and a carpet of grass, where the sun lies back like a resting traveller. It is very quiet.

At the crest of the hill, embedded in the earth by the side of the road, there stands a signpost. Rain and wind and sun have beaten against it, eroding its letters. It has become taciturn now, indicating with melancholy conviction the presence of someplace 1km—and pointing at the empty valley.


## The Coming

Beneath his face, there was a pool of something too thick to be water. He shifted his cheek muscles and was aware that the "something" oozed.

Afraid to retreat too quickly, he drew his face upward; the "something" sucked down on his skin, and then dripped. He could smell it. Just what he was afraid of. Cow shit.

He bolted upright and began to choke and splutter. "Bloody hell," he muttered, "Bloody hell!" A crow shrieked in his ear, an action that made him leap, slip and fall back into the wet, splattered cow shit; whereupon he began muttering "Bloody hell! Bloody hell!" all over again.

He looked around. He was in a paddock overgrown by weeds. Beyond the tops of huge paspallum stalks, he could see a wooden fence, and beyond that, another paddock. Further still, a blurry line of mountains. The mountains, neither very high nor very rocky, appeared to be heavily wooded, sporting a fringe of bared escarpment along their crown.

He pushed himself back up, prepared for the crow this time. When it squawked, somewhere in the paspallum, he tossed a lump of shit at the sound. A black shadow flapped up and away, reforming on the nearest fence. Its yellow eyes watched him.

"Piss off!" he yelled. The bird flapped, muttered a sound that might have been "Have a nice day!" and was gone.

The man stood, causing the valley he was in to lengthen toward the horizon. He gazed one way and then the other. He could only see beyond the field he was in by squinting, but it hardly mattered. Apart from the fences surrounding it, there was no sign of what he was looking for — human beings. Trees, shrubs, undulating fields, rocky outcrops, a cow or two — but no houses. No sheds. No dams or wind-mills. Nothing that people had made.

Wait.

There was something. He could just see it. Something. A bare ribbon of grey-brown that might have been a road. Couldn't tell from this distance. That was the way to head, no doubt. Toward the road. If it was a road. He took a step and felt squishy cow-manure ooze between his toes. He looked down in amazement. No shoes. No socks. No pants either, for that matter. Great, just great. He wasn't wearing any clothes at all.

What in God's name was he doing here, naked, with his face in a pile of shit? Had he been dumped? Did he fall from an aeroplane? Had his clothes been torn off him in a fit of passion? Perhaps he'd been making love in a haystack. Been caught by a jealous husband or angry father. Knocked out. Driven to this valley. He tried to remember, to remember anything. From ...when?...from before waking up with his face in cow shit. But there was nothing. Not only was he mystified about how he got here, he couldn't even remember his name or where he'd come from. Originally. He thought he could possibly remember his mother, but it was pretty vague. He had a memory of a woman stirring something, a shrieking kettle and "Good!" shouted angrily.

The valley itself remained nameless. Nor did any specific memories of the place come to mind. He began putting names to elements of the landscape. The scrubby undergrowth. The trees. They were eucalypts. Those others were, um, some sort of grevillea. Those, wattles. That spiky one with the odd red flowers, a banksia. They were all Australian natives at least...Ha! That was a name. Australia. A country. An island federation. Once a colony of Britain. And New South

Wales was part of Australia. Another name. New South Wales. The Premier State. So, he lived in New South Wales then. Well, maybe. He remembered New South Wales, but he didn't actually remember being born there. Or living there. Never mind.

He was suddenly so scared he staggered drunkenly. (Was that how he got where he was — in a drunken stupor?) Afraid of landing in another cow-pat — determined he would stay on his feet now he was on them — he made his way toward the fence, which was wooden and very old. Parts of it were rotted; other parts were so full of termite holes he could almost see through the palings. He reached out to support himself on the old hewn wood. To his surprise, shock even, the fence where he touched it crumbled away. It just lost its shape as though it was made of dust and his fingers had disturbed its tenuous hold on fence-reality. That might have been because he'd made contact with a particularly termite-ridden bit. But it didn't end there. He watched as the whole fence crumbled away, domino-collapsing into the distance. In a moment, there was no sign of the fence at all, anywhere on the field. It had faded like a ghost. Even the piles of dust that should have been left behind had disappeared into the grass.

The man shook, conscious that this only solid evidence of humanity, this fence, had become as unreal as the after-image of a dream. What could he do now? Would the same thing happen to him sooner or later? Was this country itself a dream? The sun that had sneaked out from behind hillcrests on his left, white-yellow and bleeding rivers of cloud, was too hot on his bare skin to be unreal, just as the grass under his feet was too spiky, the air too dusty, the cow shit too smelly.

"Is there anyone here?" he yelled, so violently his lungs hurt.

Nobody answered and his voice was sucked quickly along the length of the valley. Only a cow, many metres away, took any notice. It raised its head, looked at him and shat a steaming wad of muck onto the paddock.

Compulsively, taking the cow's actions as some kind of sign, the man walked forward, thinking that someone must own it. The cow watched him with big careless eyes until he was within a few feet, then it bellowed (the bellow sounded like "Have a nice day!') and started to plod away.

"Wait on!" said the man.

The cow stopped and gazed at him. He thought he heard it belch.

"Do you belong to anyone, eh? Where's home?" he asked.

"I was owned by a farmer once," mooed the cow, its lips twisting awkwardly, as though it wasn't used to speech (the man thought of some other names — 'Francis' and 'Mr Ed' — but he didn't know what they meant), "He disappeared. Long ago. Now I've gone wild."

"You can speak!"

"Of course I can't speak. I'm just a bloody cow. A bloody feral cow at that."

The man felt weak. He folded up his long legs and knelt next to the cow's still-warm droppings. Maybe it was his eyes. Could not seeing properly make you imagine cows speaking?

"But I can hear you!" he moaned.

"It's an illusion," the cow explained. It paused to chew. Then added: "Your mind's probably playing tricks."

"Is it?" The man rubbed his eyes. "I was afraid of that. I don't know where I am, you see, or even who I am. I don't know what I'm doing here."

"I've always found," said the cow, looking thoughtfully toward the hills, "that it's better not to worry about such things. Just be. And keep walking." It took its own advice and ambled toward the hills. Suddenly it stopped. "Yonder is a democracy," it said. "You can use it to your advantage."

"Can I?"

"Certainly."

The man sat down on the grass. "Really?" he said. Then he yelped and leapt up, rubbing his naked bottom. "Something bit me," he moaned.

"Bindii," commented the cow.

"Bindy?"

"A weed," explained the cow. "Prickly and irritating. It'll take over in the end." It yawned. "I'm going now," it added, walking away, "And, oh yeah, don't forget the road!"

Road? What road? The man looked around desperately, squinting into the sun, convinced that if there was a road, he mightn't be going mad after all. He saw the ambiguous smudge drawn through distant grass at the same moment he remembered it, and an intense relief made him clap his hands. It disappeared into and over the hill. "Thanks," he said to the cow, but it was already a long way off — too far to have travelled that distance in the time he'd been searching. He was about to chase after it, to see if it could still talk. Caution made him pause. Better not to know.

"I'm going," he said.

He had a long way to go, he was sure of that, and where he was going, the cows wouldn't say a thing.

## Bindy Daymon and the Scrub

Bindy Daymon first entered State Parliament as the member for Scrub, a thriving electorate that seemed to come into being miraculously, like a decree. I can show you the records. His nomination form, signed and witnessed. The *Herald's* account of his "startling" by-election victory — startling because he was a radical independent no one had heard of, and Scrub was rumoured to be so conservative, even the crows had voted for the Liberal Government three months before. Here, there's a photocopy from *NSW Parliamentary Debates* of Daymon's maiden speech in the Legislative Assembly — labelled "Mr Daymon (Scrub) [3.56]" — somewhat coffee-stained, because I've read over it and over it, trying to decide what exactly the man was getting at, and how what he said might have hinted at later events. Delivered in his windblown, rather ethereal, voice during a debate on something no one was particularly interested in, it was mostly about Scrub and Daymon's desires for its future.

"Of course New South Wales itself is Olympian in my ideals," he said, pounding his bony fist against the parliamentary benchtop and causing a microphone to cackle, "But Scrub — especially the glorious industrial towns centre of Mytabin — is the temple through which I will work my miracles of reform."

Yes, the evidence is concrete, a definitive mishmash of references and figures — but I'm here to tell you: Scrub is bogus, never existed.

Oh, I know, I know. Impossible, you say. You've read about it many times. You've seen the evidence. Well sure, it existed on maps all right, and in census records for most of the latter half of the twentieth century. Newspapers and books mentioned it in connection with its huge steelworks, which, according to official statistical records, accounted for 30 per cent of New South Wales' steel-products export market, and also, in connection with its port, Goninablink, the centre of a major industrial dispute during the 70s. (Yes, in this version of the legend, Scrub is a coastal region, despite the fact that other sources place it inland, about 250 kilometres west of Canberra.)

Could you write to the electors of Scrub? Sure. Last year, the electorate had 22 post offices at a time when POs other than central ones were becoming as scarce as koala bears. And it was even possible to get tourist brochures advertising the area's unique attractions. The mines. Mansgone Gorge. The surfing beach at Shimerra. Complete with photographs.

Okay, so you're sure Scrub exists. But have you ever been there? No. I didn't think so. As far as I can tell, nobody ever went there. I have no idea why, they simply never chose to, though it was always possible to find people who swore they had, despite a complete inability to remember what the place was like or what they did while enjoying its pleasures, so that, when you pressed them, they suddenly said: "Hang on, no. We were going to stay in Mytabin, but there was some trouble with accommodation..."

The *Four Corners* coverage of Bindy Daymon's by-election campaign showed modern pseudo-colonial buildings spread out in a dizzying city-plan, not unlike Canberra's, only smaller, against a vast industrial spiderweb littering the hills surrounding it. Grinning electors, screaming kids and local businessmen willing to nod on camera and mumble a few words in praise of Daymon's competence, dedication and superior drinking capacity: it was all there. But I can't find it. Scrub is nowhere.

Of course, the electorate does have a newspaper — the *Mytabin Gazette*. I've accumulated an almost complete set of its weekly issues since June 1987, *and* I've read them all. Several libraries, including the Mitchell Library in Sydney, have indicated that they hold the *Mytabin Gazette* from its first issue in 1922. Unfortunately, library staff have been either too busy or too confused to track down the whereabouts of this alleged microfilm — and, even if they do find it some day, what does it tell you about the reality of Scrub? Nothing, I insist, nothing. Newspapers are just newspapers. They lie. They are not the place itself.

You see my problem? I went to Central once and bought a ticket to North Mytabin station (it was clearly marked on State Rail timetables), but the train took me to the Victorian border before I realised we were never going to get there, no matter how many times I boarded the designated trains. When I complained to a guard, he said he thought, maybe, that particular line had been "rationalised".

But, for the time being, forget it. Never mind whether or not you were able to visit Scrub electorate, even if you'd wanted to. Assume the place! It's too important to doubt it was there, somewhere. Because it's back to Scrub that Bindy Daymon persistently harkened, whenever threatened by the depredations of his opposition or by the nagging, unavoidable spectre of lost ideals. He'd cough into his hand, take off his glasses and rub his eyes, sigh heavily — and a far-away look would creep over the intense clarity of his dark green gaze. "Scrub," he'd mutter, "I know it and it knows me. I'm part of it and it took part in my birth, right from scratch."

"You were born in Scrub somewhere?"

"My soul was. My body — that has a different ancestry."

Bindy Daymon once wrote a book — *Feral Species of Australia*. It was a voluminous, technical encyclopaedia of animals that aren't native to this country, creatures introduced since the white invasion, but which have gone wild here, a threat to the environment and the high ideals of white supremacy. Brumbies. Rabbits. Rats. Cats. Aphids. Codling Moths. Green blowies and white cabbage butterflies. Pet crocodiles berserk in the sewers. Pale, human phantoms haunting their own shadows beneath the antipodean sun.

Daymon's book was not a major contribution to the biological sciences, but it was full of pictures and sold quite well as a coffee-table item. His text was as imprecise and flowery as his speech, and, personally, I don't believe anyone ever read the thing all the way through. The bit that interested me was toward the end, after he'd discussed introduced pests, myxomatosis, the difference between dingoes and other wild dogs — and told his tale of the feral cats, which were so numerous in one area of the city that, at night, viewed from above, roads took on the appearance of a starry, Van Gogh sky.

From there, Daymon leads the theoretical reader to consider European lycanthropy as a metaphor for rebellion, and then, makes this statement: "Caucasian man in this country is an introduced species, and turns feral when his behaviour violates the integrity of the land's particular Nature. But is the wild figure which haunts the violated forests of Eden-Monaro a native to that place, or a darker, more ancient immigrant transported from the motherland? And are the woodchippers and the drivers of their tractors not themselves to be thought of as feral? Similarly, within his own society, a man may be considered feral if he violates its norms, but, if those norms are a violation of the country's aboriginal laws, then, to obey them, rather than to break them, is, on a higher level, an act of ferality."

Never mind the self-conscious didacticism and Daymon's turgid style. Focus on that hint of something monstrous, the "wild figure", lurking...where? In the forests, or in the spirits of the men who rape them, or both. What is the "wild figure"? What did Daymon believe in? Once, at a press conference, he said: "There's a monster roaming this country, and we brought it with us in the First Fleet — subdued, but eager to shatter old ties." We thought he was speaking figuratively, but now, I'm not so sure.

Coupled with his comments on lycanthropy, these words seem to indicate a belief that werewolves are at large in the backblocks of New South Wales, awaiting something. Perhaps, in the end, their time came. They found what they were looking for and dragged Bindy Daymon into the hinterland of his own philosophies.

Daymon's first day in Parliament has become part of the folklore of that institution. He was a tall, gangly man, moving along the Edwardian corridors like a marionette gone wild, limbs waving about in a tenuous rhythm that made him seem to be permanently edging toward disaster. People near him would become twitchy, expecting his arms and legs to entangle themselves at any moment and send him sprawling. You couldn't miss his approach. Jaunty thud thud thud of his thick, leather-soled shoes. The hum he'd generate, like an electric fan, singing airily. The nervous counterpoint shuffle of those walking with him. He'd turn the corner, a halo of burnt-umber hair hazing the air behind him.

If he knew you he'd yell, always from a distance: "How are you? Nice to see you. Not too civilised, I hope." Or some such thing.

On the day of his first appearance in the Legislative Assembly as the new independent member for Scrub, he turned up late, in the middle of a second-reading address, and shouted his apologies, at length, from the doorway of the House.

"Just sit down, ya mug!" screamed an older member on the Government backbenches (legend changes his identity according to the political climate).

"What?" crowed Daymon.

"I said..." yelled the old-timer, standing and poking his finger in Daymon's direction, "I said sit down. You look like a chattering camel dancing on its hind legs, for God's sake, and we didn't come here to see a bloody freak show."

At which juncture, Daymon strode across the floor and punched the venerable Member of Parliament's nose. Blood sprayed on the coats of nearby members. Daymon, then, went to his place, sat down, folded his arms and waited, as though nothing had happened. When no one said anything — except the injured MP, who was groaning in semi-conscious hysteria — Daymon remarked to the Assembly in general: "Please, carry on. I'm ready now."

Well, of course, a bit of a hoo-hah followed: medics were summoned, the Speaker babbled (only "I will not warn the honourable members again!" could be heard through his incoherence), the Clerk of the Assembly and his staff leered dangerously, journalists clambered and various members yelled at Daymon or his victim, the substance of their taunts dependent upon their political leanings.

Amidst the chaos, the Premier slithered out of his chair and tried his best to loom over Daymon, though he only succeeded in staring up at him fiercely. "You, you're a troublemaker, aren't you?" he said.

Puzzlement appeared on Daymon's face. "Troublemaker?" he muttered, as though testing the word.

"What's your name? Daymon? Well, I've got your number, Daymon, and I'll nail you to the shithouse wall if you try to undermine the sanctity of this place. *My Parliament!*"

Daymon pushed his glasses up his nose and stood. "Mr Premier," he said imperiously, "This is *not* your Parliament."

The Premier craned his neck further back in order to continue staring into Daymon's green eyes, which had become strangely luminescent, and felt a tendon tear at the top of his spine. He yowled. The Assembly suddenly stopped, riveted by the thought that Daymon might have decked the Premier. An illegal camera flashed from the press gallery.

"It's my neck!" the Premier screamed, "I've cricked my fucking neck!" Attendants helped the Premier, who was forced to stare at the lofty ceiling, as he hobbled out. The medics abandoned Daymon's first victim in order to take care of this far more influential one.

"I don't know what you're up to," whispered a short, balloon-man of an MP who yanked at Daymon's sleeve, "But I like it!" He laughed.

Someone moved an adjournment; the Speaker passed it without waiting for response from the other members, and stalked out in the Premier's wake. The old-timer with the bloodied nose crawled after him.

Stunned members expected, I guess, that something of a judicial nature would be done about Daymon and his gross breach of Standing Orders, but it transpired that the injured MP wouldn't press the matter and the Speaker quashed debate (thus initiating the rumour that the whole thing was a fraud, that both the MP and the Speaker were in cahoots with Daymon. Once I would've said this theory was a bit fantastic, except that in hindsight, everything about Daymon seems essentially fantastic). At any rate, during the time it took the House to regain its composure, Daymon sat in his place, smiling ineffably.

The second-reading address started again from the top. Afterwards, even the journalists had trouble remembering whom Daymon had slugged, though that Daymon had done the slugging was clearly enshrined in legend. Of course, the incident never appeared in *Hansard*; officially forgotten, it instead entered Parliamentary folklore and public imagination almost immediately. A contraband portrait of the Premier cringing in Daymon's shadow and yowling in discomfort mysteriously appeared on the Premier's desk. Others were pinned to the noticeboard in the foyer of Parliament House and took up most of the front page of several major newspapers by the end of the week. Daymon had made his mark.

That afternoon, the debate occurred in which Daymon gave his maiden speech. The usual arguments and insults were being bandied about when Daymon received the nod from the Speaker.

He rose endlessly and the whole House fell silent.

Smiling, as though at something about a metre to the right and upward of the Speaker's chair, Daymon cleared his throat.

"Mr Speaker and honourable members," he said...and stopped.

Everyone waited. Several MPs well-known for their garrulous manner ahemmed as though about to make some sardonic remark, but memory of the morning's violence made them cautious. Finally, a journalist, no doubt feeling safe enough in the public gallery, yelled: "Who pressed the pause button?"

Daymon looked around and smiled.

"As I rise to speak," he said, pushing his glasses further up the bridge of his nose, "newly a member of the New South Wales Legislative Assembly, representing the good people of Scrub—"

"They need a scrub 'cause they're a bunch of dirty scoundrels, eh?" someone rashly interjected. "Like their representative?"

"—I am conscious of the fact that not all those who find a place within these walls are worthy to hold such a high and responsible office. Some are bloody idiots who do not have the intelligence that allows them to differentiate between a Parliamentary motion and the sort of pollutants regularly spilling into our coastal waters and out of their own foul mouths."

Daymon glared in the general direction of the interjector while the House tittered.

"Mr Speaker," said a voice, "is the honourable member for...what was it? Scrub? Is he ever going to speak to the issue?"

The Speaker looked glum. "Perhaps the honourable member for Tooly-Ooly would hold it in mind that this *is* the honourable member for Scrub's maiden speech, and, therefore, allow him his customary silence. I'm sure he will speak to the issue shortly."

"Thank you, Mr Speaker." Daymon straightened his suit-coat and nudged his glasses. "I would like to do two things at this time: one, make my maiden speech as a tribute to my electorate of Scrub, and two, direct remarks specifically toward the discussion presently underway."

There were a few barely suppressed groans from various parts of the House, which Daymon ignored.

"I am indebted to the dedicated members of my team. They are, of course, merely symbolic of Scrub's earnest and forthright voters — but they are also themselves the pillars on which my success was built. Let me name them: my campaign director, Gabriel Johnson; my operations director, Michael Watergrass; my finance director, Ithuriel Smith; and, of course, God, without whose existence, I would be nothing."

This caused a certain incredulity to rustle through the Assembly. Aulder Pugwandell, Member for Urydimbar, who had been absent from the morning's session but had come after lunch to see what this arrogant newcomer might do next, wrote something on a piece of paper and passed it to Samantha Hersey, member for West Sydney, who laughed. Daymon did not look at them.

"Scrub electorate is a place which not only I, its representative, but also the entire Parliament, should look to and protect, whatever our origins. It is industrial and pastoral, metropolitan and rural, a region of sunshine and rain, of wealth and poverty; within Scrub, ignorance and enlightenment, greed and altruism, science and art, exploitation and nurture, apathy and zeal contend — it is a microcosm of Australian, perhaps even global, society which can provide a useful background for the legislation this Parliament so carelessly initiates and sends out willy-nilly into the world, most often little knowing whether or not the people want it, whether such Laws are not rather an imposition and a burden to the very electors we thus so capriciously represent."

Daymon did not pause for breath, though the effort of listening to that sentence would have left the Chamber silent even if he had.

"If you, the governors of this State, come to understand and revere Scrub, then you will understand and revere all of New South Wales, indeed, all of Australia. For they are one and the same."

"Pretentious ratbag!" someone muttered at last, but Daymon, if he heard, was too wound up. He drew a complex, wordy portrait of the electorate and its towns, mentioning, it was claimed afterwards (only semi-facetiously), every inhabitant from Bob Montey, the corporate mogul who owned 70 per cent of the multi-national Mytabin steelworks, to Joan Fairweather, the aging half-caste who consistently got herself thrown in gaol for daubing her muddy handprints over the duco of whiter citizens' cars.

Daymon spoke of Scrub's weather, industries, arts, educational and welfare needs, economic future, road systems, debts, unemployment and other social problems. Also its murder rate. He went on to describe, in ecstatic detail, the beauty of Scrub's threatened rainforests and (later) its polluted beaches. Those listening, of whom there were very few, could not decide afterwards at what point he finished with Scrub and began on New South Wales itself. It hardly mattered. Even in reading his speech, one is stupefied to such an extent that accurate differentiation becomes impossible.

"I am neither provincial nor reactionary," he said,

fixing the eye of a Government backbencher who had leaned toward his neighbour and whispered "provincial" and "reactionary" like a threat in his ear. "Only prophetic. I am, first and foremost, an Australian, and my aims are those which, in benefiting my electorate of Scrub, will benefit all of Australia, every man, woman, and child. Who are you to sit there and snidely whisper? I speak out, forthrightly, openly, honestly. Those who do not listen will be the first to experience the vengeance of Azrael, Angel of Death, when wild things emerge once more from the heart's scrubland, to tear the soul of ferality from the corpse of its own desolation! You will listen, and you will listen in silence!"

From that point on, there was no question of interruption, all being compelled by the words that poured from Daymon's lips like the hypnotic power of a Svengalian high-priest. First his green eyes, then his skin began to blaze, as his passion rose, igniting an inner fire of righteous conviction that threatened to catch on the benches and sweep along the polished wood and leather, feeding on reports and memos and illuminating the Assembly like a druidic torch. As he spoke of the Government's failure to address fundamental issues of spiritual enlightenment — rather it added, he said, to the sum of national decay through its regressive policies and totalitarian denial of a grassroot passion for justice — lights throughout the old Parliamentary building flickered; and a thunderclap, like the shockwave of an earthquake, turned solid matter everywhere to tremulous echoes of itself. Lightning cracked the air, visible even through walls and ornamental ceilings. The Assembly was plunged into thick darkness.

"Power failure," someone whispered.

Daymon's voice went on, clear as though his microphone alone were unaffected. It was like an incantation, a chant for the beginning of a bloody harvest.

"Rape the environment!" he screamed from the black. "Deny the poor! Tell the common people they are worthless! Spit upon virtue and art! Send democracy into exile! Let corporate lust dispossess us of the possibility of love! Do all these things, give strength to these dreams of Power, and what are you left with?"

*Silence and darkness.*

The moment stretched on for what seemed like an eternity, but nobody moved within the Assembly. Then, suddenly, woosh! Light strikes back and shadows dart for cover after-effects of concussion linger briefly before reverberating into the calm tones of Daymon's speech.

"...economic needs of Scrub and, beyond them, the needs of the State: the destruction of the education system, economic failure, environmental degradation — these are priority issues which the present Government fails to address, in some cases, deliberately obfuscating the true significance of facts we can see emblazoned every day in the papers, the world around us..."

MPs looked at each other puzzled, confused. Some thought they'd nodded off, others that Daymon's microphone had, after all, been silenced and the words they swore they'd heard were simply the echoes of thunder. In a few moments, Daymon's invective had been all but forgotten.

But, not in the mind of Aulder Pugwandell. The one-time journalist, touted future leader of the Party, could not rid himself of either the words or the emotions. They sat in him, hard and ulcer-inflaming, awaiting digestion without hope of it. He slumped, nodded when addressed, waving away enquiries from his colleagues.

"What was it Daymon said?" Samantha Hersey muttered at him, as a Government spokesman eulogised his administration's Budgetary foresight, "Something about corporate lust?" Pugwandell looked at her blankly.

"I meant to write it down," the member for West Sydney continued, "Could have used it. I hope the journos were paying attention. I think I missed a bit." Pugwandell said nothing. Hersey nudged him jovially. "What's up with you?"

"Nothing." Pugwandell glanced toward Daymon, but, for a moment, couldn't find him. He seemed to have blurred away, a ghost. He blinked. No, Daymon was there. In his seat. Arms folded. Smug. Cheerful. Pugwandell felt as though he'd been personally threatened. "I don't like him," he said at last.

Hersey shrugged. "I don't know, seems like he might bring a bit of life to the place. An eccentric, don't you think? They're always good for a laugh. But harmless. Yeah, harmless."

"Harmless? He's dangerous, Samantha."

"To whom? You mean to the Party?"

"Not exactly."

"To whom then?"

Pugwandell didn't answer.

## Feral Business in the Front Benches

Of course, I'm not actually sure how much of the following exchange is true. A lot of it's in *Hansard*, and you could read the account there, but I've elaborated it here and I think, in the end, it doesn't really matter whether it's true or not, or to what extent. Truth becomes a little irrelevant in circumstances like these.

Certainly in the weeks that followed the Apocalypse, no reports concerning what I'm about to tell you made it into the newspapers. Everyone was too busy with what seemed like Great Matters to bother about politicians. In fact, the Right Honourable Daymon's subsequent disappearance was put down to his being in the House when the giant demon-lizard from the Outer Darkness trod on it. A junior reporter for the *Telegraph-Mirror* even identified a particularly large red-brown smudge as the ex-Member for Scrub; it was rather hairy and its one unsquashed limb was dog-legged, but it was wearing a Bond's singlet stamped "Mytabin YMCA" on the back, so the identification was relatively certain. Detail I was given about the emergency sitting that preceded the Apocalypse was sketchy, but, if you'd been a fly on the wall — or in the public gallery — you might have witnessed the following scene:

"Why was this bloody sitting called anyway?" said Premier Daymon, the Member for Scrub, leaning forward and ruffling memos on the huge table facing the Opposition benches. He grabbed something that looked like an agenda. "Says here it was a decision of the Chair. What's this about, Mr Speaker?"

Jimmy McGlitch, the Speaker, wheezed and pointed

toward a thick bundle of paper. "This document has been tabled by...someone or other."

The Premier read the top page of the bundle; his face went even redder than normal. "Where the fuck did this come from?"

"Language!" yelled someone from the Independent Moralist Party.

"Better be important," the Opposition leader — Sir Harry Filby — muttered into a cup of what looked like molasses — or coagulated blood, perhaps. He hadn't noticed the Premier's reaction. "I was busy."

"Order! Order!" muttered Jimmy McGlitch.

"It's not important, not at all." The Premier laughed falsely. "We might as well go home."

The few other MPs who'd gathered that day watched this interplay, Government members nervously, Opposition members curiously. Aulder Pugwandell picked at his teeth with the tip of a pencil, scowling the whole time in a vengeful manner.

"I want to read that document!" yelled Sir Filby.

"Fuck off!" yelled the Premier. "Where'd this stuff come from, Jimmy? Who the bloody hell tabled it? I want an explanation."

Aulder Pugwandell, now the independent Member for Tooly-Ooly, saw cunning and a touch of panic twitch across the Premier's face and smiled to himself.

Jimmy shrugged. "Anyone want to speak on the motion?"

"What motion?" screamed the Premier.

"No-confidence motion," the Speaker said, "...against you."

"What? I should have had notice."

The House was suddenly in an uproar.

"What's this about, Bindy?" whispered the Deputy Premier to the Premier.

The Premier said nothing.

The Deputy Premier, who was shorter than the Premier and less cadaver-like, cleared her throat and shuffled anxiously. "Um...I think you should have told us something was up."

"I didn't expect it to come out till later." The Premier folded his spindly arms across his chest and glared at the Member for Tooly-Ooly. "But who cares? There's maybe an hour in it."

"Mr Speaker," said Pugwandell suddenly, his voice so penetrating that everyone fell silent immediately. "May I speak?"

"Please do."

Duncan Kandinski, the Treasurer, who hated Premier Daymon for reasons never made entirely clear — though the fact that vast areas of his electorate kept disappearing into Daymon's, at least administratively (despite the fact that the two seats didn't seem to share any common boundaries), might have had something to do with it — scowled. "Perhaps this should be clarified, Mr Premier?"

Daymon grinned. "Sure," he said carelessly. "It doesn't matter anyway."

Pugwandell frowned. Didn't matter? "It was me that tabled the documentation," he blurted.

Again, there was uproar. The Speaker pounded away with his gavel. Only when someone yelled, "You're a bloody ratbag, Pugwandell! A traitor!" did relative quiet fall.

Pugwandell scowled and rubbed his double chin. "I'm not the ratbag," he said. "The real ratbaggery emanates from the highest levels of responsibility. You lot threw me out of the Party to take on this...this...ghoul. So whatever happens, you deserve it."

The Minister for Education ruffled her thick mane of red hair, emanating wrath. "Save the rhetoric for those who respond to it! I knew it was a mistake to treat you as an equal. You should have been ejected from Parliament long ago."

Pugwandell wrinkled his thick lips. "Daymon's the one should be thrown out!"

"Mine is the safest seat in the state," the Premier remarked calmly.

"For God's sake, what's it about, Duncan?" Eddie Olivetti, Opposition Member for Someplace, came around the central table and snatched the paper out of the Treasurer's hand. He began to read it. "15 October, last year...to Zedlines-Inferno Pty Ltd. What's that?"

"A demolition company," explained the Premier.

"Keep reading," muttered Pugwandell.

"Don't you dare!" roared the Premier suddenly, in a sudden change of demeanour. He leapt to his feet and began chasing Olivetti in a loping stride around the Chamber. Everyone was yelling. The Speaker banged his gavel some more.

"'In response to suggestions made Thursday last,'" Olivetti read, while leaping over the front benches, "'I think the State would be more than willing to participate in your scheme to de-construct Sydney along post-modern lines drawn up at that meeting...' De-construct Sydney? What meeting, Mr Premier?"

"Read!" screamed Pugwandell.

"No," yelled the Premier. "I want to read it. It's my project."

"'...given that the Assembly and the Upper House will provide all the appropriate legislation. Monies will be approved by the Treasury, outwardly through funding for extension to the Harbour Tunnel and other public works...'. This never went through the House."

"I protest," yelled the Premier, finally collapsing, utterly winded, into an empty seat toward the back of the back-benches. He was getting old. At the beginning, he could have chased MPs around the Chamber all day and still had enough energy at the end to punch them on the nose. Observers might have remarked that he seemed to have become broader across the shoulders and more hunched. Teeth were protruding through his lower lip.

Pugwandell thumped the table in front of him with his knotty finger. He was holding some other papers. "I have figures to prove that the money's already gone. And into accounts that were apparently approved by Cabinet. A large Federal grant was diverted—"

"It's not true," screamed the Treasurer.

"How much, Daymon?" shouted the Shadow Minister for Roads.

"$12 billion," the Premier said coolly. "Give or take a few billion. What's it matter?"

"What?"

"Might be more."

Most of the Parliament looked like someone had just thrown a bucket of cold porridge over them. Daymon looked like he might have done the throwing. "What in

God's name is this project?" said Olivetti.

Daymon smiled evenly, his snout lengthening: "Maybe Mr Pugwandell, as he's been so fiendishly clever as to find me out, should be the one to explain?"

"Bullshit!" someone in the back yelled.

"Among other things," Pugwandell said, uncertain, "It involves the demolition of everything from Darling Harbour eastwards to Macquarie Street and southwards to Marrickville — followed by sale of the freed land for massive re-development."

"Fuck a duck!" cried Sir Filby, too flabbergasted to press his political advantage.

"What the hell has the Premier got to do with this project?" shouted someone else.

Pugwandell loomed forward. "Simple. I've managed to trace the ownership of companies that will receive the lucrative contracts involved, including the re-development plans. Many of these companies boast the Premier as a major shareholder."

"Is that it?" commented the Member for Scrub scornfully.

"Do you deny the facts?"

"I deny nothing, Pugwandell." The Premier was looking positively canine. The others stared at him, waiting for explanation.

"Moreover..." said Pugwandell, his anxiety increasing as the Premier failed to display even the most elementary signs of discomfort, "I have proof that Daymon has been engaging in certain arcane rituals—"

"Rituals? What sort of rituals?" the Deputy Premier asked.

"Demonic ones. I don't know what they are for, but

they involve, among other atrocities, human sacrifice."

"Human sacrifice?" Hersey looked ill. "That's absurd..." She didn't sound entirely convinced about that judgement even as she made it. "Is there any substance to this accusation, or are you merely appealing to the sensationalist press under the protection of parliamentary privilege?"

Daymon growled loudly. "Of course there's substance to the claim," he said. "There's no point in hiding it. The end is too near to bother."

The entire House sat in stunned silence. Journalists went crazy in the gallery.

"I don't understand," said Sir Filby at last. "What's this Satanic stuff got to do with the re-development plans?"

"They're intricately connected," commented Daymon, picking at his fangs with a clawed finger. "Intricately connected."

"Here," said Pugwandell, pulling a video cassette cartridge from his suit-pocket. He suspected Daymon of diverting the debate from the key issues. "I have the recording of a meeting that took place between the Premier and a Mr Lucifer—"

"Who the devil is he?" asked the Minister for Education.

"A representative of Zedlines-Inferno Pty Ltd. Shall I play the tape, Mr Premier?"

The Premier smiled. Veins were standing out all over his hairy forehead and his bulging capillaries looked as though they might burst. "A tape? Where did you get that then, Pugwandell?"

"I never betray a leak."

The Premier smiled in a way that told Pugwandell exactly where the tape — which had appeared on his desk only yesterday — had come from. The Independent Member for Tooly-Ooly collapsed suddenly, crashing like a large sack of lumpy custard into his chair.

"Yes, it's all true," said Daymon. "You don't have to play the tape. That was for your personal edification, Pugwandell. I thought I was rather good in it." He turned to the rest of the House. "The re-development will cost the State billions...but we'll get it back. With interest."

"How?" yelled the Treasurer, "What goddam difference will it make? We'd never get away with demolishing Sydney."

"Why not? Who'd notice?"

"We'll have to stop it."

"We can't," the Premier said.

"Why not?"

Daymon tossed yet another pile of papers onto the table. "There's copies of the papers, signed by all members of the Cabinet and relevant public servants. Pugwandell has copies. It's official. Sydney's on the way out."

There was sudden turmoil; all the MPs began screaming at once.

"Shut up!" Sir Filby's voice cracked through the babble. "Just shut up! Look, it's ridiculous. Development like that would require special legislation—"

"Look it up. The first reading, the second reading, with an introductory speech by myself, an hour's debate...it was passed through both Houses during September."

"I don't remember that."

"No one remembers it, but it's in *Hansard*."

"But how?"

"It was achieved," said Daymon, as his suit burst from his expanding biceps, "using new reality manipulation methodologies developed by a company called Magic-Time — owned, incidentally, by the Zedlines-Inferno board of management. There's no legal precedent. You can take it to court, but it's watertight. There's been massively clever malpractice at the highest level—"

"More than that...massive fraud."

"But, surely, no one here signed those documents," someone commented.

Daymon began rifling through the pages. "Myself...the Treasurer...the Deputy Premier...the Minister for Construction...Industrial Relations...Roads ...There's also papers signed by the Mayor of Sydney...the Attorney-General...even the Governor. And that's only the beginning."

"But I didn't sign anything," said Duncan Kandinski.

"They're all real, Duncan. Maybe you were drunk." Daymon grinned. "And what's more...*Hansard* records the Sydney Metropolitan Demolition Bill was passed through both Houses without a single dissenting voice."

"Rubbish!"

"Bullshit!"

"The Premier must be joking," yelled Sir Filby. "Surely this thing can be stopped! It's an obvious fraud.

No one even remembers the debate."

"Reality manipulation or not, it can't be allowed."

"Work starts today," growled Daymon calmly. "By the time the issue goes through the Court, the Court will have been demolished." His words cut through the babble like a thunder clap. There was sudden, and utter silence. "Today," Daymon repeated, waving a sheaf of papers in the air above his head, "This afternoon at three o'clock, Zedlines-Inferno — whom I called up especially for the purpose — has the legal right to demolish the City of Sydney. Plans are underway. You can't even use the military to stop them, because the deal included the use of the military to take part in the demolition." He grinned. "Yes, the trumpets are blowing, gentlemen, and we can only wait upon them. But while we do..." He loomed over the table, his wolfish maw slavering. "...I think the Honourable members deserve to have their most urgent questions answered."

"Questions?"

"Yes." He glanced meaningfully around the dumbfounded Chamber.

Pugwandell looked like he was about to collapse inward. His face sank, his belly sagged. Words popped out of his mouth like gas forced from him by his shrinking stature. "What questions?" he said.

"First off..." Daymon raised his voice so that the entire House could hear him clearly. "...you'll want to know..." He paused meaningfully. "What do *you* get out of this?"

"Hear! Hear!" shouted the Honourable Members, in unison.

A while later, the Demolition began. It was said that, when it started, Bindy Daymon was in the middle of an impassioned speech concerning the triumph of ferality — and, by thus succumbing to his garrulous nature, he guaranteed his own downfall. Most of the other MPs had cleared the Chamber by the time the trembling of the ground reached a peak, so when the giant lizardman from the Outer Darkness appeared, losses were minimised.

Bindy Daymon never lived to see the culmination of his re-creation plans and wasn't around to oversee their implementation. Nevertheless, no one seemed to notice in the General Chaos that a rider to the Sydney Metropolitan Demolition Bill stated that: "All lands cleared under this Act shall henceforth be known as 'Scrub'." It also provided the entire area would be given over to farming — specifically to the cross-breeding of chooks and a hitherto obscure species of small green lizard.

The subsequent history of these provisions is not within the province of this account.

# Previously Published Stories

*The following stories have been previously published:*

'The Black Lake's Fatal Flood', *Eidolon* #19, vol. 5, no. 2, October 1995

'Dreams of Death' *Alfred Hitchcock's Mystery Magazine*, vol. 35, no. 7, July 1990

'Rotting Eggplant on the Bottom Shelf of a Fridge' in *Eidolon* #14, vol. 4, no. 2, April 1994

'Rotten Times' in *Aurealis* #27/28, 2001, and on *Ideomancer Speculative Fiction* website, February 2003

'Groundswell' in *Aurealis* #5, 1991

'Heartless' in *Aurealis* #31, 2003

'Separating Lenore' in *Book of Shadows* (Canada), November 1991

'The Slimelight, And How To Step Into It' in *Iniquities: the Magazine of Great Wickedness and Wonder*, no. 2, 1991

'Casual Visitors' in *Scarp* vol. 2, no. 2, May 1989

'You're A Sick Man, Mr Antwhistle' in *Mattoid* #36, 1990 and *The Year's Best Horror Stories: XIX*, edited by Karl Edward Wagner, New York, DAW, 1991

'Lo Que No Asusta' was written as a Guest of Honour contribution to the Borderlands: That Which Scares Us convention booklet, Perth, 7 to 8 September 2002

'Creeping in Reptile Flesh', 'Unravelling' and 'Getting Rid of Mother' were previously unpublished and original to this collection.

'Scrubbed' first published in *AustrAlien Absurdities*, edited by Chuck McKenzie and Tansy Raynor Roberts, Agog! Press, 2002.

# Other books by Robert Hood:

*Day-dreaming on Company Time* (Five Islands Press, 1988)

*Backstreets* (Hodder Headline, 1999)

*Shades 1*: Shadow Dance (Hodder Headline, 2001)

*Shades 2*: Night Beast (Hodder Headline, 2001)

*Shades 3*: Ancient Light (Hodder Headline, 2001)

*Shades 4*: Black Sun Rising (Hodder Headline, 2001)

*Immaterial. Ghost Stories* (MirrorDanse Books, 2002)

# Books edited by Robert Hood

*Crosstown Traffic* (with Stuart Coupe and Julie Ogden,
Five Islands Press, 1993)

*Bonescribes. Year's Best Australian Horror*: 1995
(with Bill Congreve, MirrorDanse Books, 1996)

*Daikaiju! Giant Monster Tales* (with Robin Pen, Agog! Press,
2005)

*Daikaiju! 2*: Revenge of the Giant Monsters
(with Robin Pen, Agog! Press/Prime Books, 2007)

*Daikaiju! 3*: Giant Monsters vs the World
(with Robin Pen, Agog! Press/Prime Books, 2007)

# REVIEWS

"Robert Hood has been writing chilling, sickening, funny and thoughtful horror for longer than he cares to remember. *Creeping in Reptile Flesh* brings together some of the best from his twistedly evil mind…. There are many types of horror here to suit many tastes and all of them will please the discerning reader who enjoys good tales told well."

**Keith Stevenson, *Aurealis* #43**

"Simply a class act…A must-have addition to any horror fan's bookcase, it will have you wanting to check out more Robert Hood material."

**Jeff Ritchie, *ScaryMinds* website**

"An impressive, very personal and thematically cohesive collection of stories from horror writer, Robert Hood…*Creeping* shows the significant contribution Robert has made to the Australian horror genre."

**13th Annual Aurealis Awards:**
**Best Anthology/Collection Category Judges' Report**

"Hood's collection *Creeping in Reptile Flesh*…was the finest Aussie collection released in 2008. [It] contains several of Hood's best stories and spans two decades of his career."

**Shane Jiraiya Cummings, Australian Shadows**
**Award 2008 Judges' Comments**

"The central theme for Hood is menacing decay, both bodily an environmental, and this focus showcases his ability to move from old-fashioned confessional-style horror, complete with tentacled tropes, to rather wonderful absurdism."

**Talie Helene,** *Black: Australian Dark Culture*

# OTHER COMMENTS

"Aussie horror's wicked godfather."

*Black Magazine*

"Hood has gone on [from *Day-dreaming on Company Time*] to produce many fine horror stories and establish himself as one of this country's leading horror authors."

**Steven Paulsen and Sean McMullen,**
**"The Hunt for Australian Horror" in *Aurealis* #14**

"Rob Hood is Australia's master of dark fantasy, seducing the reader with stories that are lavishly grim and rife with a quirky, unpredictable inventiveness. He takes us along streets we prefer not to travel, even in daylight, and finds humanity in the blackest of shadows."

**Sean Williams, best-selling author of the Orphans**
**trilogy, *Metal Fatigue*, *The Resurrected Man* & more**

"Rob Hood is a brilliant fantasist. I've seen work penned by Hood that is absolutely luminous, unnerving, and original. This man can write!"

**Jack Dann, author of *The Memory Cathedral*, *The***
***Rebel* and numerous other works, & editor of the**
**award-winning anthology, *Dreaming Downunder*)**

# ABOUT THE AUTHOR

Robert Hood's many stories, which have appeared in major Australian and international genre magazines and anthologies, range from crime to science fiction to dark fantasy, often mixed. Some of these are in his three collections to date: *Day-Dreaming on Company Time* (Five Islands Press, 1988), *Immaterial: Ghost Stories* (MirrorDanse Books, 2002) and *Creeping in Reptile Flesh*. His novel, *Backstreets*, was published by Hodder Headline in 1999. The Shades series — four connected YA supernatural thrillers — appeared in 2001, also from Hodder Headline.

He has co-edited five anthologies, including the award-winning *Daikaiju! Giant Monster Tales* and its two sequels (Agog! Press, 2006-2007), and has published many short children's books and stories.

Frequently nominated for Aurealis and Ditmar Awards, (most recently for 'Wasting Matilda' from *Zombie Apocalypse!* from Robinson Press/Running Press and for *Creeping in Reptile Flesh* itself — both as collection and a novella), he has won the Australian Golden Dagger Award for short crime fiction and two William Atheling Awards for genre commentary and review.

Coming up, he has stories in *Anywhere But Earth* (edited by Keith Stevenson for Coeur De Lion), *In the Footsteps of Gilgamesh* (edited Karen Newman and Pete

Kempshall for Gilgamesh Press) and *Exotic Gothic 4* (edited by Danel Olson for PS Publishing).

Hood lives in NSW, Australia, with his partner, writer, artist and editor Cat Sparks. His website is: www.roberthood.net. He also has an award-winning blog, Undead Backbrain (www.roberthood.net/blog/).

# AVAILABLE NOW-

## HOW TO MAKE MONSTERS
## by GARY McMAHON

Since the dawn of mankind, we have always made our own monsters: the terrors of capitalism and corruption, the things between the cracks, the ghosts of self...terrible beasts of desire, debt, regret, racism...of family ties, and the things that get in the way of our aspirations...the familiar monsters of our own faces, of tradition, rejection, and the darkness that lives deep inside our own hearts...

Can you identify the component parts of your own monster?

Can you afford to pay the dreadful price of its construction?

# AVAILABLE NOW-

## VOICES edited by
## MARK S. DENIZ & AMANDA PILLAR

# AVAILABLE NOW-

## DEAD SOULS
### edited by MARK S. DENIZ

Before God created light, there was darkness. Even after He illuminated the world, there were shadows — shadows that allowed the darkness to fester and infect the unwary.

The tales found within *Dead Souls* explore the recesses of the soul; those people and creatures that could not escape the shadows. From the inherent cruelness of humanity to malevolent forces, *Dead Souls* explores the depths of humanity as a lesson to the ignorant, the naive and the unsuspecting.

God created light, but it is a temporary grace that will ultimately fail us, for the darkness is stronger and our souls...are truly dead.

# AVAILABLE NOW-

## THE PHANTOM QUEEN AWAKES
### edited by Mark S. Deniz & Amanda Pillar

The Phantom Queen, goddess of death, love and war, returns to strike fear into the hearts of mortals in the anthology, *The Phantom Queen Awakes*.

Meet a washerwoman on the shores of the river; cleaning the clothes of the soon-to-be-dead; try to bargain with the capricious goddess of war; hear the songs of the dead as they cry for justice; walk with heroes of the past

Revisit the world of the Celts; a land of mystical beauty, avarice, lust and war through stories told by Katharine Kerr, C.E. Murphy, Elaine Cunningham and Anya Bast, among many other talented authors.

# AVAILABLE NOW-

## GRANTS PASS
### edited by Amanda Pillar & Jennifer Brozek

Humanity was decimated by bio-terrorism; three engineered plagues were let loose on the world. Barely anyone has survived.

Just a year before the collapse, Grants Pass, Oregon, USA, was publicly labelled as a place of sanctuary in a whimsical online, "what if" post. Now, it has become one of the last known refuges, and the hope, of mankind.

Would you go to Grants Pass based on the words of someone you've never met?

# AVAILABLE NOW-

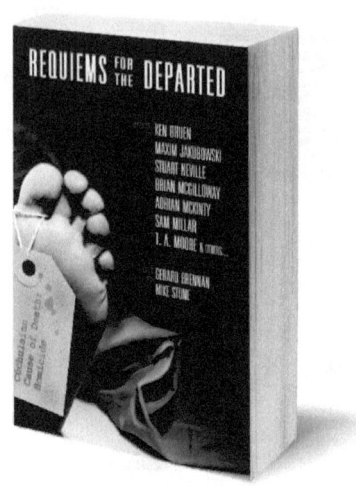

## REQUIEMS FOR THE DEPARTED
### edited by Gerard Brennan & Mike Stone

*Requiems for the Departed* contains seventeen short stories, inspired by Irish mythology, from some of the finest contemporary writers in the business.

Watch the children of Conchobar return to their mischievous ways, meet ancient Celtic royalty, and follow druids and banshees as they are set loose in the new Irish underbelly, murder and mayhem on their minds.

Featuring top shelf tales by Ken Bruen, Maxim Jakubowski, Stuart Neville, Brian McGilloway, Adrian McKinty, Sam Millar, John Grant, Garry Kilworth, T.A. Moore and many more.

# AVAILABLE NOW-

## SCENES FROM THE SECOND STOREY
## edited by Amanda Pillar & Pete Kempshall

*Scenes from the Second Storey* is an anthology that pays homage to the album, *Scenes from the Second Storey*, by The God Machine. Quirky, dark, insightful and sometimes downright disturbing, these tales reflect the emotions and images our authors experienced when they heard 'their' song from *Scenes from the Second Storey*.

In *Scenes*, you will meet a girl struggling to find cleanliness in a world full of corruption with Kaaron Warren; follow the twisted mental pathways of the egocentric with Robert Hood; watch two men search for enlightenment down a dark path with Paul Haines; and dance with a girl struggling to find her role within society with Cat Sparks.

# COMING SOON-

## THE WHISPER JAR
## by Carole Lanham

Some secrets are kept in jars — others, in books. Some are left forgotten in musty rooms — others, created in old barns. Some are brought about by destiny — others, born in blood.

Secrets — they are the hidden heart of this collection. In these pages, you will encounter a Blood Digger who bonds two children irrevocably together; a young woman who learns of her destiny through the random selection of a Bible verse; and a boy whose life begins to reflect the stories he reads...

Most importantly, though, if someone should ever happen to offer you a Jilly Jally Butter Mint, just say "No!"

www.ingramcontent.com/pod-product-compliance
Lightning Source LLC
Chambersburg PA
CBHW020819180626
46814CB00001B/20